SPARKS!

WRITTEN BY **IAN BOOTHBY**

ART BY **NINA MATSUMOTO**
WITH COLOR BY DAVID DEDRICK

graphix

An Imprint of
■SCHOLASTIC

Dedicated to the real-life Charlie and August!
—Ian Boothby and Nina Matsumoto

Library of Congress Control Number: 2017943774

ISBN 978-1-338-02947-5 (hardcover)
ISBN 978-1-338-02946-8 (paperback)

10 9 8 7 6 5 4 3 2 1   18 19 20 21 22

Printed in China   38
First edition, March 2018
Edited by Adam Rau
Color by David Dedrick
Book design by Phil Falco
Creative Director: David Saylor

CHAPTER ONE

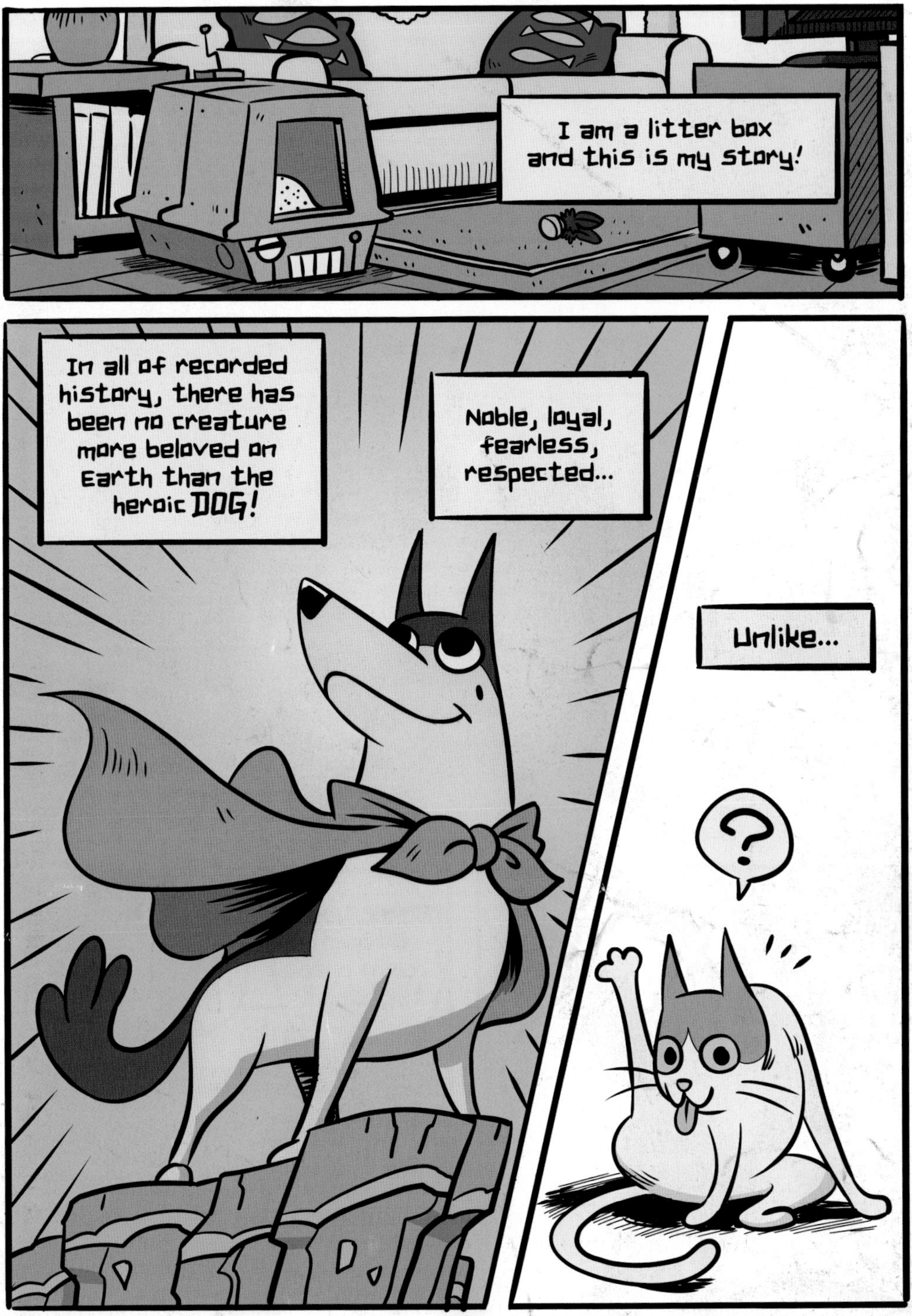
I am a litter box and this is my story!
In all of recorded history, there has been no creature more beloved on Earth than the heroic DOG!
Noble, loyal, fearless, respected...
Unlike...
?

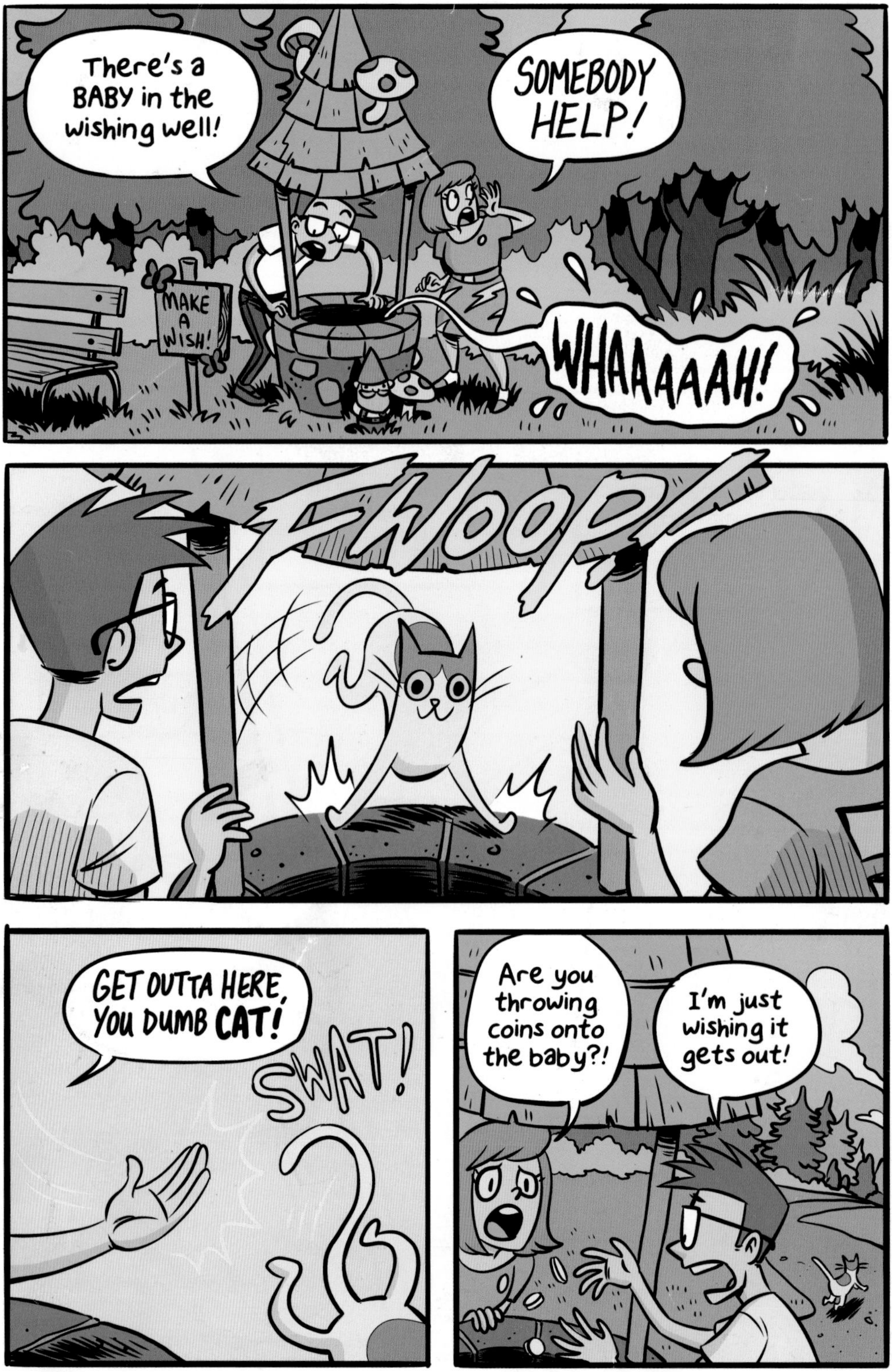
There's a BABY in the wishing well!
SOMEBODY HELP!
MAKE A WISH!
WHAAAAAH!
FWOOP!
GET OUTTA HERE, YOU DUMB CAT!
SWAT!
Are you throwing coins onto the baby?!
I'm just wishing it gets out!

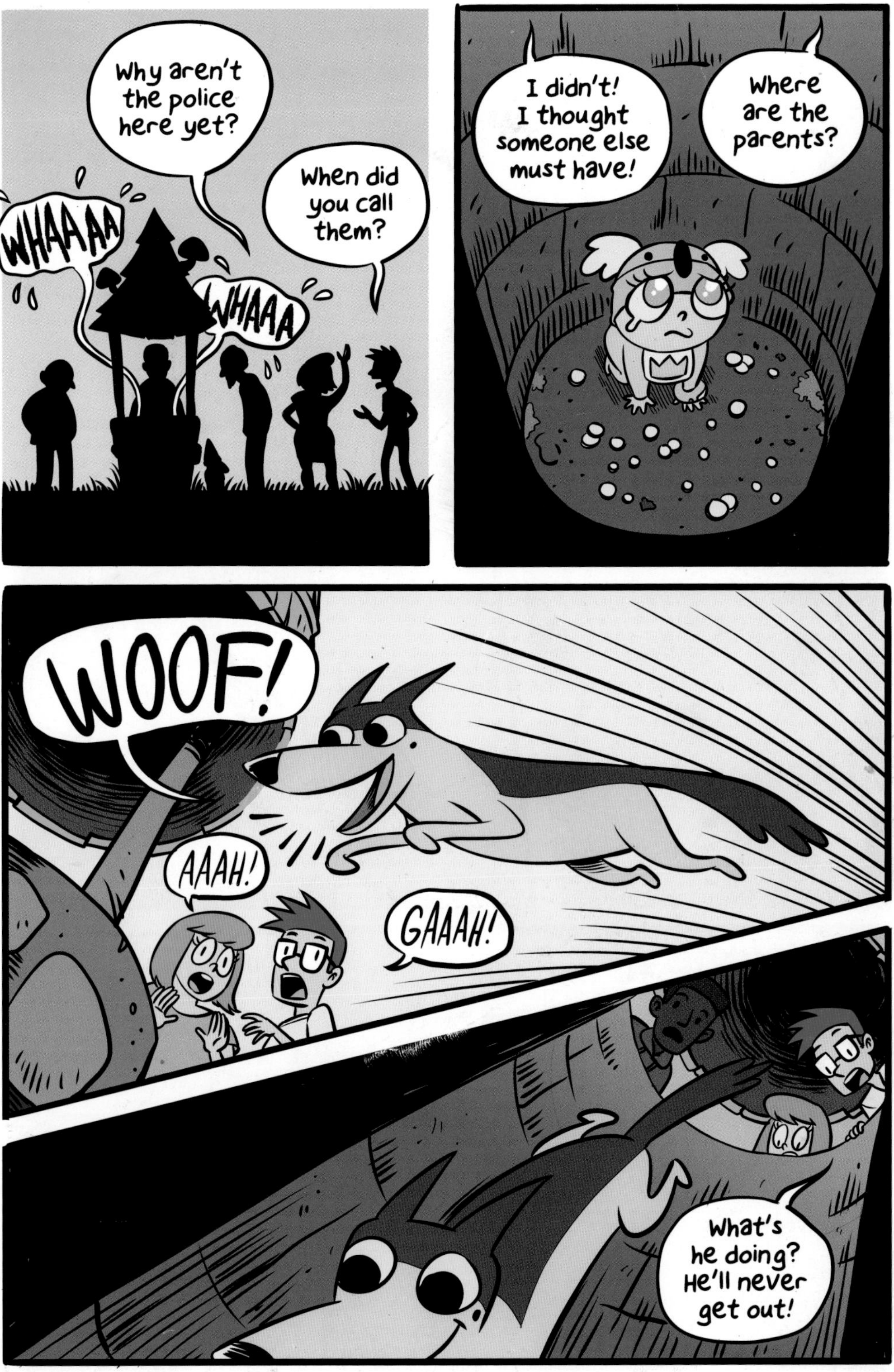

Why aren't the police here yet?
WHAAAAA
WHAAA
When did you call them?
I didn't! I thought someone else must have!
Where are the parents?
WOOF!
AAAH!
GAAAH!
What's he doing? He'll never get out!

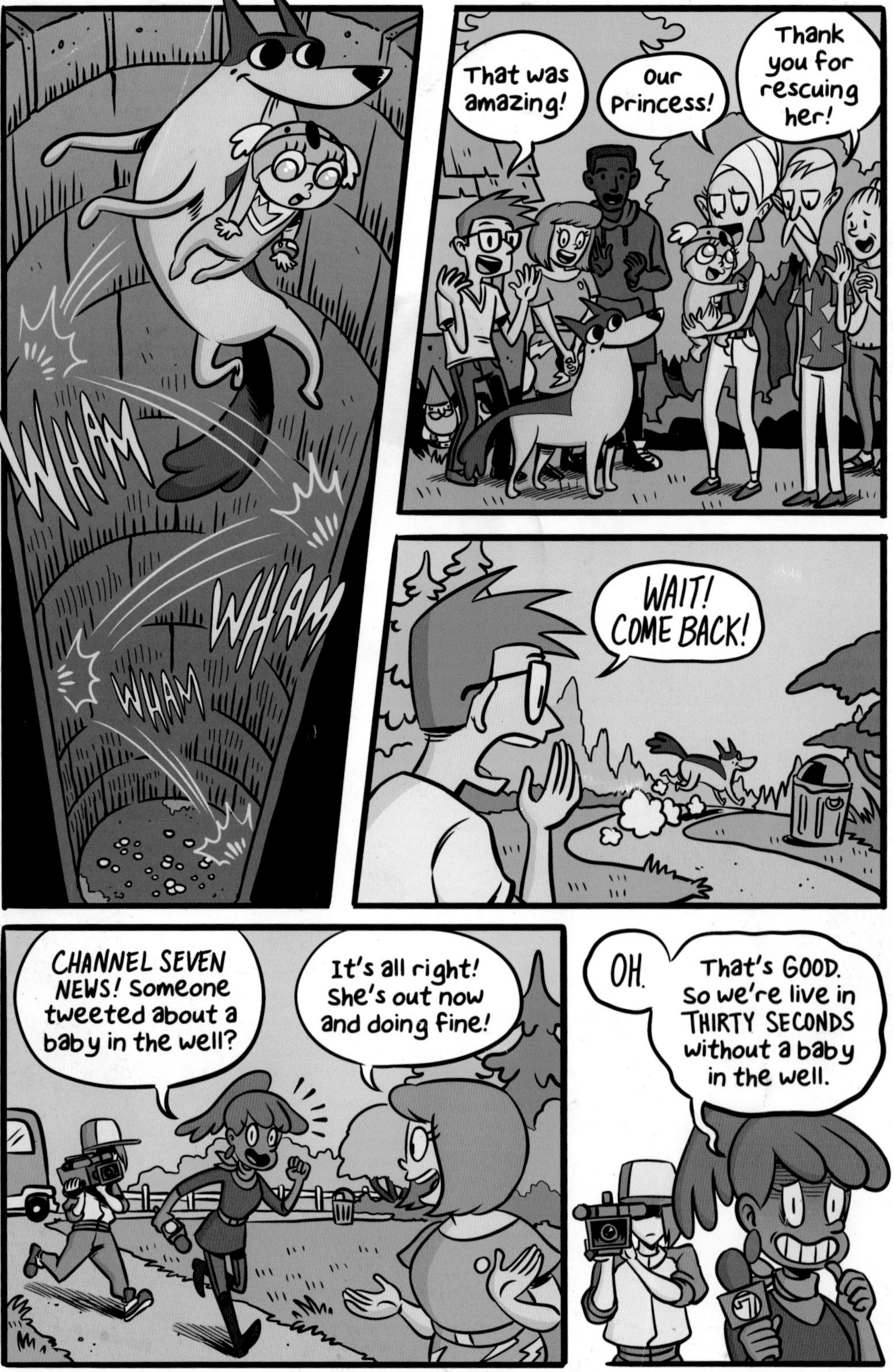
WHAM
WHAM
WHAM
That was amazing!
Our Princess!
Thank you for rescuing her!
WAIT! COME BACK!
CHANNEL SEVEN NEWS! Someone tweeted about a baby in the well?
It's all right! She's out now and doing fine!
OH.
That's GOOD. So we're live in THIRTY SECONDS without a baby in the well.

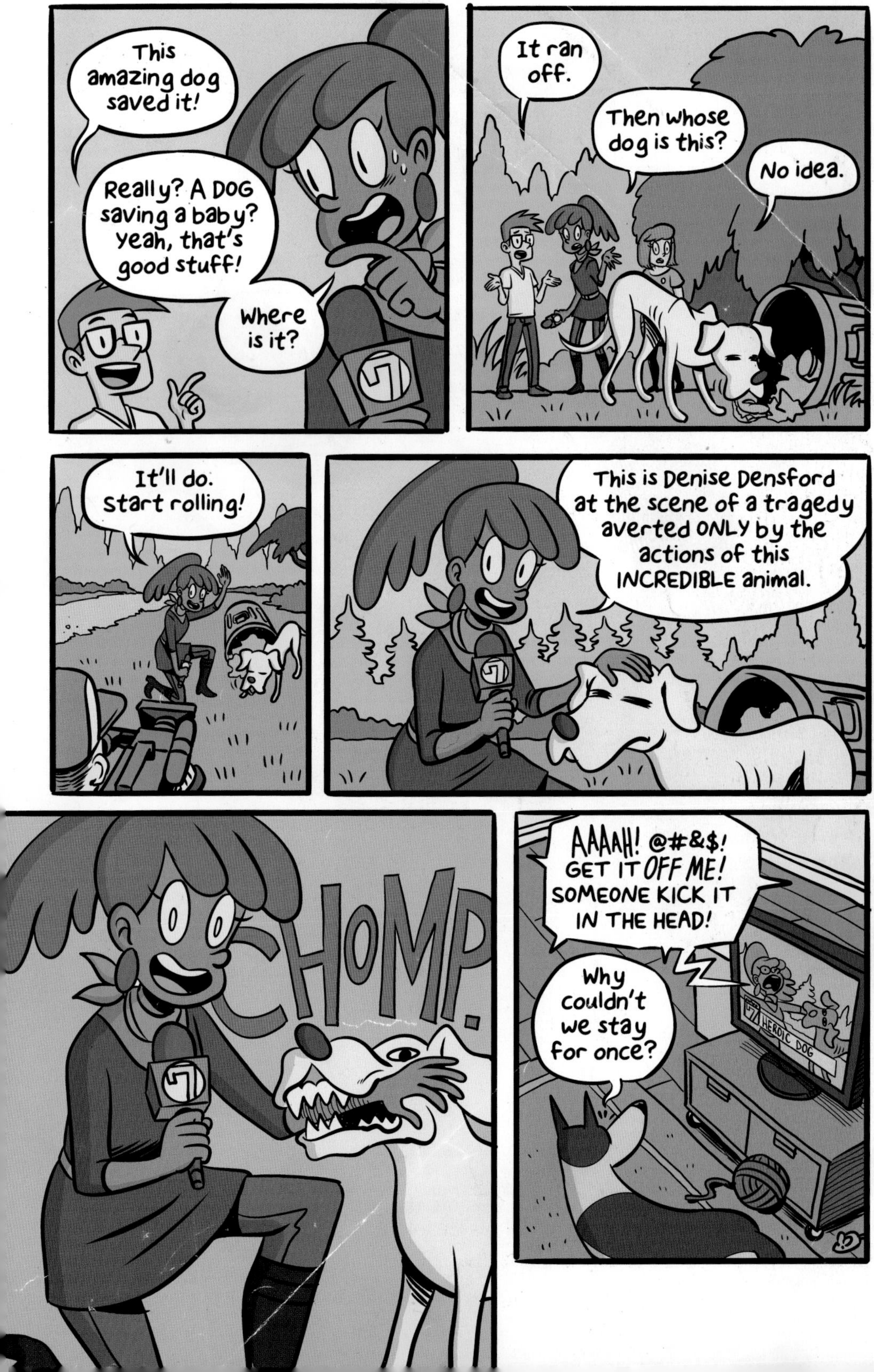
This amazing dog saved it!
Really? A DOG saving a baby? Yeah, that's good stuff!
Where is it?
It ran off.
Then whose dog is this?
No idea.
It'll do. Start rolling!
This is Denise Densford at the scene of a tragedy averted ONLY by the actions of this INCREDIBLE animal.
CHOMP.
AAAAH! @#&$! GET IT OFF ME! SOMEONE KICK IT IN THE HEAD!
HEROIC DOG
Why couldn't we stay for once?

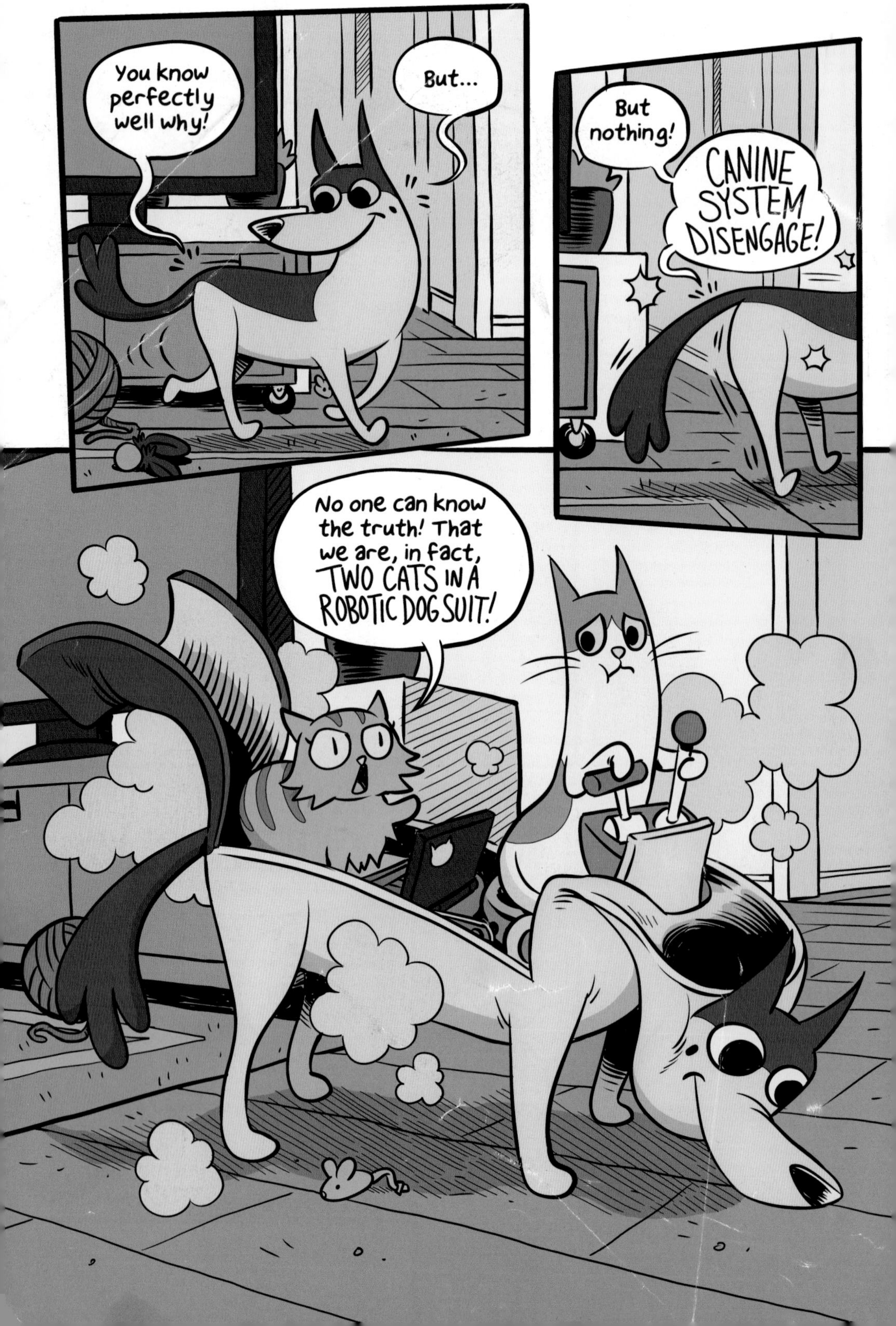
You know perfectly well why!
But...
But nothing!
CANINE SYSTEM DISENGAGE!
No one can know the truth! That we are, in fact, TWO CATS IN A ROBOTIC DOG SUIT!

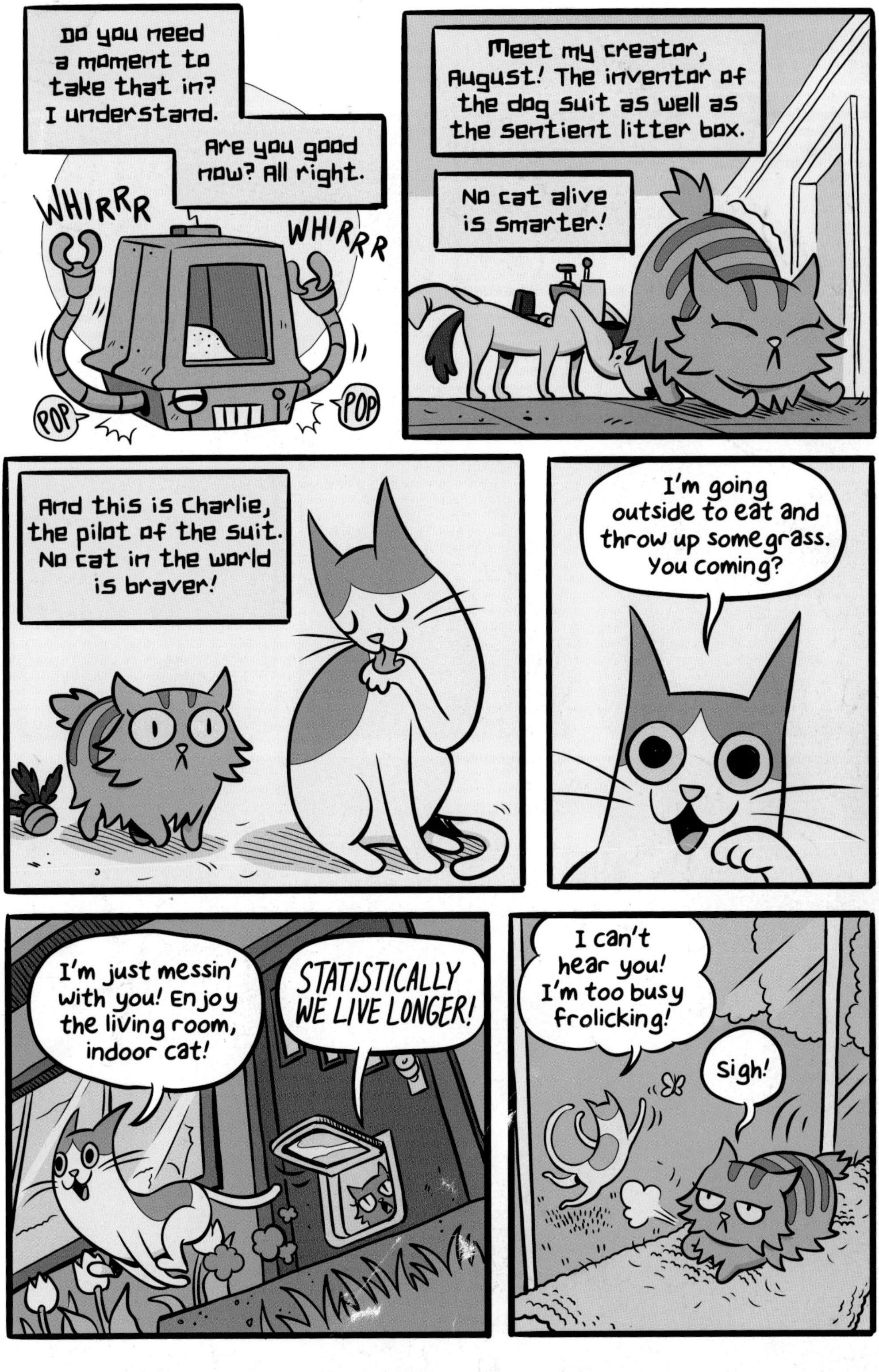
Do you need a moment to take that in? I understand.
Are you good now? All right.
WHIRRR
WHIRRR
POP
POP
Meet my creator, August! The inventor of the dog suit as well as the sentient litter box.
No cat alive is smarter!
And this is Charlie, the pilot of the suit. No cat in the world is braver!
I'm going outside to eat and throw up some grass. You coming?
I'm just messin' with you! Enjoy the living room, indoor cat!
STATISTICALLY WE LIVE LONGER!
I can't hear you! I'm too busy frolicking!
Sigh!

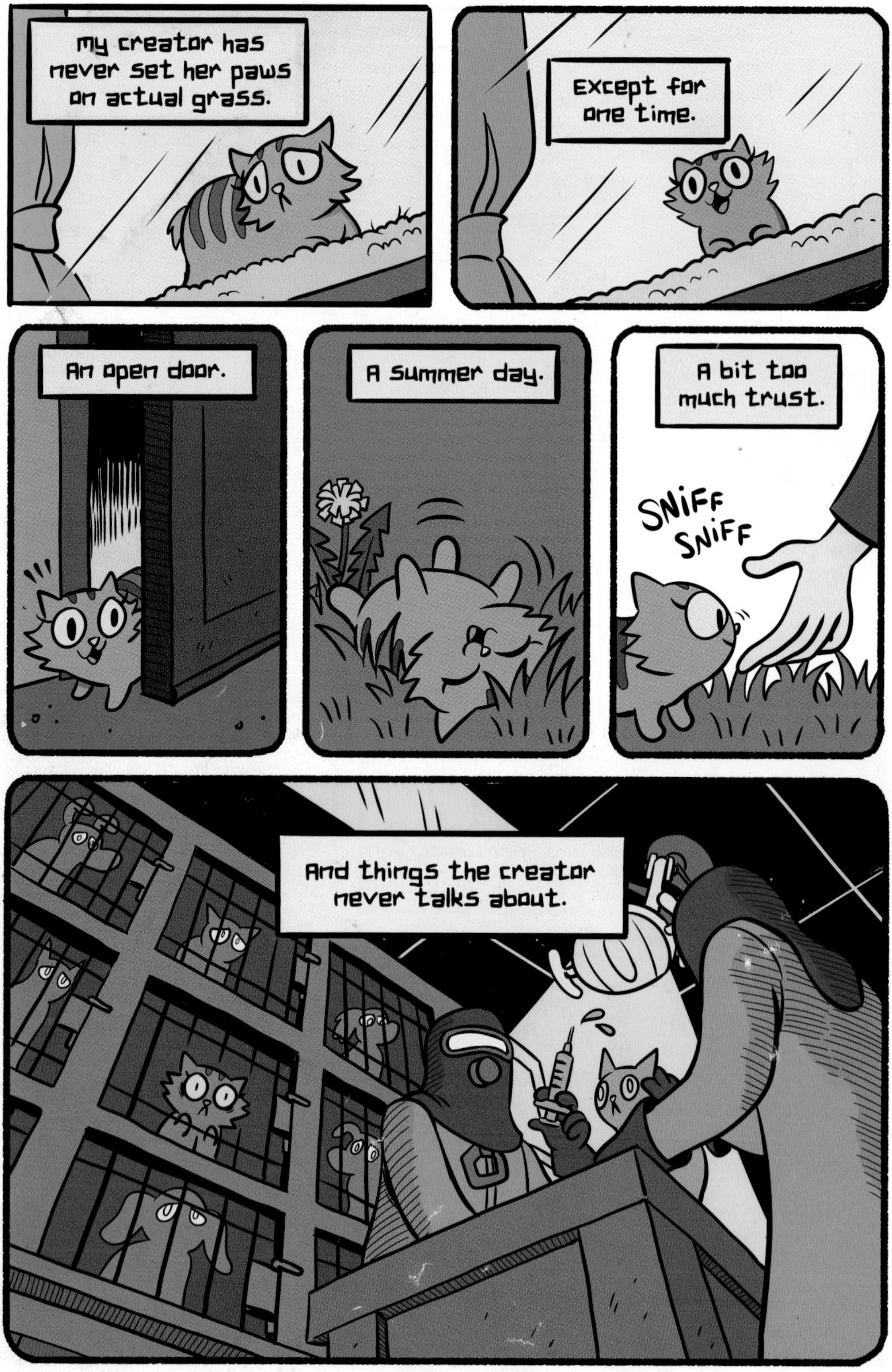
my creator has never set her paws on actual grass.
Except for one time.
An open door.
A summer day.
A bit too much trust.
SNIFF SNIFF
And things the creator never talks about.

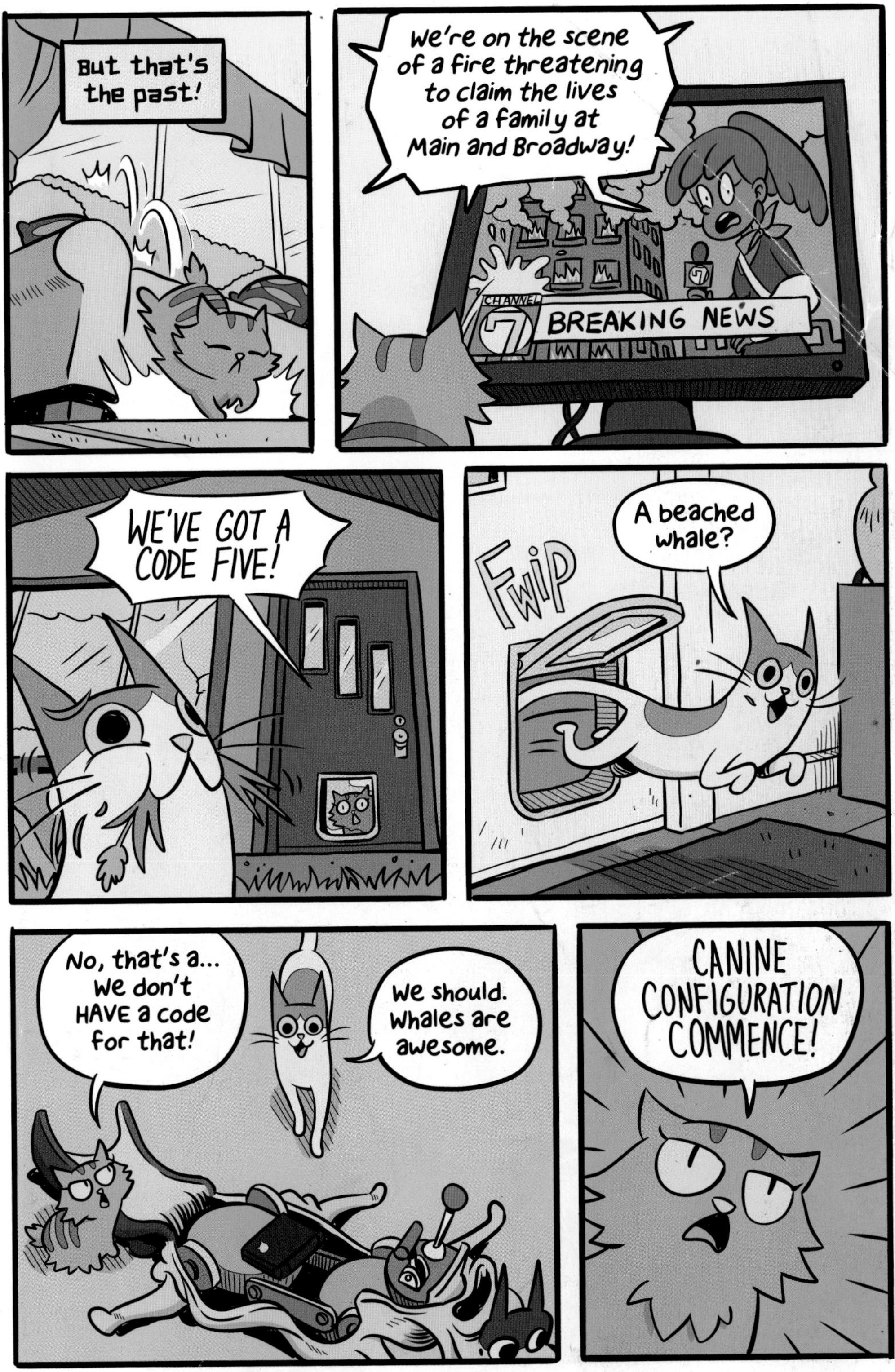

But that's the past!
We're on the scene of a fire threatening to claim the lives of a family at Main and Broadway!
CHANNEL 7
BREAKING NEWS
WE'VE GOT A CODE FIVE!
FWIP
A beached whale?
No, that's a... We don't HAVE a code for that!
We should. Whales are awesome.
CANINE CONFIGURATION COMMENCE!

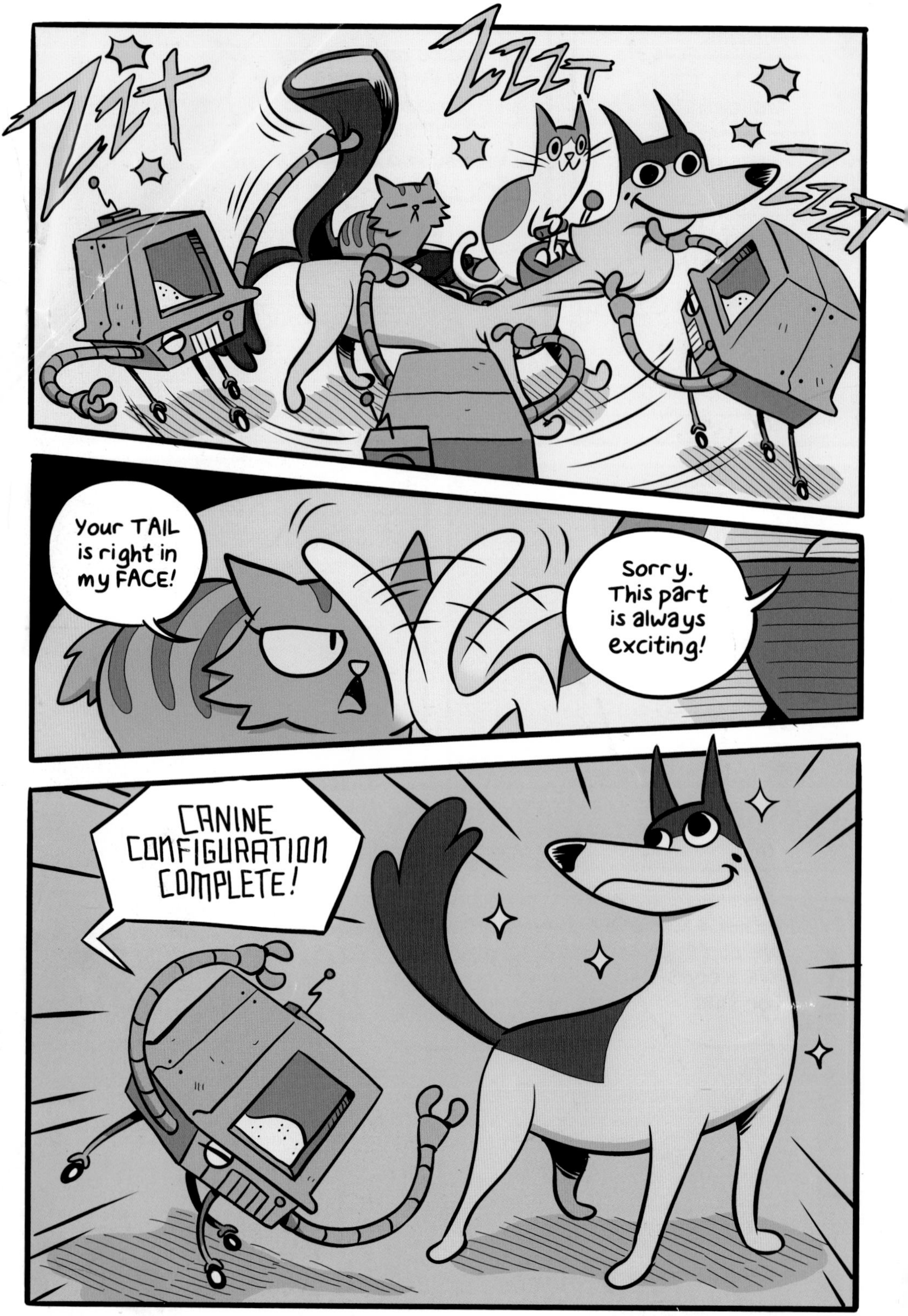
ZZZT
ZZZT
ZZZT
Your TAIL is right in my FACE!
Sorry. This part is always exciting!
CANINE CONFIGURATION COMPLETE!

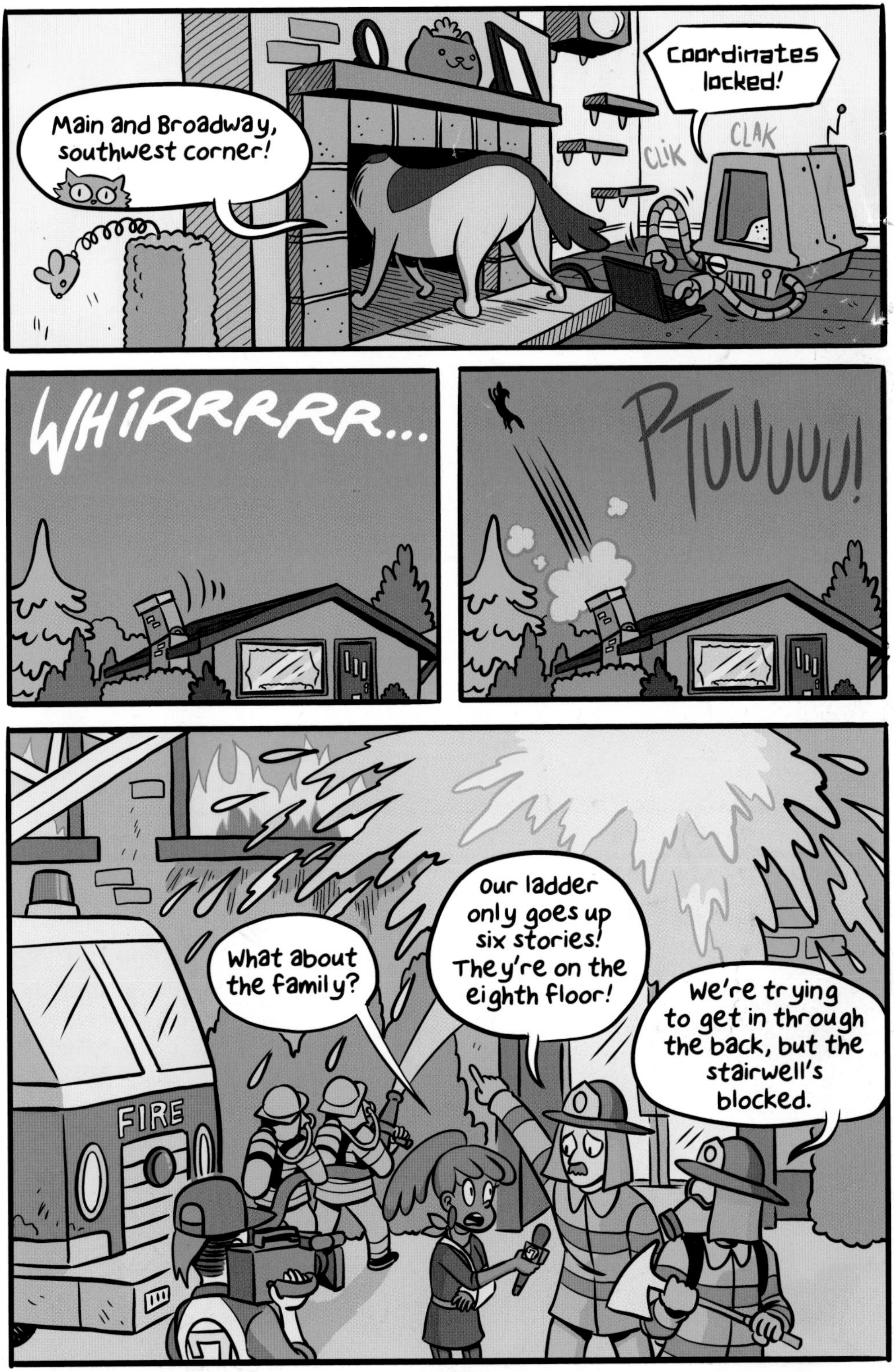
Main and Broadway, southwest corner!
Coordinates locked!
CLIK
CLAK
WHiRRRRR...
PTUUUUU!
What about the family?
Our ladder only goes up six stories! They're on the eighth floor!
We're trying to get in through the back, but the stairwell's blocked.
FIRE

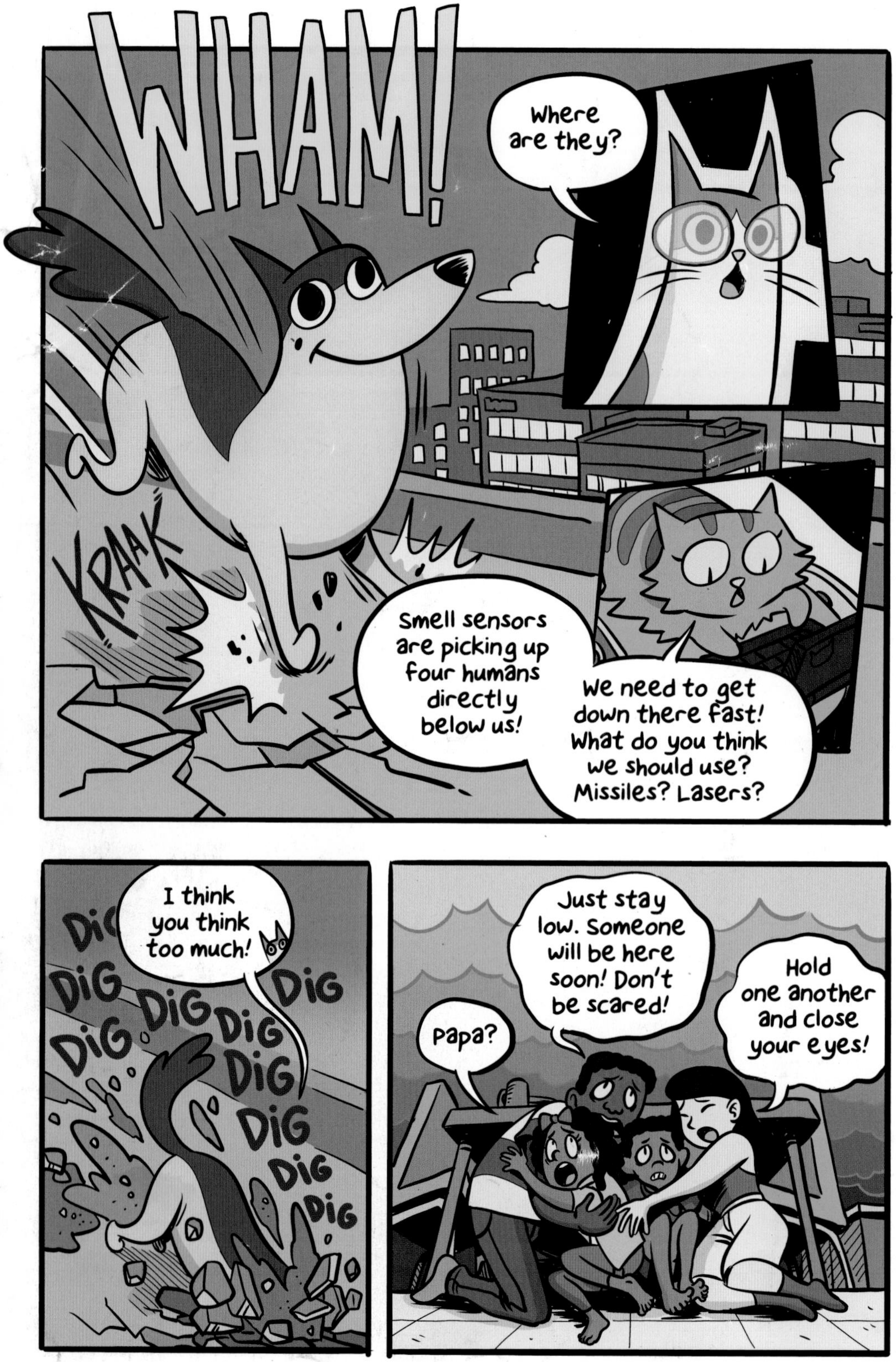
WHAM!
Where are they?
KRAAK
Smell sensors are picking up four humans directly below us!
We need to get down there fast! What do you think we should use? Missiles? Lasers?
I think you think too much!
DIG DIG DIG DIG DIG DIG DIG DIG DIG DIG DIG
Papa?
Just stay low. Someone will be here soon! Don't be scared!
Hold one another and close your eyes!

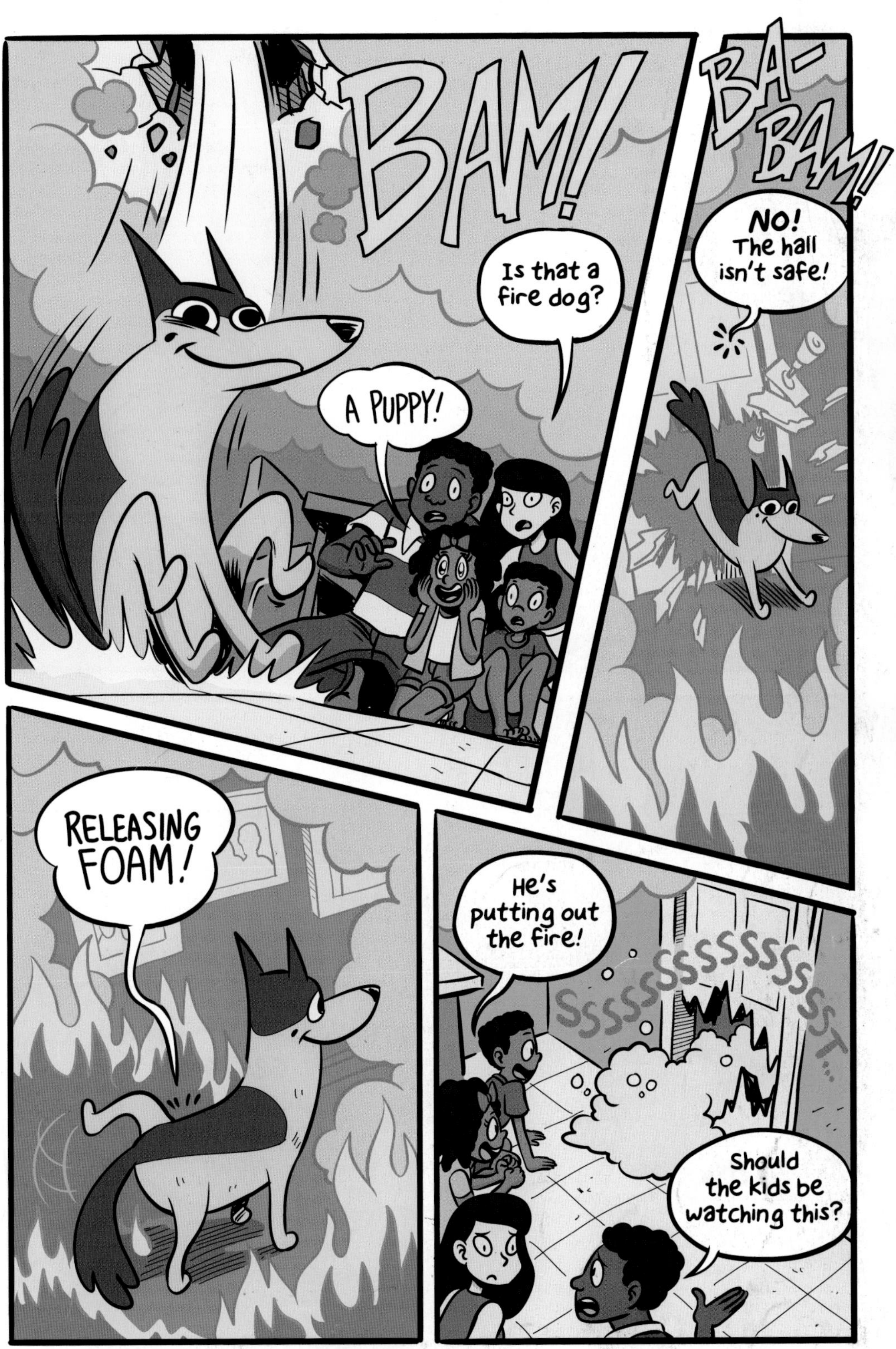
BAM!
Is that a fire dog?
A PUPPY!
BA-BAM!
NO! The hall isn't safe!
RELEASING FOAM!
He's putting out the fire!
SSSSSSSSSSSSSSSST...
Should the kids be watching this?

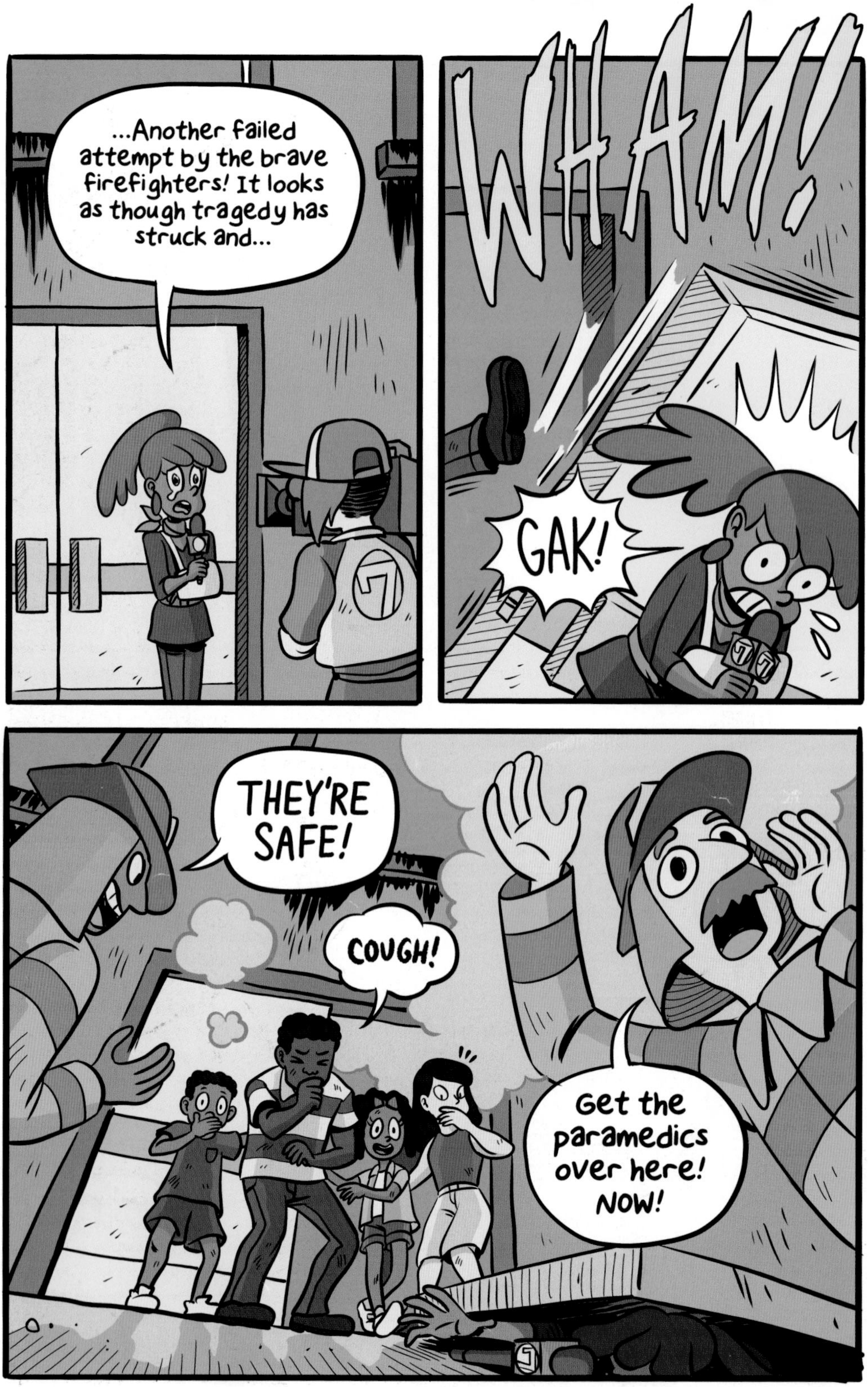
...Another failed attempt by the brave firefighters! It looks as though tragedy has struck and...
WHAM!
GAK!
THEY'RE SAFE!
COUGH!
Get the paramedics over here! NOW!

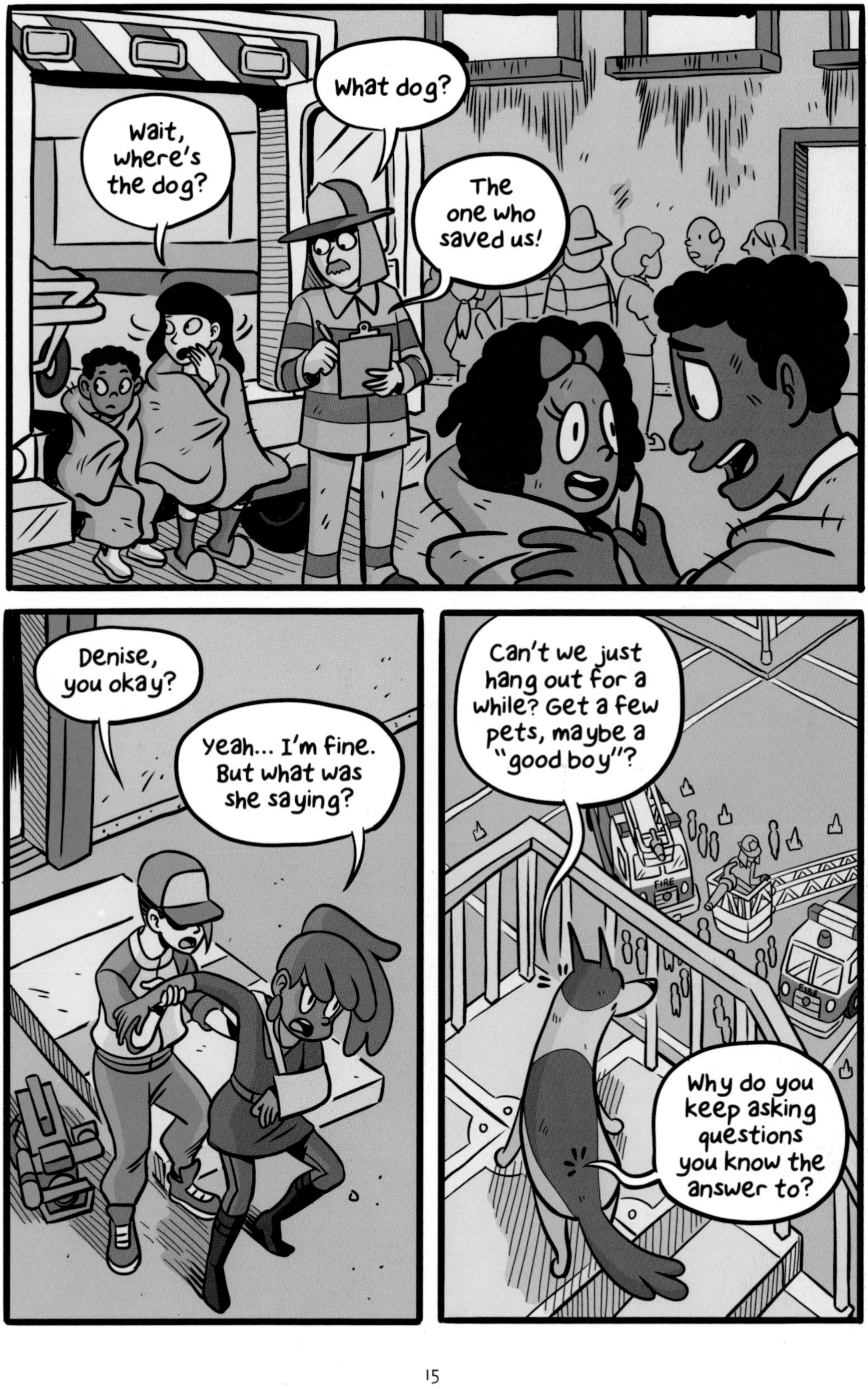
Wait, where's the dog?
What dog?
The one who saved us!
Denise, you okay?
Yeah... I'm fine. But what was she saying?
Can't we just hang out for a while? Get a few pets, maybe a "good boy"?
Why do you keep asking questions you know the answer to?

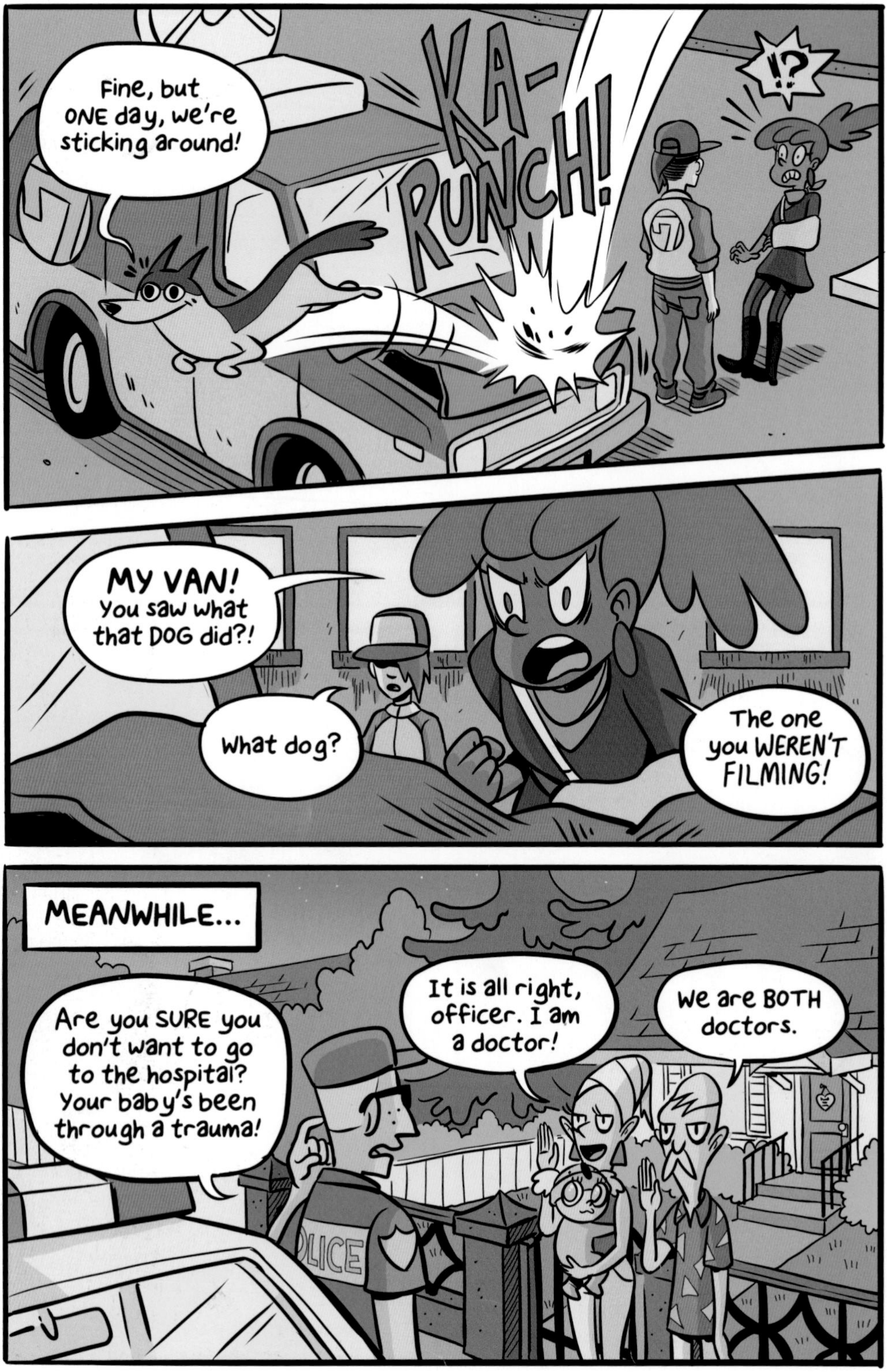

Fine, but ONE day, we're sticking around!
KA-RUNCH!
!?
MY VAN! You saw what that DOG did?!
What dog?
The one you WEREN'T FILMING!
MEANWHILE...
Are you SURE you don't want to go to the hospital? Your baby's been through a trauma!
It is all right, officer. I am a doctor!
We are BOTH doctors.
POLICE

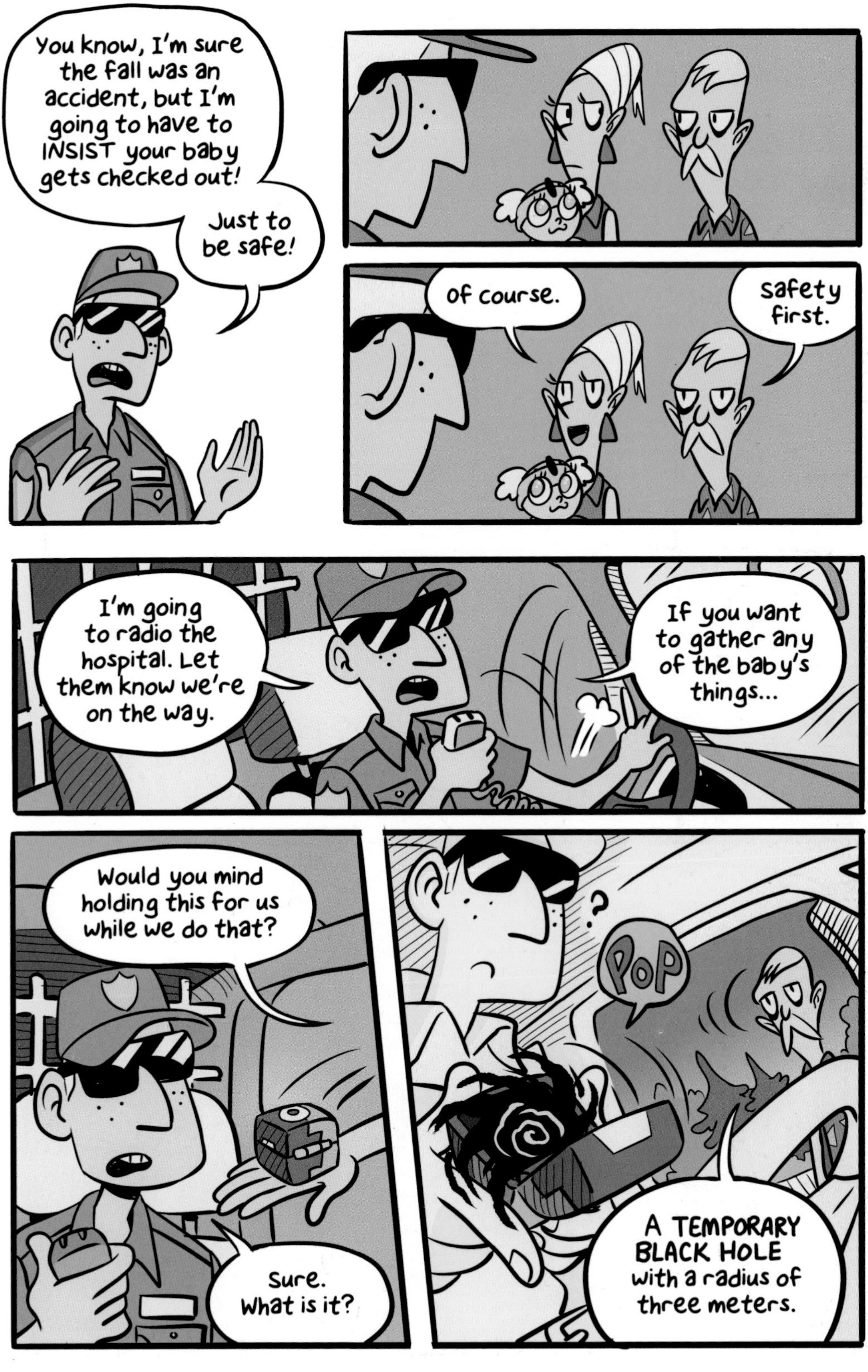
You know, I'm sure the fall was an accident, but I'm going to have to INSIST your baby gets checked out!
Just to be safe!
Of course.
Safety first.
I'm going to radio the hospital. Let them know we're on the way.
If you want to gather any of the baby's things...
Would you mind holding this for us while we do that?
Sure. What is it?
?
POP
A TEMPORARY BLACK HOLE with a radius of three meters.

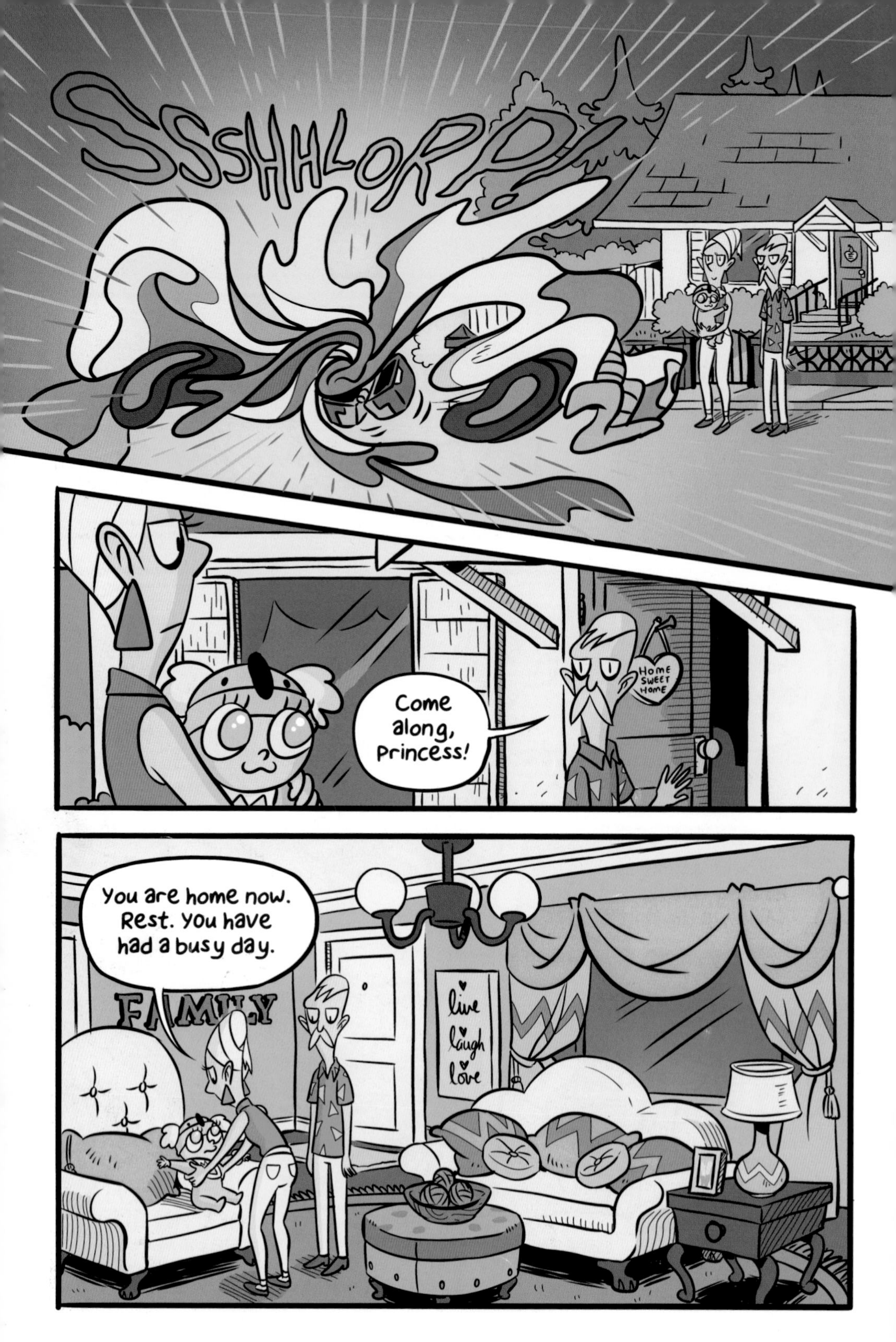
SSSHHLORPP!
Come along, princess!
HOME SWEET HOME
You are home now. Rest. You have had a busy day.
FAMILY
live laugh love

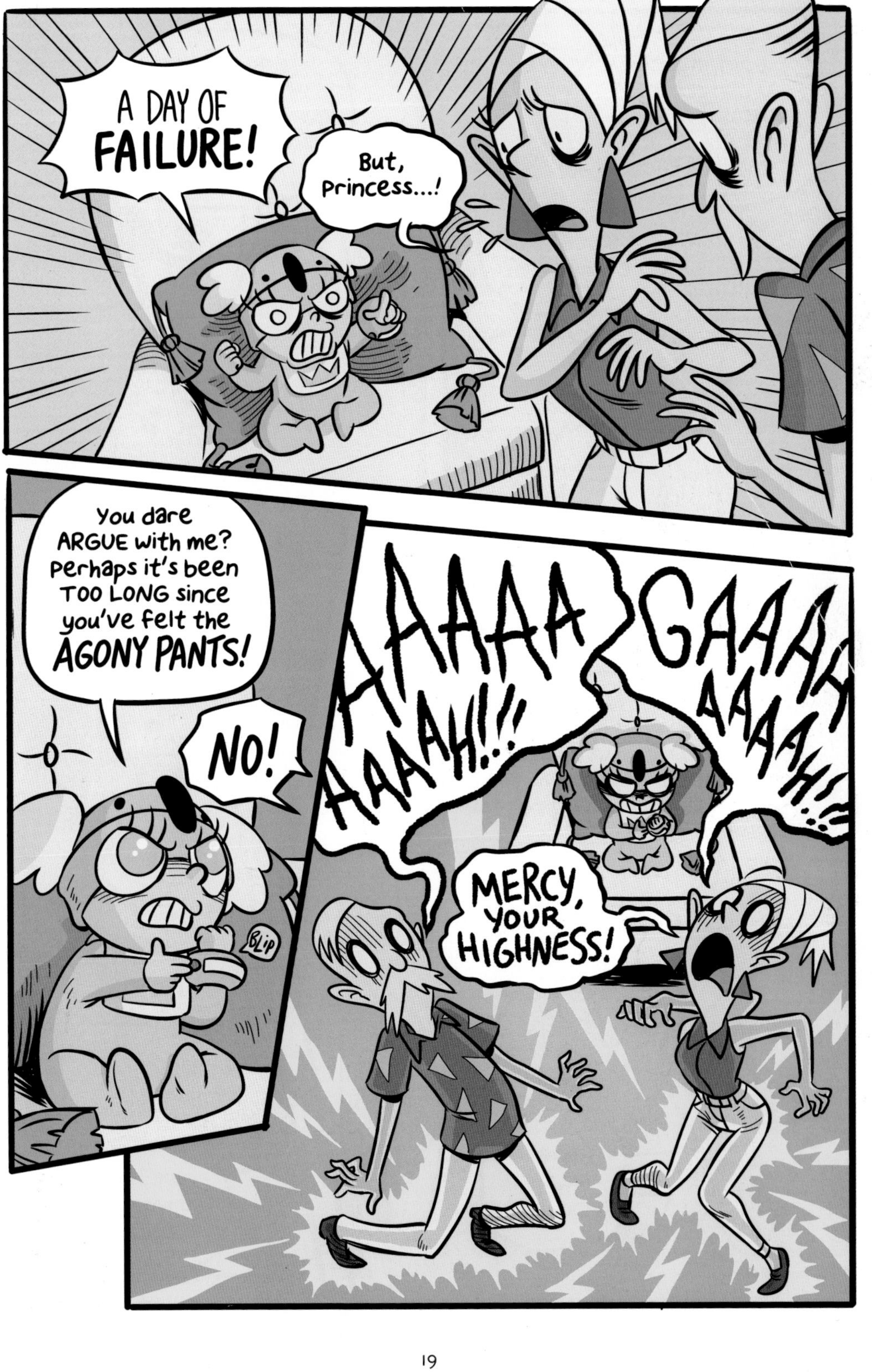

A DAY OF FAILURE!
But, Princess...!
You dare ARGUE with me? Perhaps it's been TOO LONG since you've felt the AGONY PANTS!
NO!
BLIP
AAAAAAAAAH!!!
GAAAHAAAAH!!!
MERCY, YOUR HIGHNESS!

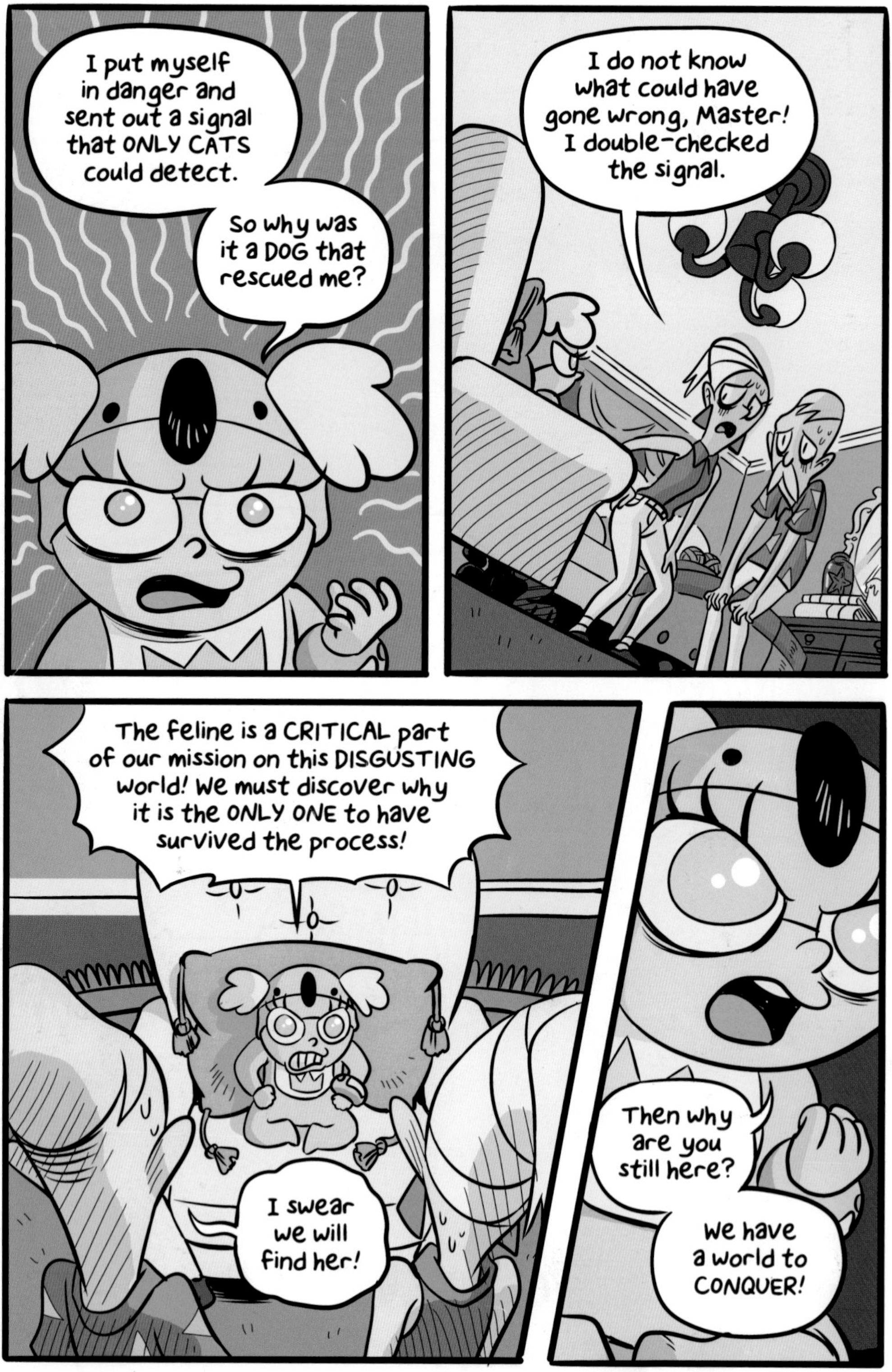
I put myself in danger and sent out a signal that ONLY CATS could detect.
So why was it a DOG that rescued me?
I do not know what could have gone wrong, Master! I double-checked the signal.
The feline is a CRITICAL part of our mission on this DISGUSTING world! We must discover why it is the ONLY ONE to have survived the process!
I swear we will find her!
Then why are you still here?
We have a world to CONQUER!

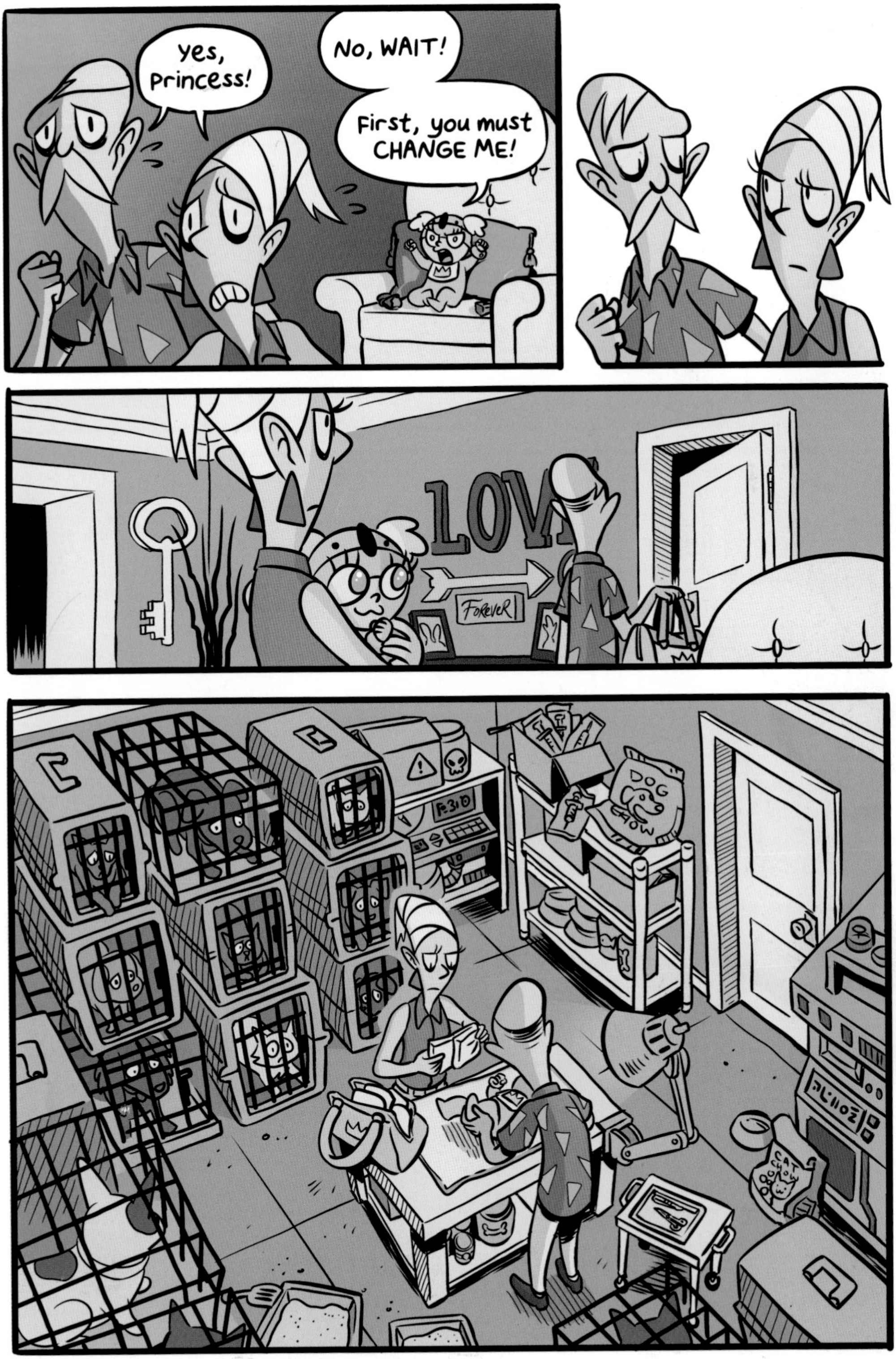
yes, Princess!
No, WAIT!
First, you must CHANGE ME!
LOVE
FOREVER
DOG CHOW
CAT CHOW

CHAPTER TWO

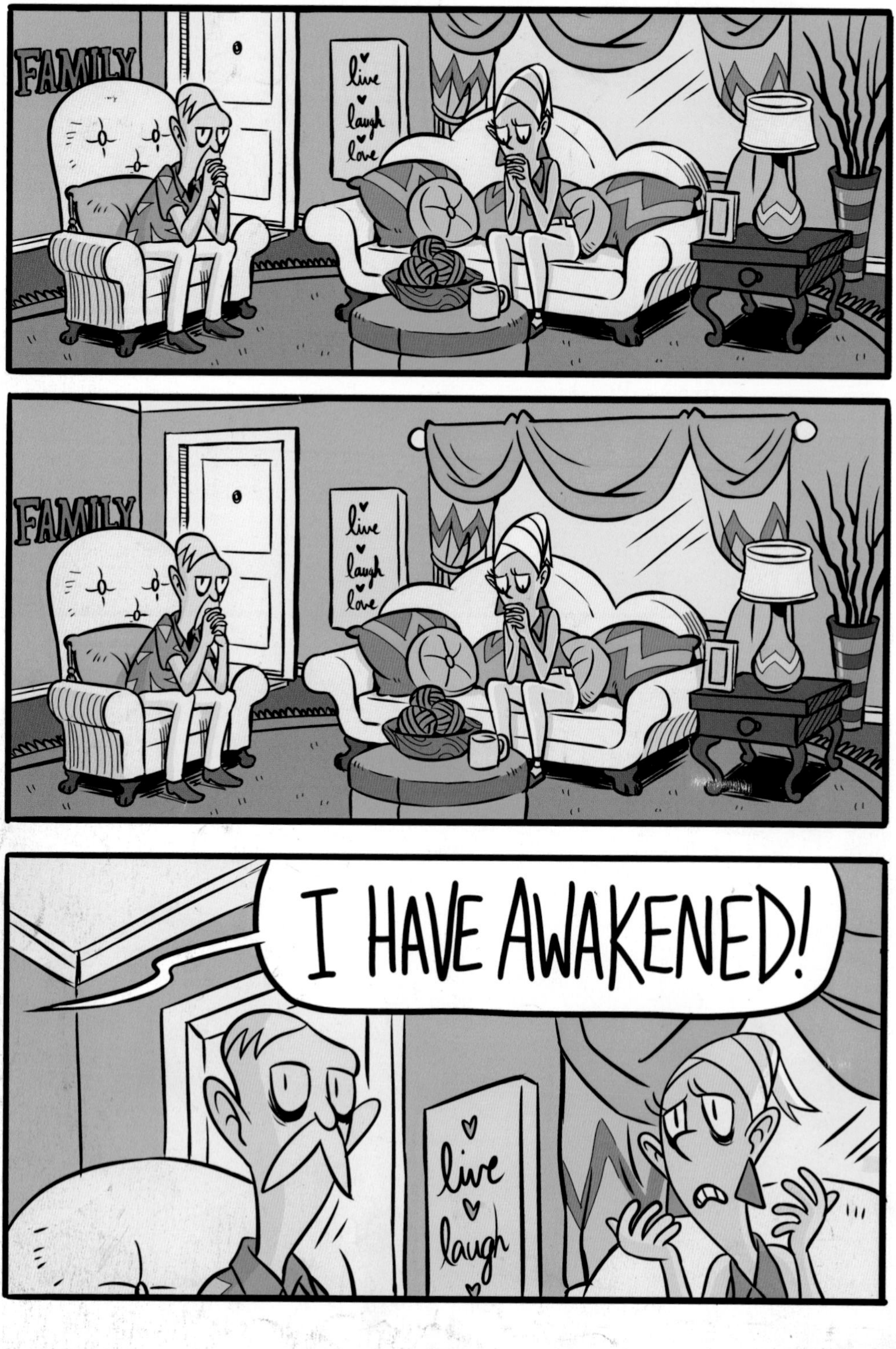
FAMILY
live
laugh
love
FAMILY
live
laugh
love
I HAVE AWAKENED!
live
laugh

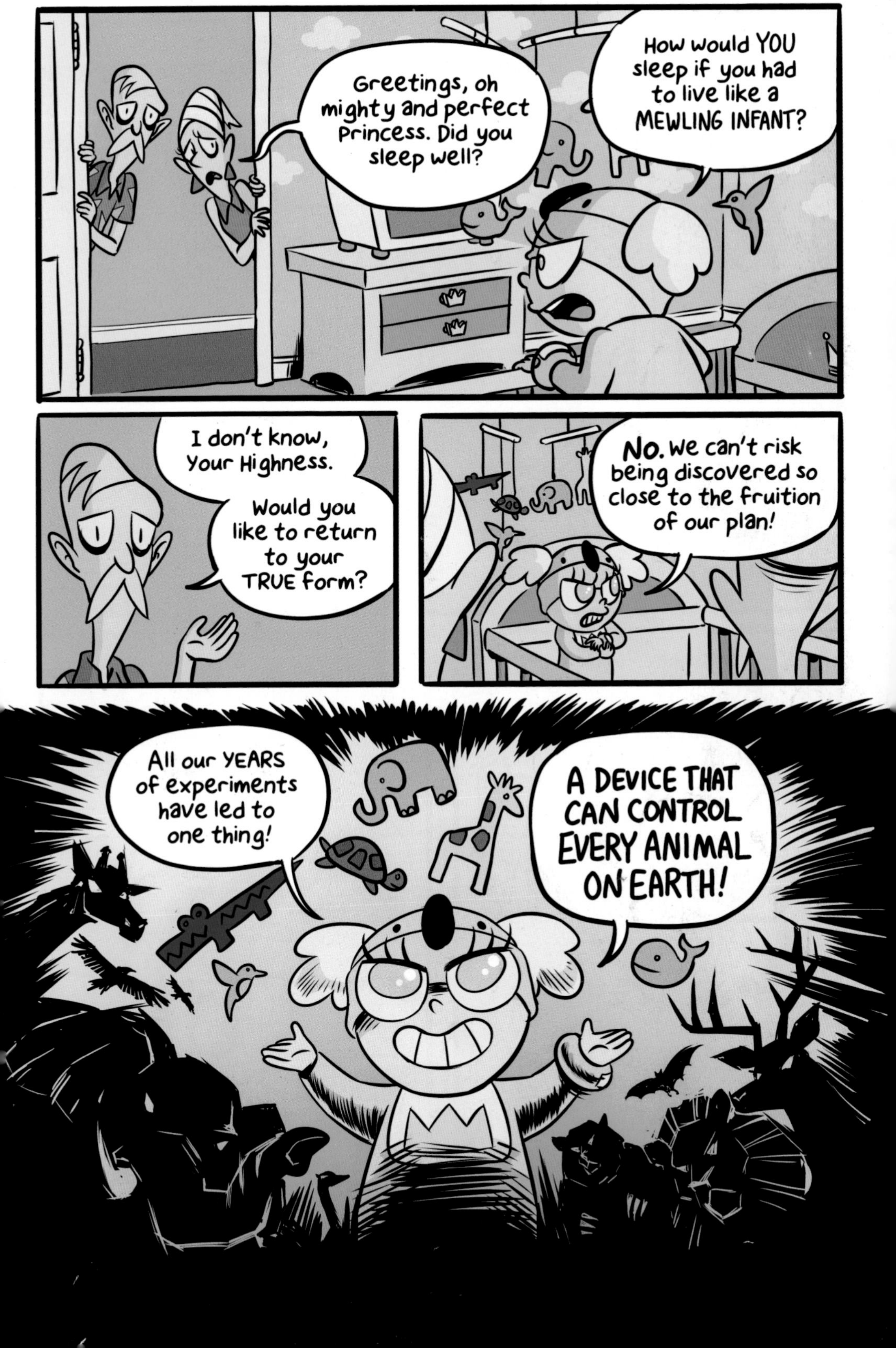
Greetings, oh mighty and perfect Princess. Did you sleep well?
How would YOU sleep if you had to live like a MEWLING INFANT?
I don't know, Your Highness.
Would you like to return to your TRUE form?
NO. We can't risk being discovered so close to the fruition of our plan!
All our YEARS of experiments have led to one thing!
A DEVICE THAT CAN CONTROL EVERY ANIMAL ON EARTH!

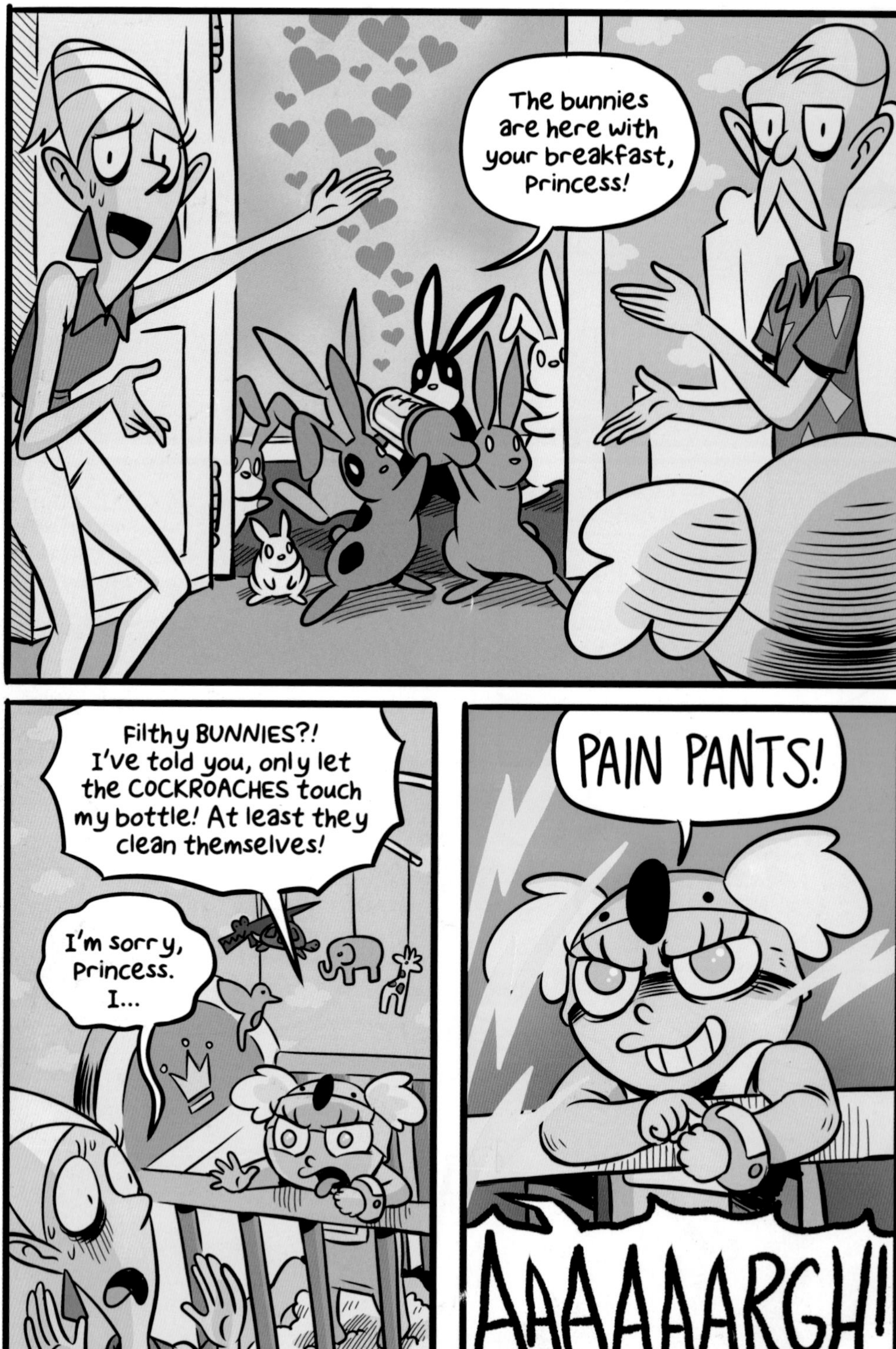
The bunnies are here with your breakfast, Princess!
Filthy BUNNIES?! I've told you, only let the COCKROACHES touch my bottle! At least they clean themselves!
I'm sorry, Princess. I...
PAIN PANTS!
AAAAAARGH!

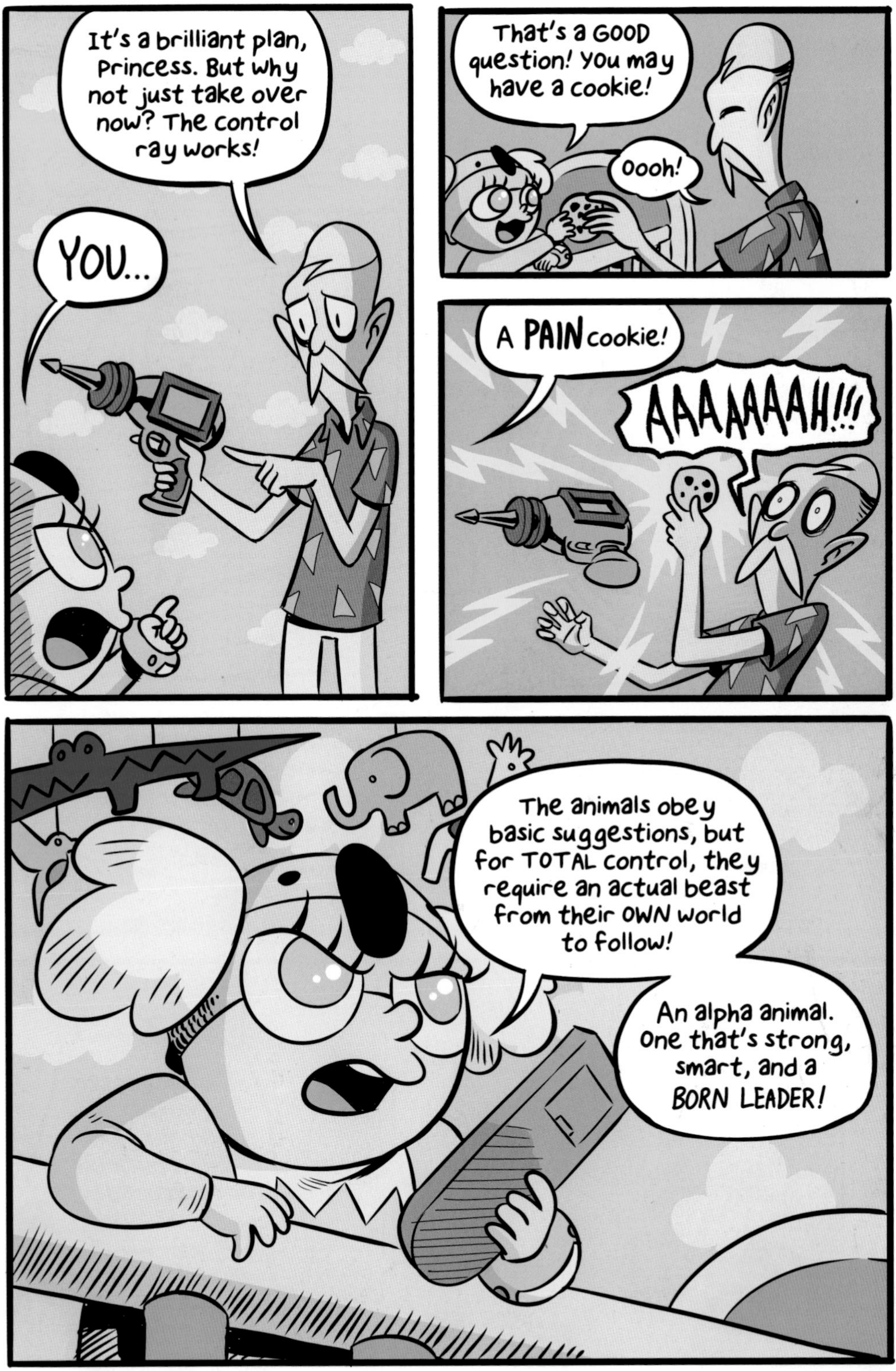
It's a brilliant plan, Princess. But why not just take over now? The control ray works!
YOU...
That's a GOOD question! You may have a cookie!
Oooh!
A PAIN cookie!
AAAAAAAH!!!
The animals obey basic suggestions, but for TOTAL control, they require an actual beast from their OWN world to follow!
An alpha animal. One that's strong, smart, and a BORN LEADER!

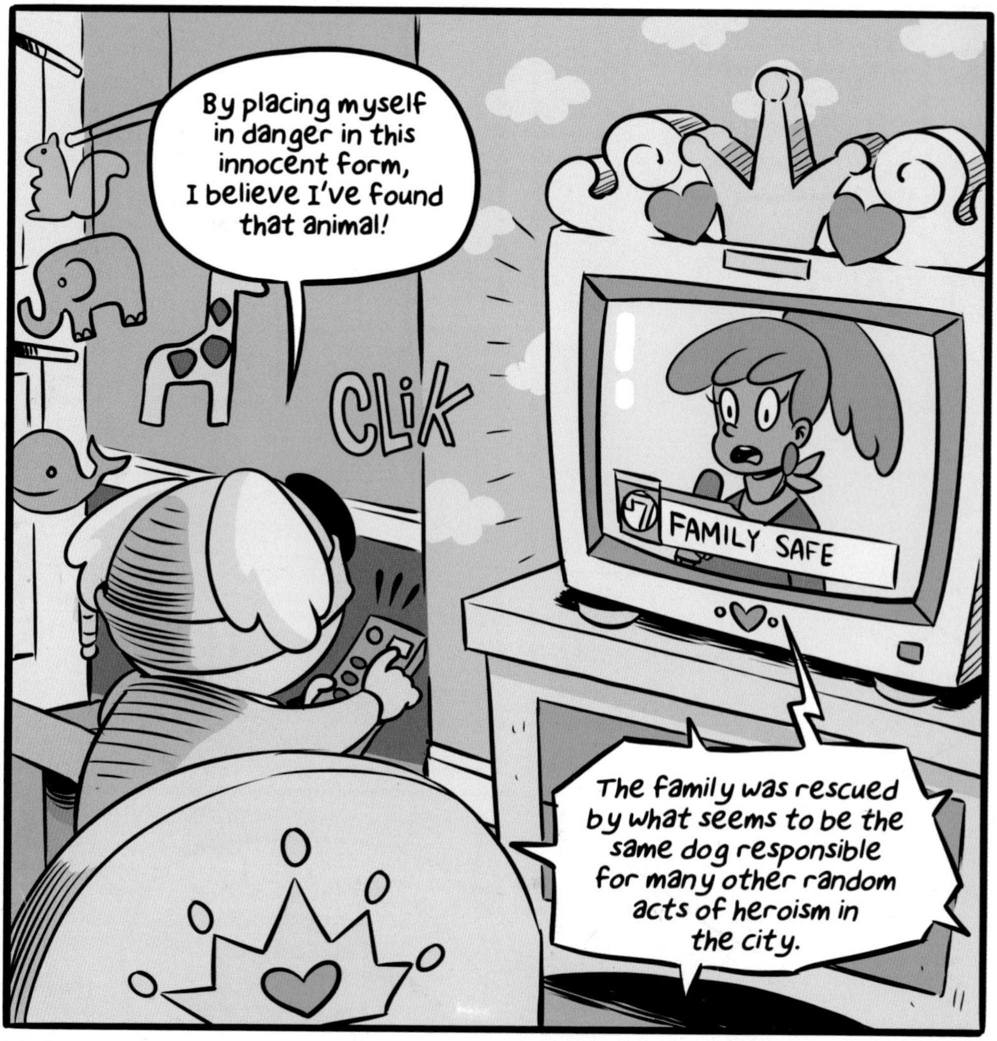
By placing myself in danger in this innocent form, I believe I've found that animal!
CLIK
FAMILY SAFE
The family was rescued by what seems to be the same dog responsible for many other random acts of heroism in the city.

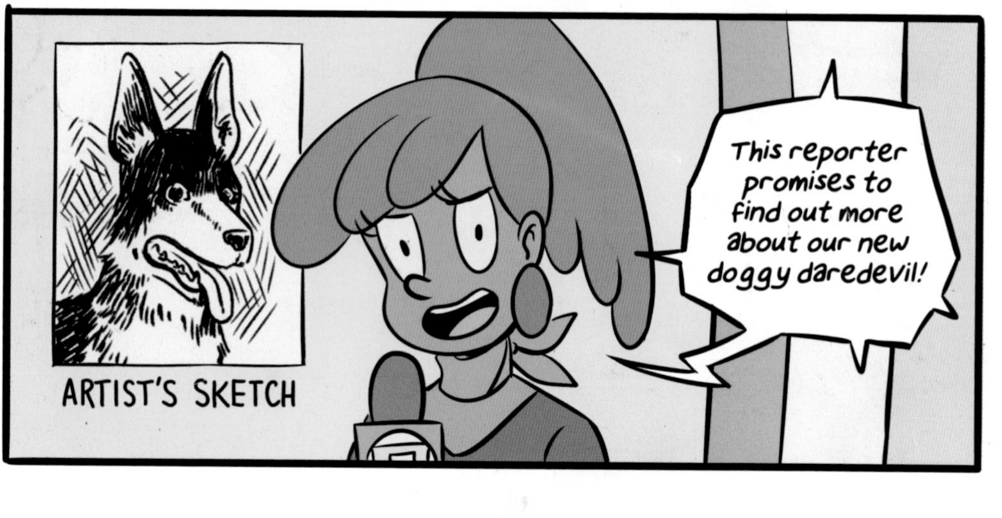
ARTIST'S SKETCH
This reporter promises to find out more about our new doggy daredevil!

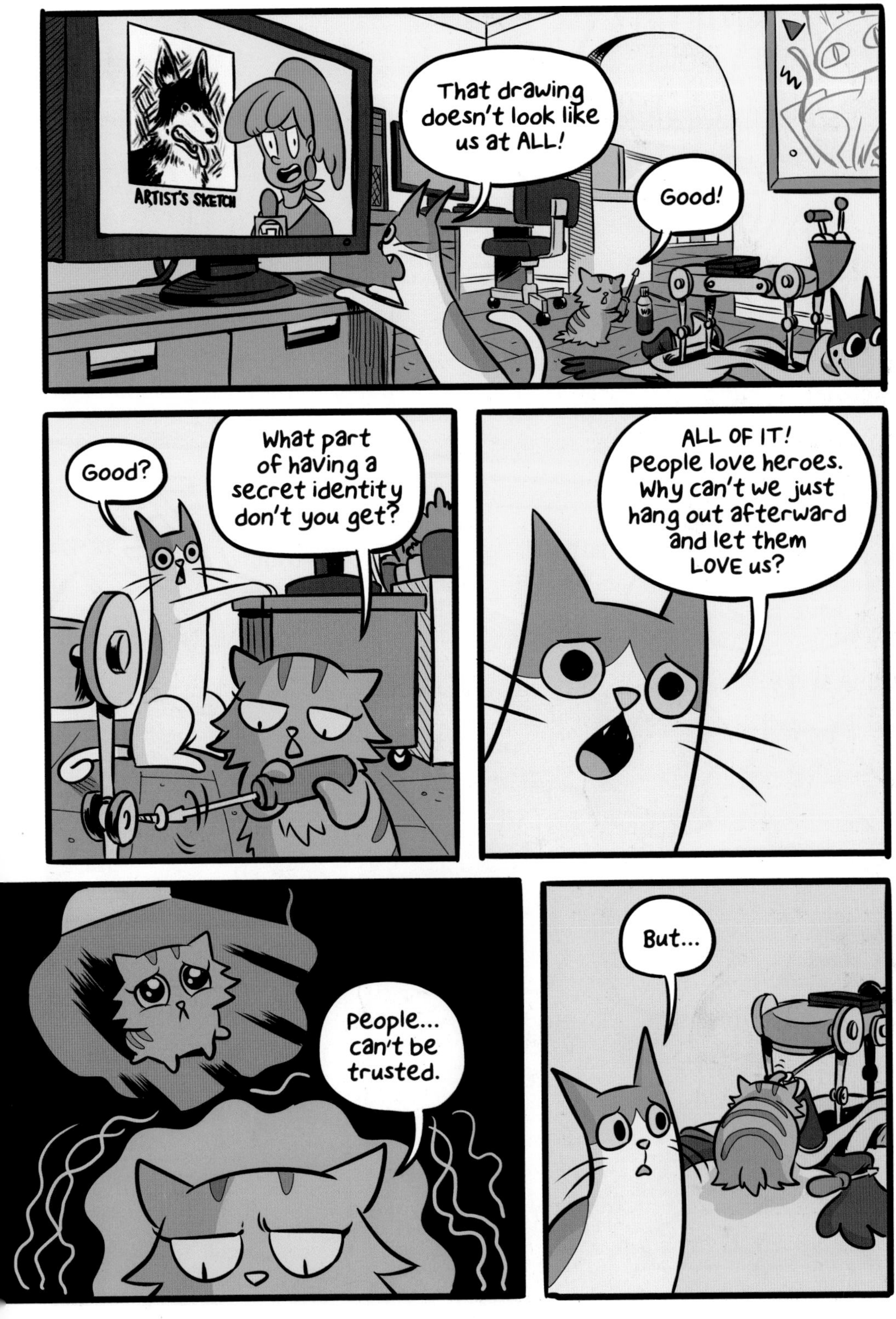
ARTIST'S SKETCH
That drawing doesn't look like us at ALL!
Good!
Good?
What part of having a secret identity don't you get?
ALL OF IT! People love heroes. Why can't we just hang out afterward and let them LOVE us?
People... can't be trusted.
But...

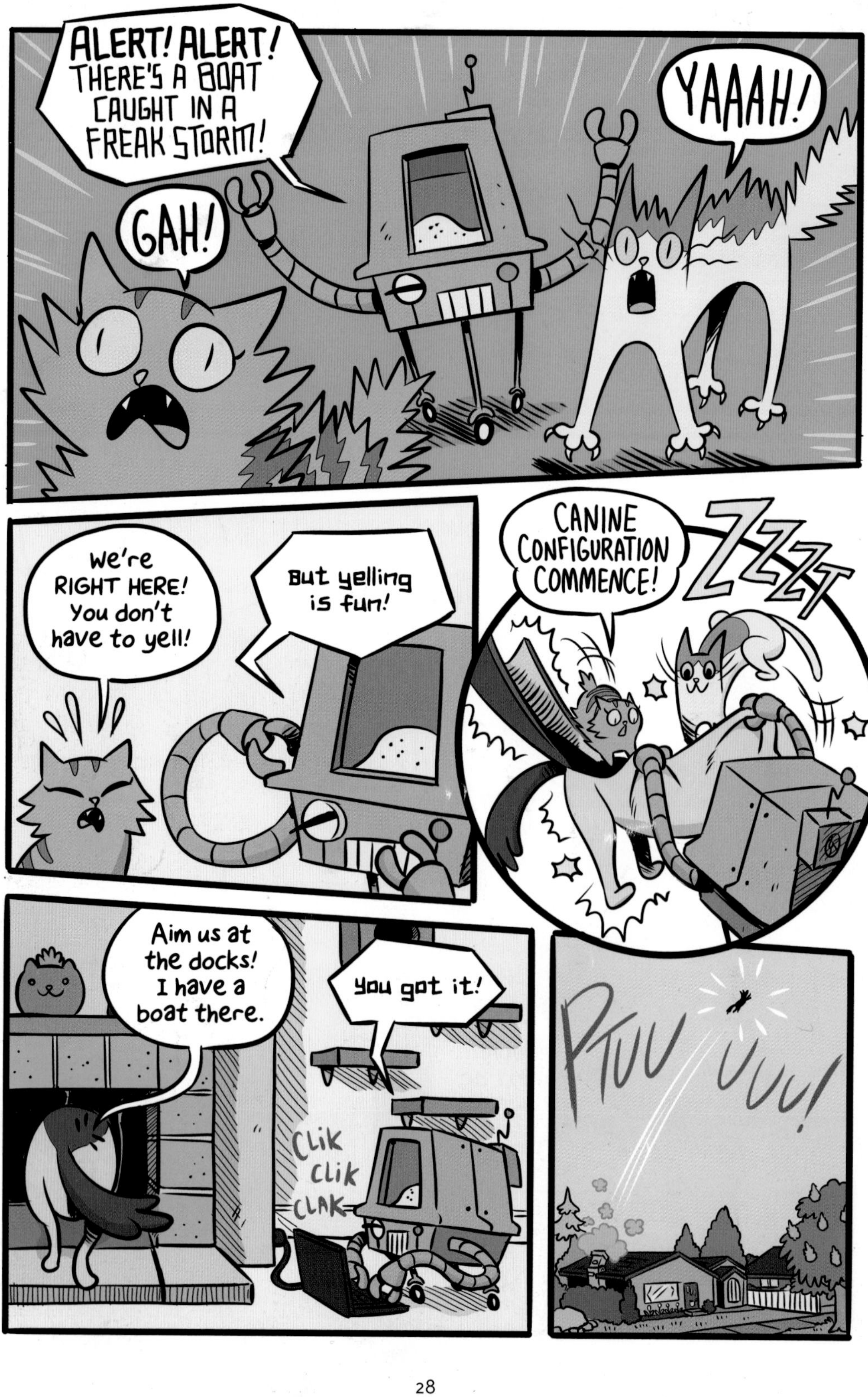
ALERT! ALERT! THERE'S A BOAT CAUGHT IN A FREAK STORM!
YAAAH!
GAH!
We're RIGHT HERE! You don't have to yell!
But yelling is fun!
CANINE CONFIGURATION COMMENCE!
ZZZT
Aim us at the docks! I have a boat there.
You got it!
CLIK
CLIK
CLAK
PTUUUUU!

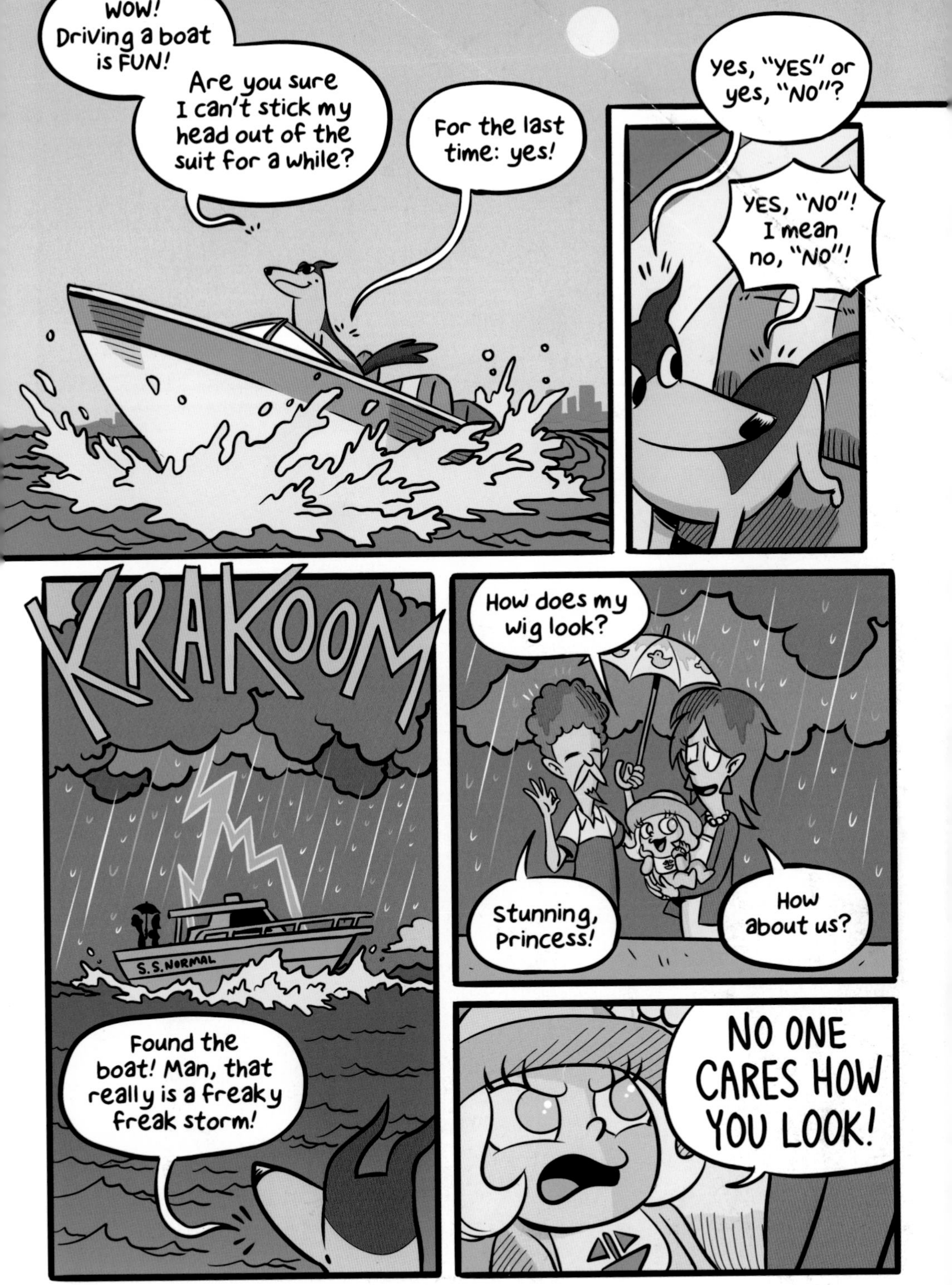
WOW! Driving a boat is FUN!
Are you sure I can't stick my head out of the suit for a while?
For the last time: yes!
yes, "YES" or yes, "NO"?
YES, "NO"! I mean no, "NO"!
KRAKOOM
S.S. NORMAL
Found the boat! Man, that really is a freaky freak storm!
How does my wig look?
Stunning, Princess!
How about us?
NO ONE CARES HOW YOU LOOK!

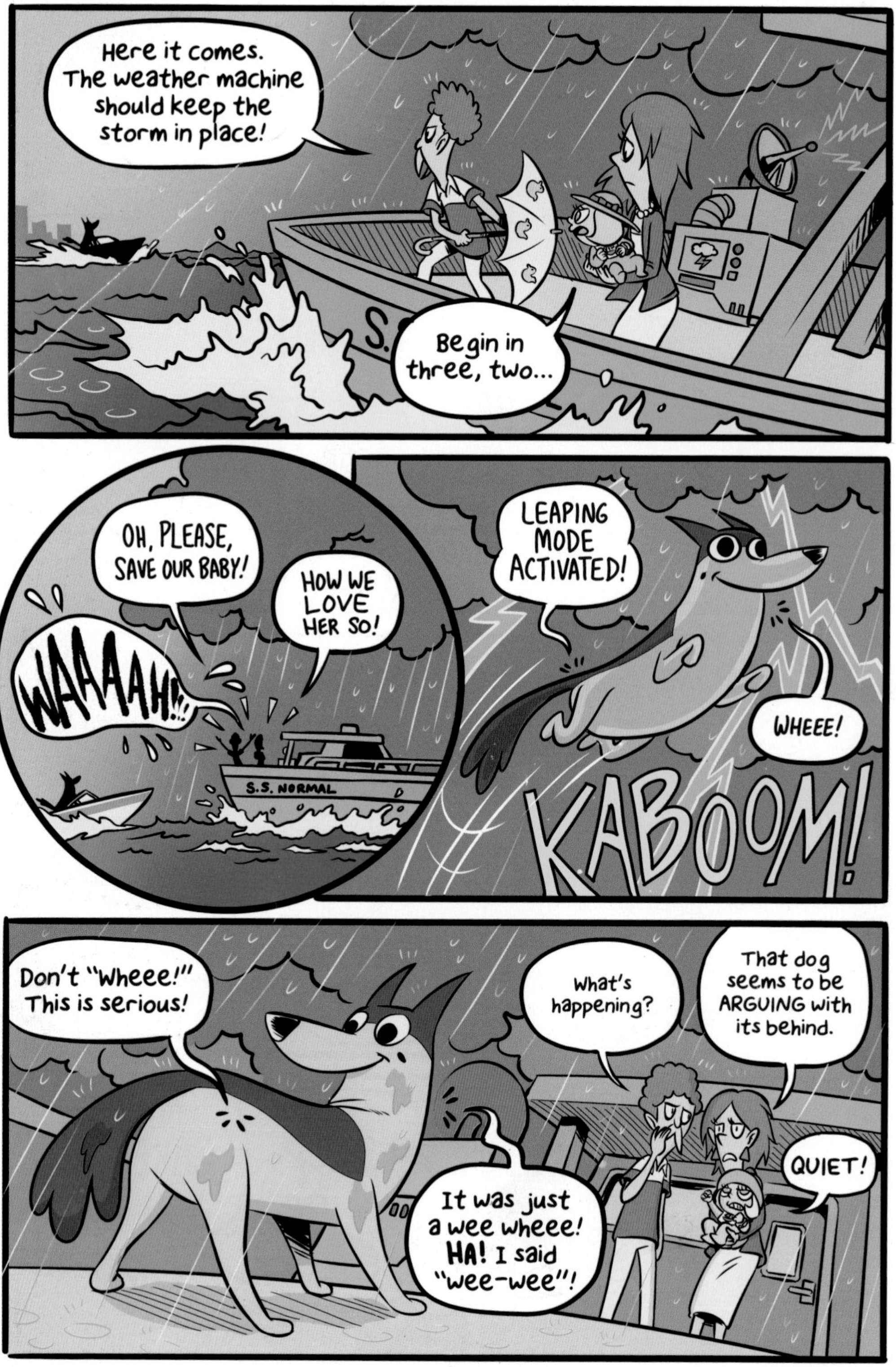
Here it comes. The weather machine should keep the storm in place!
S.S.
Begin in three, two...
OH, PLEASE, SAVE OUR BABY!
HOW WE LOVE HER SO!
WAAAAH!!!
S.S. NORMAL
LEAPING MODE ACTIVATED!
WHEEE!
KABOOM!
Don't "Wheee!" This is serious!
What's happening?
That dog seems to be ARGUING with its behind.
It was just a wee wheee! **HA!** I said "wee-wee"!
QUIET!

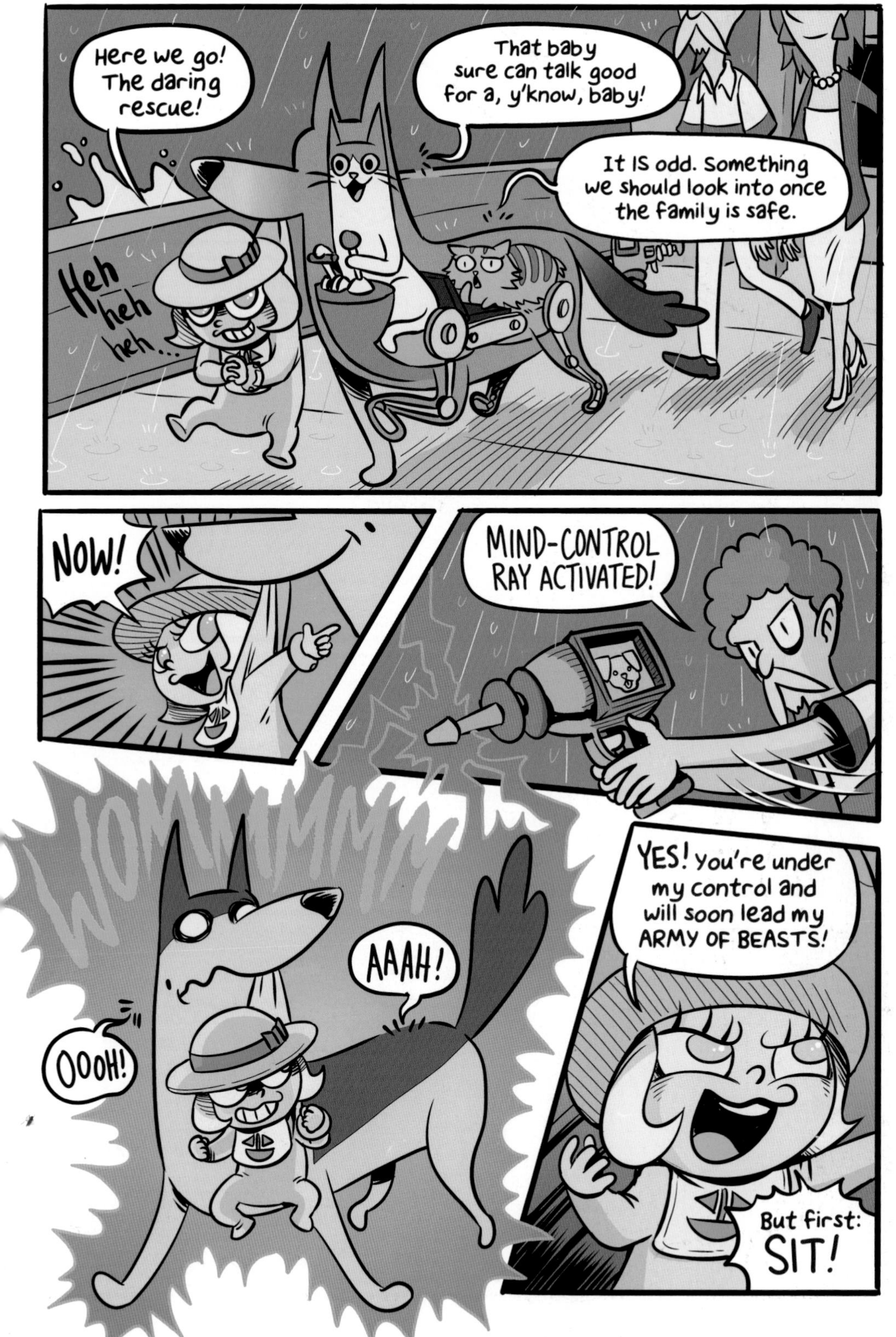
Here we go! The daring rescue!
That baby sure can talk good for a, y'know, baby!
It IS odd. Something we should look into once the family is safe.
Heh heh heh...
NOW!
MIND-CONTROL RAY ACTIVATED!
WOMMMMM
AAAH!
OOOH!
YES! You're under my control and will soon lead my ARMY OF BEASTS!
But first: SIT!

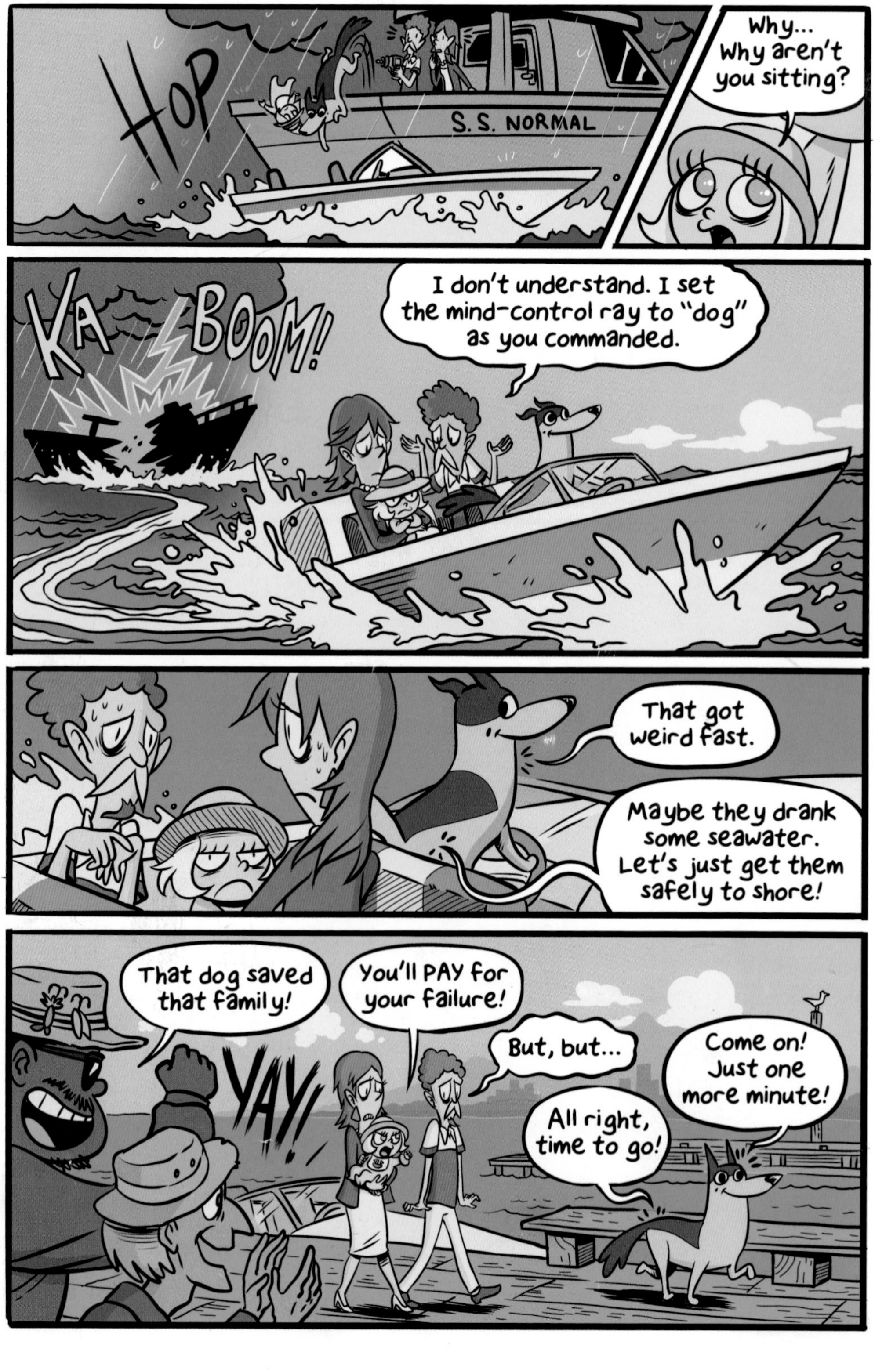
HOP
S.S. NORMAL
Why... Why aren't you sitting?
KA BOOM!
I don't understand. I set the mind-control ray to "dog" as you commanded.
That got weird fast.
Maybe they drank some seawater. Let's just get them safely to shore!
That dog saved that family!
YAY!
You'll PAY for your failure!
But, but...
Come on! Just one more minute!
All right, time to go!

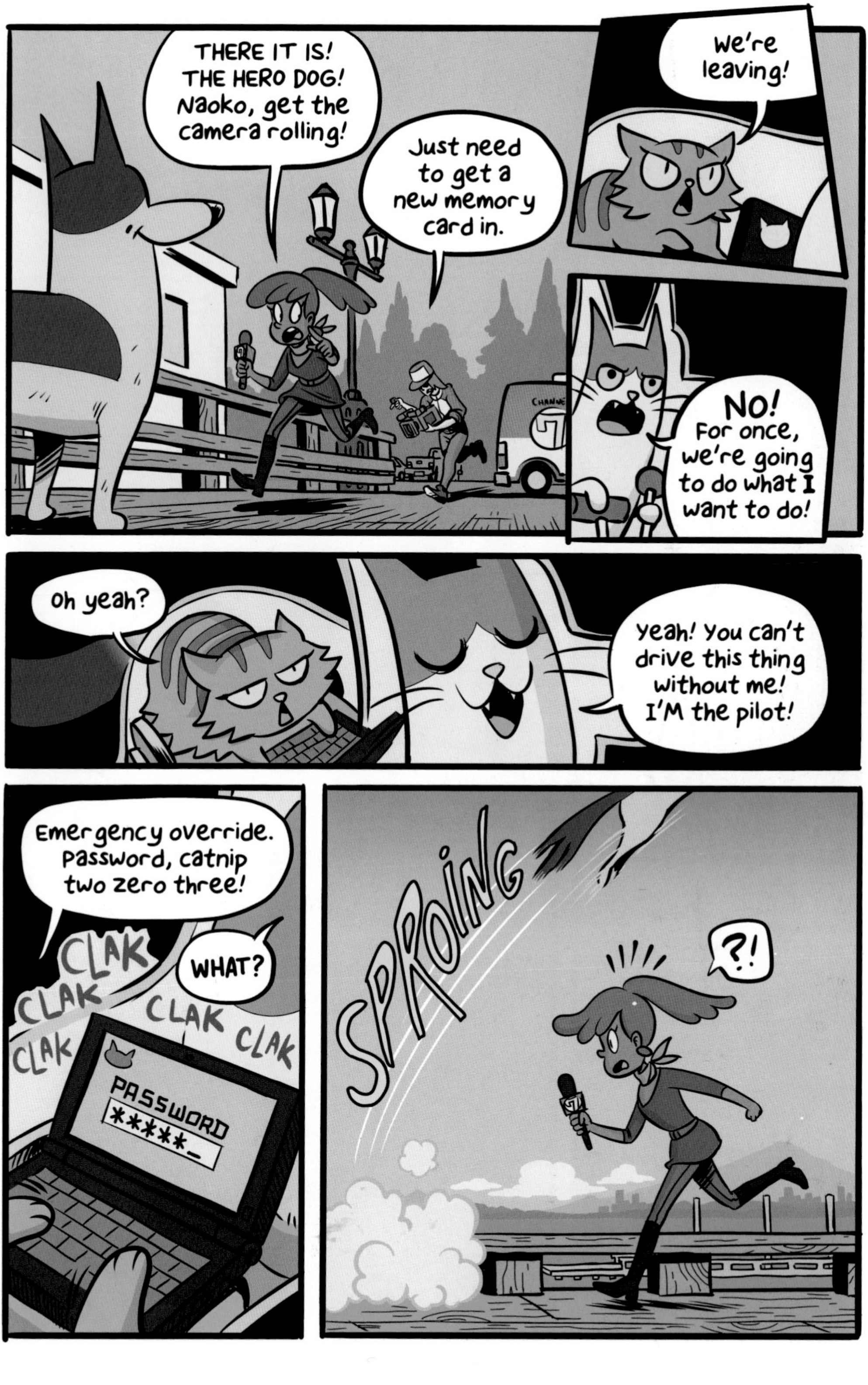
THERE IT IS! THE HERO DOG! Naoko, get the camera rolling!
Just need to get a new memory card in.
We're leaving!
CHANNE
NO! For once, we're going to do what I want to do!
Oh yeah?
Yeah! You can't drive this thing without me! I'M the pilot!
Emergency override. Password, catnip two zero three!
CLAK
CLAK
CLAK
WHAT?
CLAK
CLAK
PASSWORD
*****_
SPROING
?!

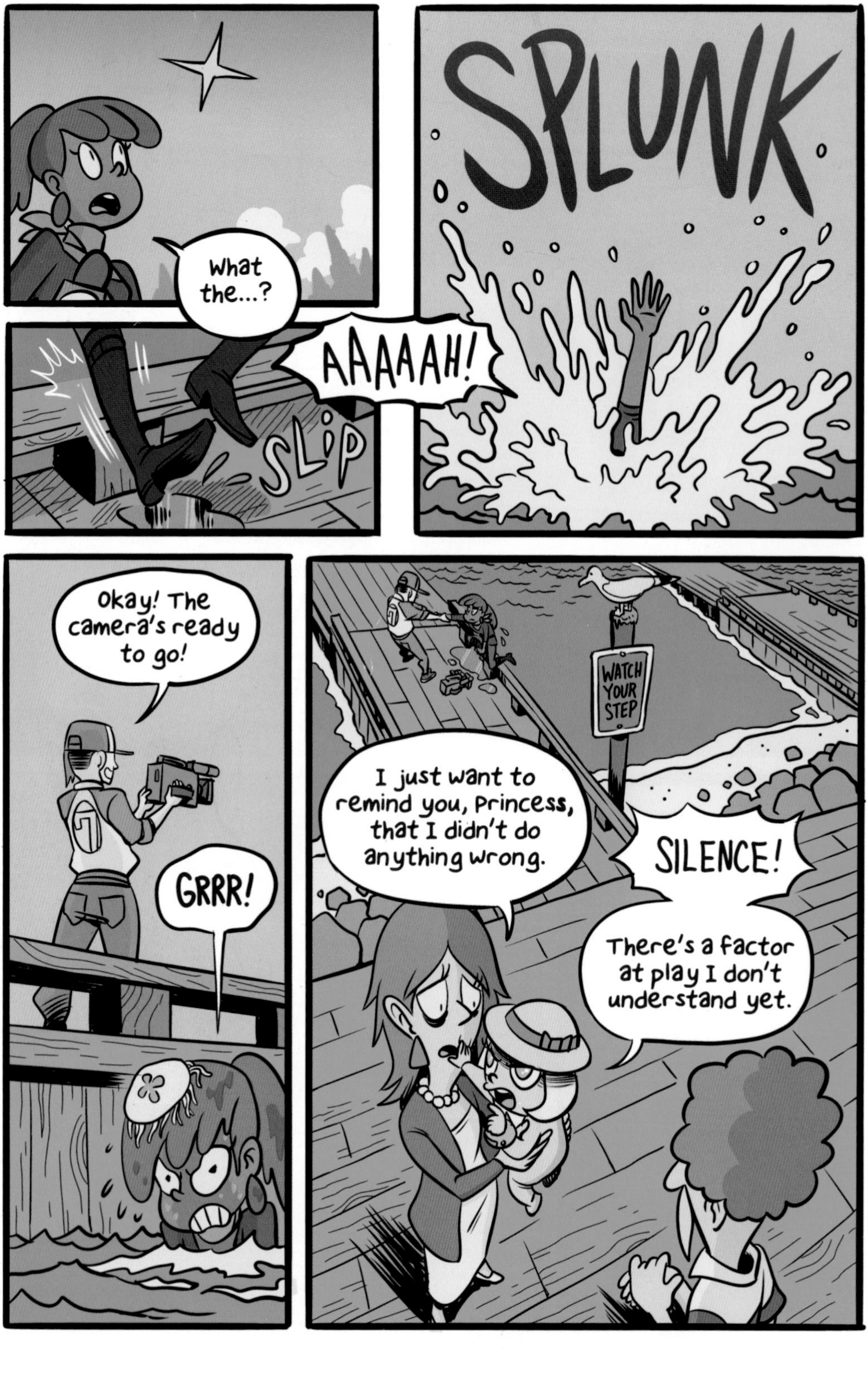
What the...?
AAAAAH!
SLIP
SPLUNK
Okay! The camera's ready to go!
GRRR!
WATCH YOUR STEP
I just want to remind you, Princess, that I didn't do anything wrong.
SILENCE!
There's a factor at play I don't understand yet.

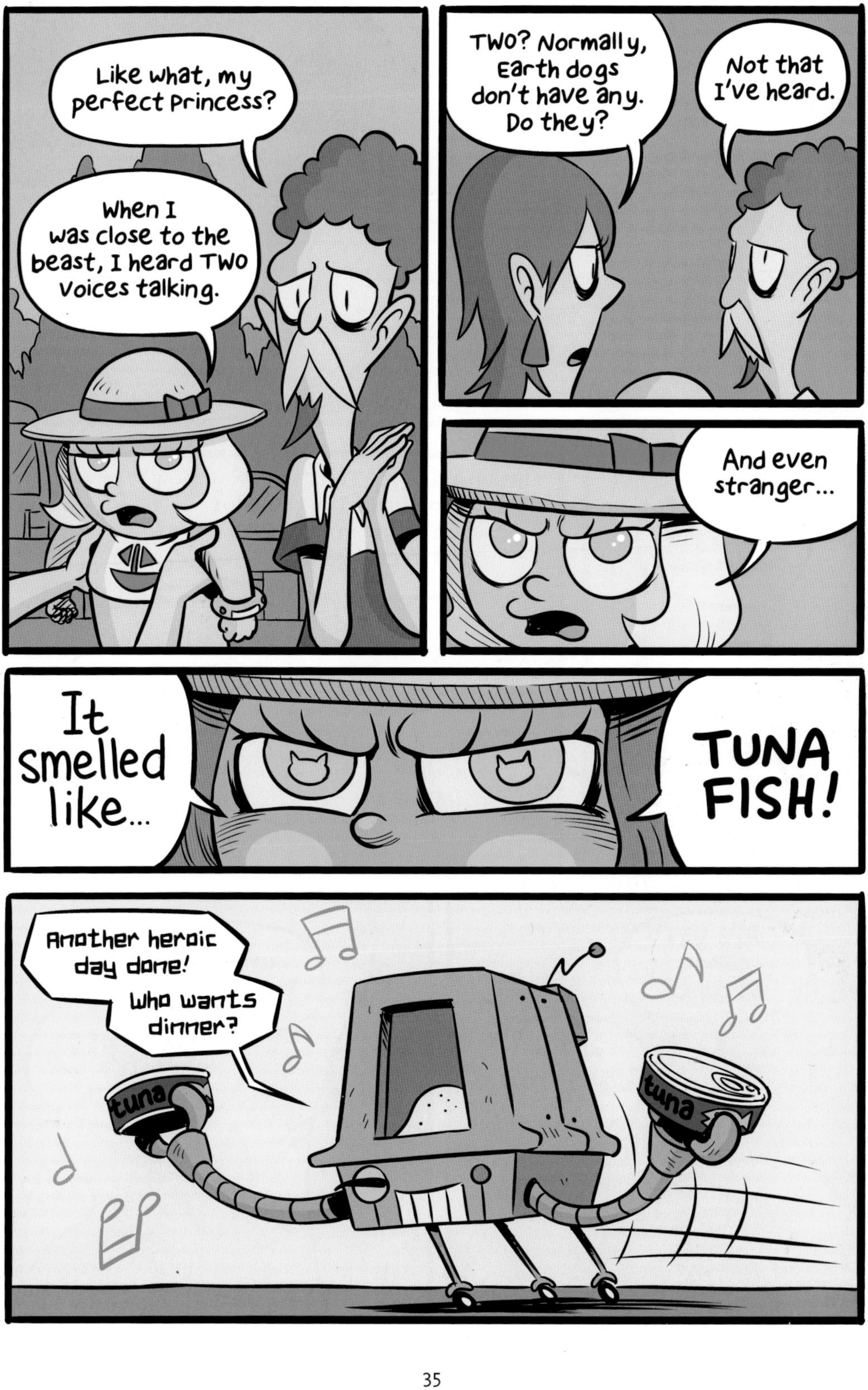
Like what, my perfect Princess?
When I was close to the beast, I heard TWO voices talking.
TWO? Normally, Earth dogs don't have any. Do they?
Not that I've heard.
And even stranger...
It smelled like...
TUNA FISH!
Another heroic day done!
Who wants dinner?
tuna
tuna

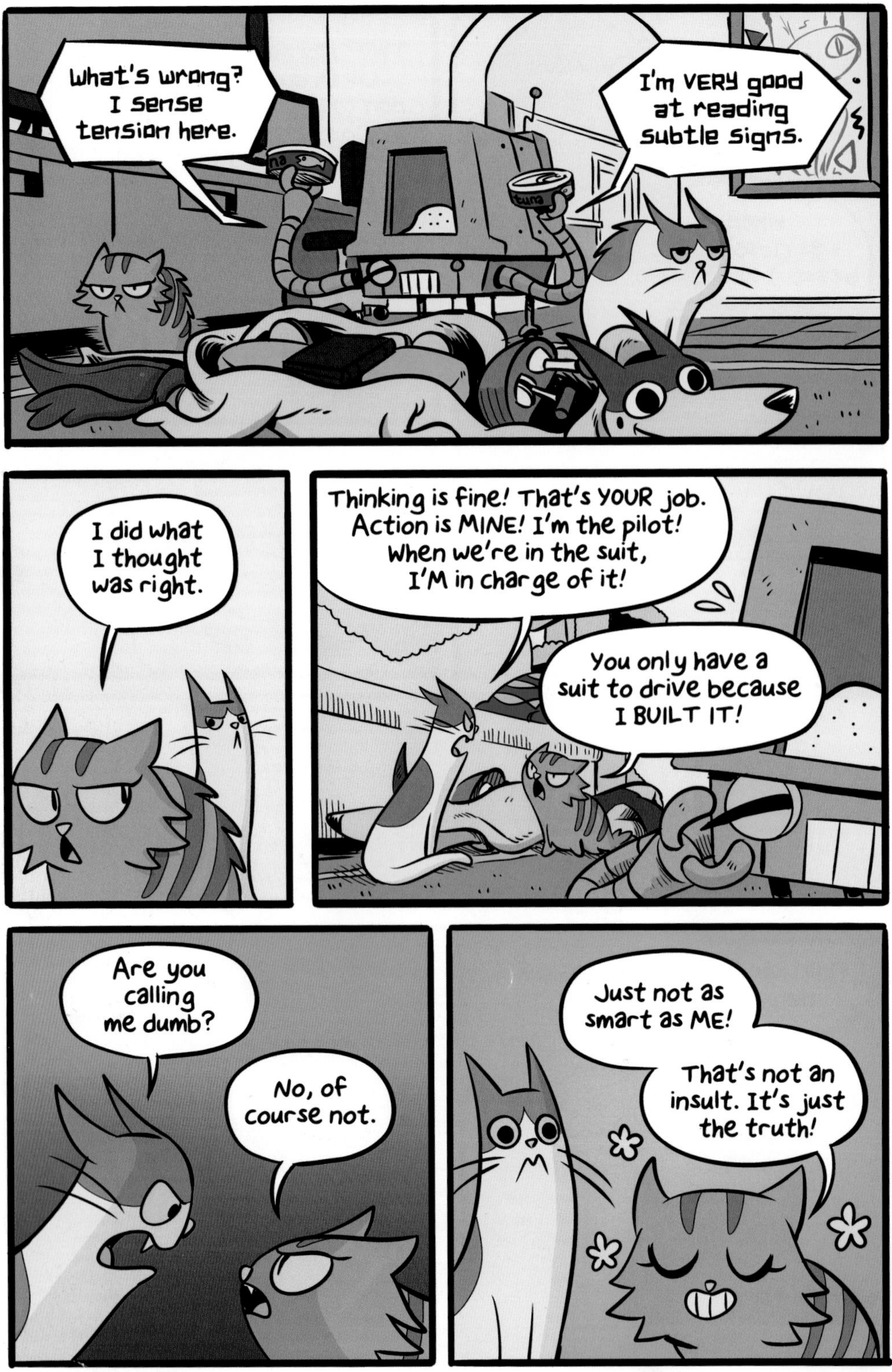
What's wrong? I sense tension here.
I'm VERY good at reading subtle signs.
I did what I thought was right.
Thinking is fine! That's YOUR job. Action is MINE! I'm the pilot! When we're in the suit, I'M in charge of it!
You only have a suit to drive because I BUILT IT!
Are you calling me dumb?
No, of course not.
Just not as smart as ME!
That's not an insult. It's just the truth!

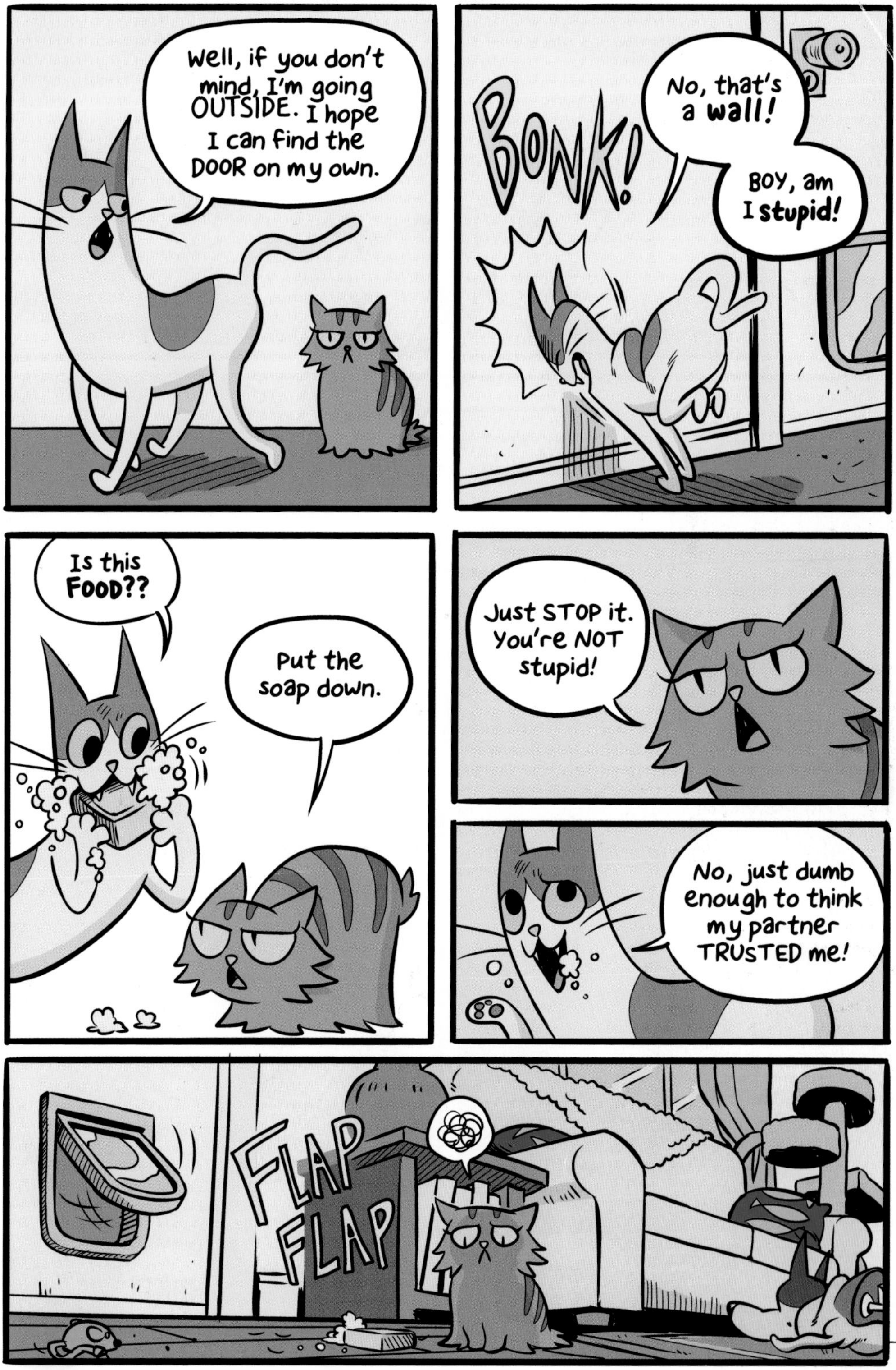
Well, if you don't mind, I'm going OUTSIDE. I hope I can find the DOOR on my own.
BONK!
No, that's a wall!
BOY, am I stupid!
Is this FOOD??
Put the soap down.
Just STOP it. You're NOT stupid!
No, just dumb enough to think my partner TRUSTED me!
FLAP FLAP

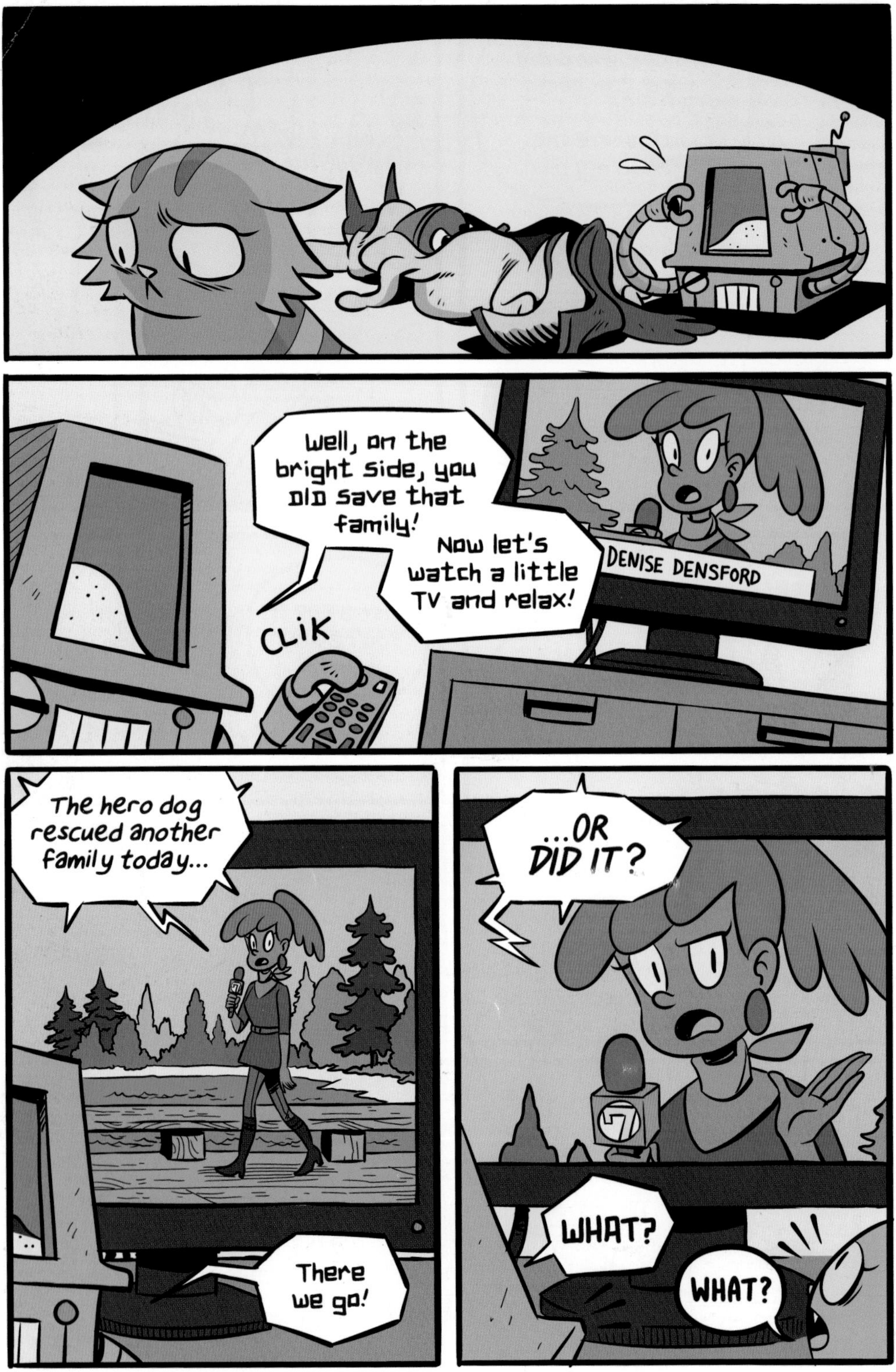

Well, on the bright side, you DID save that family!
Now let's watch a little TV and relax!
CLIK
DENISE DENSFORD
The hero dog rescued another family today...
There we go!
...OR DID IT?
WHAT?
WHAT?

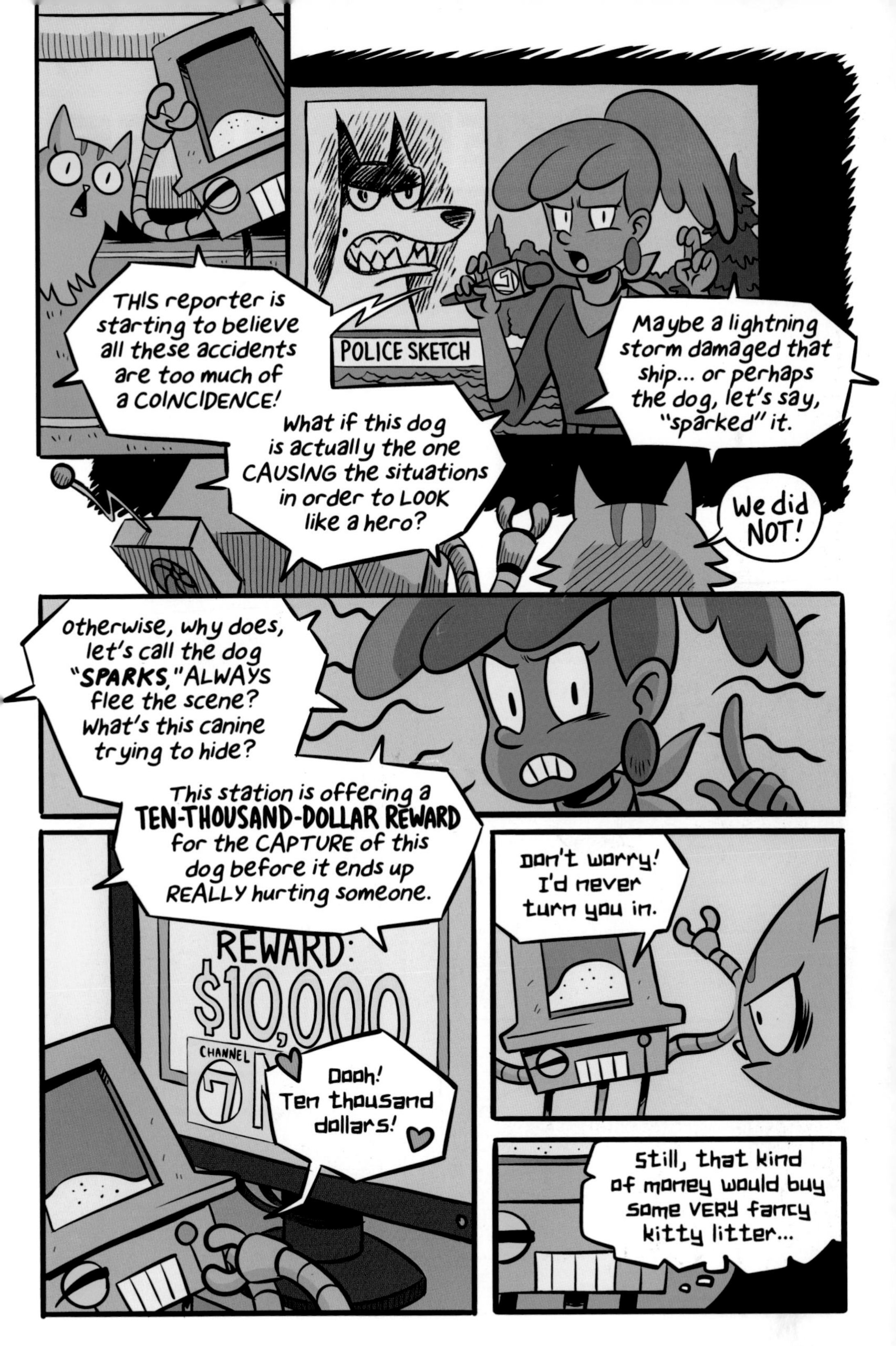
THIS reporter is starting to believe all these accidents are too much of a COINCIDENCE!
POLICE SKETCH
Maybe a lightning storm damaged that ship... or perhaps the dog, let's say, "sparked" it.
What if this dog is actually the one CAUSING the situations in order to LOOK like a hero?
We did NOT!
Otherwise, why does, let's call the dog "SPARKS," ALWAYS flee the scene? What's this canine trying to hide?
This station is offering a TEN-THOUSAND-DOLLAR REWARD for the CAPTURE of this dog before it ends up REALLY hurting someone.
REWARD: $10,000
CHANNEL 7
Oooh! Ten thousand dollars!
Don't worry! I'd never turn you in.
Still, that kind of money would buy some VERY fancy kitty litter...

CHAPTER THREE

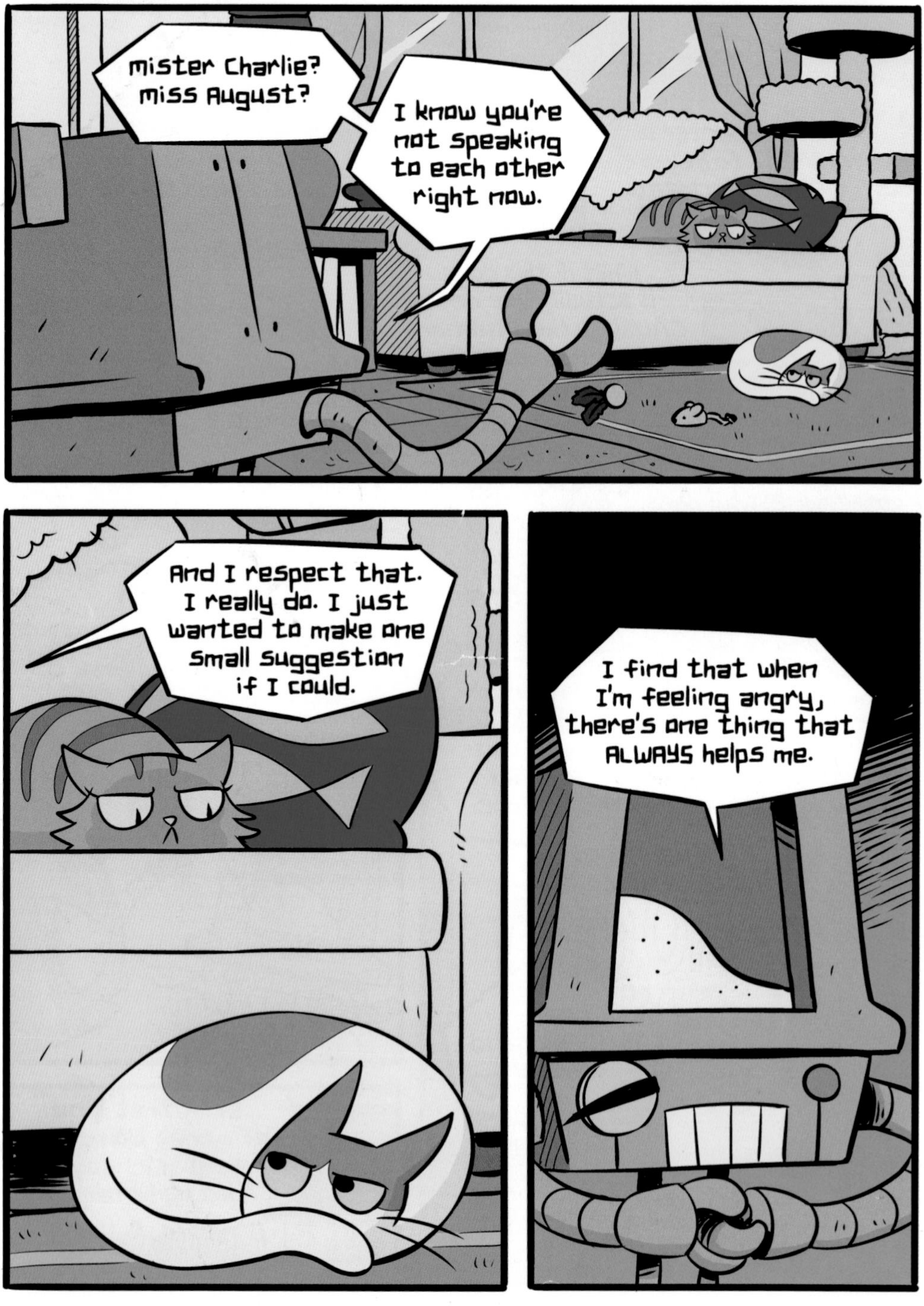

mister Charlie? miss August?
I know you're not speaking to each other right now.
And I respect that. I really do. I just wanted to make one small suggestion if I could.
I find that when I'm feeling angry, there's one thing that ALWAYS helps me.

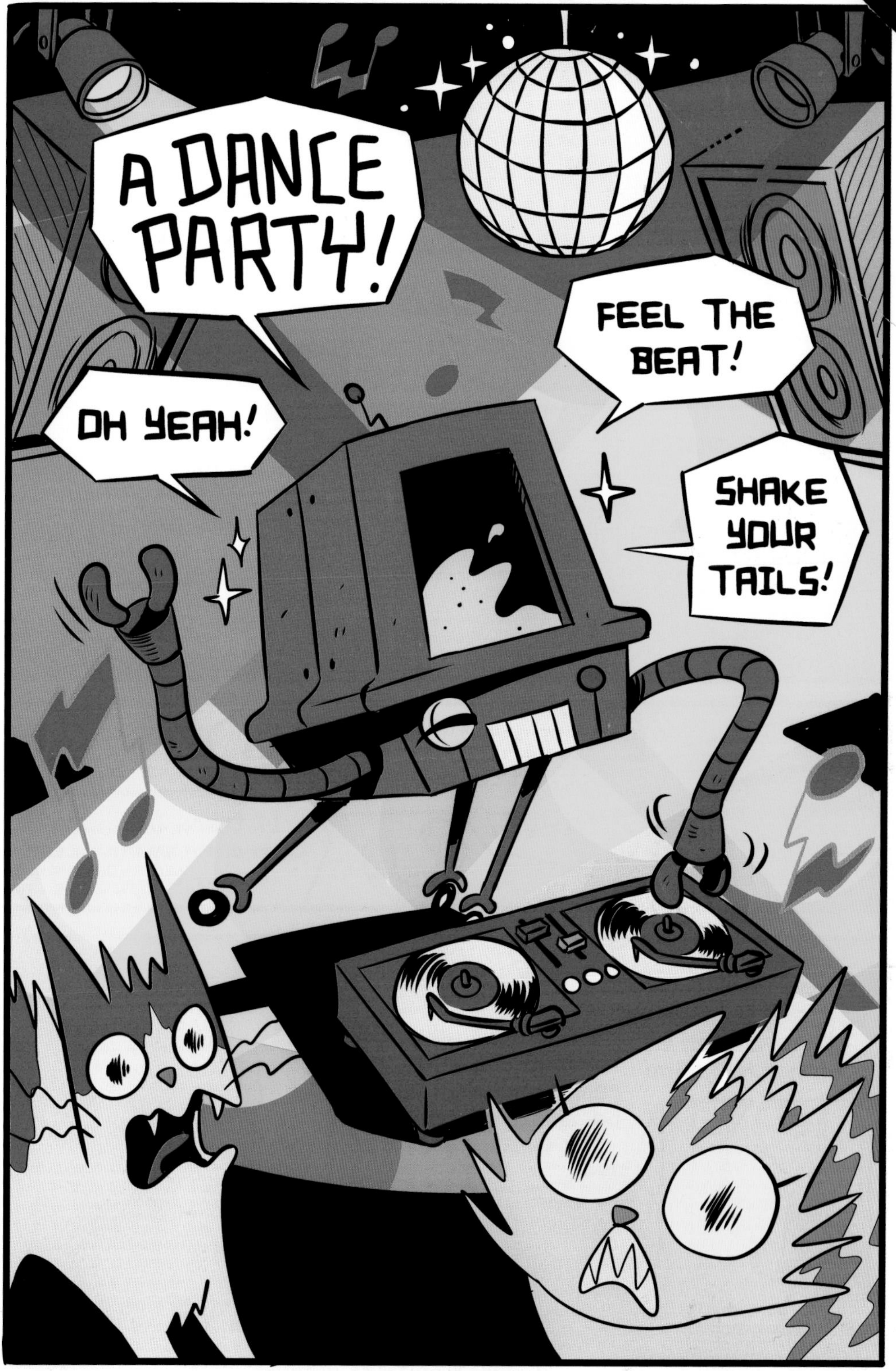
A DANCE PARTY!
OH YEAH!
FEEL THE BEAT!
SHAKE YOUR TAILS!

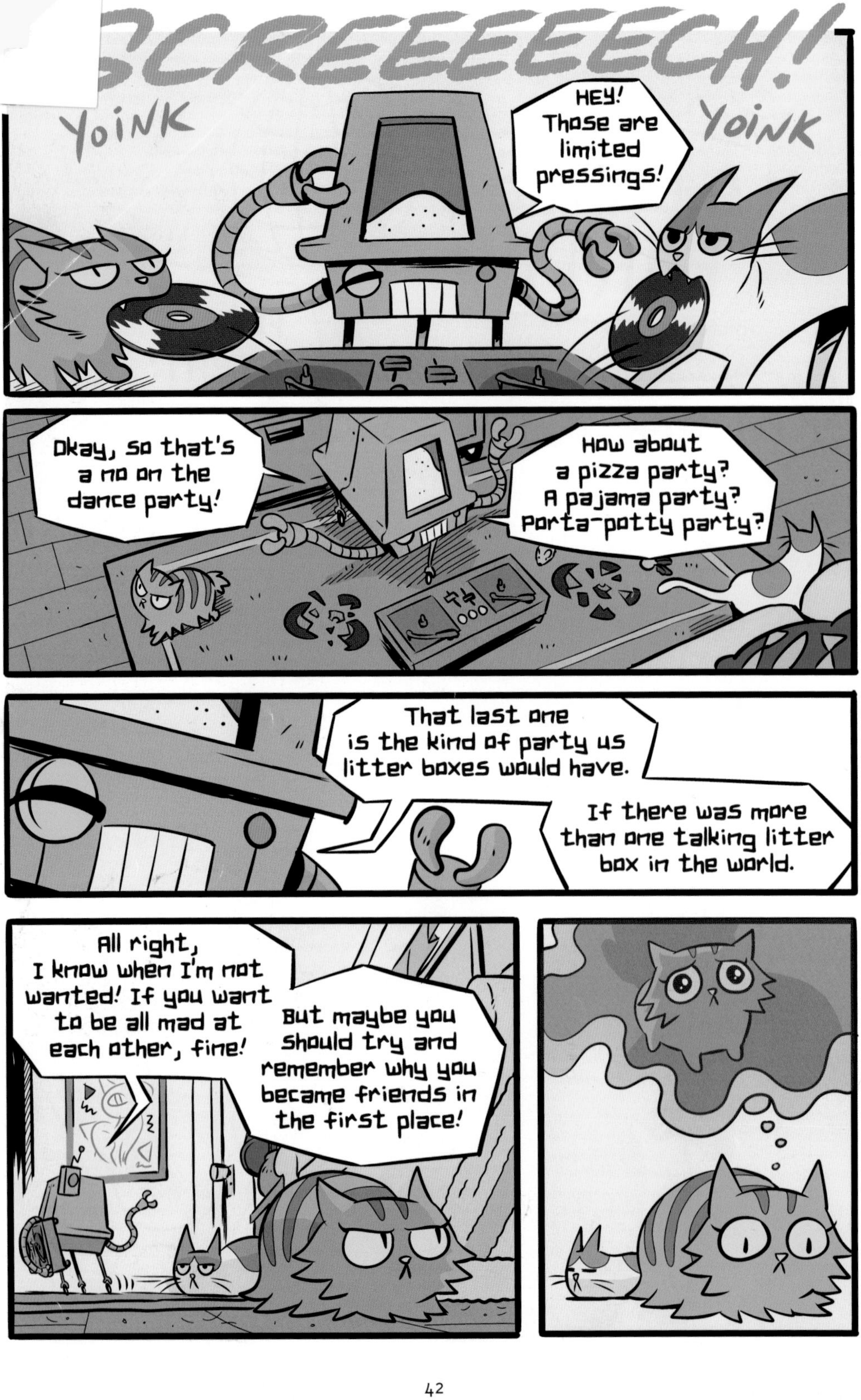
SCREEEEECH!
YOINK
HEY! Those are limited pressings!
YOINK
Okay, so that's a no on the dance party!
How about a pizza party? A pajama party? Porta-potty party?
That last one is the kind of party us litter boxes would have.
If there was more than one talking litter box in the world.
All right, I know when I'm not wanted! If you want to be all mad at each other, fine!
But maybe you should try and remember why you became friends in the first place!

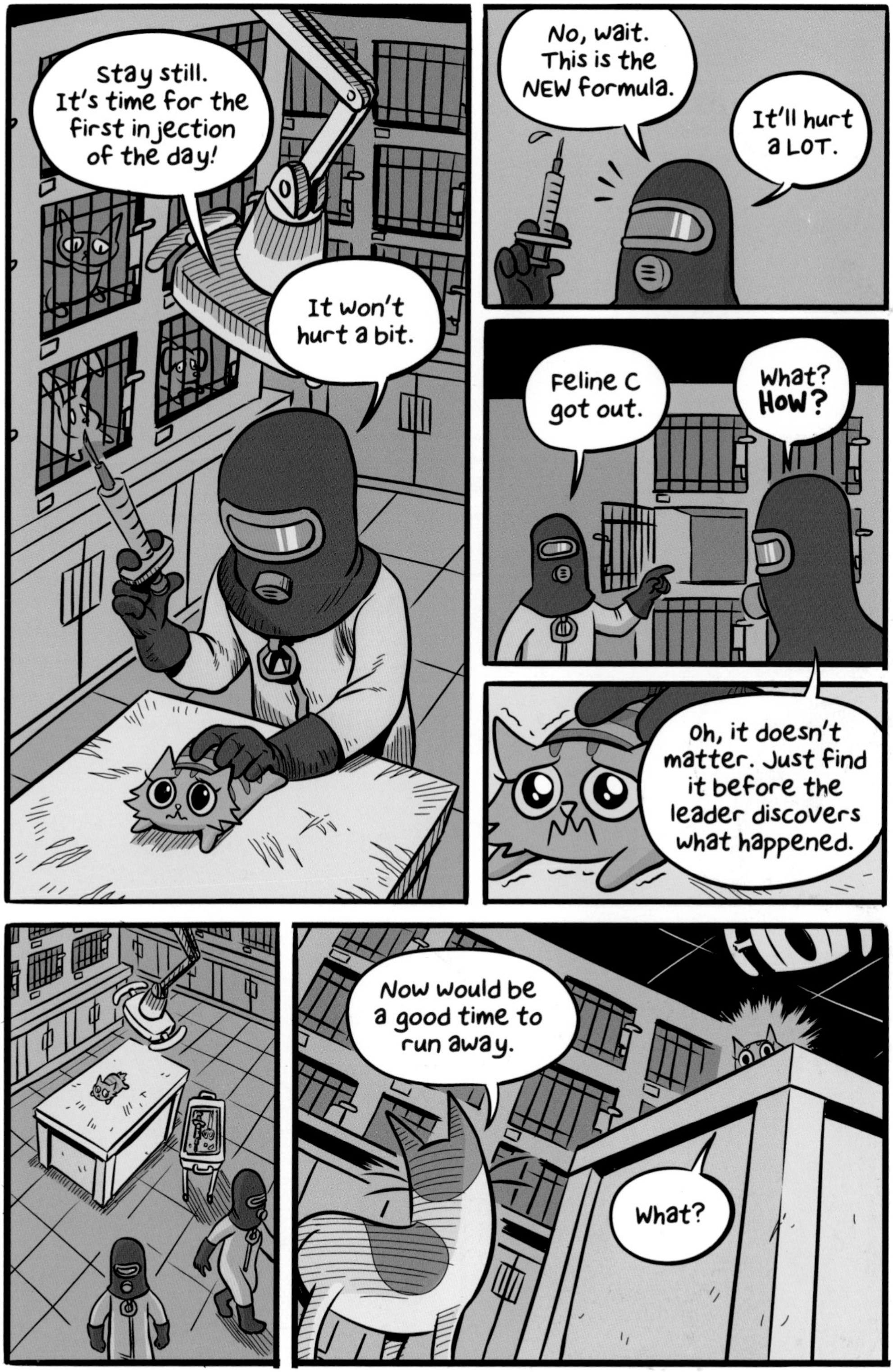
Stay still. It's time for the first injection of the day!
It won't hurt a bit.
No, wait. This is the NEW formula.
It'll hurt a LOT.
Feline C got out.
What? HOW?
Oh, it doesn't matter. Just find it before the leader discovers what happened.
Now would be a good time to run away.
What?

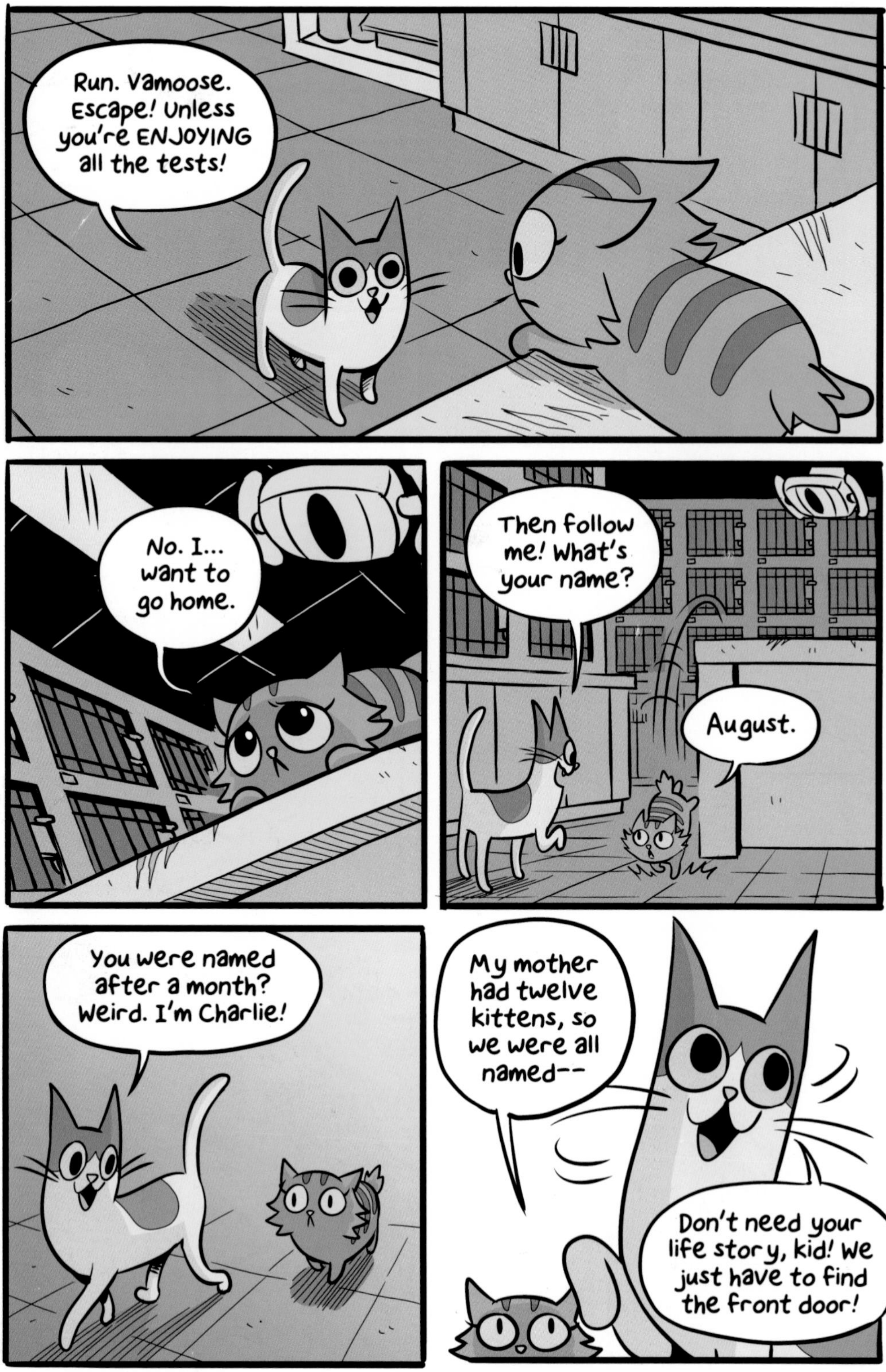
Run. Vamoose. Escape! Unless you're ENJOYING all the tests!
No. I... want to go home.
Then follow me! What's your name?
August.
You were named after a month? Weird. I'm Charlie!
My mother had twelve kittens, so we were all named--
Don't need your life story, kid! We just have to find the front door!

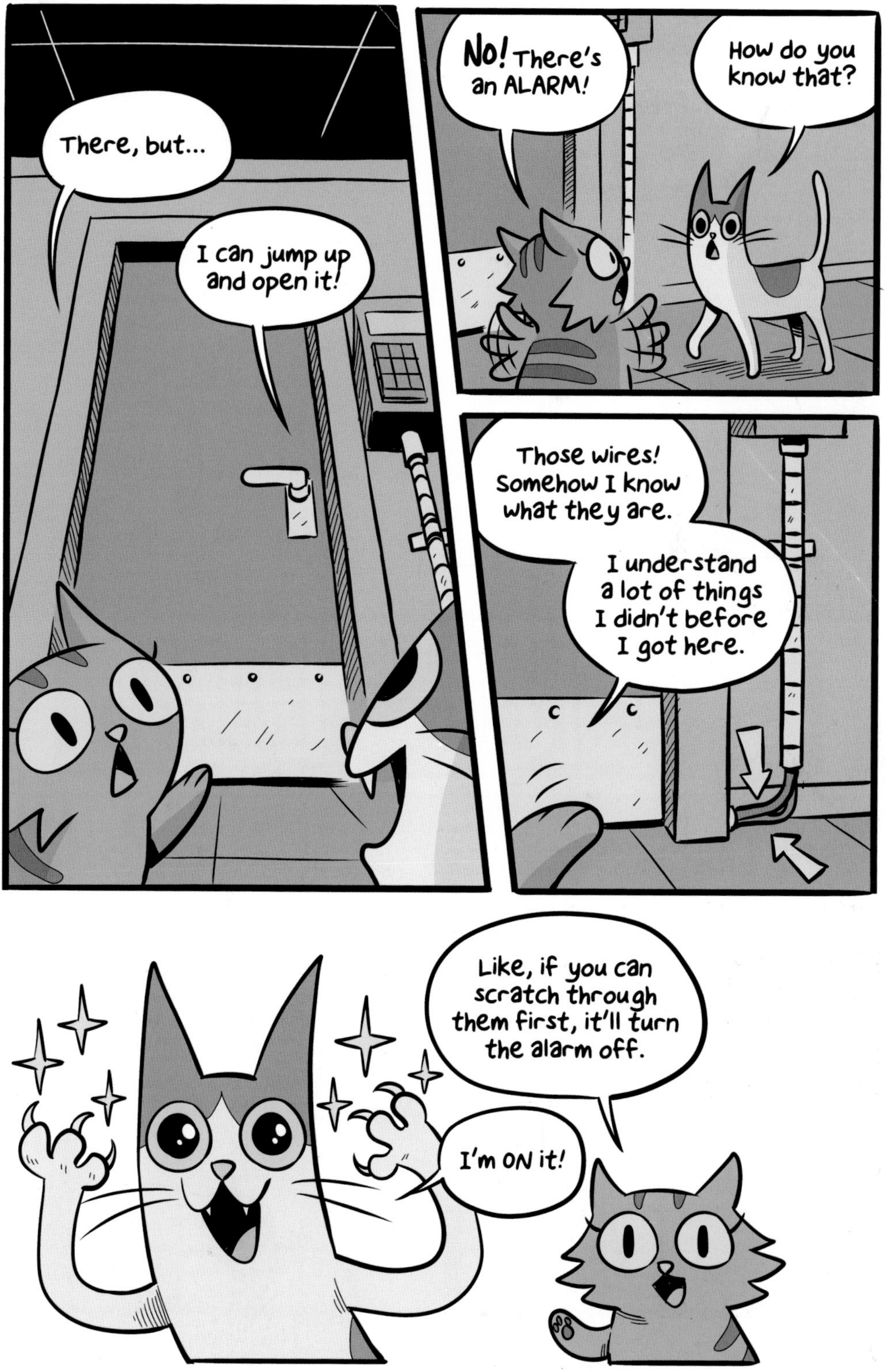
There, but...
I can jump up and open it!
No! There's an ALARM!
How do you know that?
Those wires! Somehow I know what they are.
I understand a lot of things I didn't before I got here.
Like, if you can scratch through them first, it'll turn the alarm off.
I'm ON it!

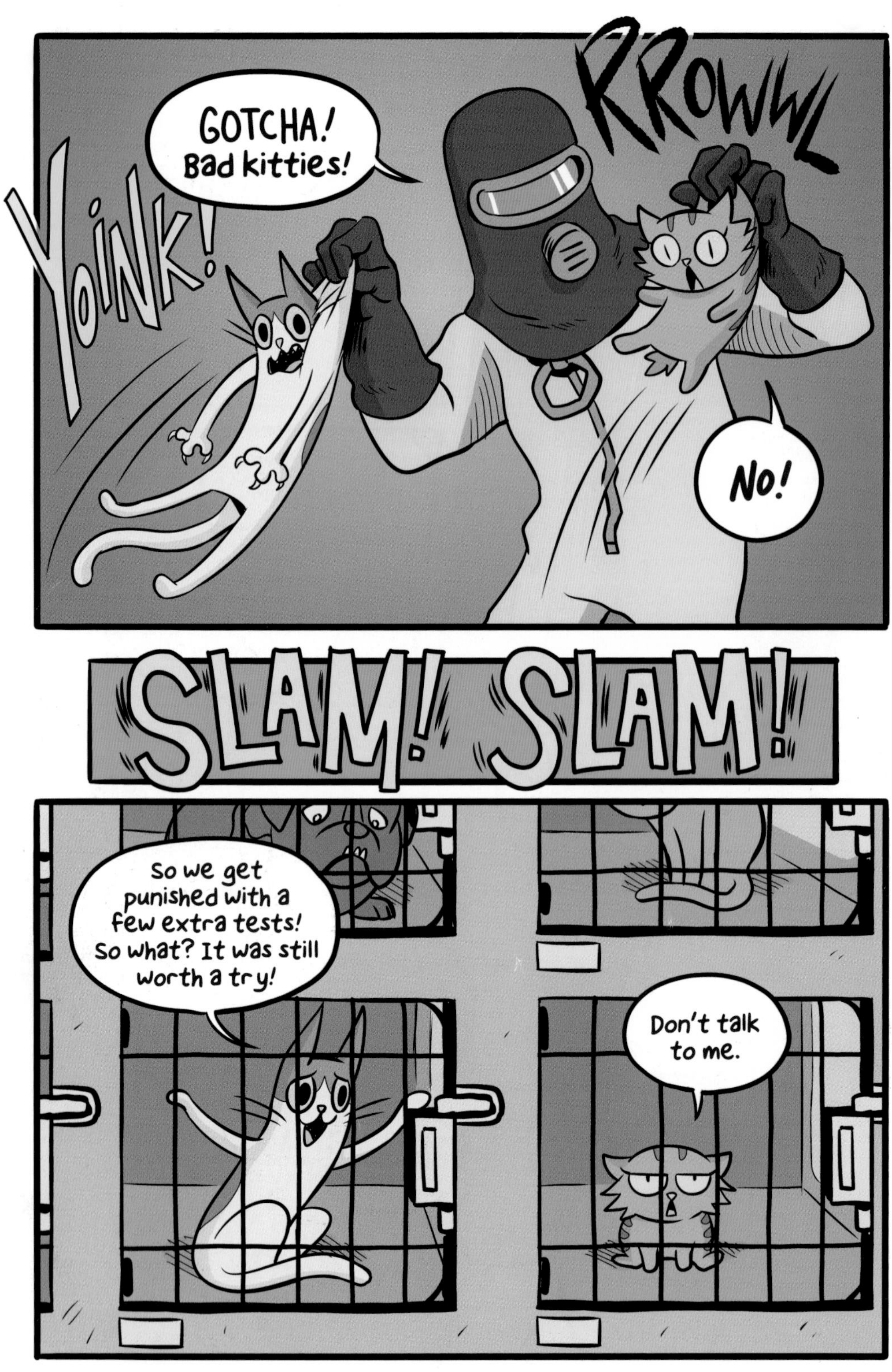
YOINK!
GOTCHA! Bad kitties!
RROWWL
No!
SLAM! SLAM!
So we get punished with a few extra tests! So what? It was still worth a try!
Don't talk to me.

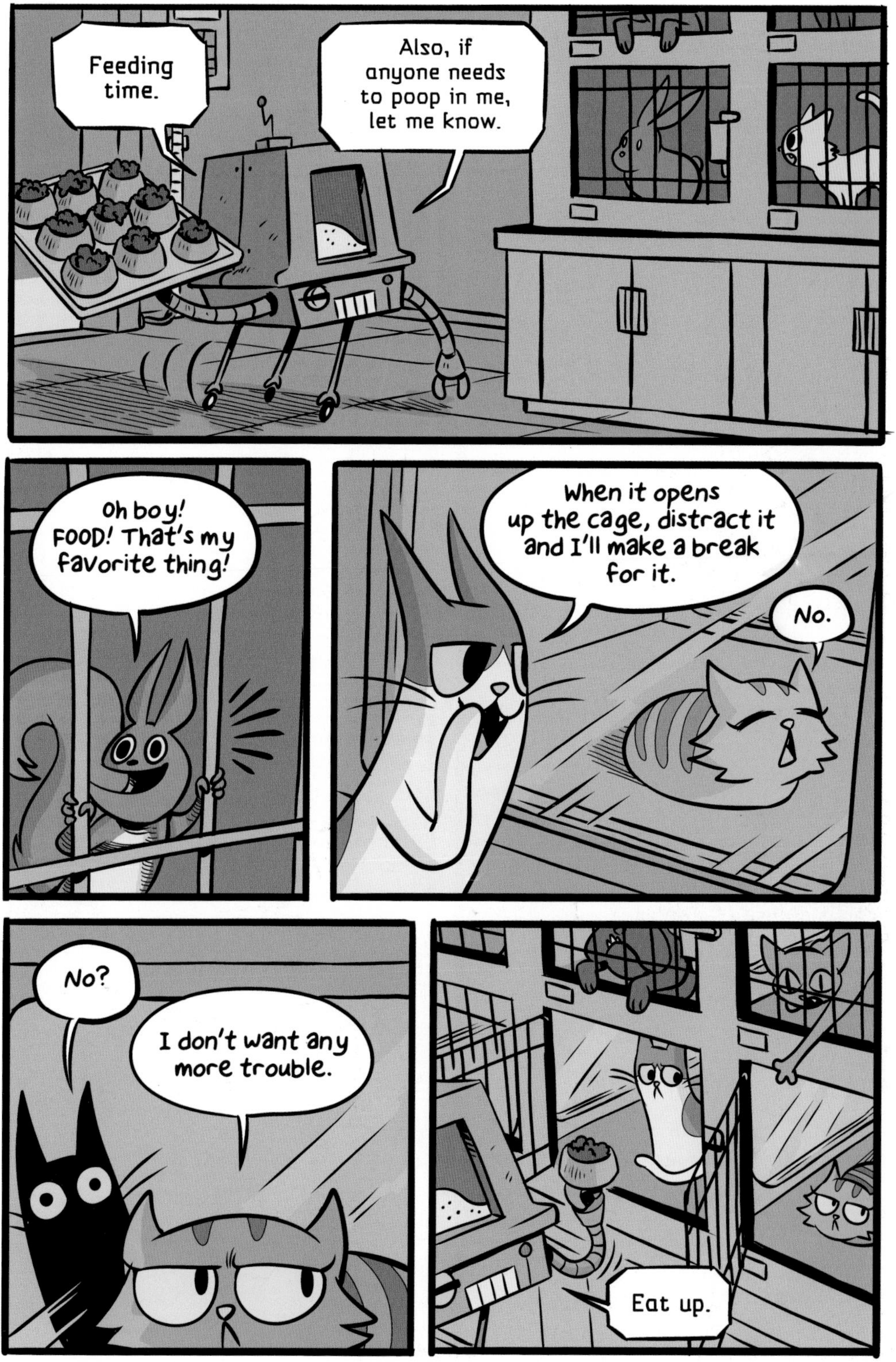
Feeding time.
Also, if anyone needs to poop in me, let me know.
Oh boy! FOOD! That's my favorite thing!
When it opens up the cage, distract it and I'll make a break for it.
No.
No?
I don't want any more trouble.
Eat up.

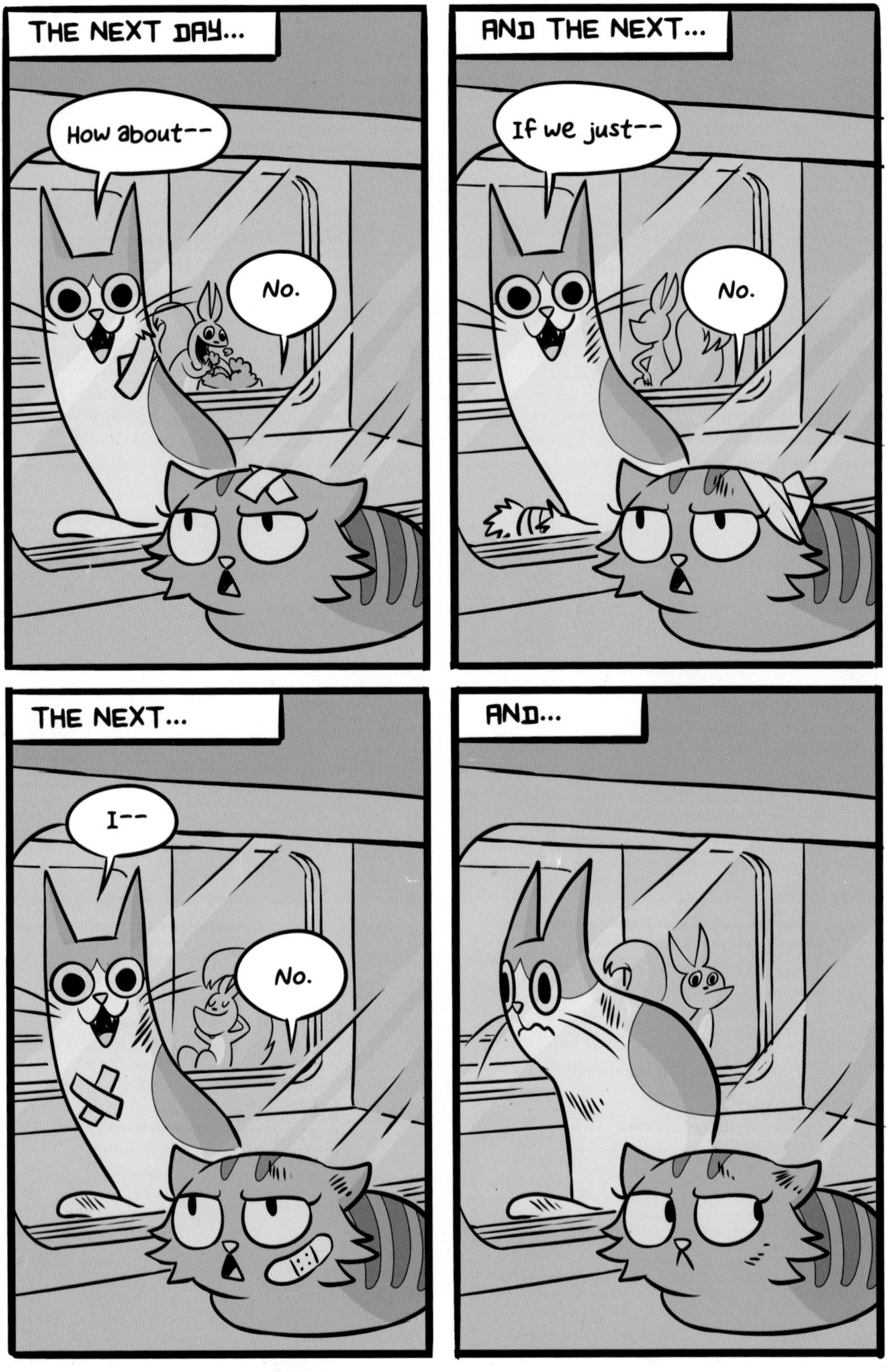
THE NEXT DAY...
How about--
No.
AND THE NEXT...
If we just--
No.
THE NEXT...
I--
No.
AND...

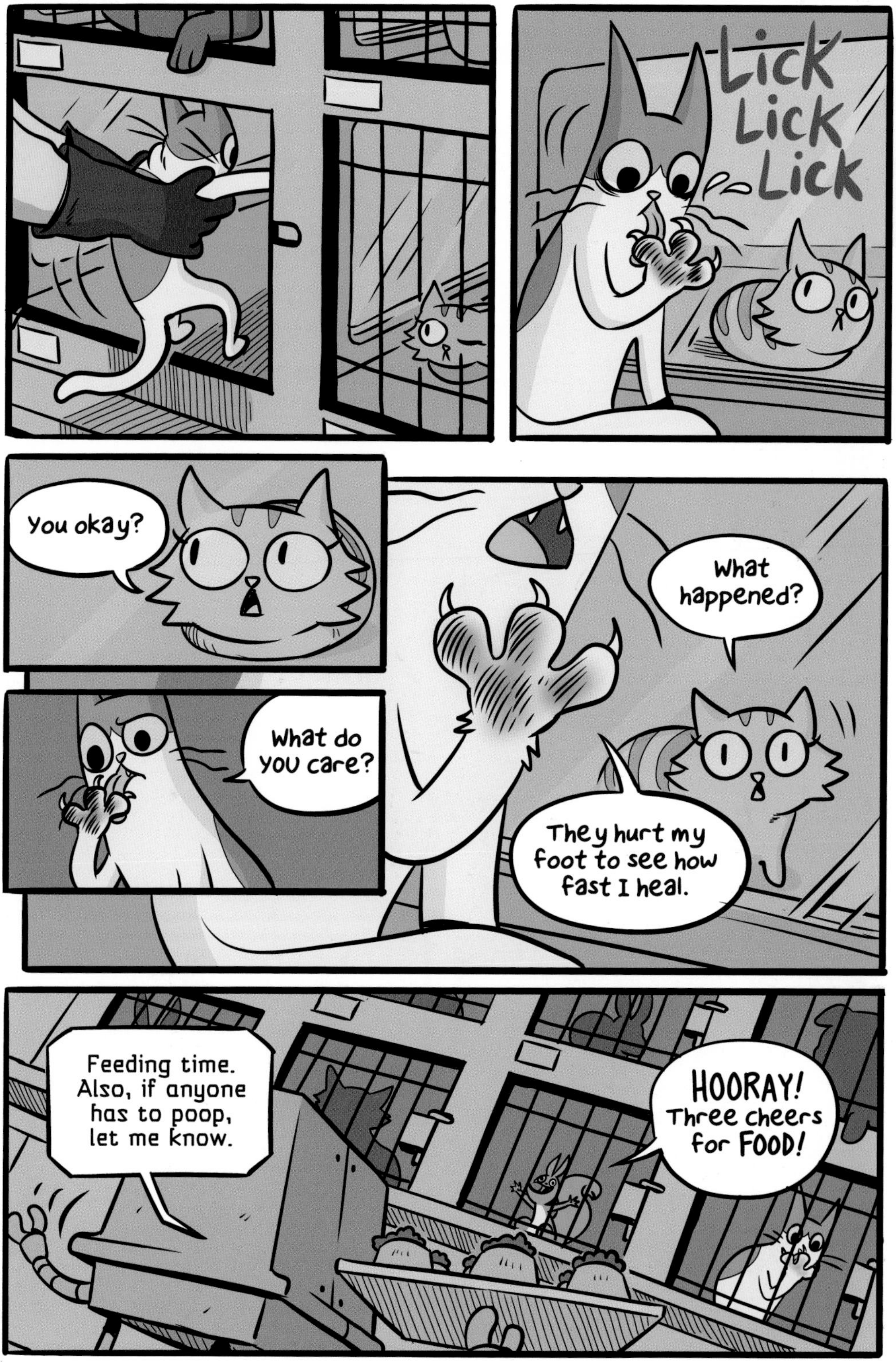
Lick
Lick
Lick
You okay?
What happened?
What do you care?
They hurt my foot to see how fast I heal.
Feeding time. Also, if anyone has to poop, let me know.
HOORAY! Three cheers for FOOD!

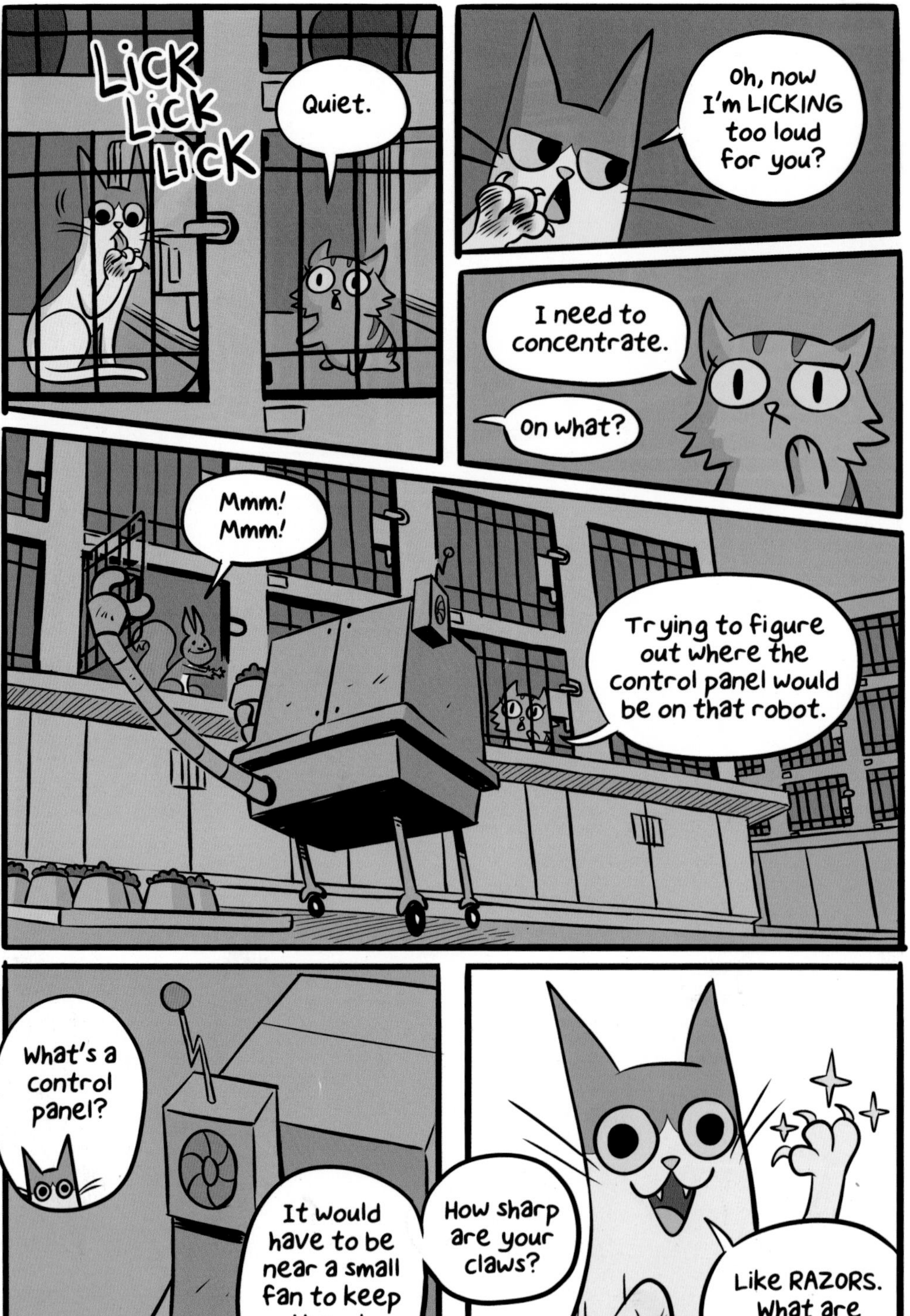
Lick Lick Lick
Quiet.
Oh, now I'm LICKING too loud for you?
I need to concentrate.
On what?
Mmm! Mmm!
Trying to figure out where the control panel would be on that robot.
What's a control panel?
It would have to be near a small fan to keep it cool.
How sharp are your claws?
Like RAZORS. What are you thinking?

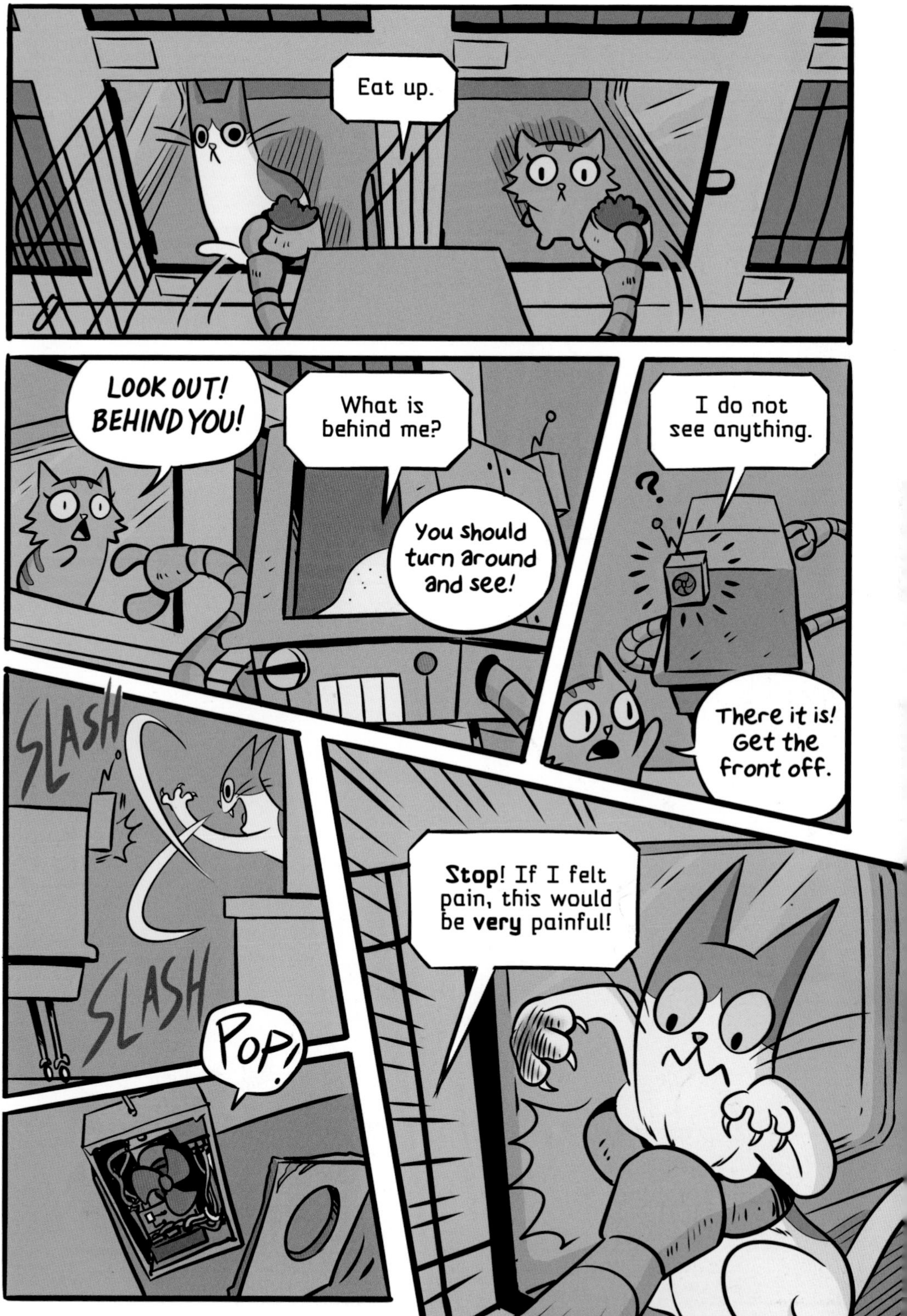
Eat up.
LOOK OUT! BEHIND YOU!
What is behind me?
You should turn around and see!
I do not see anything.
There it is! Get the front off.
SLASH
SLASH
POP!
Stop! If I felt pain, this would be very painful!

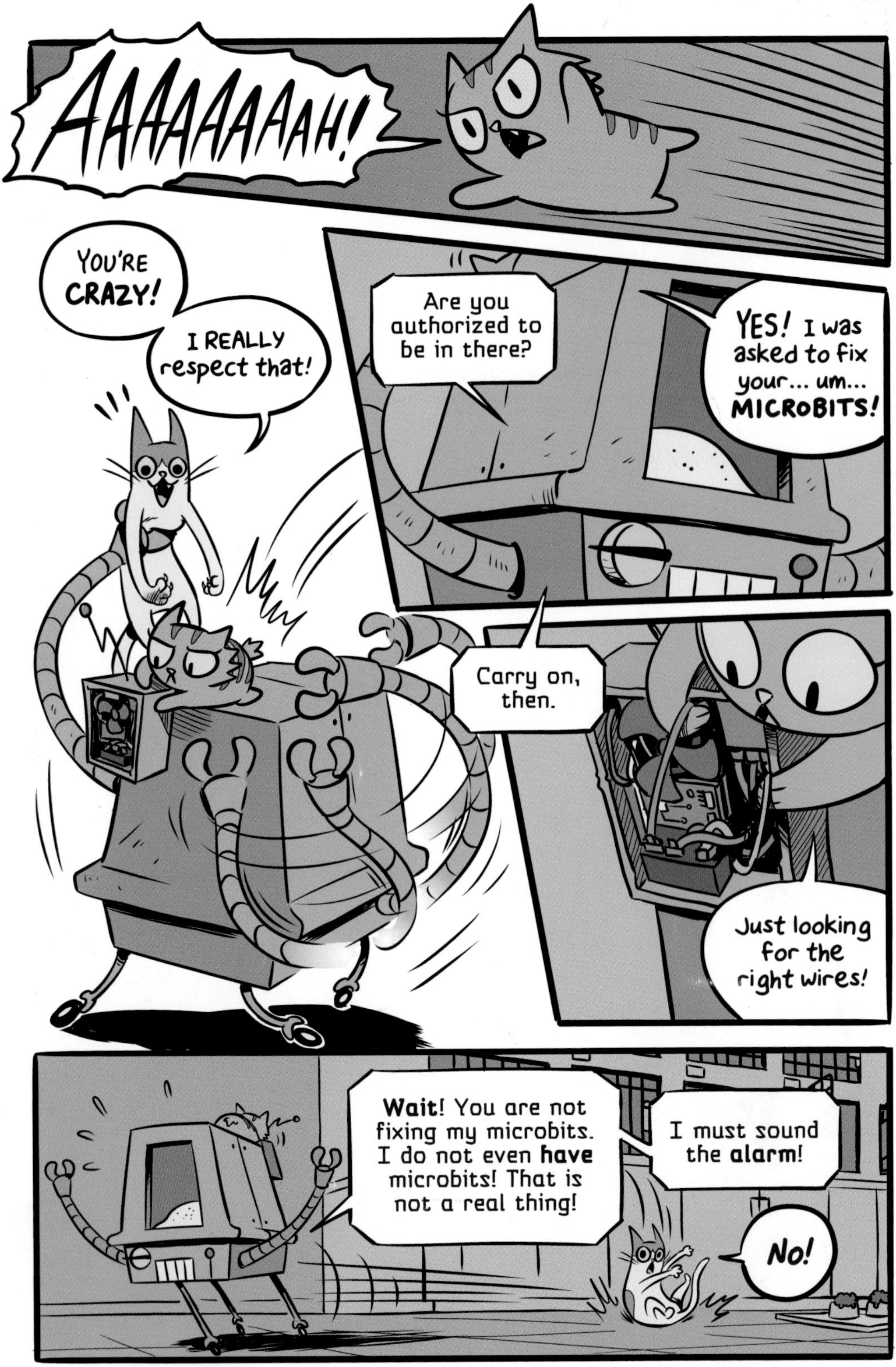
AAAAAAAAAH!
YOU'RE CRAZY!
I REALLY respect that!
Are you authorized to be in there?
YES! I was asked to fix your... um... MICROBITS!
Carry on, then.
Just looking for the right wires!
Wait! You are not fixing my microbits. I do not even have microbits! That is not a real thing!
I must sound the alarm!
No!

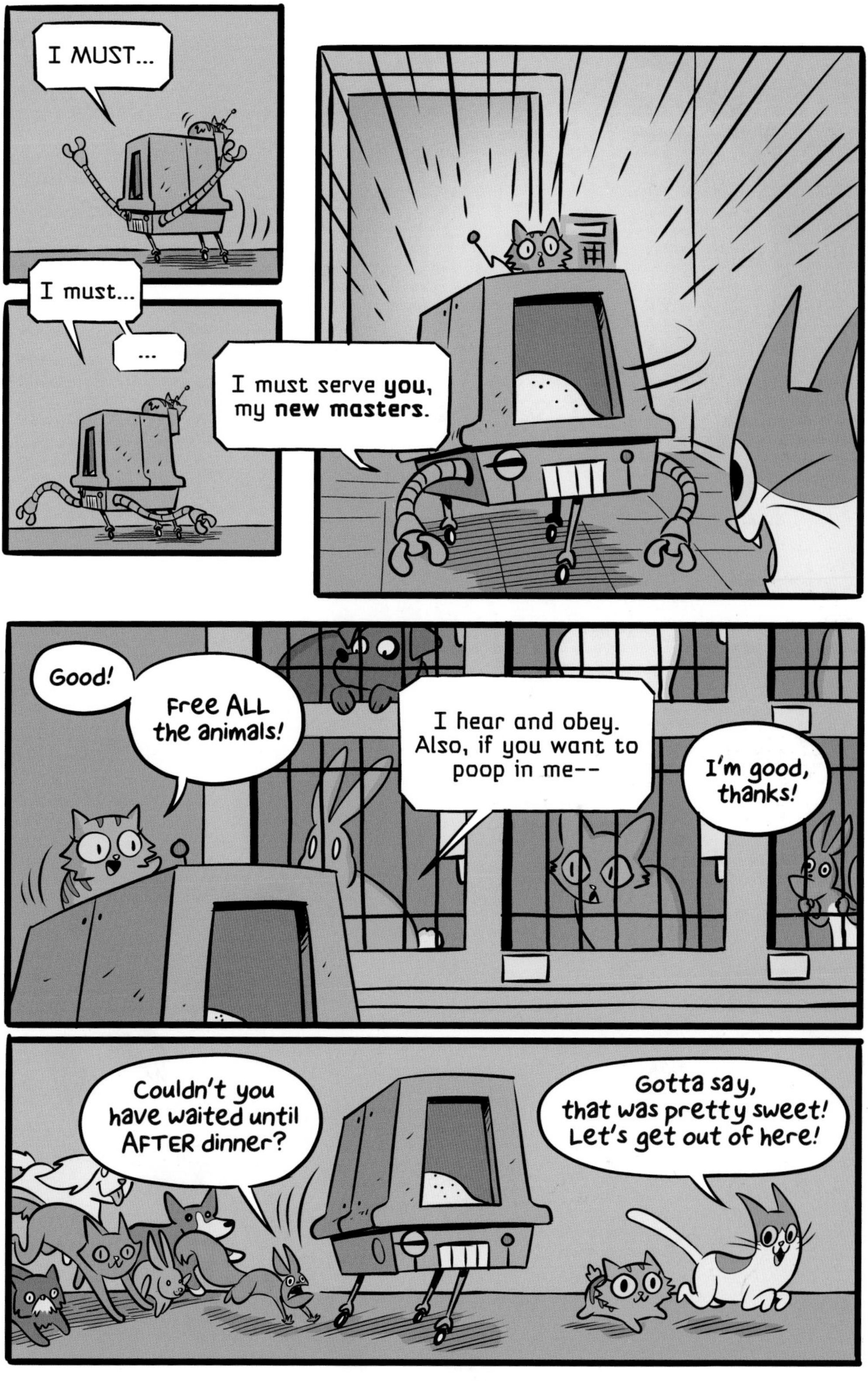
I MUST...
I must...
...
I must serve you, my new masters.
Good!
Free ALL the animals!
I hear and obey. Also, if you want to poop in me--
I'm good, thanks!
Couldn't you have waited until AFTER dinner?
Gotta say, that was pretty sweet! Let's get out of here!

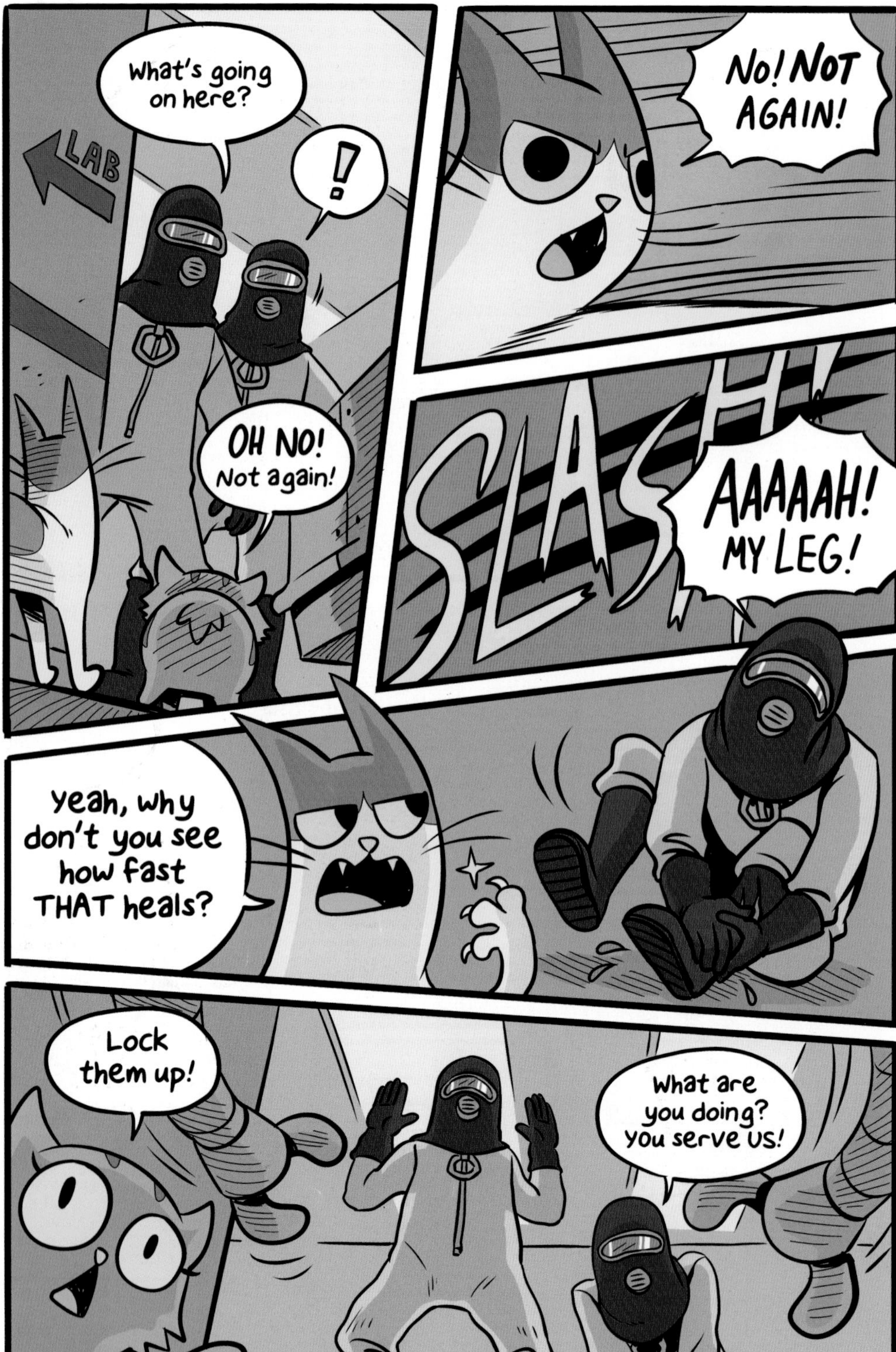
What's going on here?
LAB
!
OH NO! Not again!
No! NOT AGAIN!
SLASH!
AAAAAH! MY LEG!
yeah, why don't you see how fast THAT heals?
Lock them up!
What are you doing? You serve US!

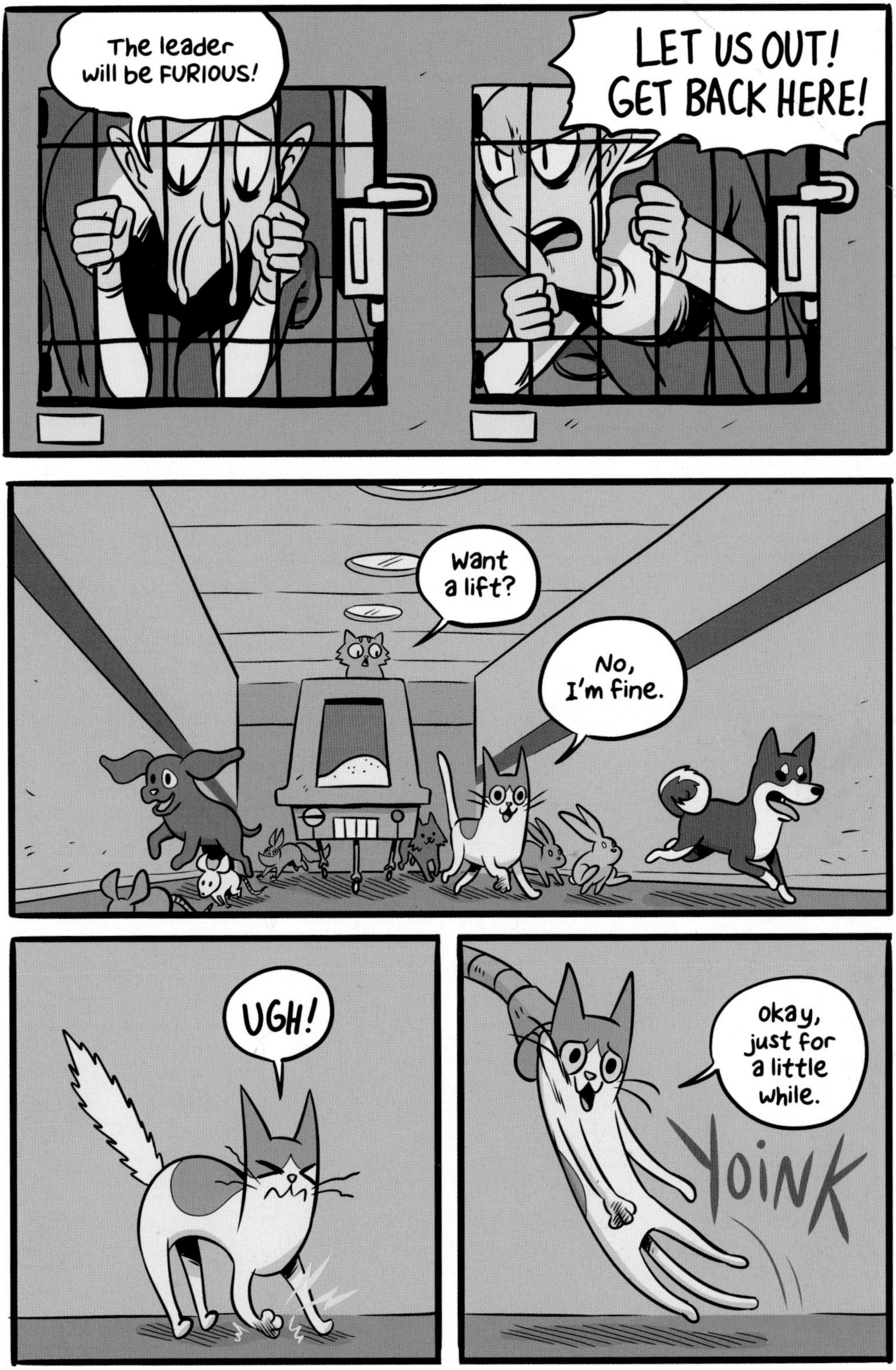
The leader will be FURIOUS!
LET US OUT! GET BACK HERE!
Want a lift?
No, I'm fine.
UGH!
okay, just for a little while.
YOINK

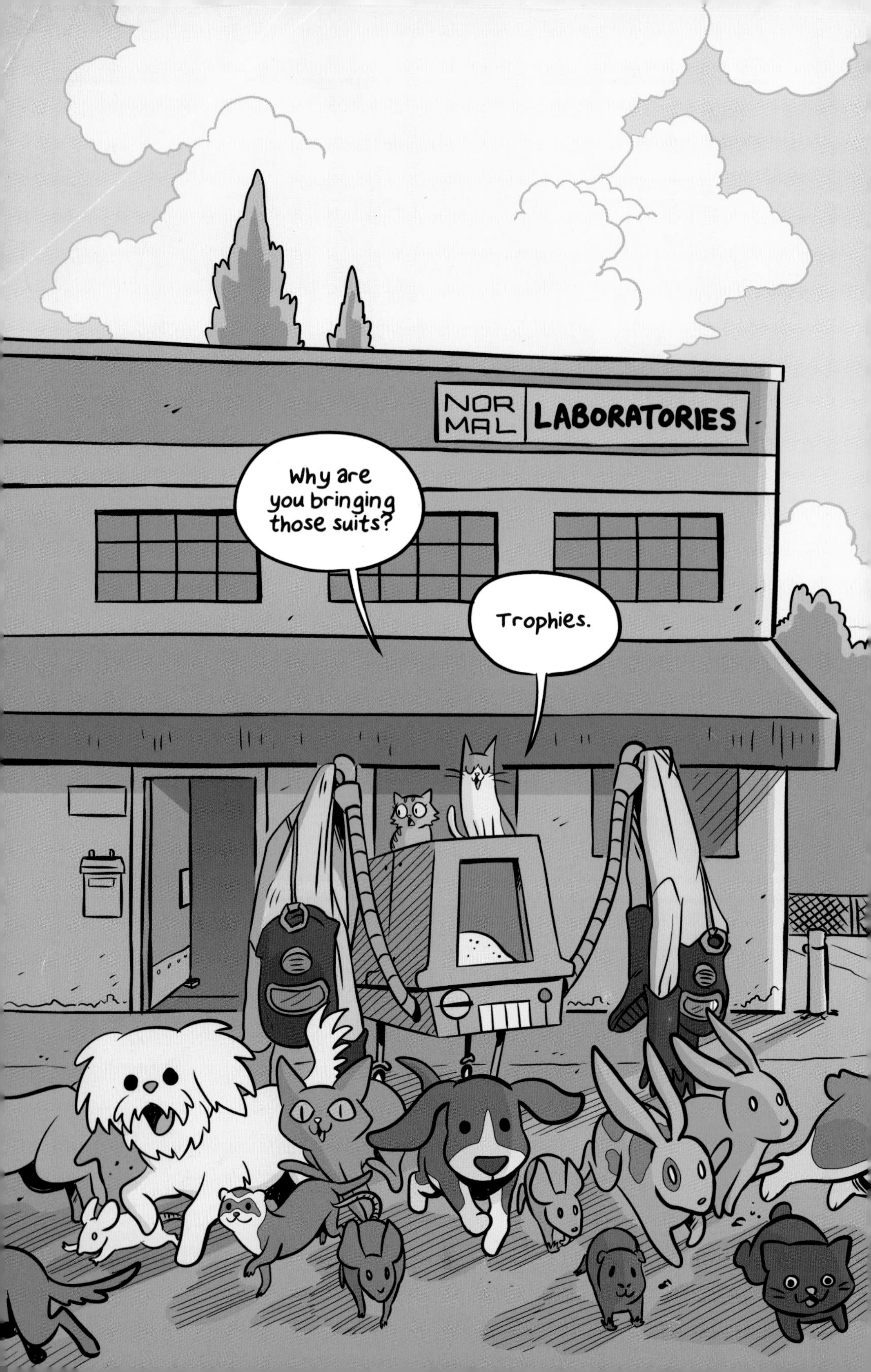
NORMAL LABORATORIES
Why are you bringing those suits?
Trophies.

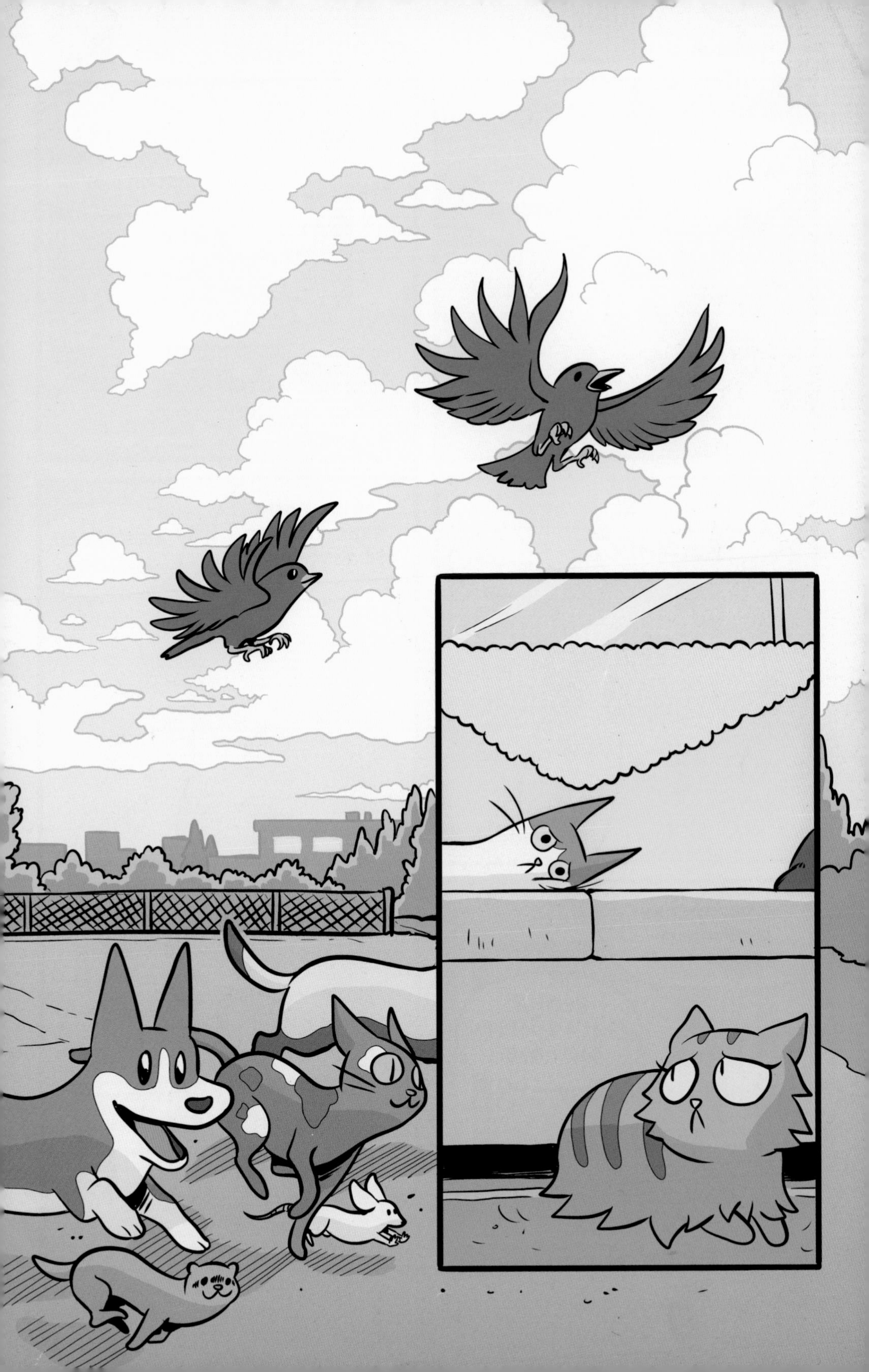

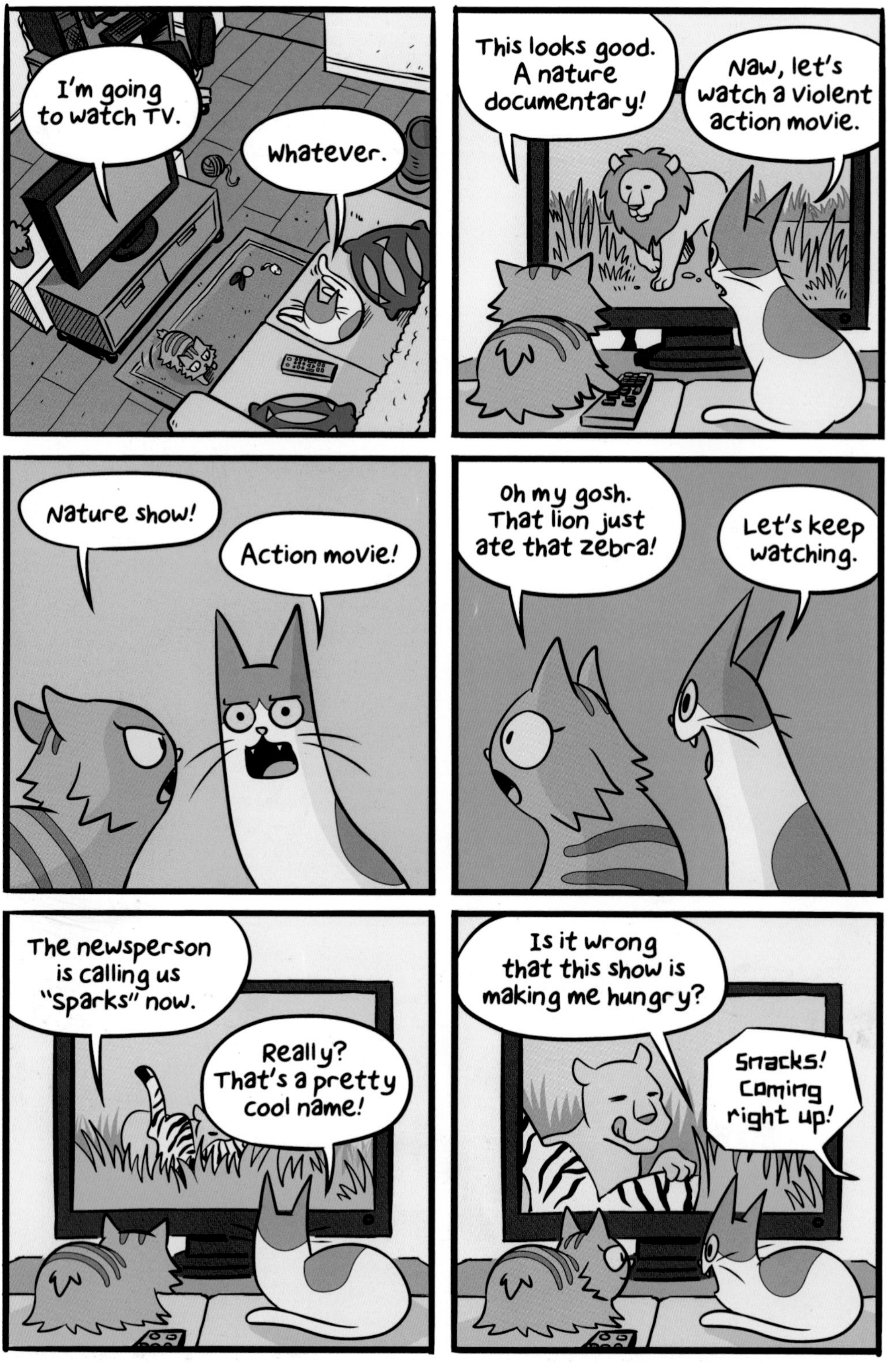
I'm going to watch TV.
Whatever.
This looks good. A nature documentary!
Naw, let's watch a violent action movie.
Nature show!
Action movie!
Oh my gosh. That lion just ate that zebra!
Let's keep watching.
The newsperson is calling us "Sparks" now.
Really? That's a pretty cool name!
Is it wrong that this show is making me hungry?
Snacks! Coming right up!

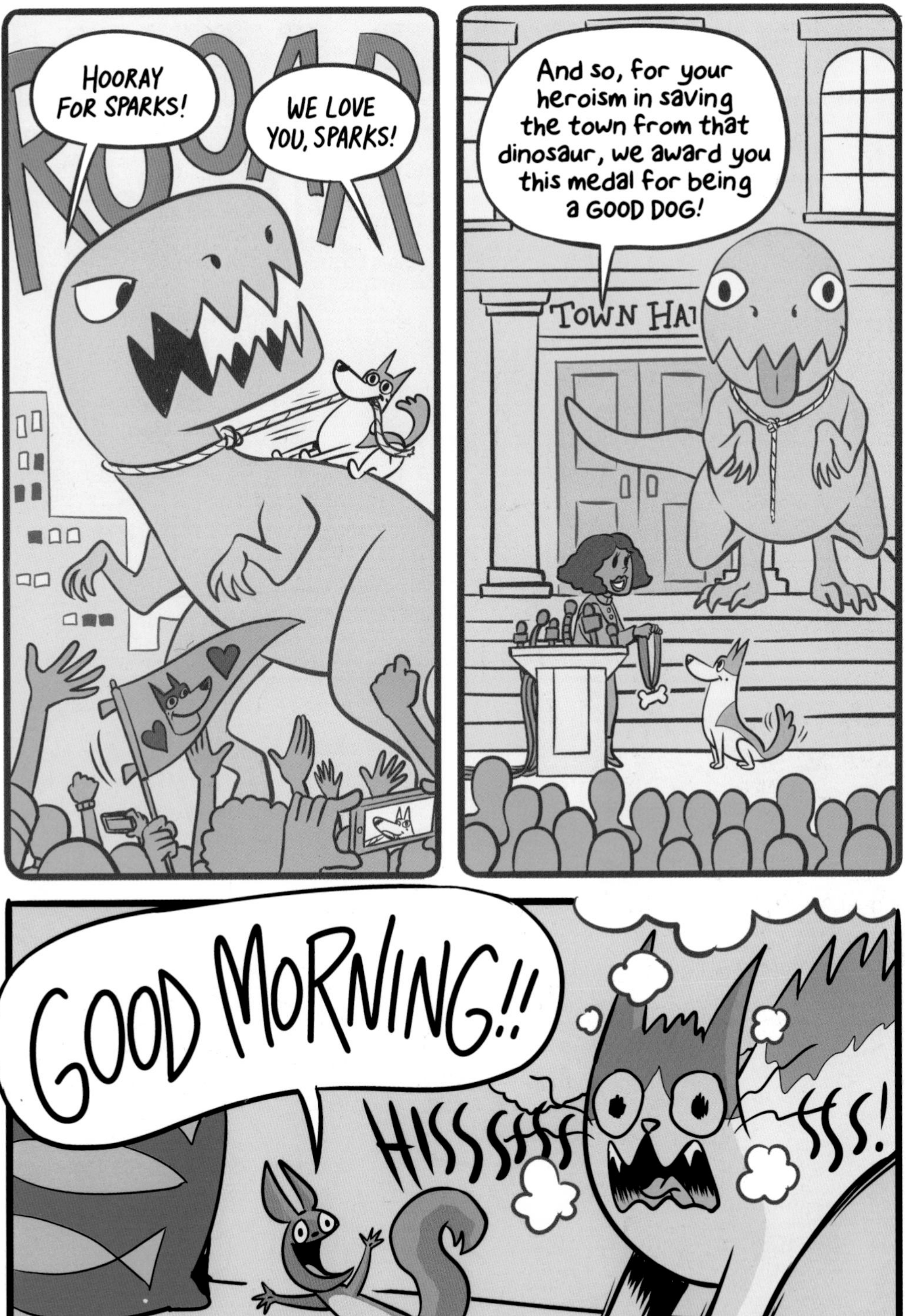
ROOAR
HOORAY FOR SPARKS!
WE LOVE YOU, SPARKS!
And so, for your heroism in saving the town from that dinosaur, we award you this medal for being a GOOD DOG!
TOWN HA
GOOD MORNING!!
HISSSSSSSSS!

CHAPTER FOUR

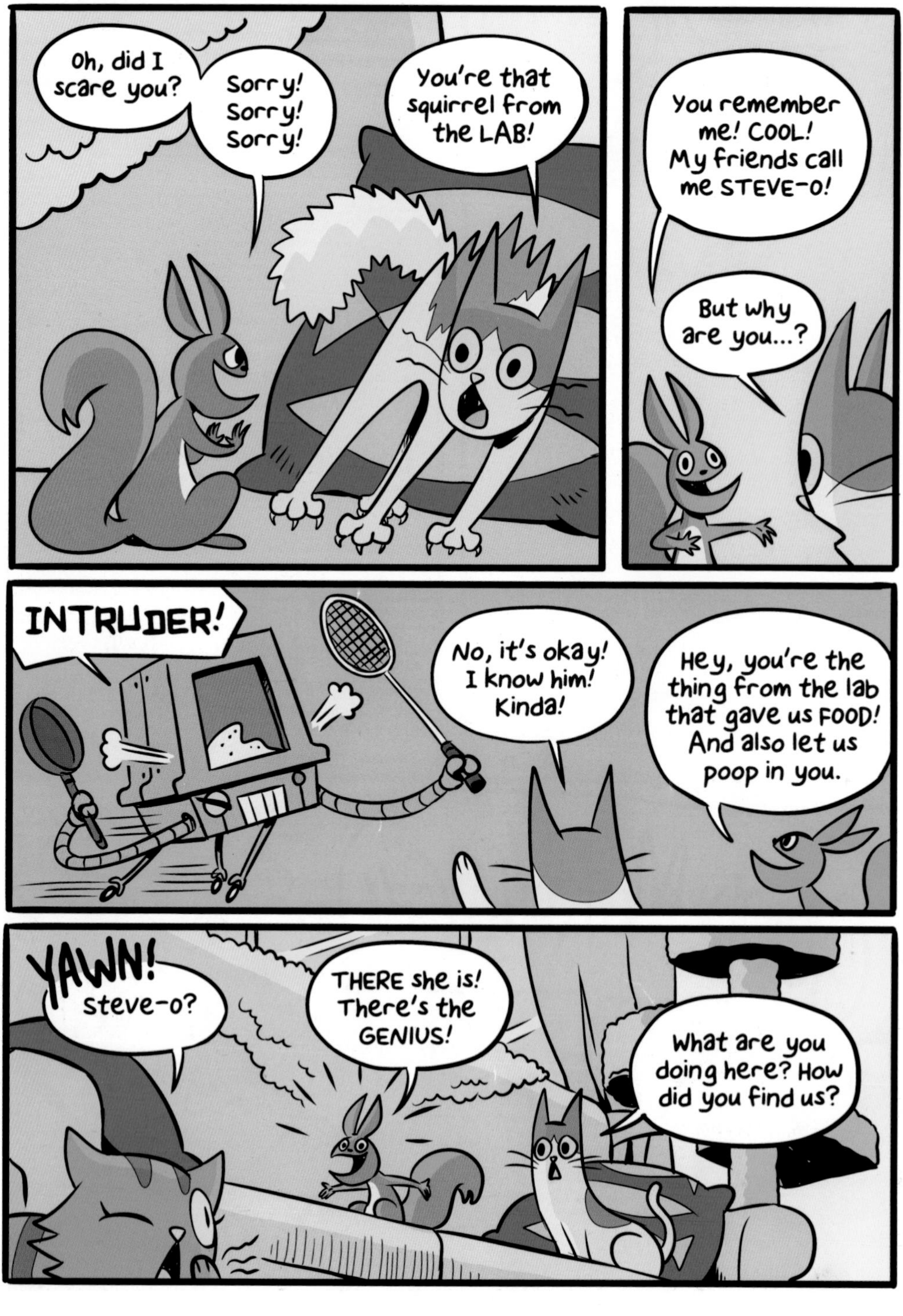
Oh, did I scare you?
Sorry! Sorry! Sorry!
You're that squirrel from the LAB!
You remember me! COOL! My friends call me STEVE-O!
But why are you...?
INTRUDER!
No, it's okay! I know him! Kinda!
Hey, you're the thing from the lab that gave us FOOD! And also let us poop in you.
YAWN! steve-o?
THERE she is! There's the GENIUS!
What are you doing here? How did you find us?

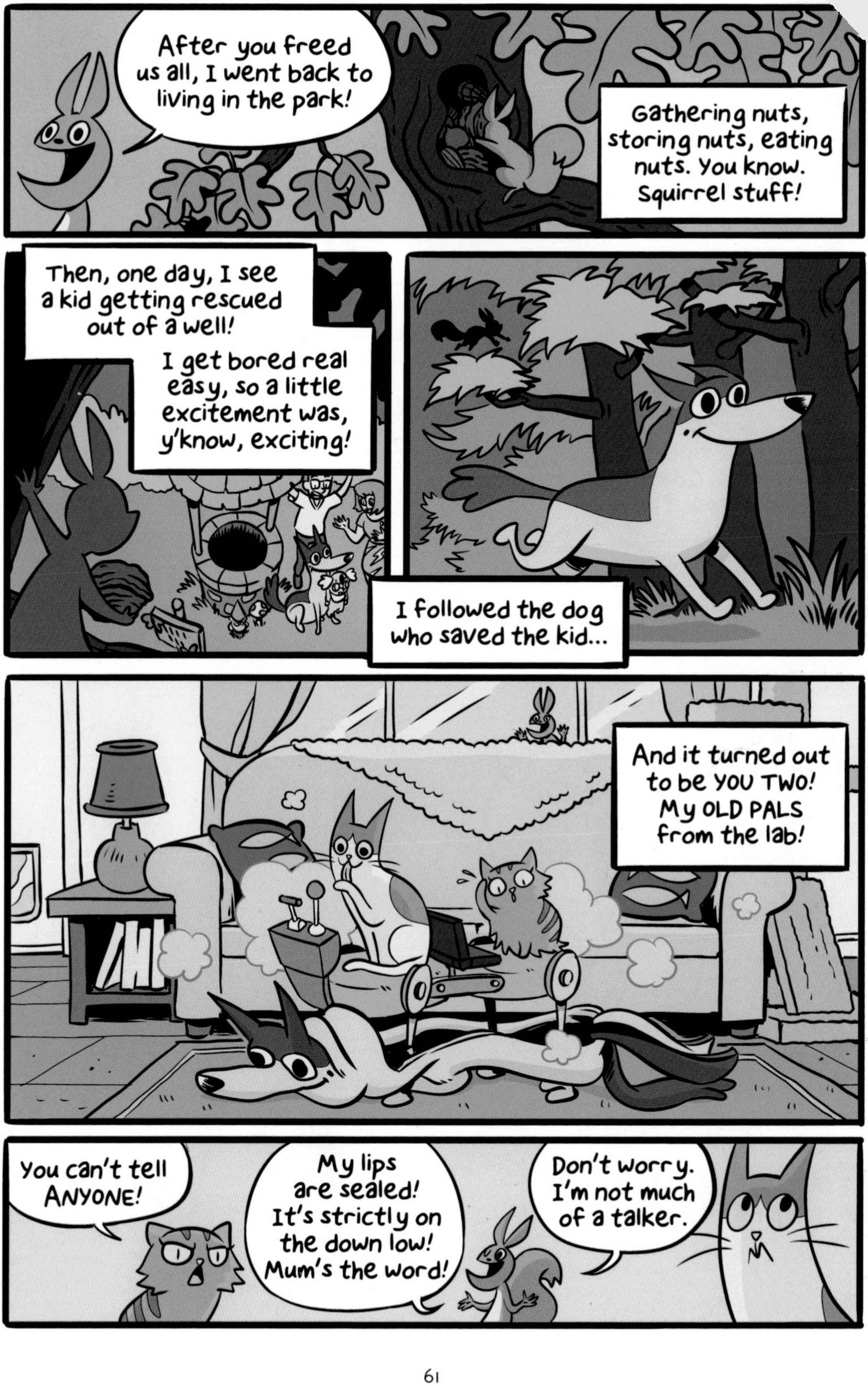
After you freed us all, I went back to living in the park!
Gathering nuts, storing nuts, eating nuts. You know. Squirrel stuff!
Then, one day, I see a kid getting rescued out of a well!
I get bored real easy, so a little excitement was, y'know, exciting!
I followed the dog who saved the kid...
And it turned out to be YOU TWO! My OLD PALS from the lab!
You can't tell ANYONE!
My lips are sealed! It's strictly on the down low! Mum's the word!
Don't worry. I'm not much of a talker.

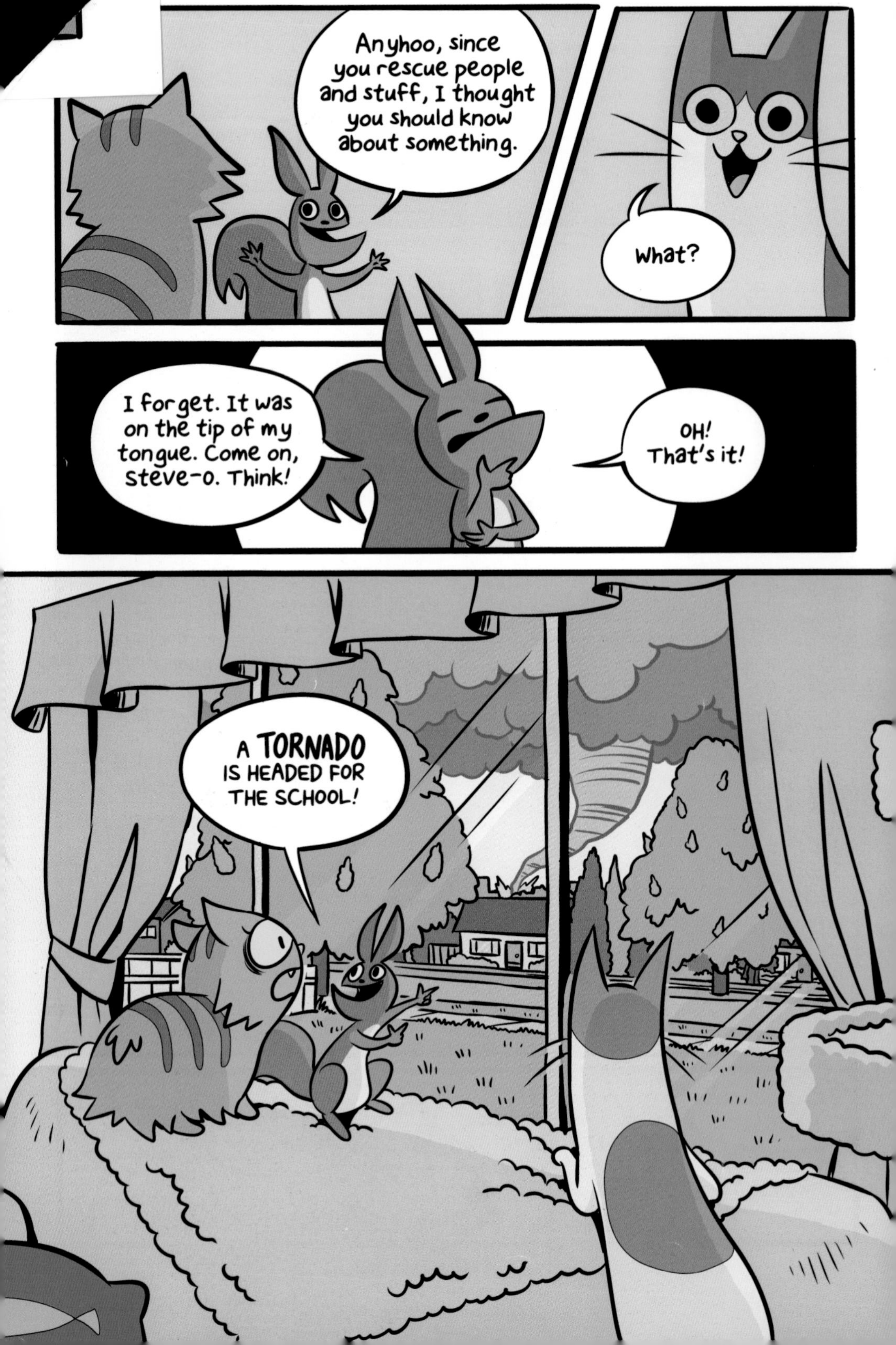
Anyhoo, since you rescue people and stuff, I thought you should know about something.
What?
I forget. It was on the tip of my tongue. Come on, steve-o. Think!
OH! That's it!
A TORNADO IS HEADED FOR THE SCHOOL!

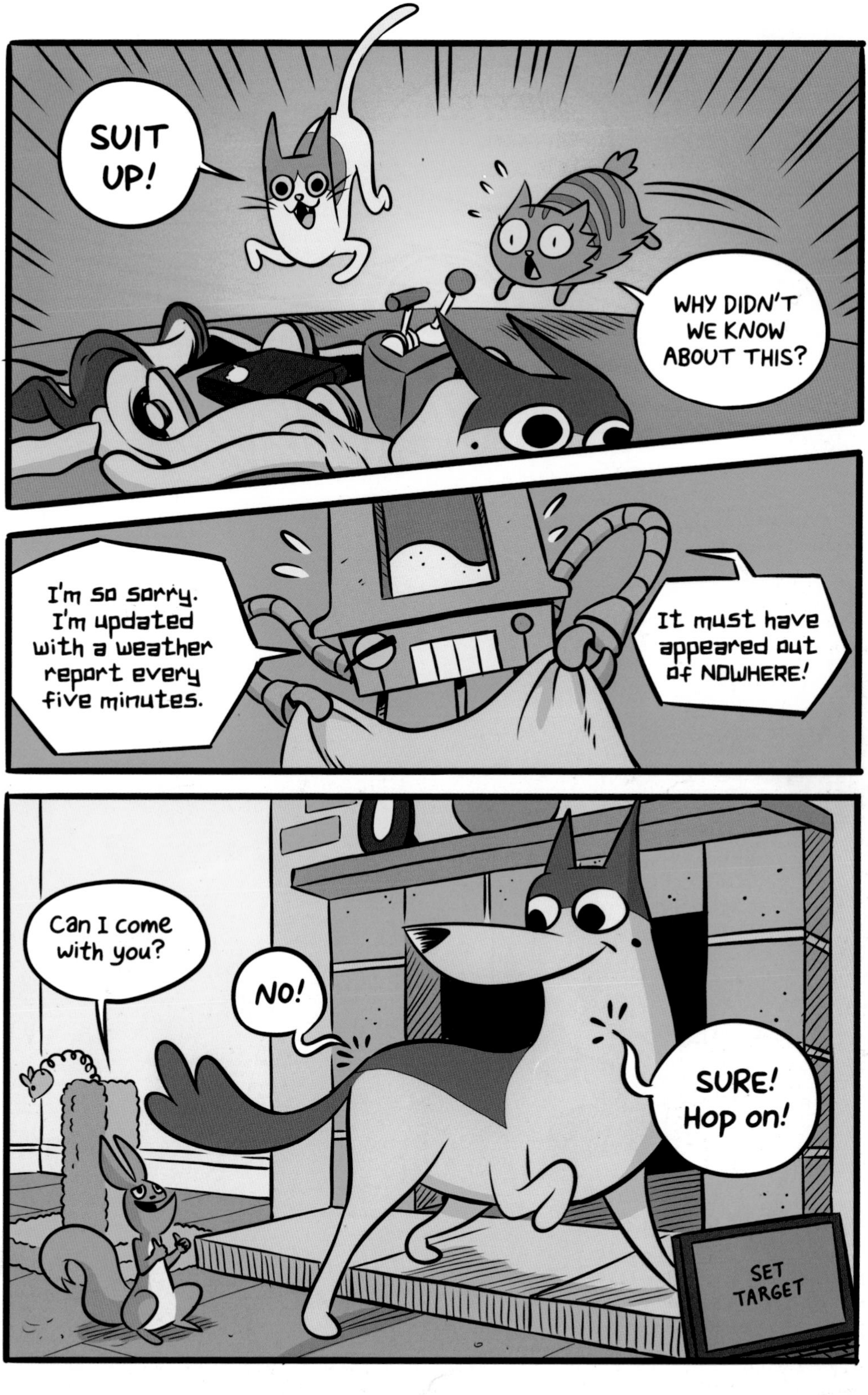
SUIT UP!
WHY DIDN'T WE KNOW ABOUT THIS?
I'm so sorry. I'm updated with a weather report every five minutes.
It must have appeared out of NOWHERE!
Can I come with you?
NO!
SURE! Hop on!
SET TARGET

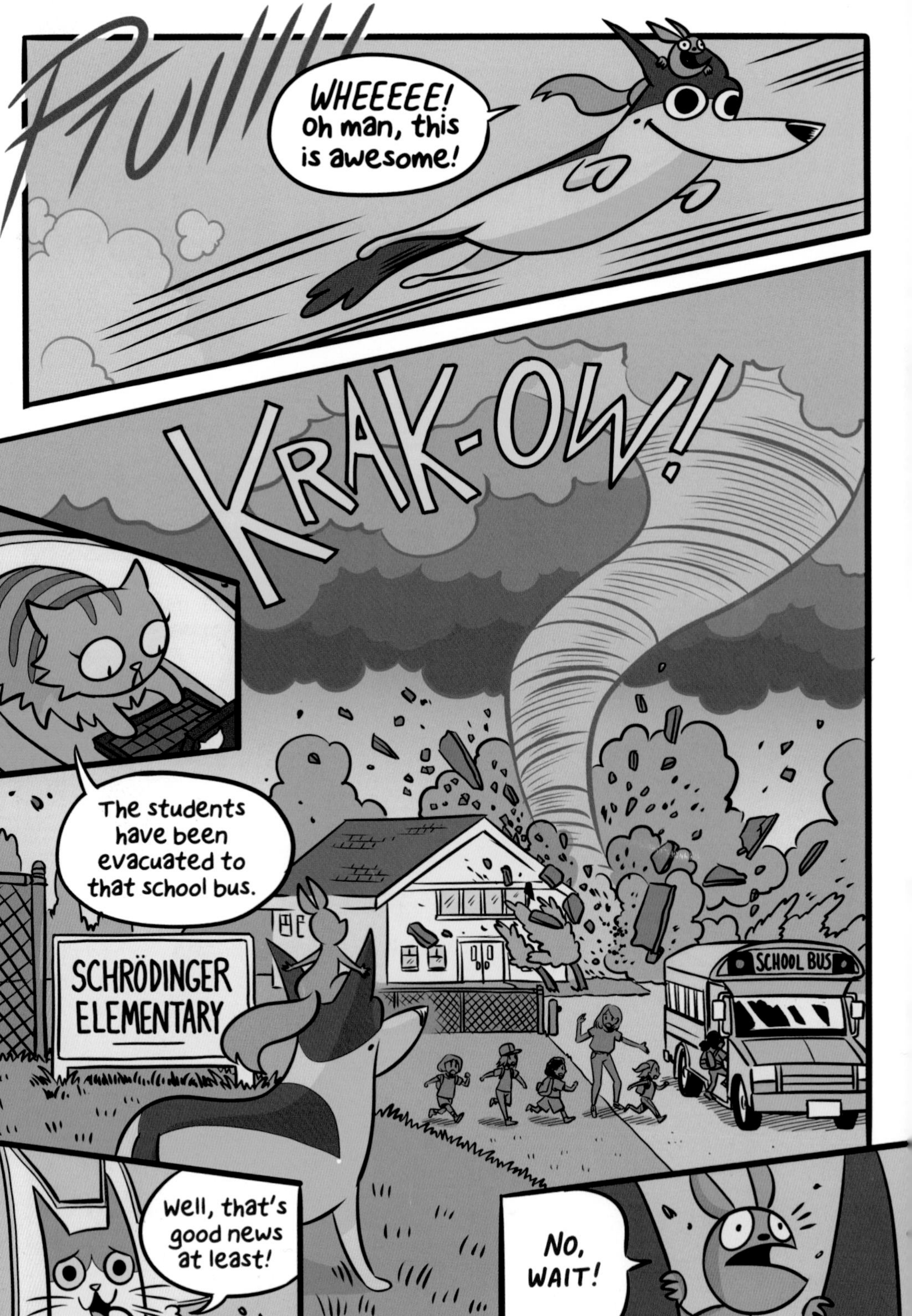

PFUIIII!
WHEEEEE! Oh man, this is awesome!
KRAK-OW!
The students have been evacuated to that school bus.
SCHRÖDINGER ELEMENTARY
SCHOOL BUS
Well, that's good news at least!
No, WAIT!

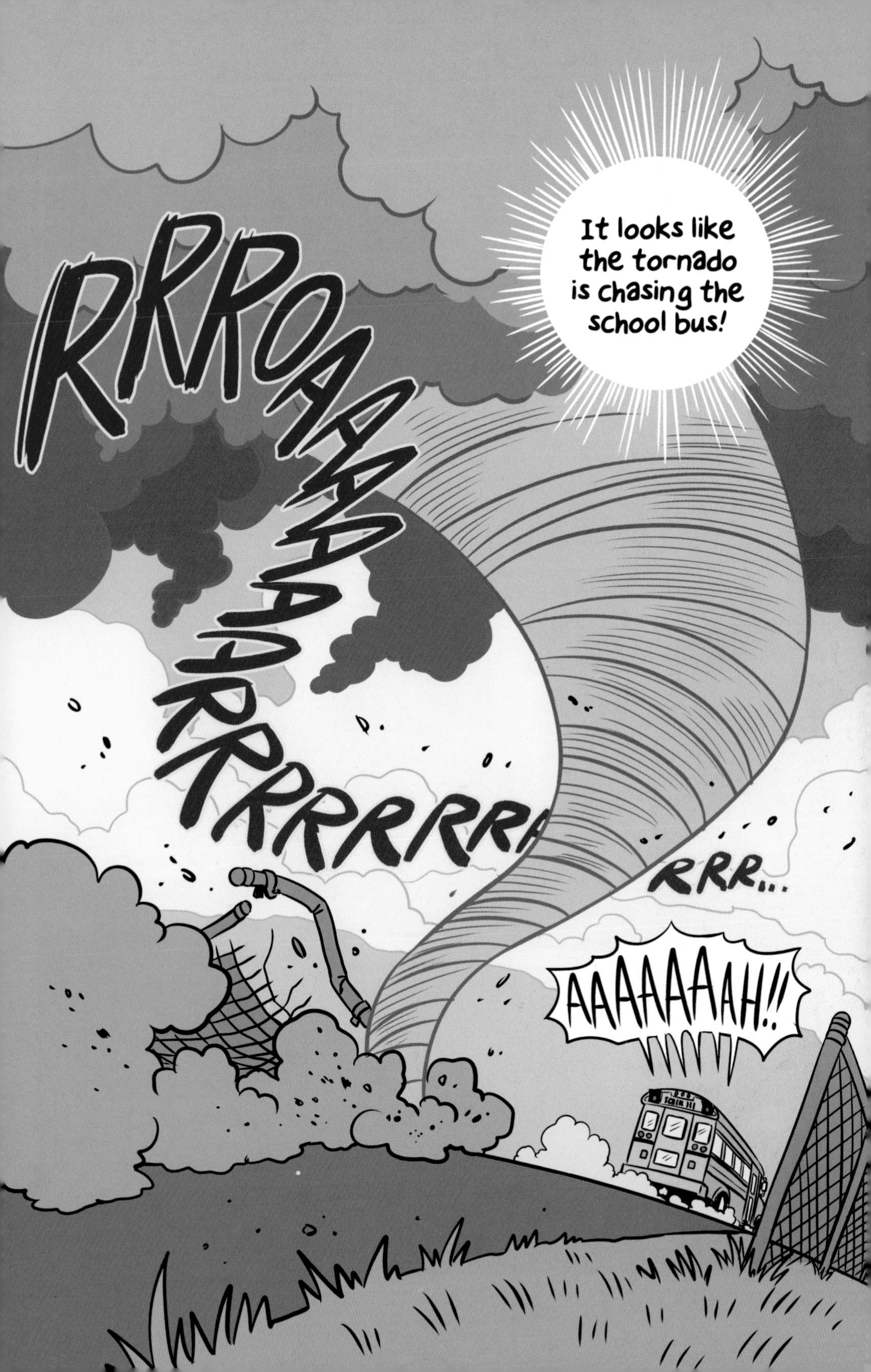
It looks like the tornado is chasing the school bus!
RRROAAAAAARRRRRRRRA
RRR...
AAAAAAAH!!

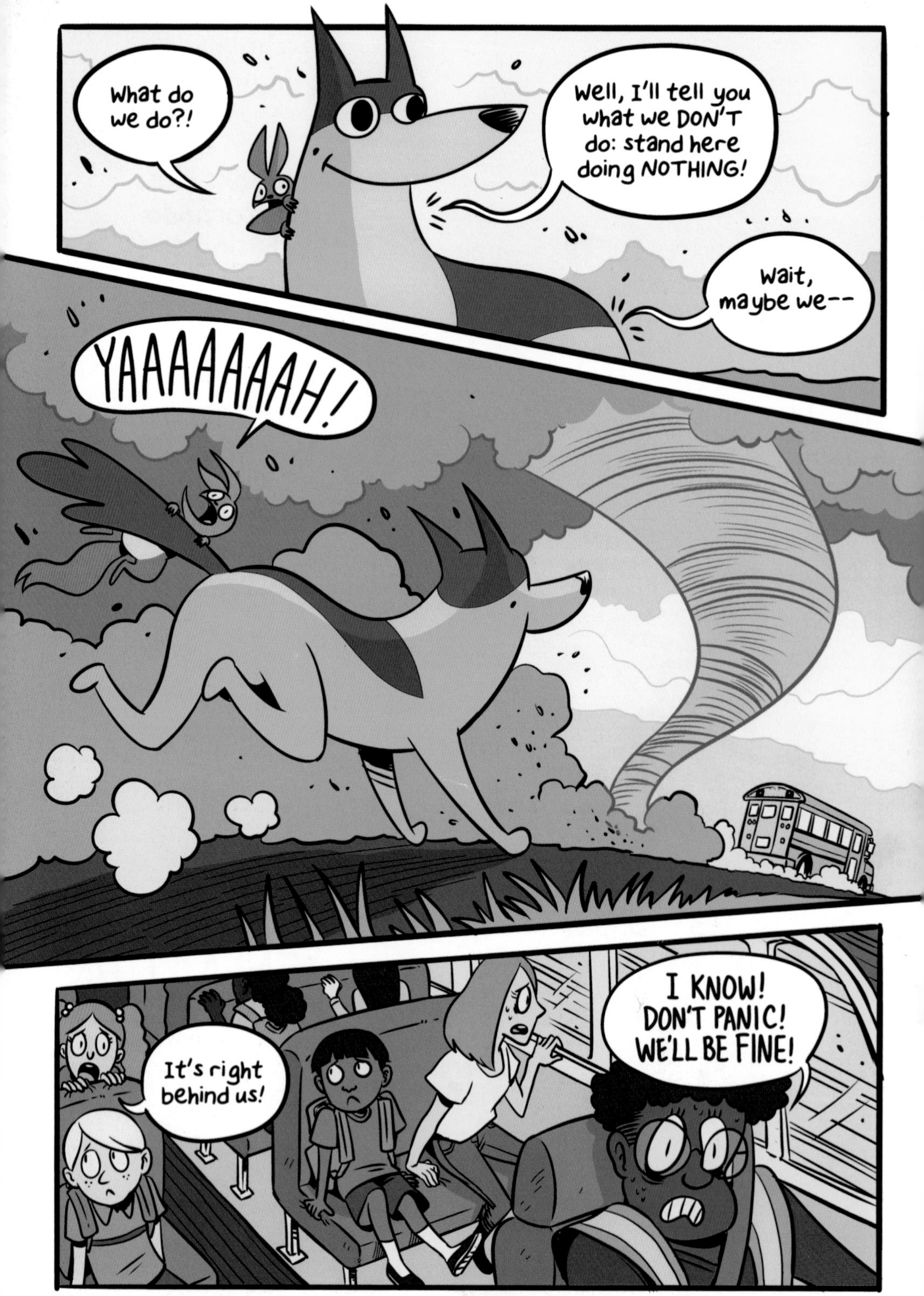
What do we do?!
Well, I'll tell you what we DON'T do: stand here doing NOTHING!
Wait, maybe we--
YAAAAAAAH!
It's right behind us!
I KNOW! DON'T PANIC! WE'LL BE FINE!

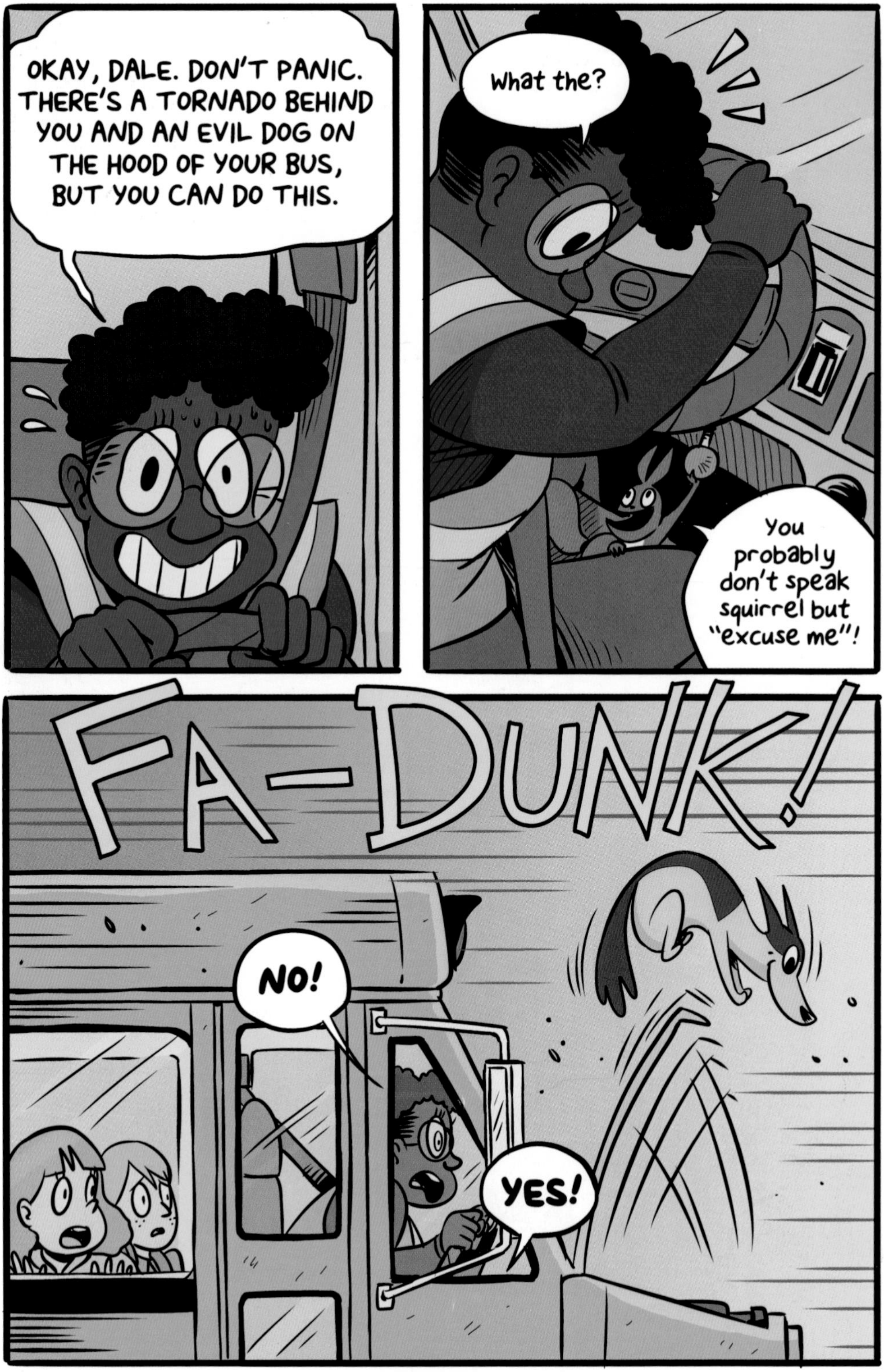
OKAY, DALE. DON'T PANIC. THERE'S A TORNADO BEHIND YOU AND AN EVIL DOG ON THE HOOD OF YOUR BUS, BUT YOU CAN DO THIS.
What the?
You probably don't speak squirrel but "excuse me"!
FA-DUNK!
NO!
YES!

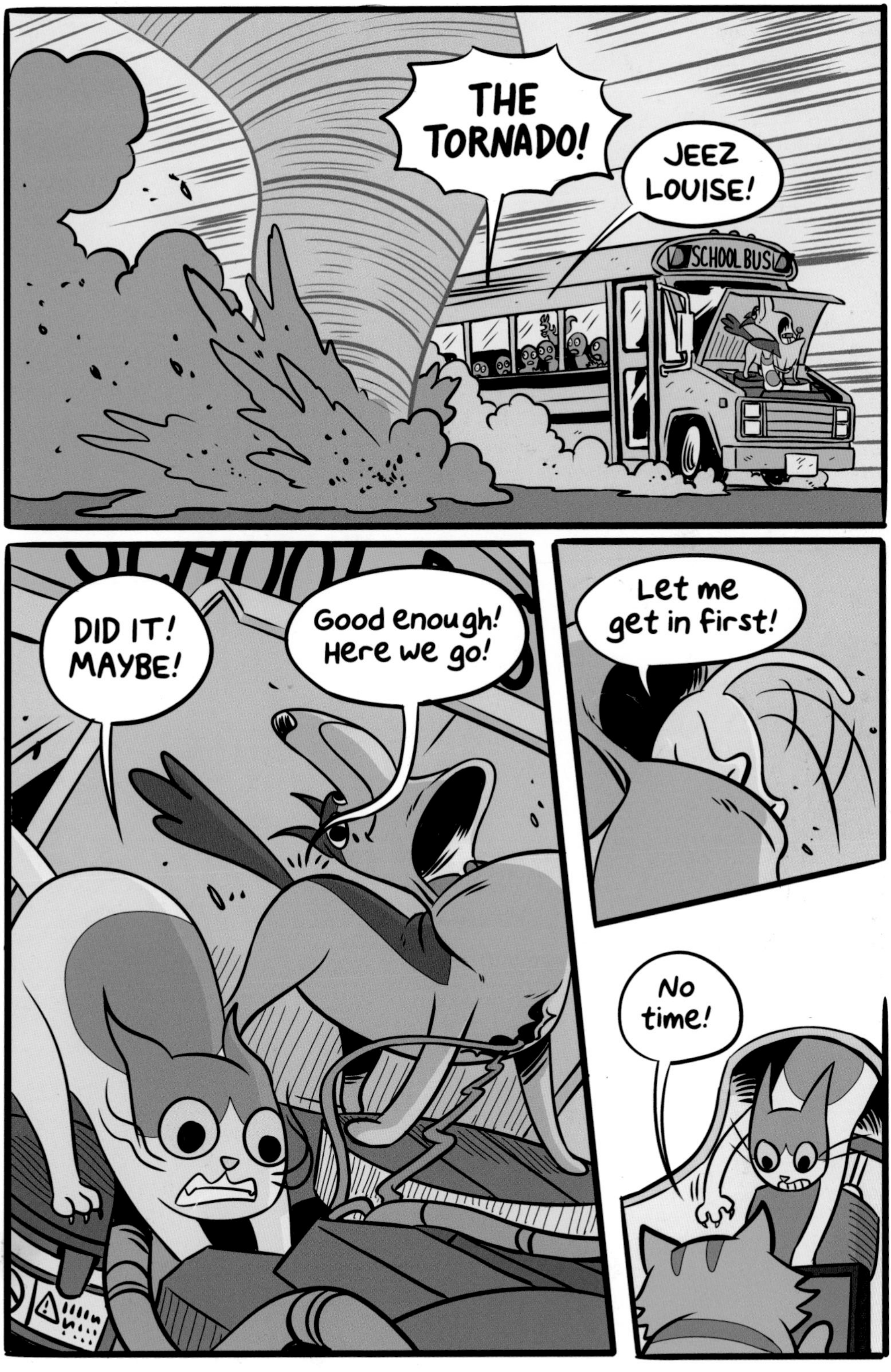
THE TORNADO!
JEEZ LOUISE!
SCHOOL BUS
DID IT! MAYBE!
Good enough! Here we go!
Let me get in first!
No time!

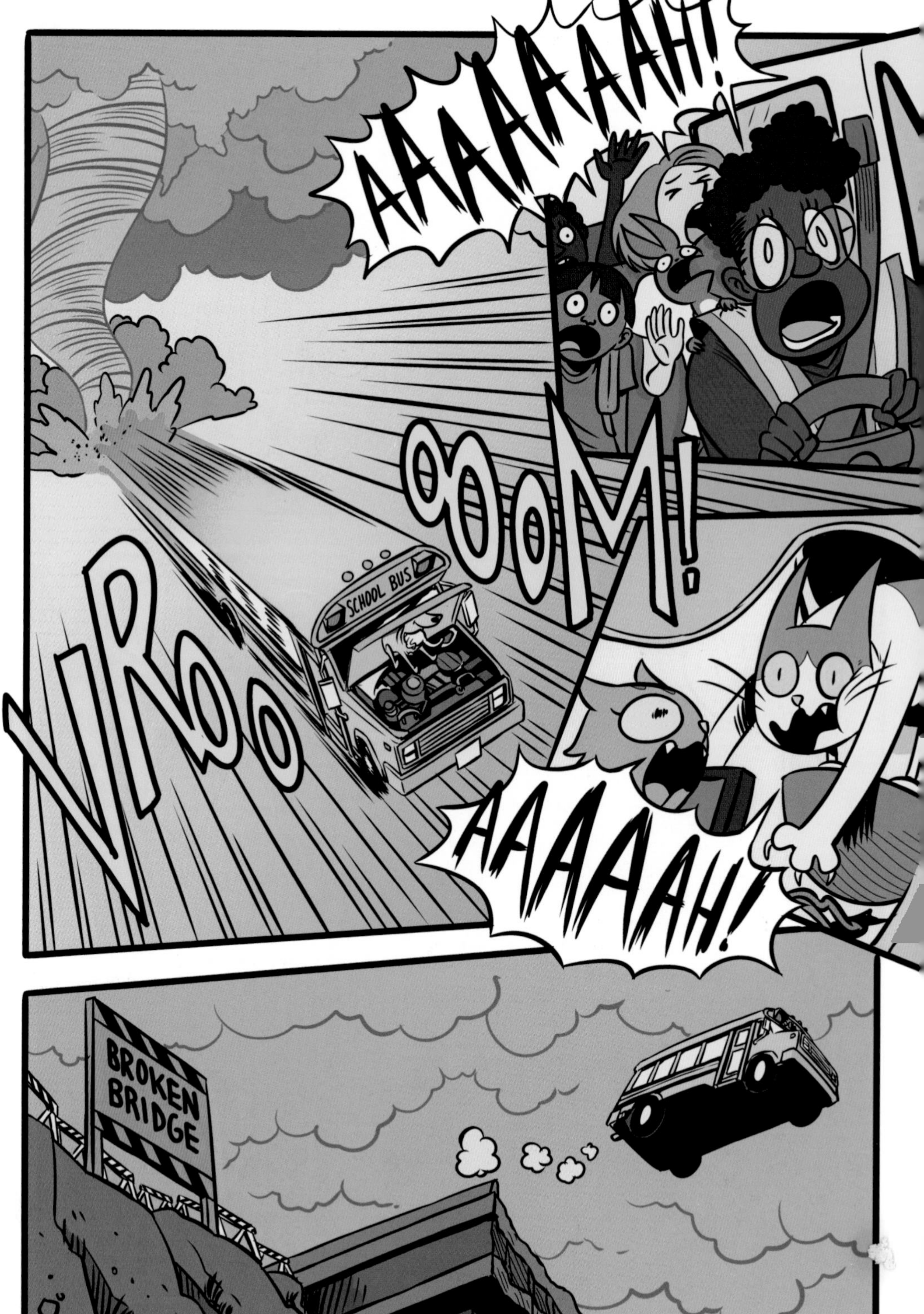
AAAAAAAAH!
VROOOOOM!
SCHOOL BUS
AAAAAAH!
BROKEN BRIDGE

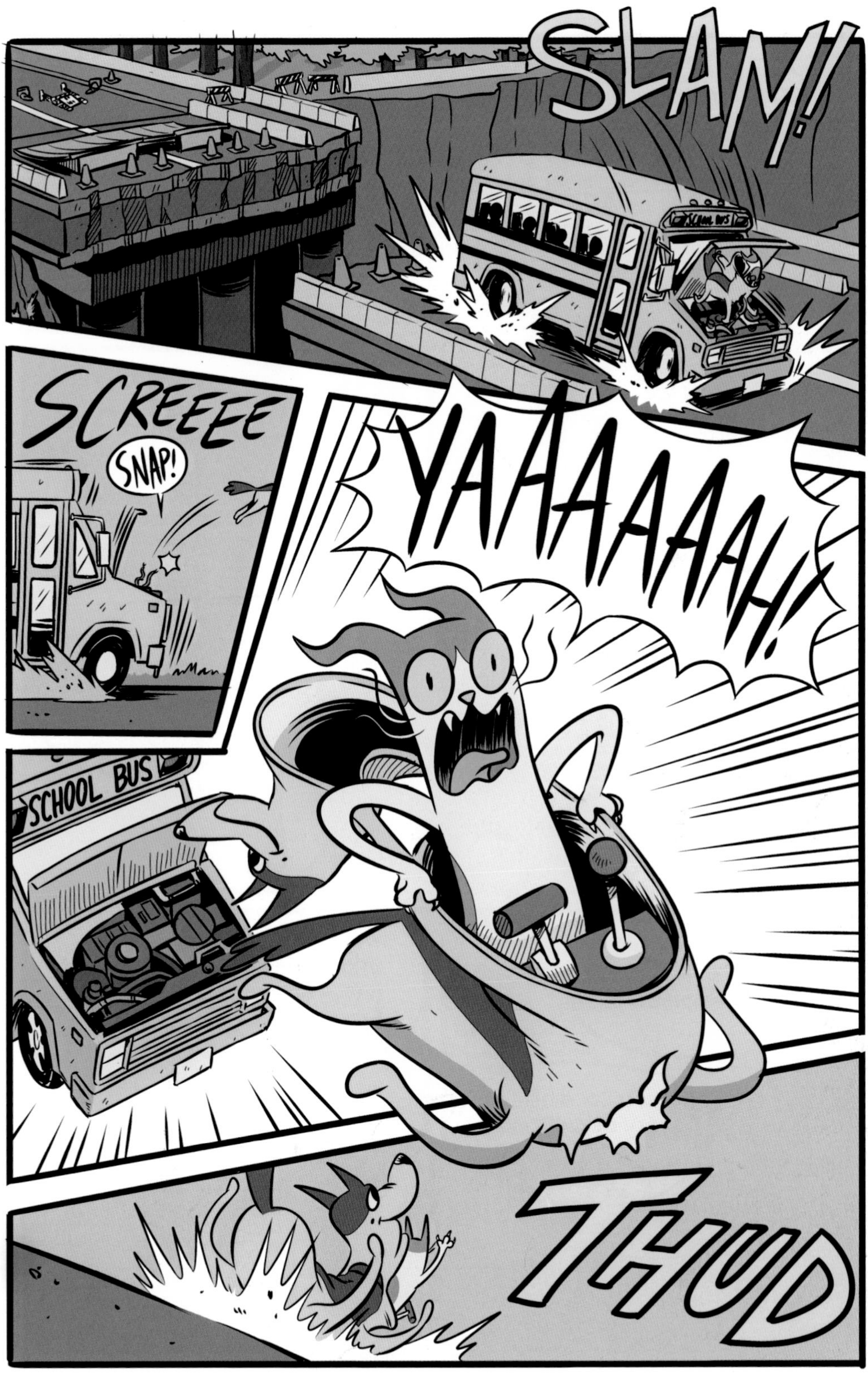
SLAM!
SCHOOL BUS
SCREEEE
SNAP!
YAAAAAAAH!
SCHOOL BUS
THUD

CHAPTER FIVE

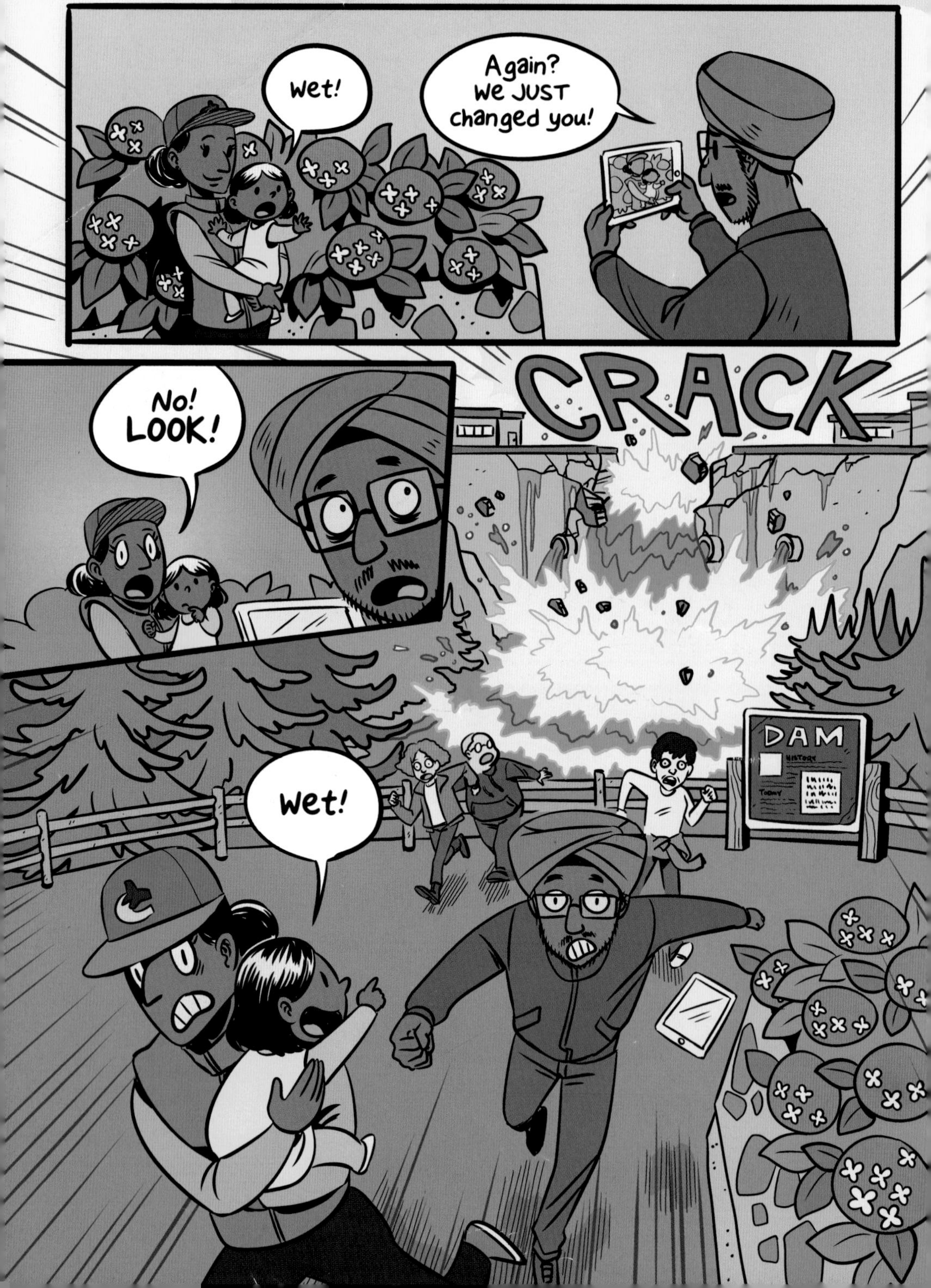
Wet!
Again? We JUST changed you!
No! LOOK!
CRACK
DAM
Wet!

79

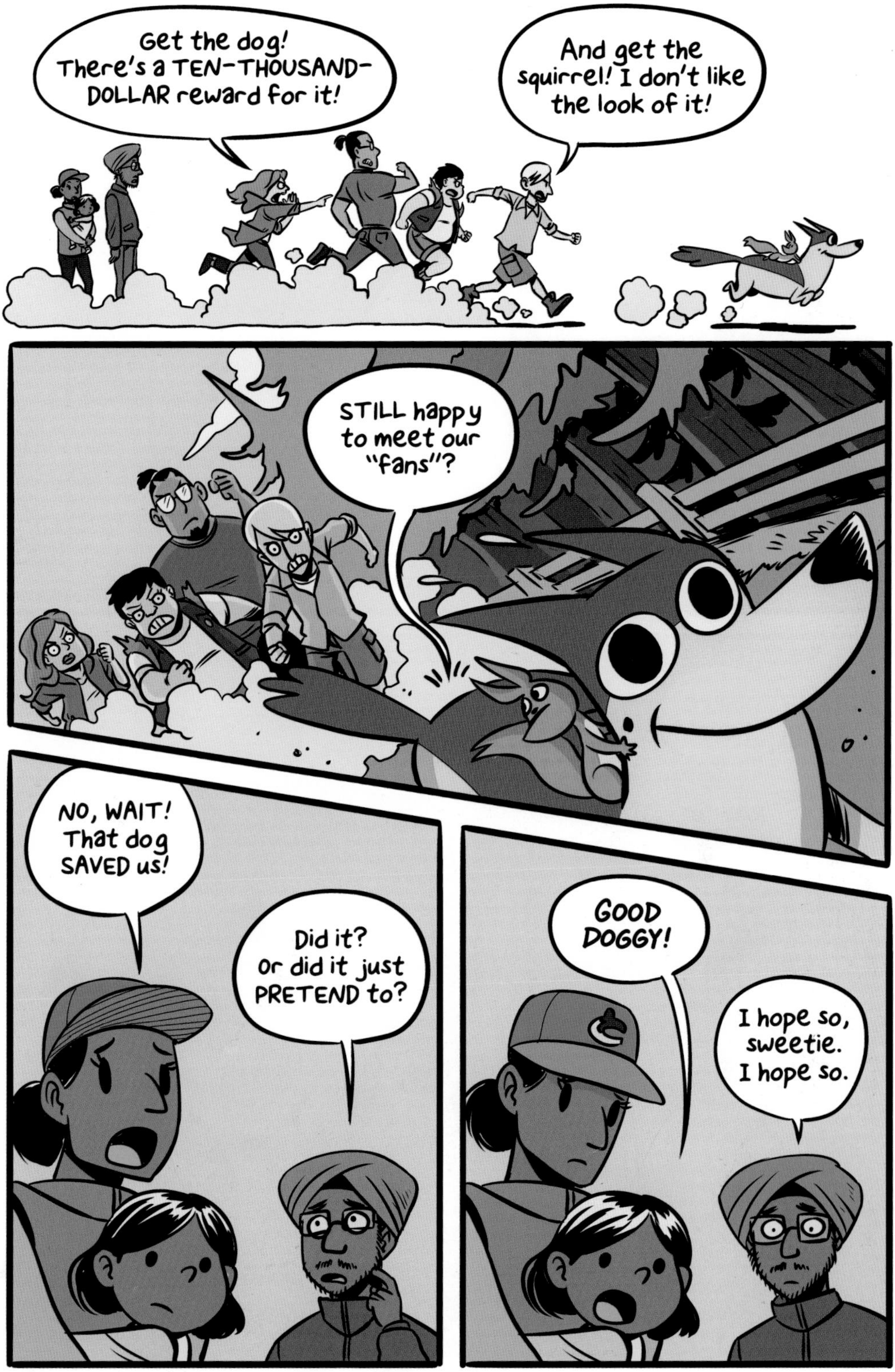
Get the dog! There's a TEN-THOUSAND-DOLLAR reward for it!
And get the squirrel! I don't like the look of it!
STILL happy to meet our "fans"?
NO, WAIT! That dog SAVED us!
Did it? Or did it just PRETEND to?
GOOD DOGGY!
I hope so, sweetie. I hope so.

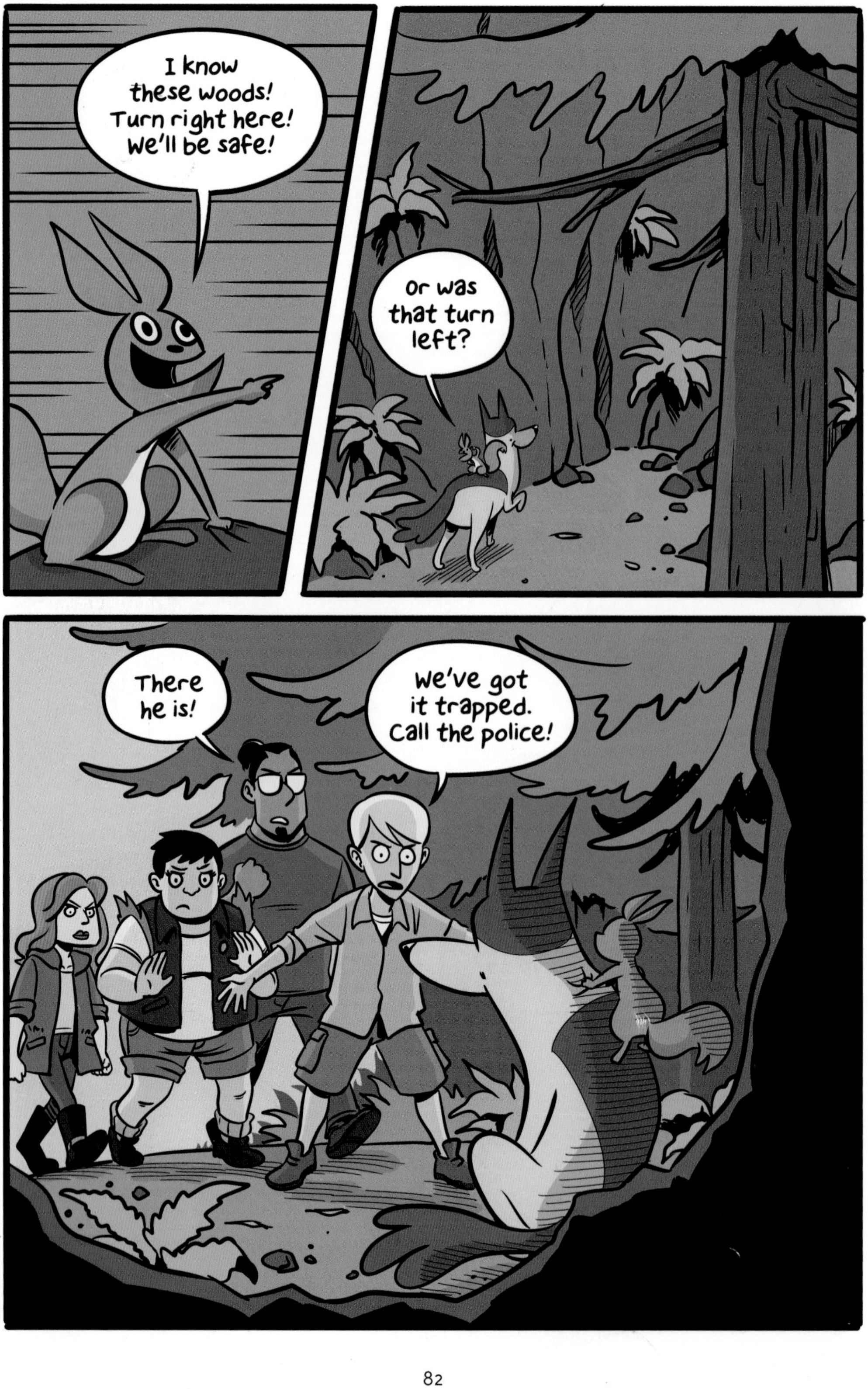
I know these woods! Turn right here! We'll be safe!
Or was that turn left?
There he is!
We've got it trapped. Call the police!

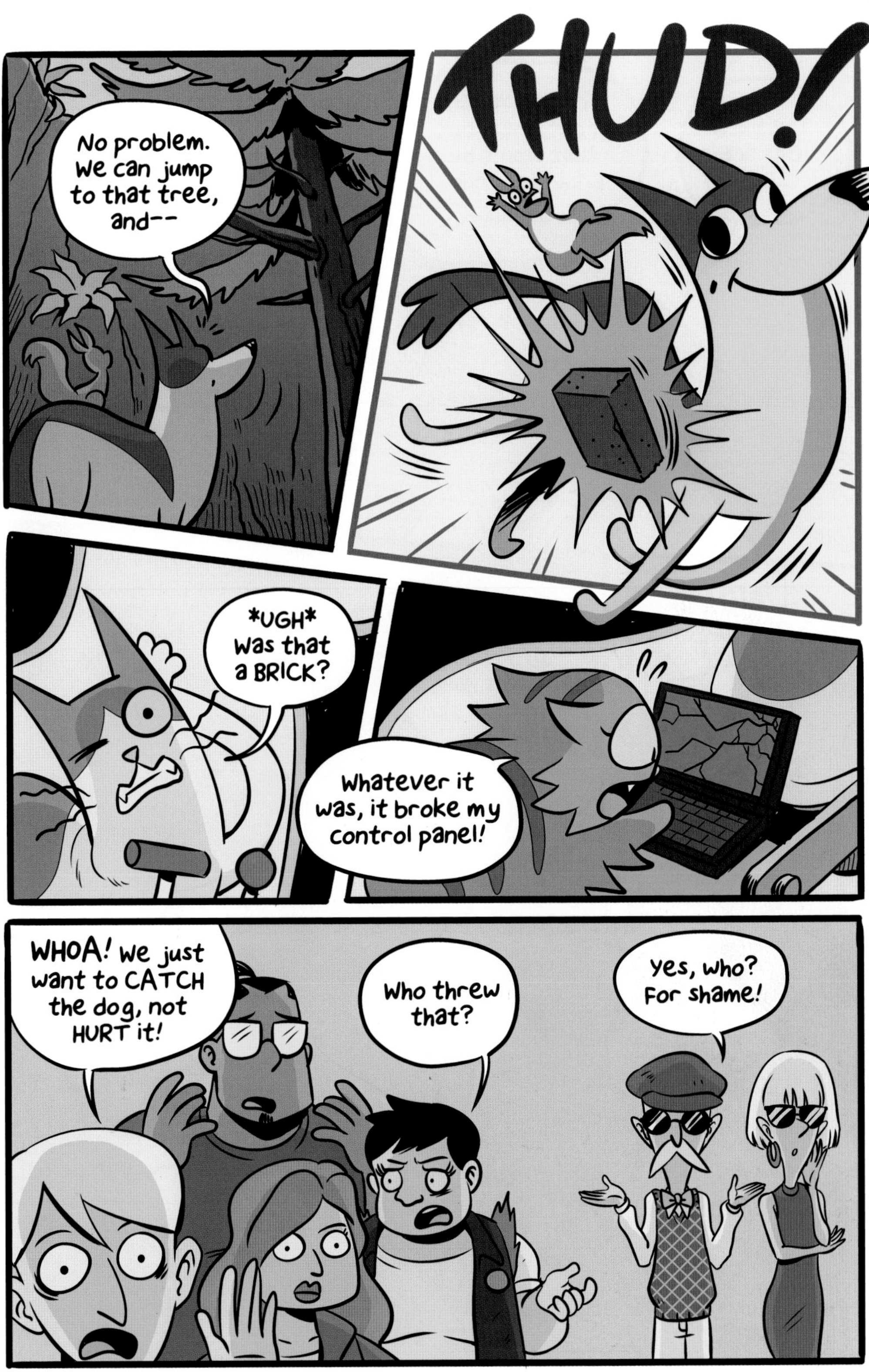
No problem. We can jump to that tree, and--
THUD!
UGH Was that a BRICK?
Whatever it was, it broke my control panel!
WHOA! We just want to CATCH the dog, not HURT it!
Who threw that?
Yes, who? For shame!

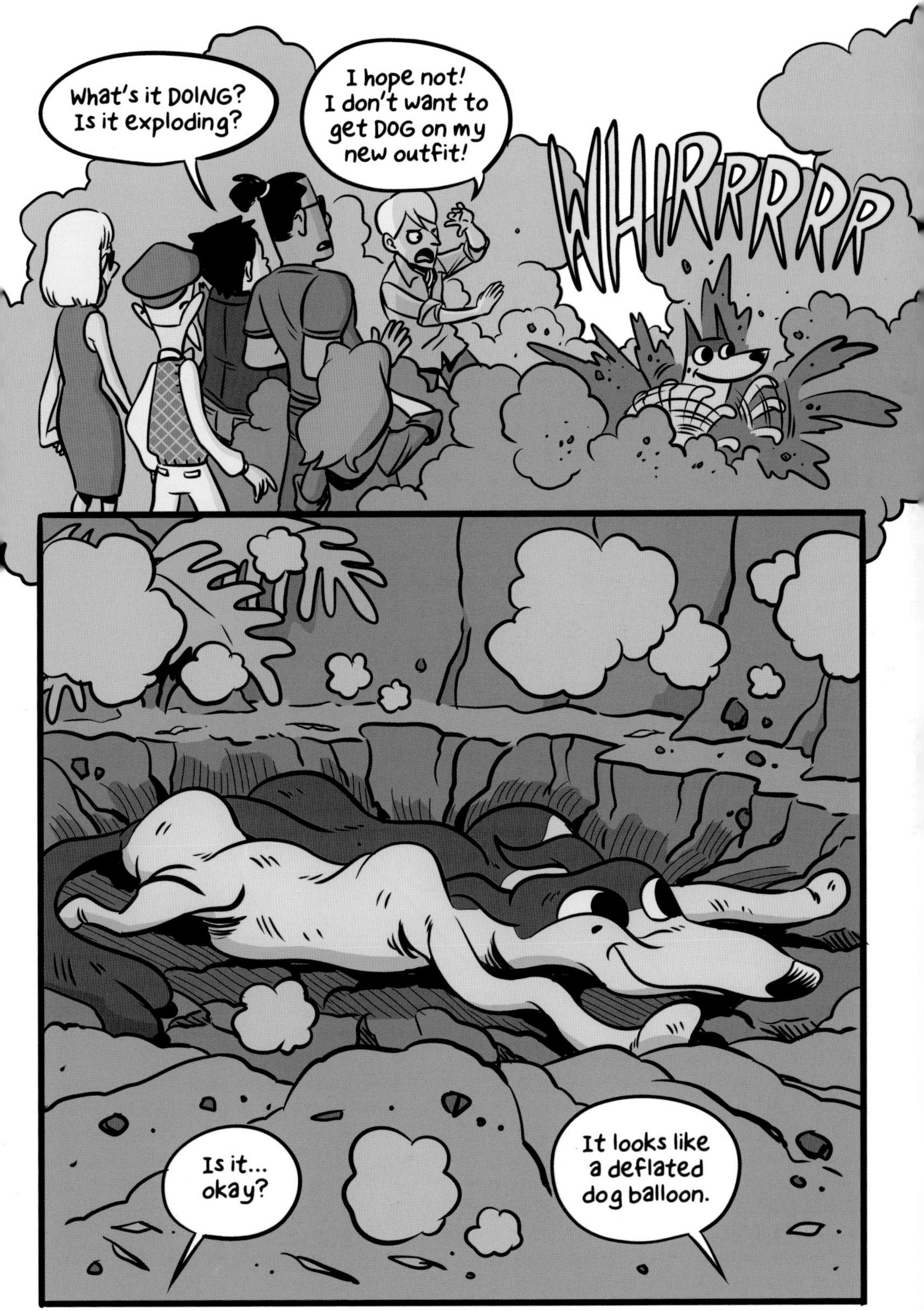
What's it DOING? Is it exploding?
I hope not! I don't want to get DOG on my new outfit!
WHIRRRRRR
Is it... okay?
It looks like a deflated dog balloon.

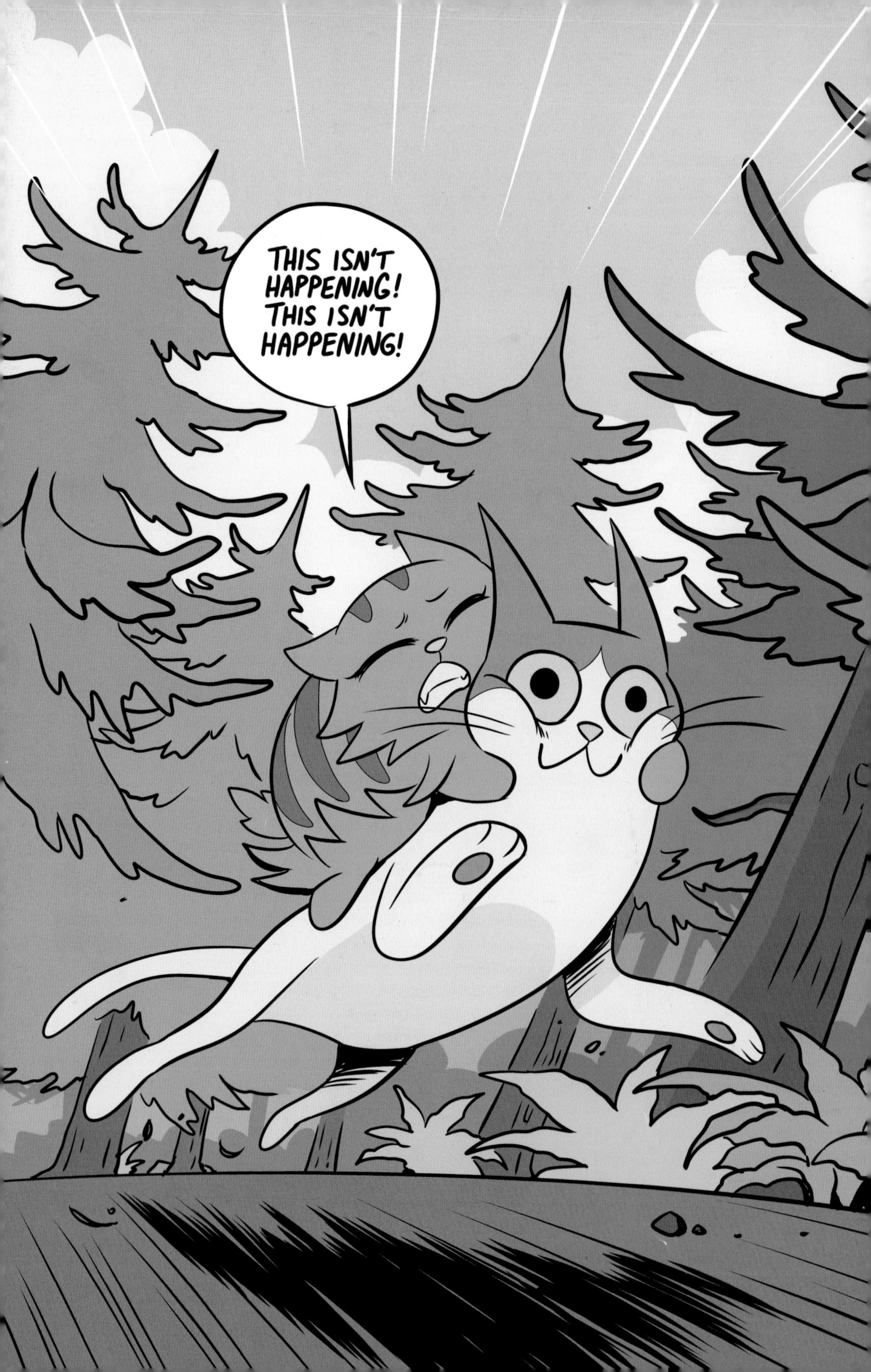
THIS ISN'T HAPPENING! THIS ISN'T HAPPENING!

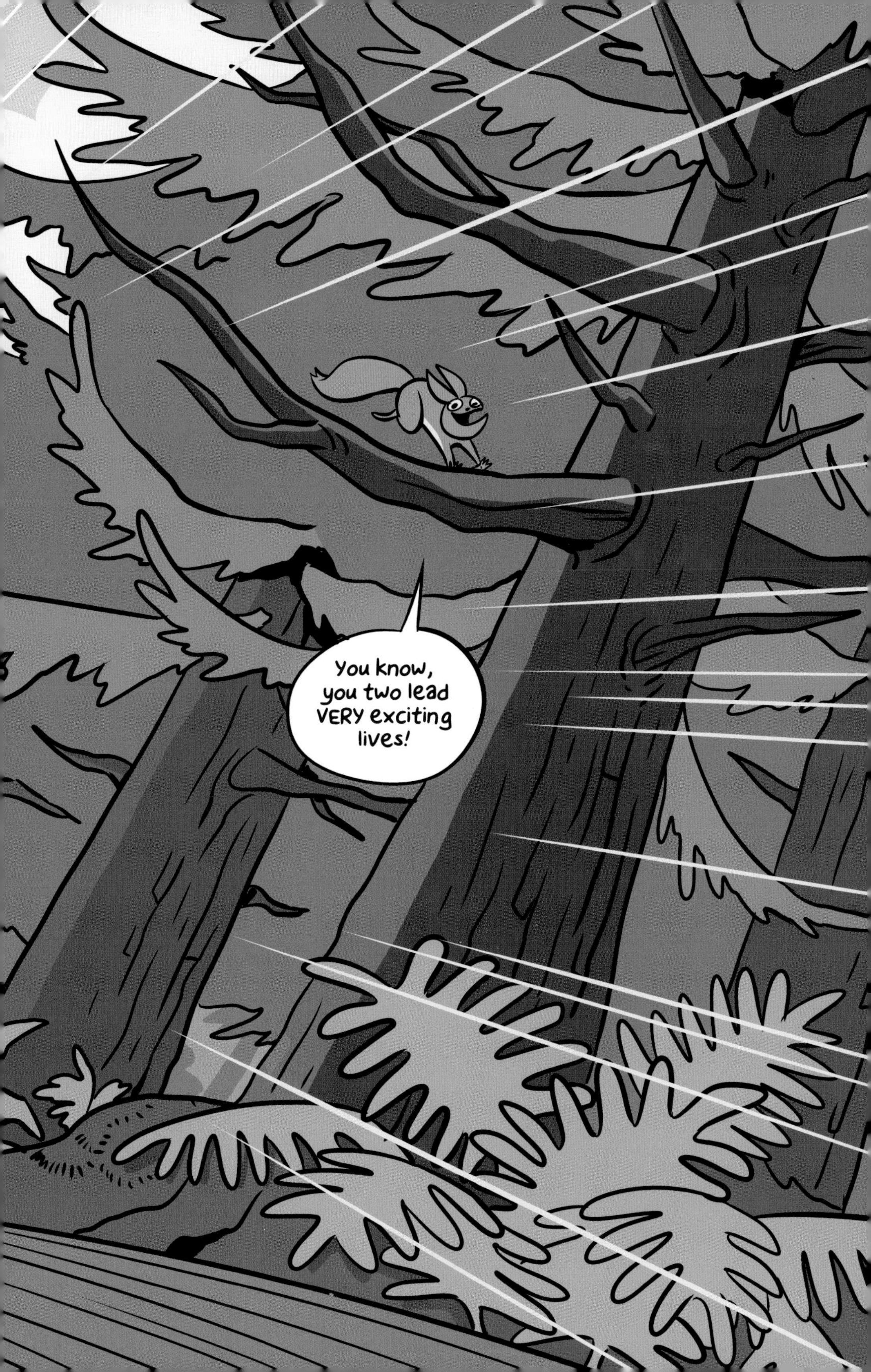
You know, you two lead VERY exciting lives!

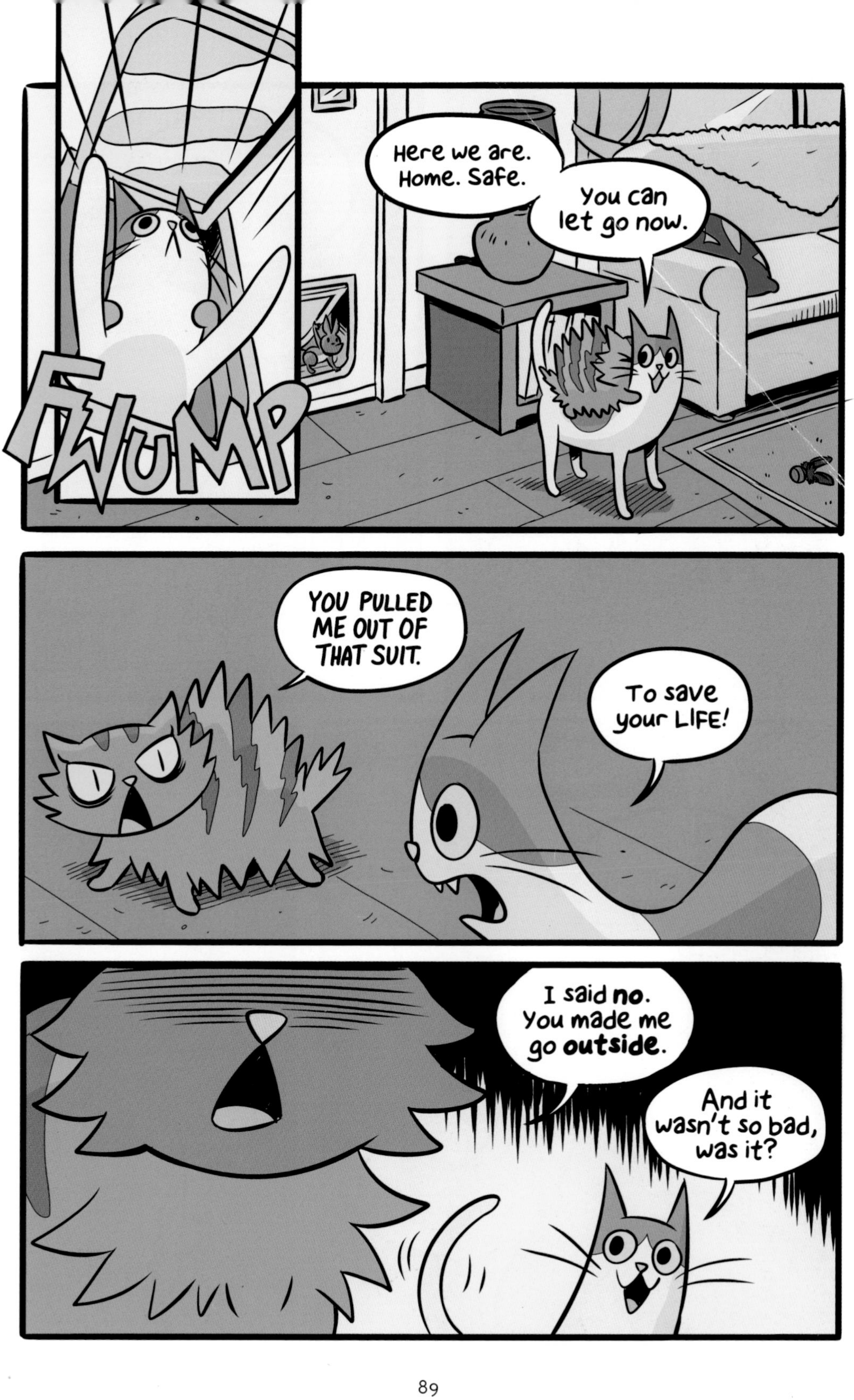
FWUMP
Here we are. Home. Safe.
You can let go now.
YOU PULLED ME OUT OF THAT SUIT.
To save your LIFE!
I said **no**. You made me go **outside**.
And it wasn't so bad, was it?

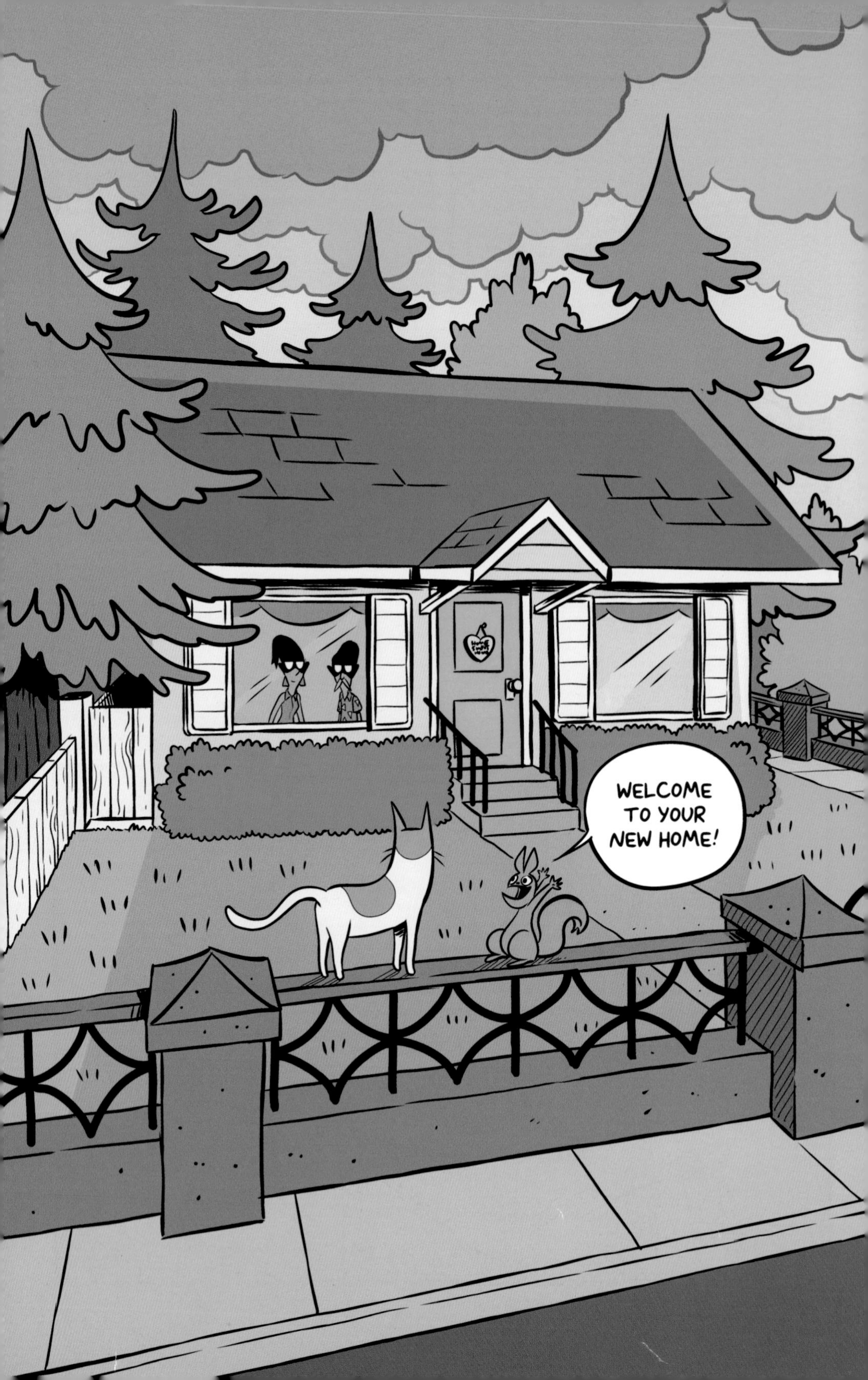
WELCOME TO YOUR NEW HOME!

CHAPTER SIX

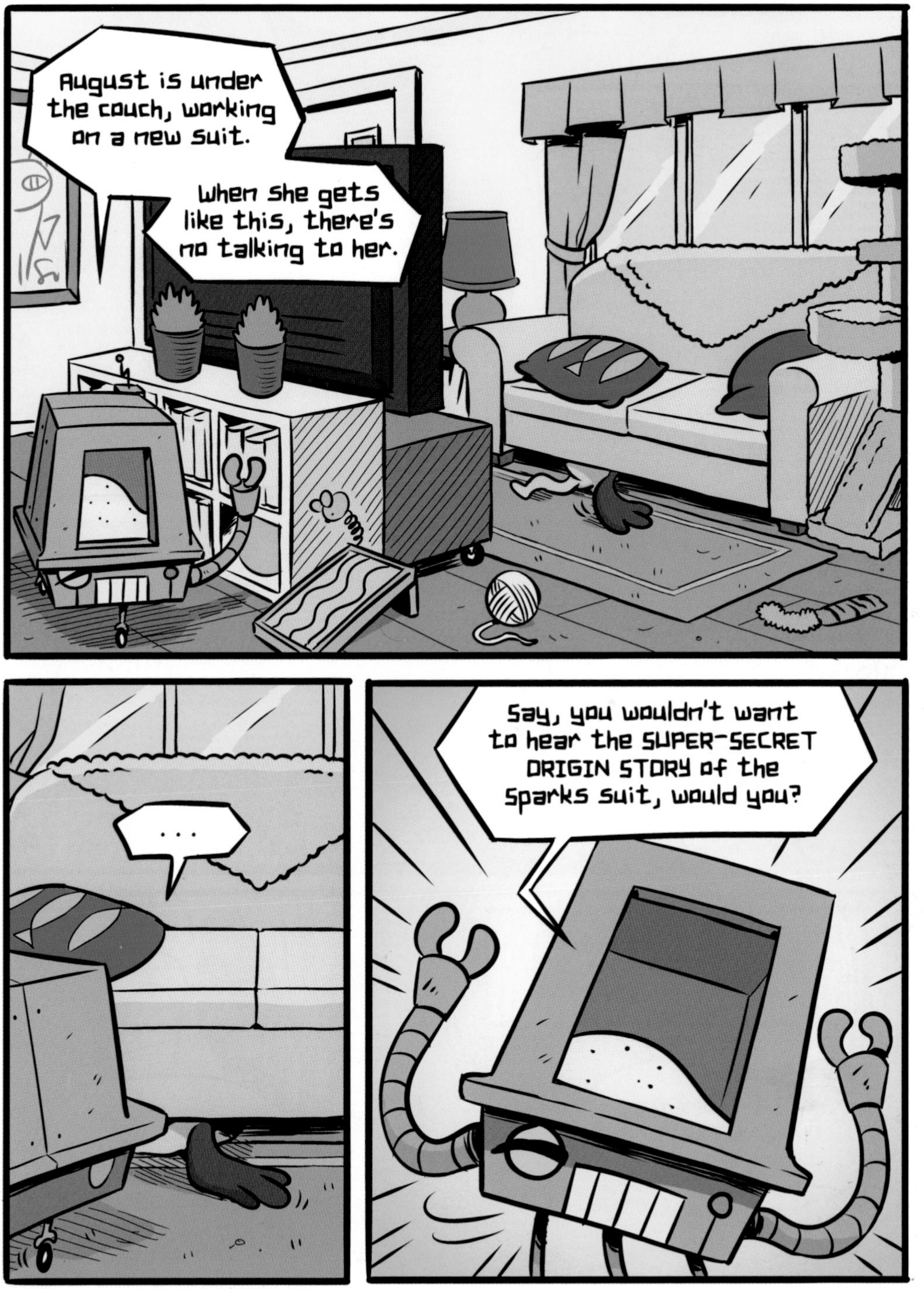
August is under the couch, working on a new suit.
When she gets like this, there's no talking to her.
. . .
Say, you wouldn't want to hear the SUPER-SECRET ORIGIN STORY of the Sparks suit, would you?

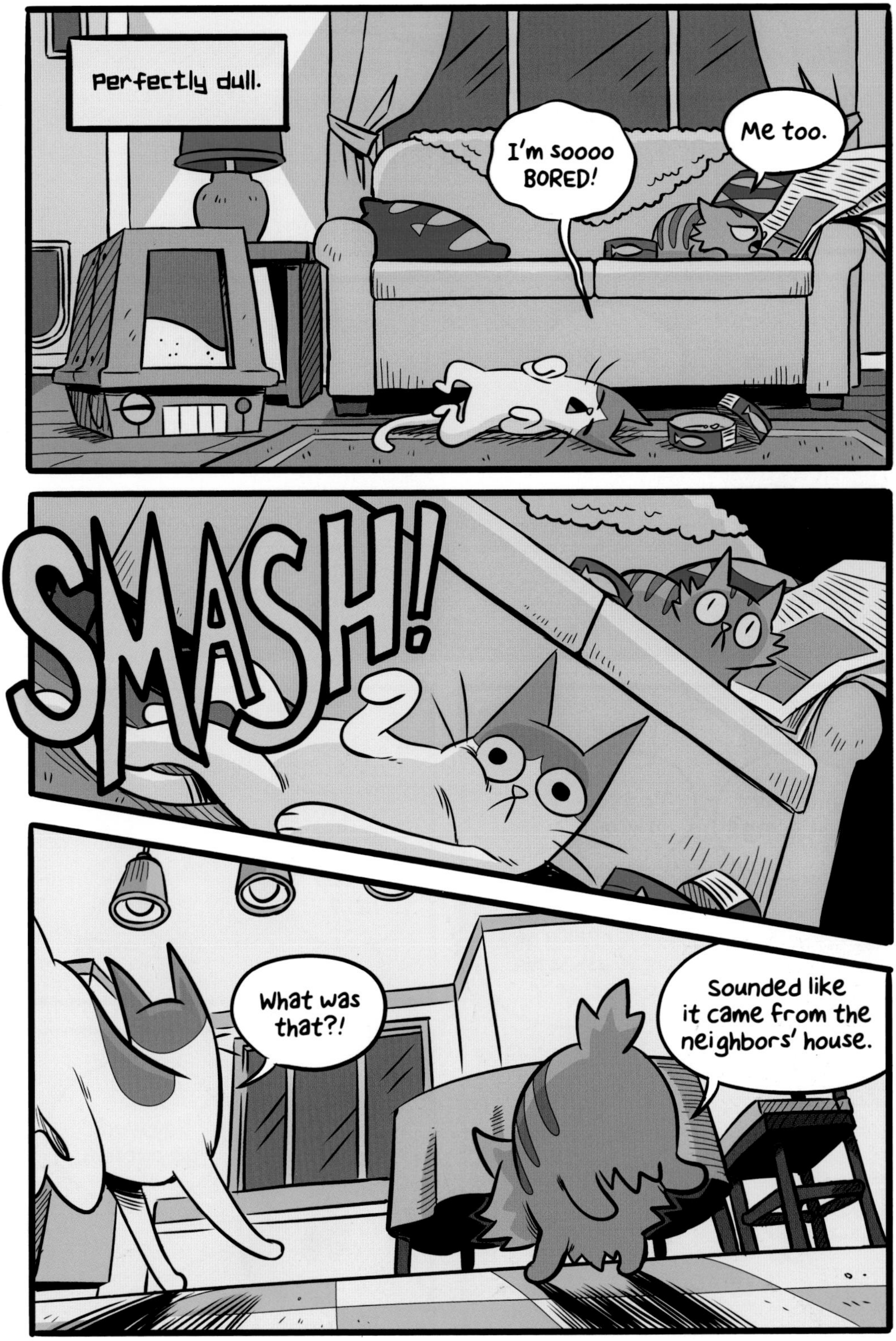
Perfectly dull.
I'm soooo BORED!
Me too.
SMASH!
What was that?!
Sounded like it came from the neighbors' house.

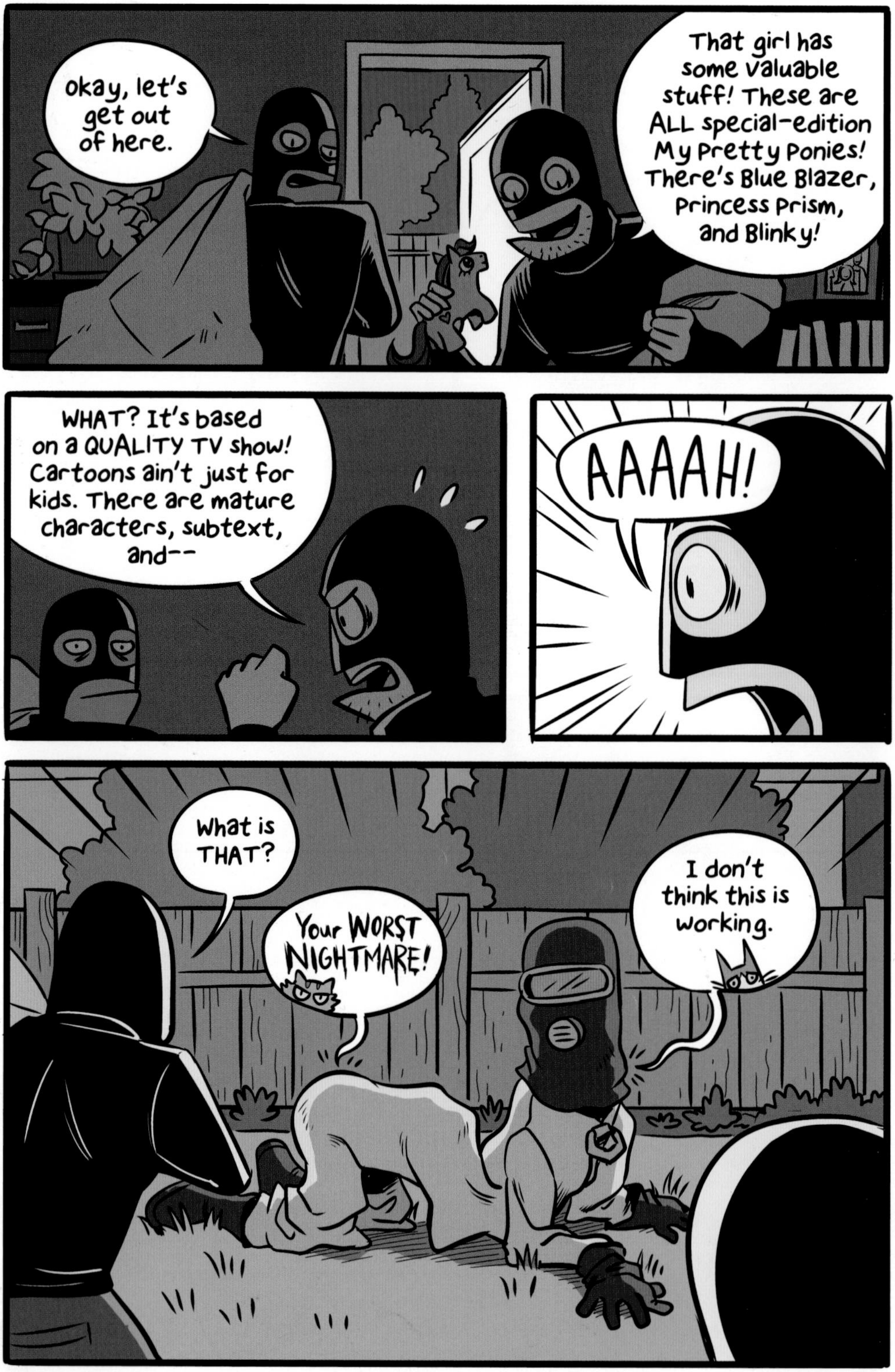
okay, let's get out of here.
That girl has some valuable stuff! These are ALL special-edition My Pretty Ponies! There's Blue Blazer, Princess Prism, and Blinky!
WHAT? It's based on a QUALITY TV show! Cartoons ain't just for kids. There are mature characters, subtext, and--
AAAAH!
What is THAT?
Your WORST NIGHTMARE!
I don't think this is working.

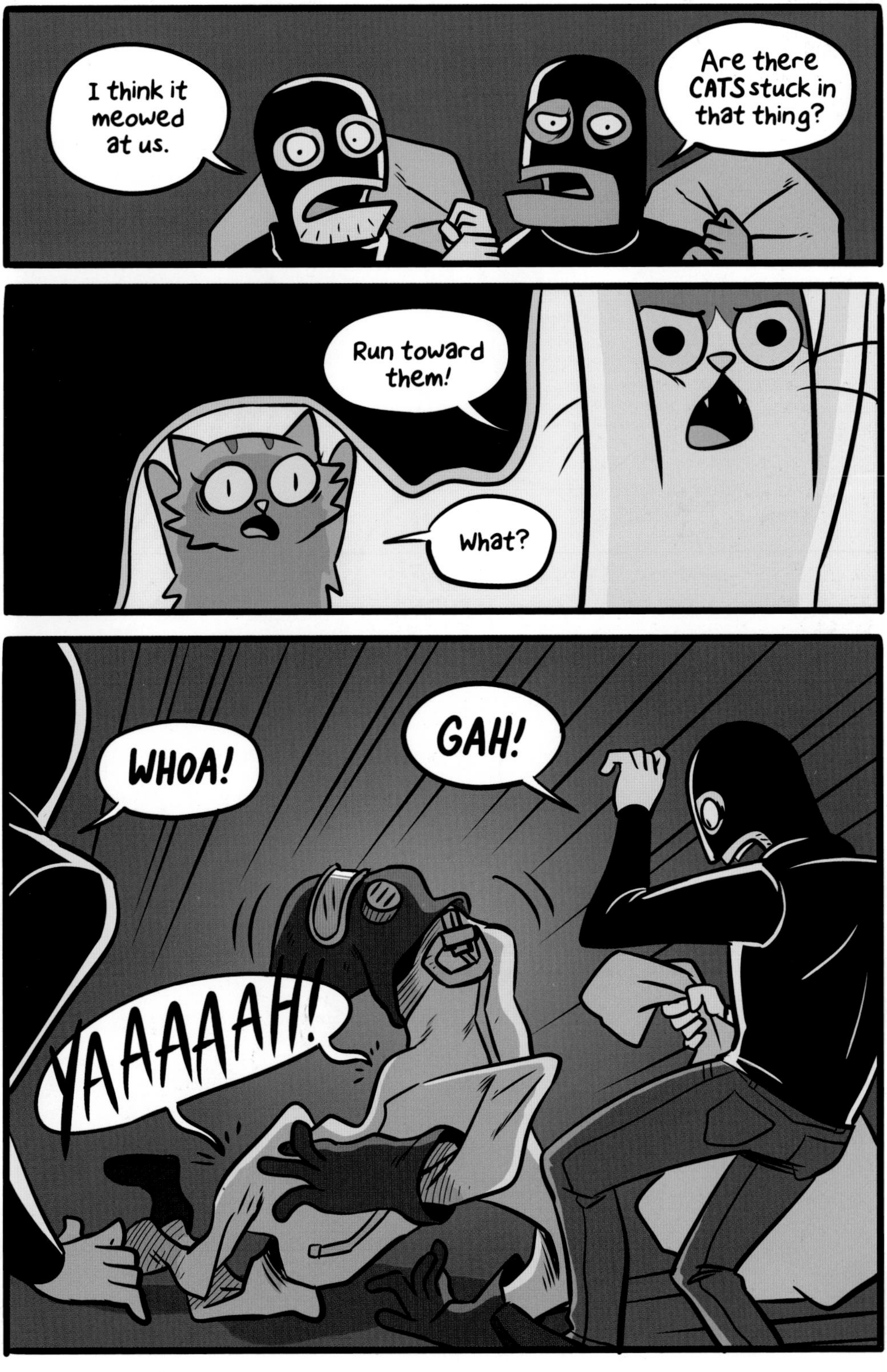
I think it meowed at us.
Are there CATS stuck in that thing?
Run toward them!
What?
WHOA!
GAH!
YAAAAAH!

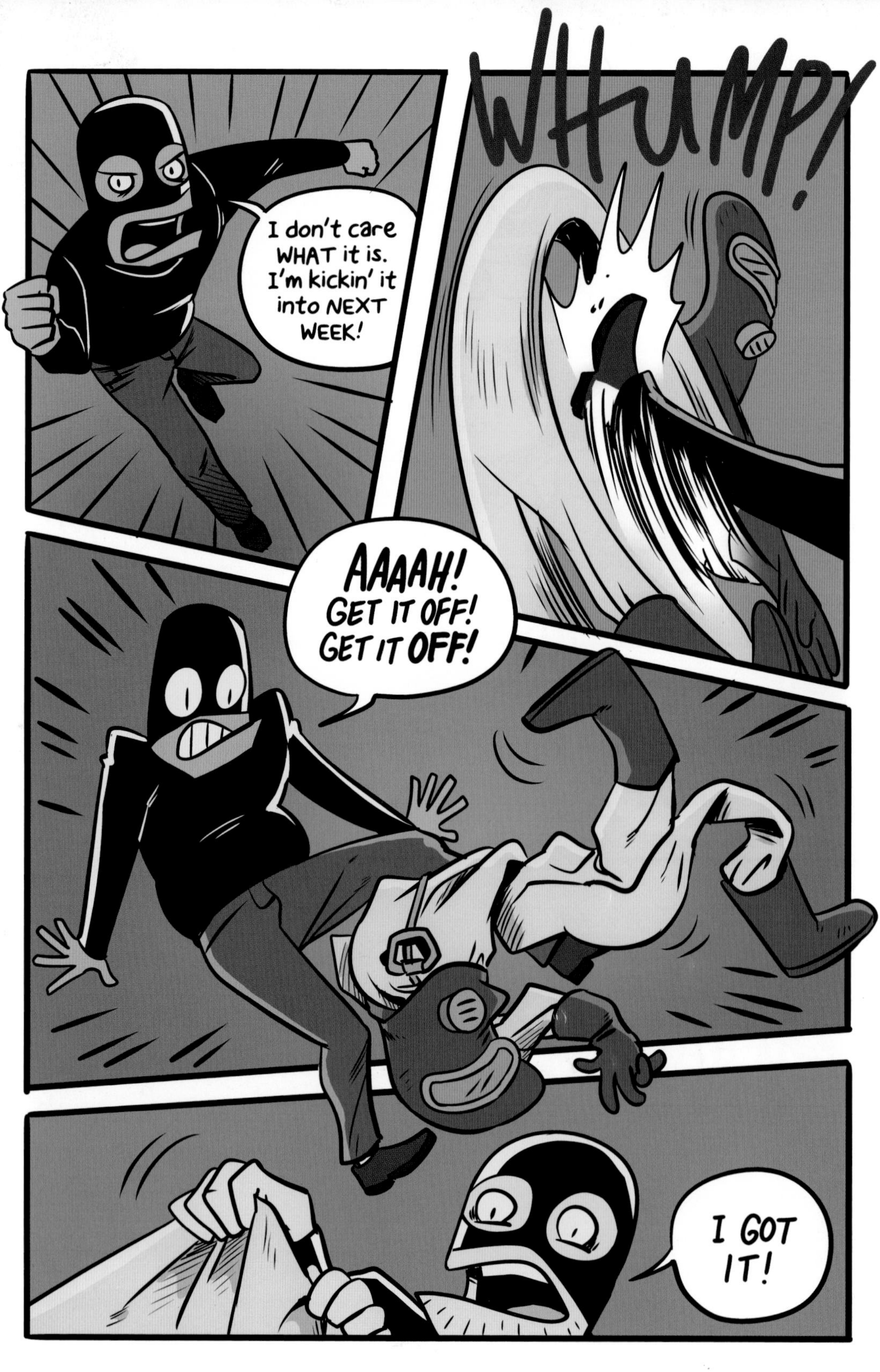
I don't care WHAT it is. I'm kickin' it into NEXT WEEK!
WHUMP!
AAAAH! GET IT OFF! GET IT OFF!
I GOT IT!

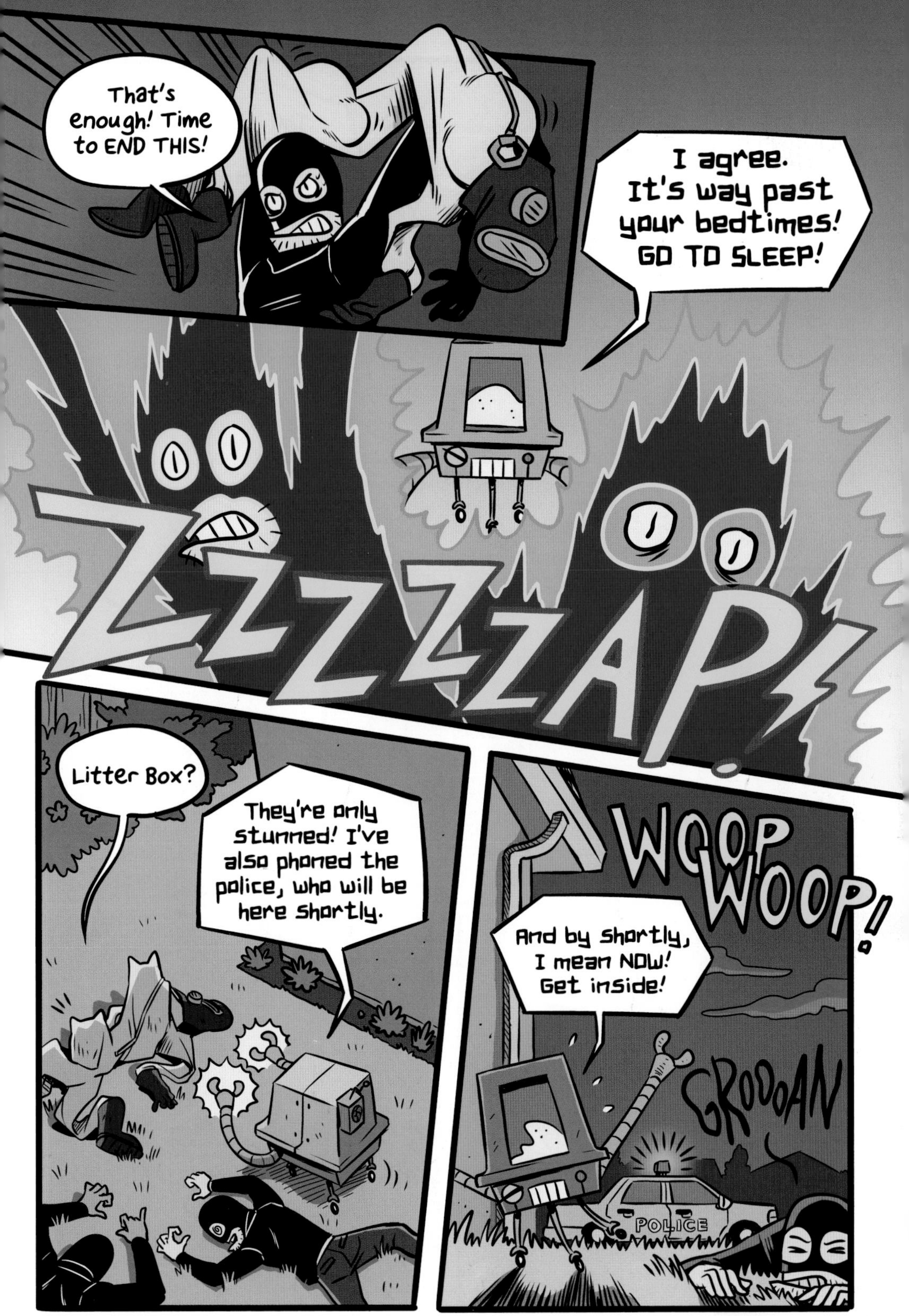
That's enough! Time to END THIS!
I agree. It's way past your bedtimes! GO TO SLEEP!
ZZZZZAP!
Litter Box?
They're only stunned! I've also phoned the police, who will be here shortly.
WOOP WOOP!
And by shortly, I mean NOW! Get inside!
GROOOAN
POLICE

108

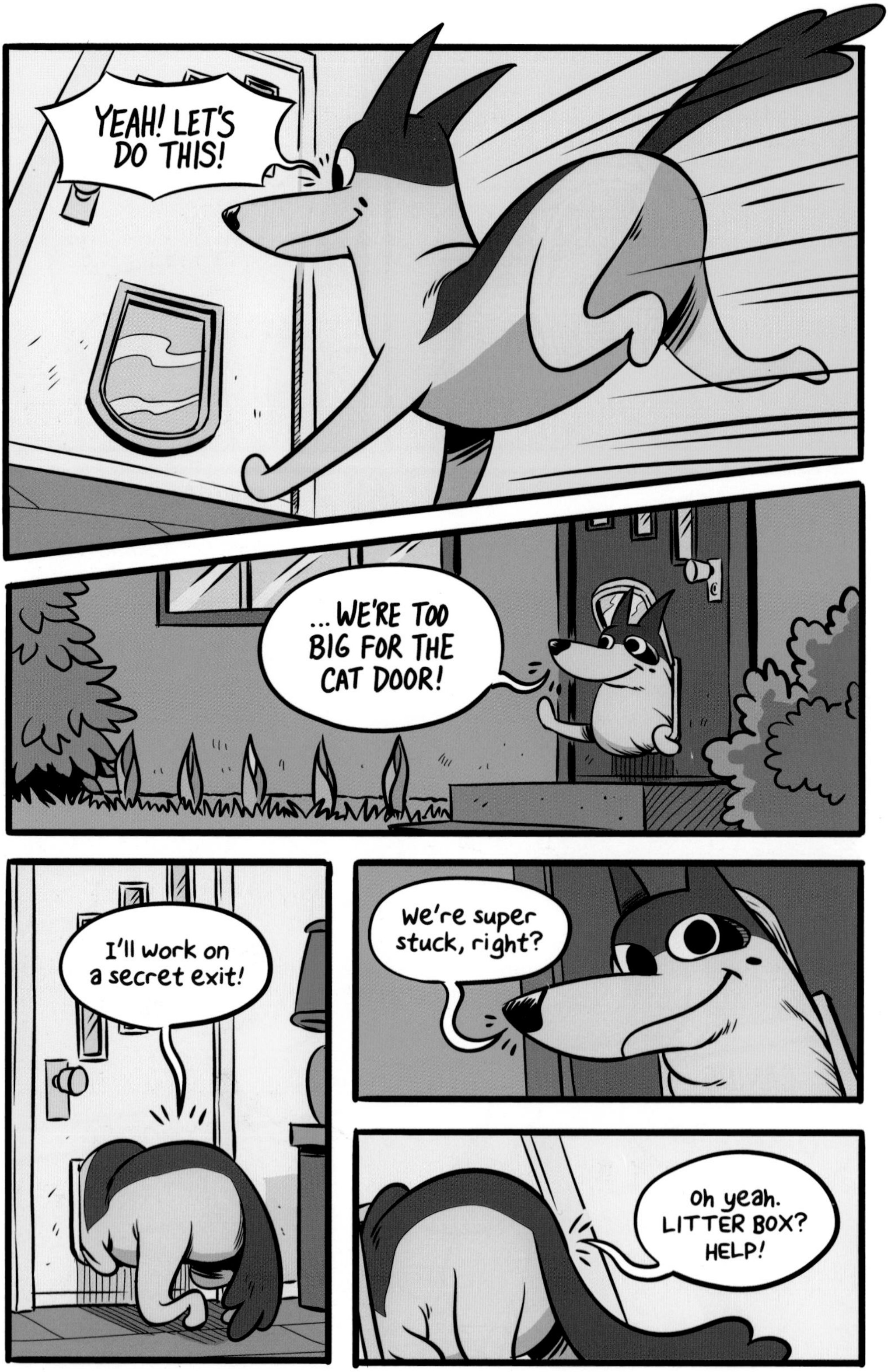
YEAH! LET'S DO THIS!
...WE'RE TOO BIG FOR THE CAT DOOR!
I'll work on a secret exit!
We're super stuck, right?
Oh yeah. LITTER BOX? HELP!

CHAPTER SEVEN

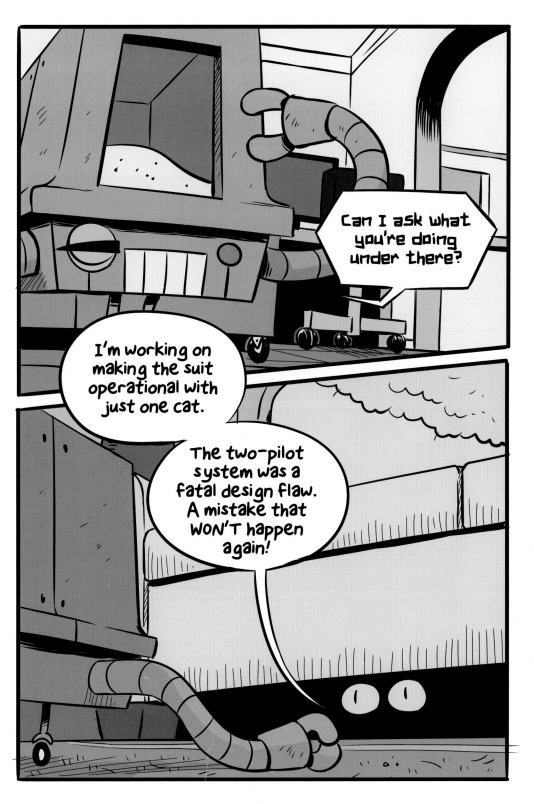

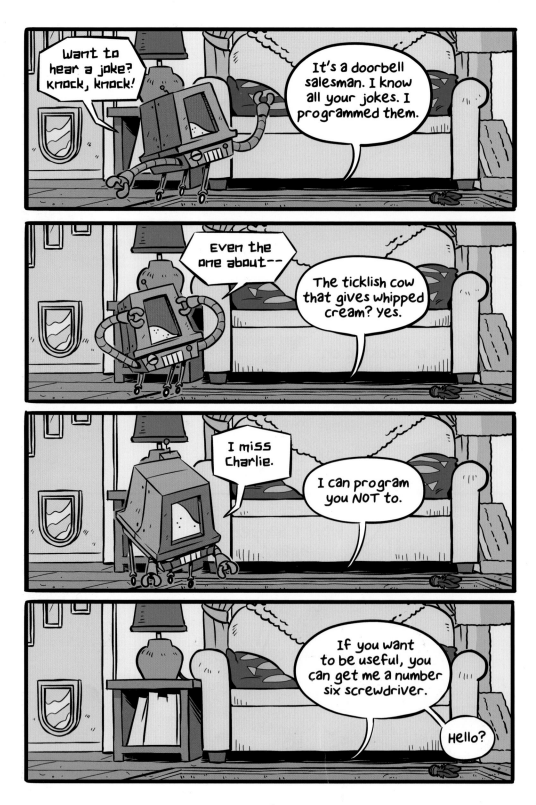

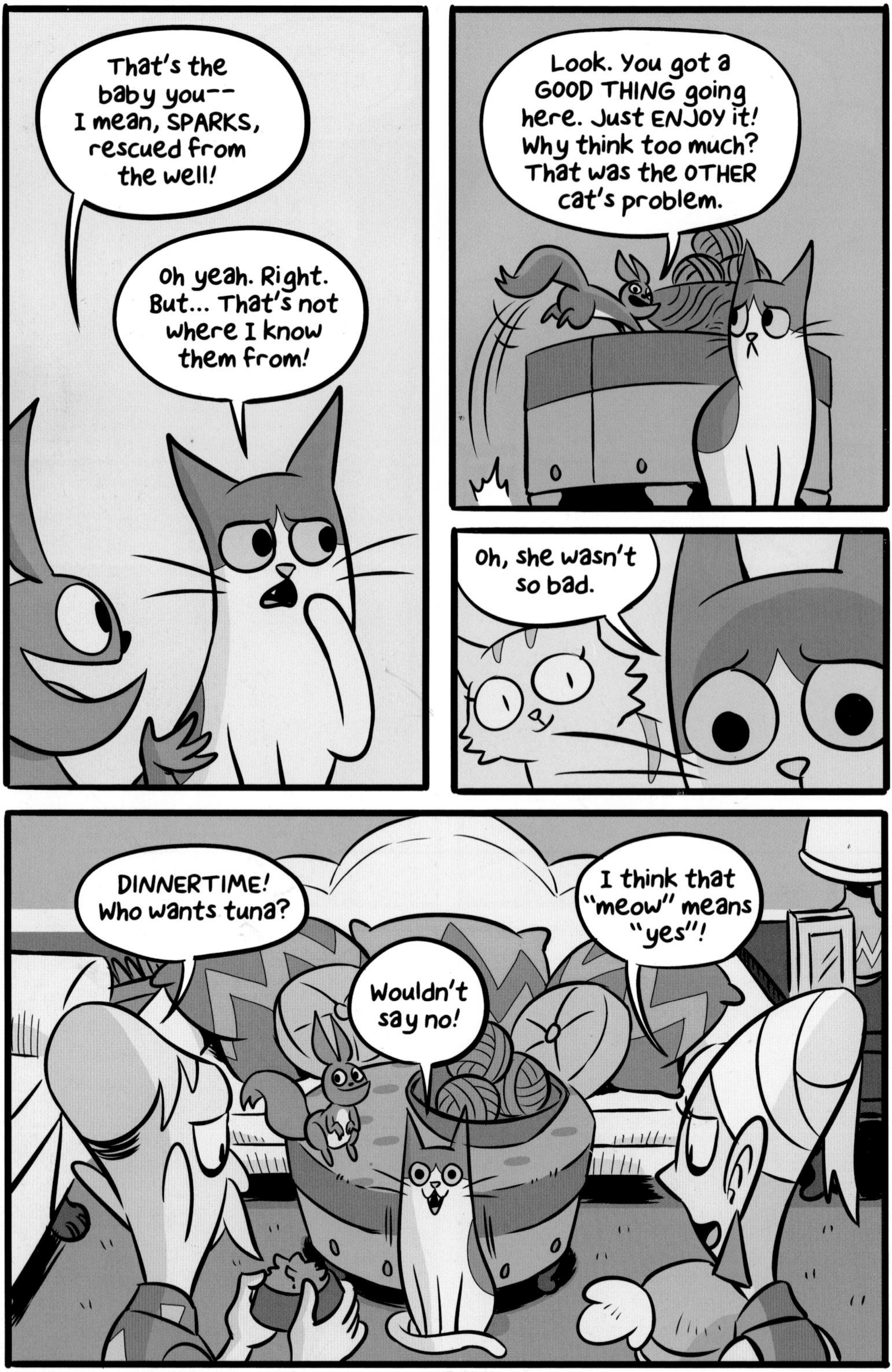
That's the baby you-- I mean, SPARKS, rescued from the well!
Oh yeah. Right. But... That's not where I know them from!
Look. You got a GOOD THING going here. Just ENJOY it! Why think too much? That was the OTHER cat's problem.
Oh, she wasn't so bad.
DINNERTIME! Who wants tuna?
Wouldn't say no!
I think that "meow" means "yes"!

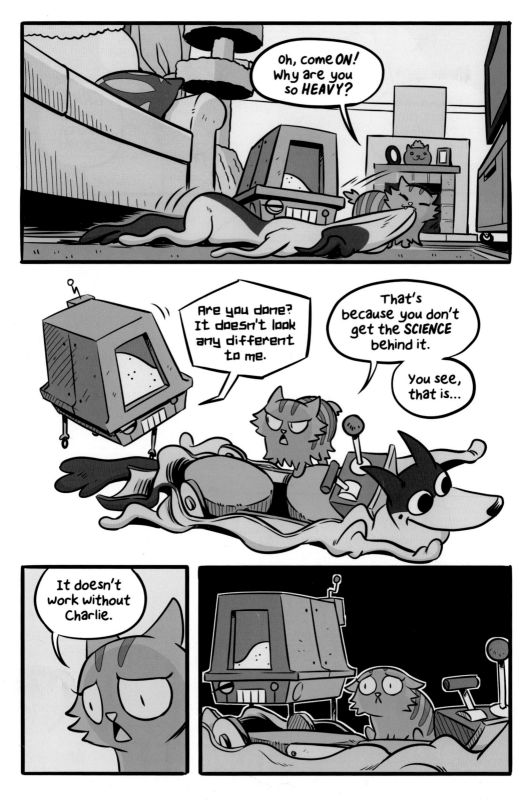

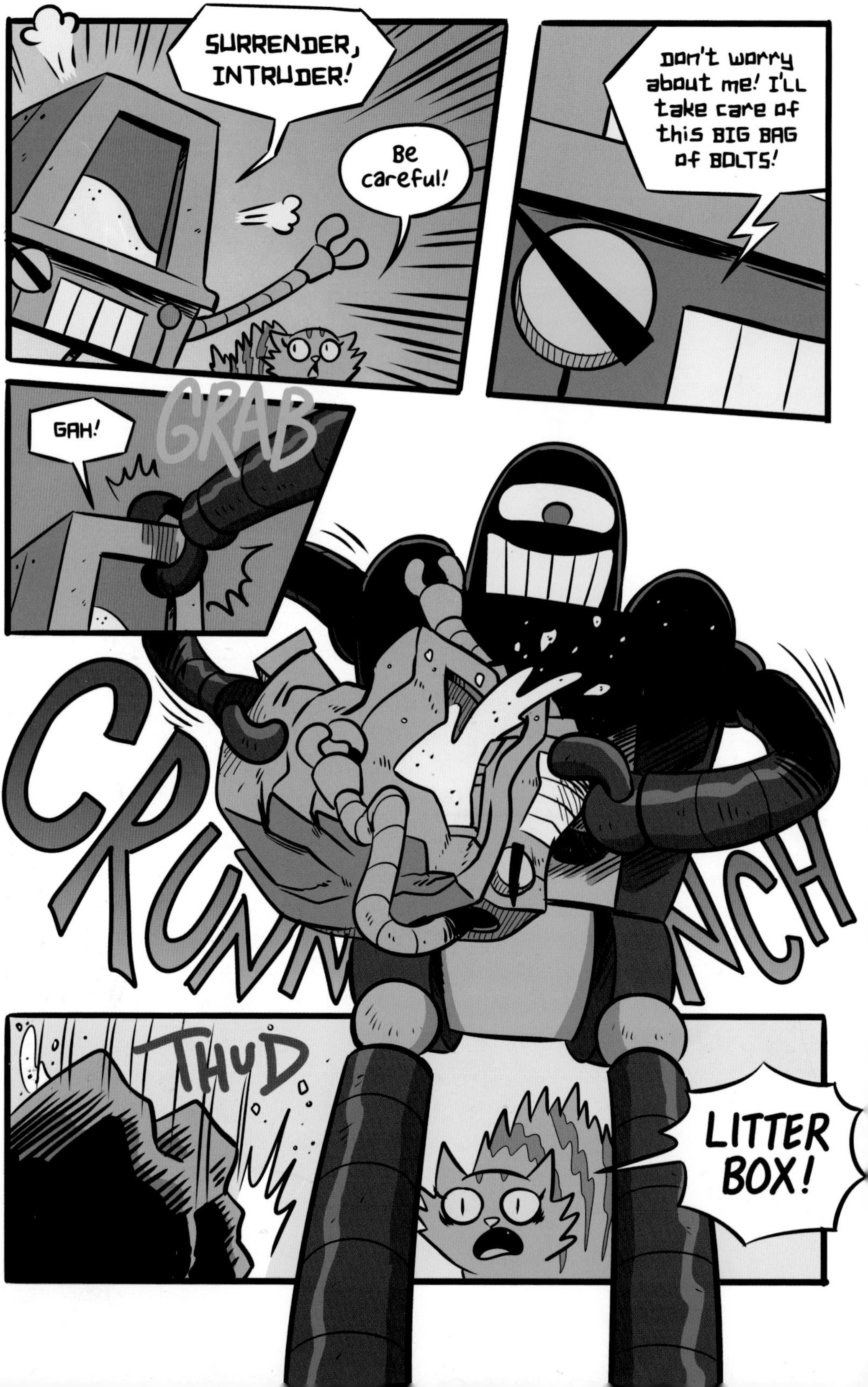
SURRENDER, INTRUDER!
Be careful!
Don't worry about me! I'LL take care of this BIG BAG of BOLTS!
GAH!
GRAB
CRUNNNCH
THUD
LITTER BOX!

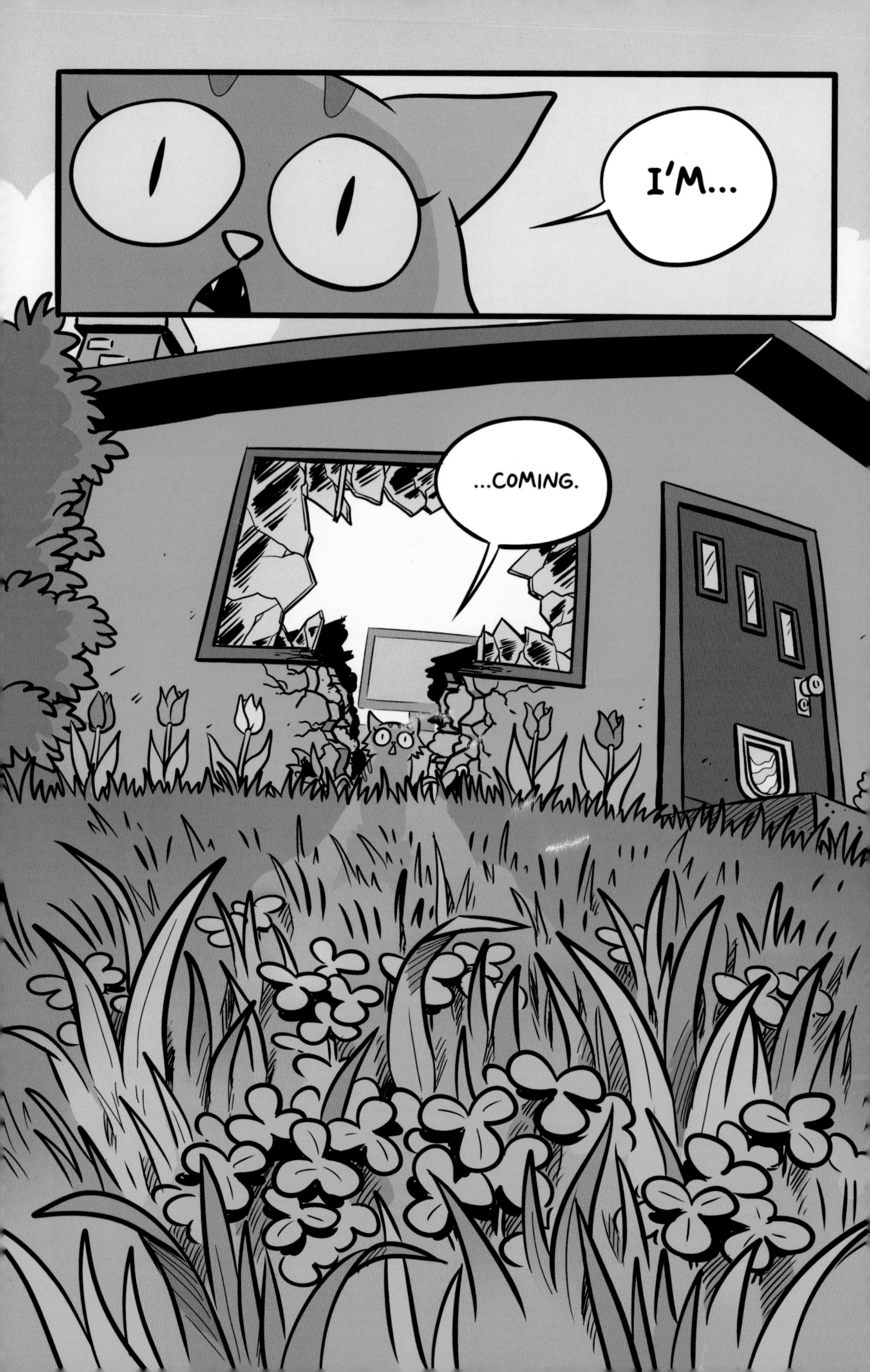
I'M...
...COMING.

CHAPTER EIGHT

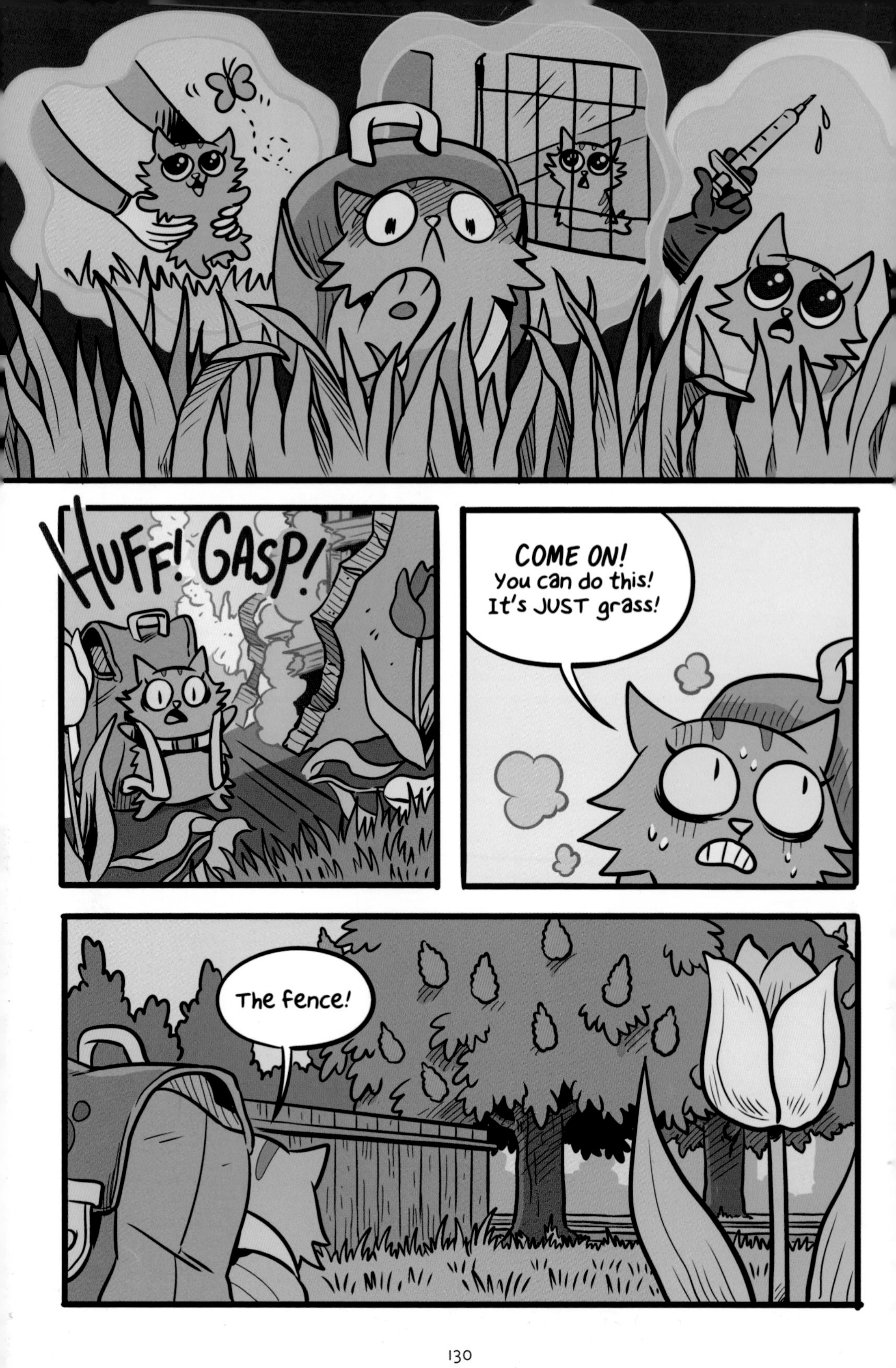
HUFF! GASP!
COME ON! You can do this! It's JUST grass!
The fence!

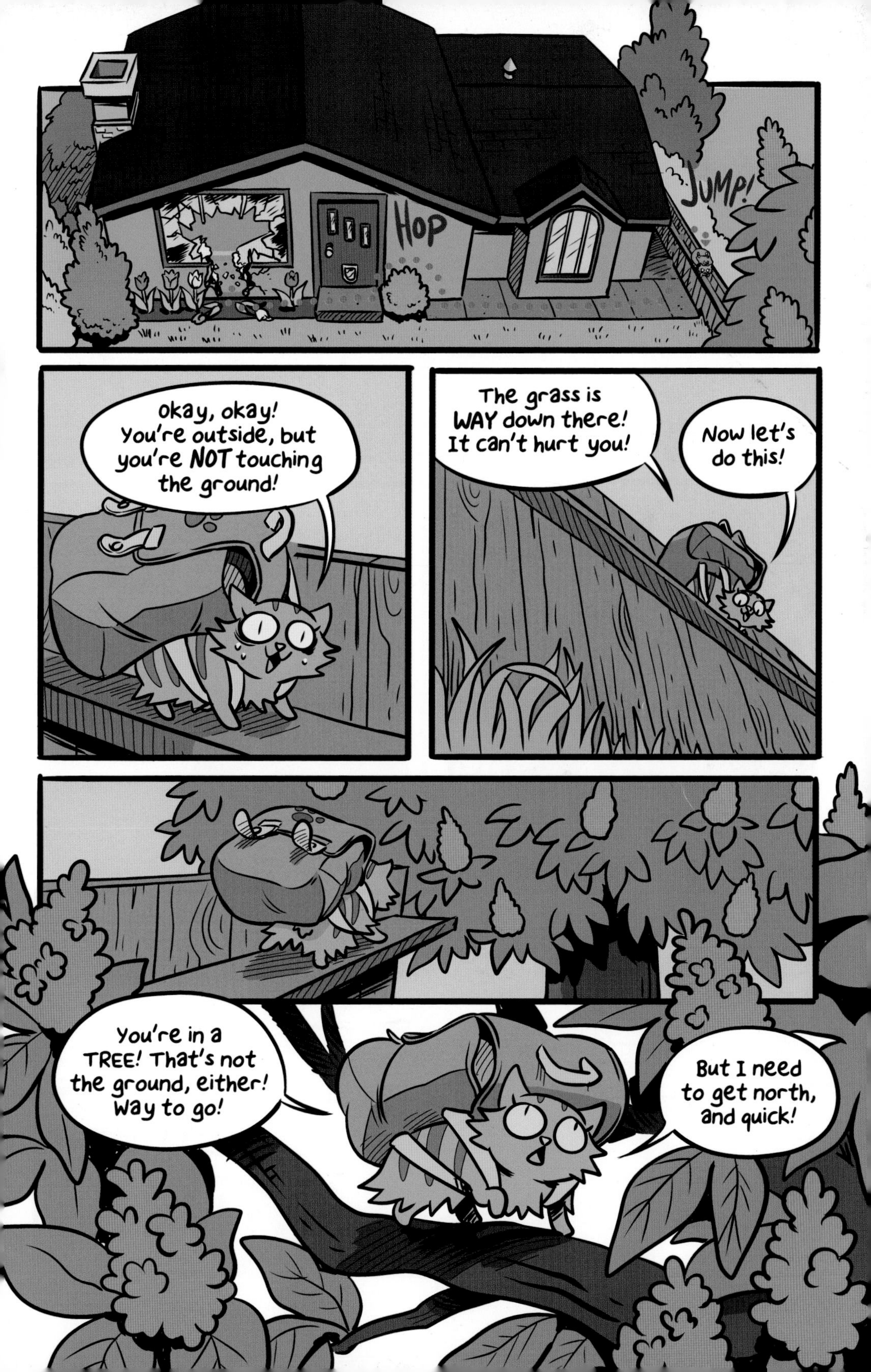
HOP
JUMP!
Okay, okay! You're outside, but you're NOT touching the ground!
The grass is WAY down there! It can't hurt you!
Now let's do this!
You're in a TREE! That's not the ground, either! Way to go!
But I need to get north, and quick!

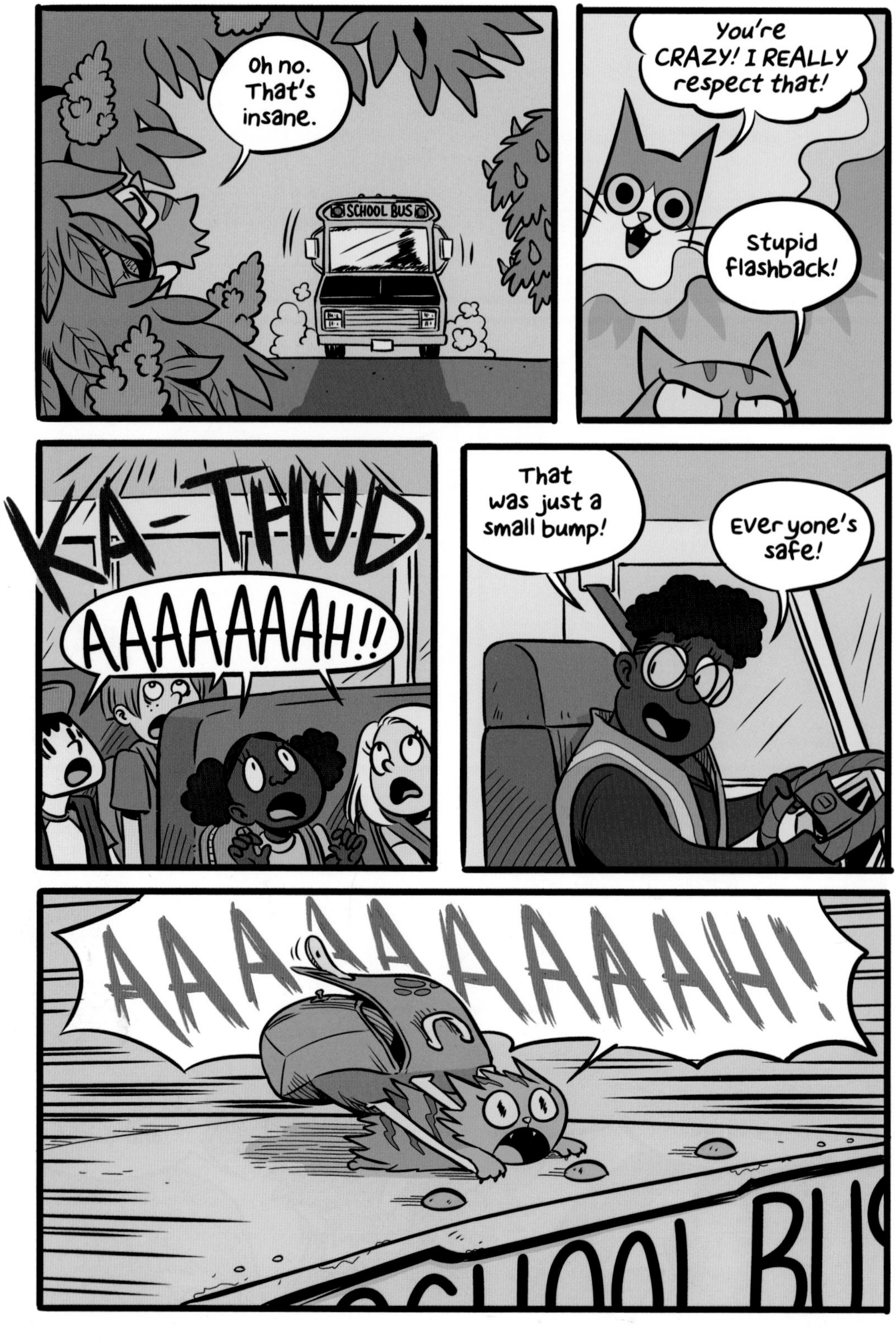
Oh no. That's insane.
SCHOOL BUS
You're CRAZY! I REALLY respect that!
Stupid flashback!
KA-THUD
AAAAAAAH!!
That was just a small bump!
Everyone's safe!
AAAAAAAAAAH!
SCHOOL BUS

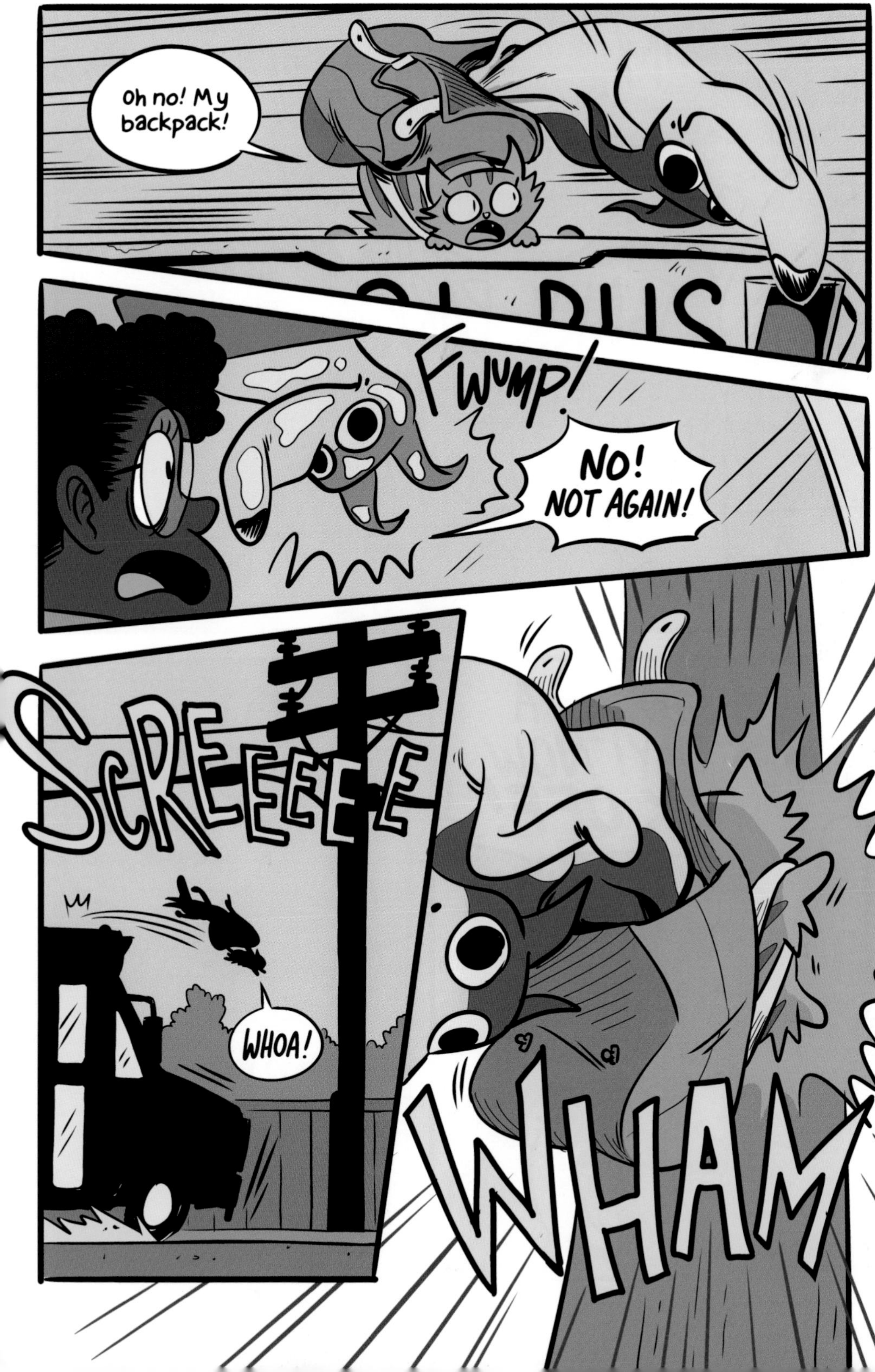
Oh no! My backpack!
FWUMP!
NO! NOT AGAIN!
SCREEEEE
WHOA!
WHAM

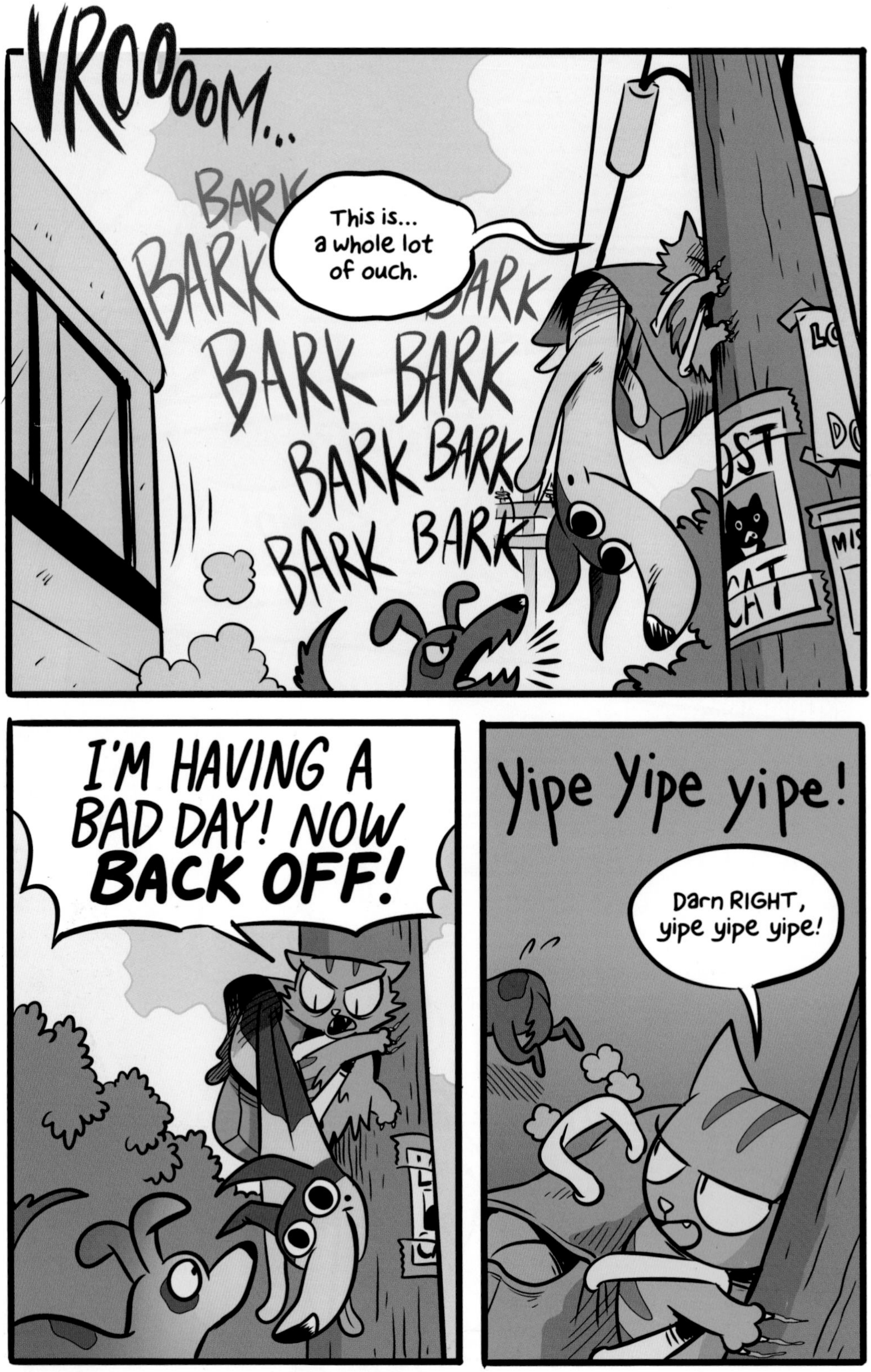
VROOooM...
BARK BARK BARK BARK BARK BARK BARK BARK BARK
This is... a whole lot of ouch.
I'M HAVING A BAD DAY! NOW BACK OFF!
Yipe yipe yipe!
Darn RIGHT, yipe yipe yipe!

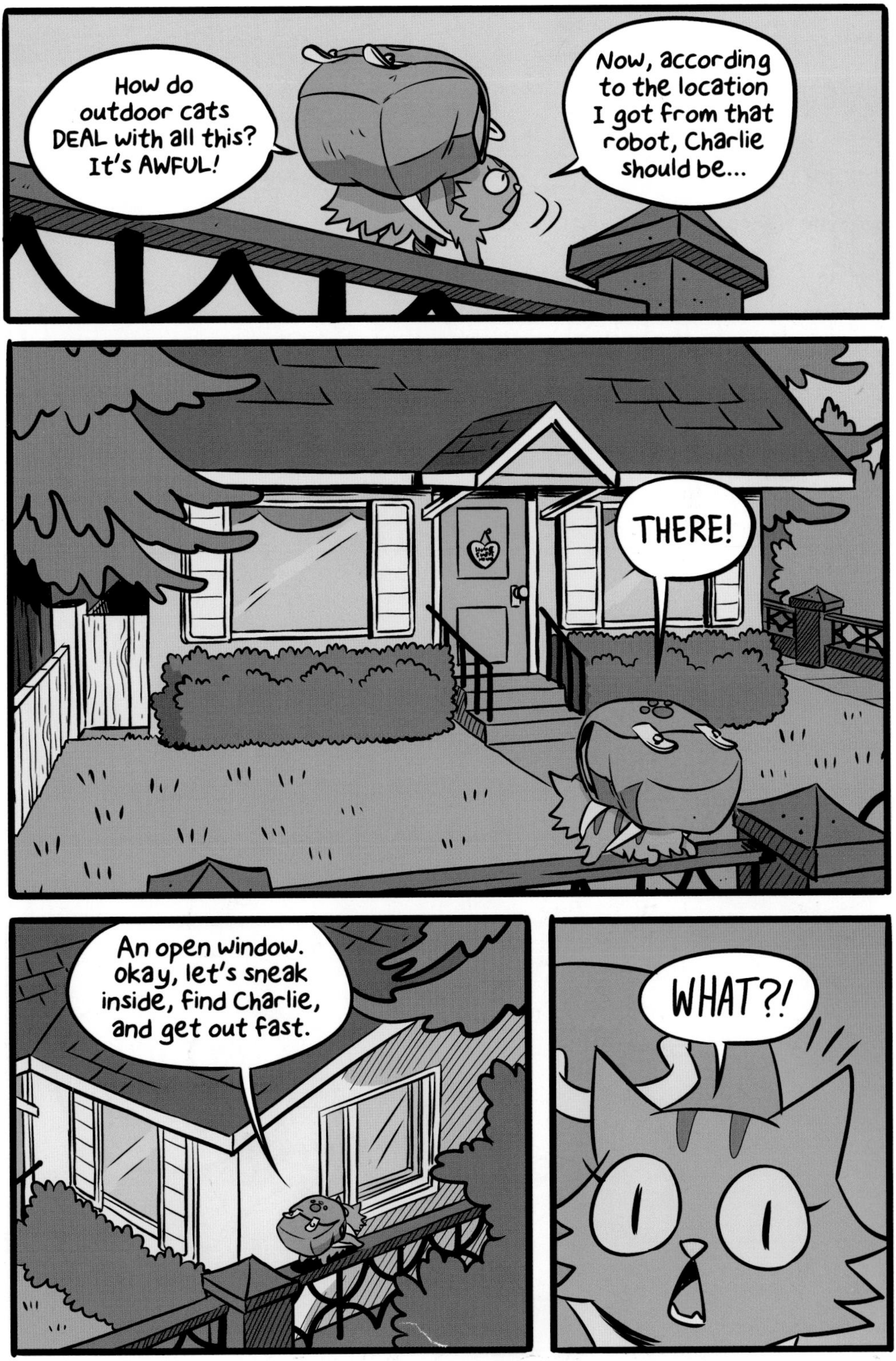
How do outdoor cats DEAL with all this? It's AWFUL!
Now, according to the location I got from that robot, Charlie should be...
THERE!
An open window. okay, let's sneak inside, find Charlie, and get out fast.
WHAT?!

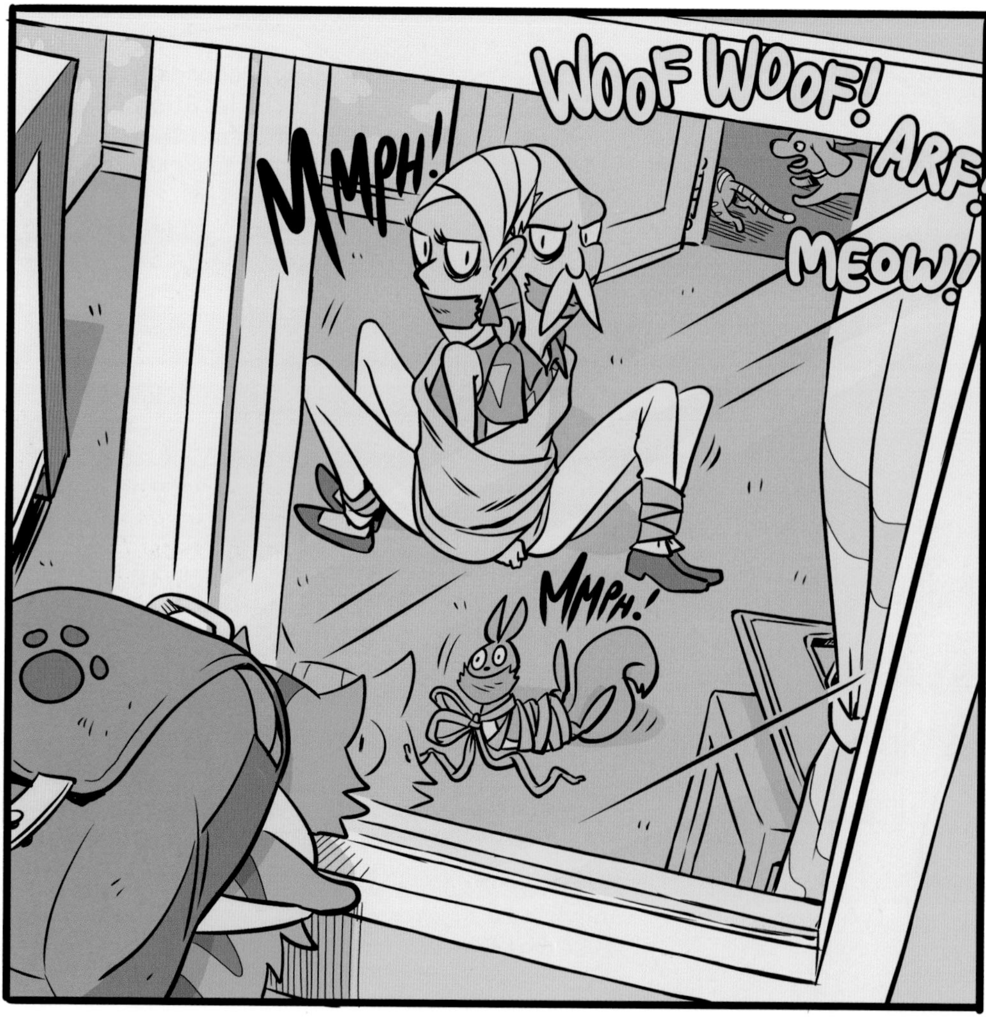
WOOF WOOF!
MMPH!
ARF!
MEOW!
MMPH!

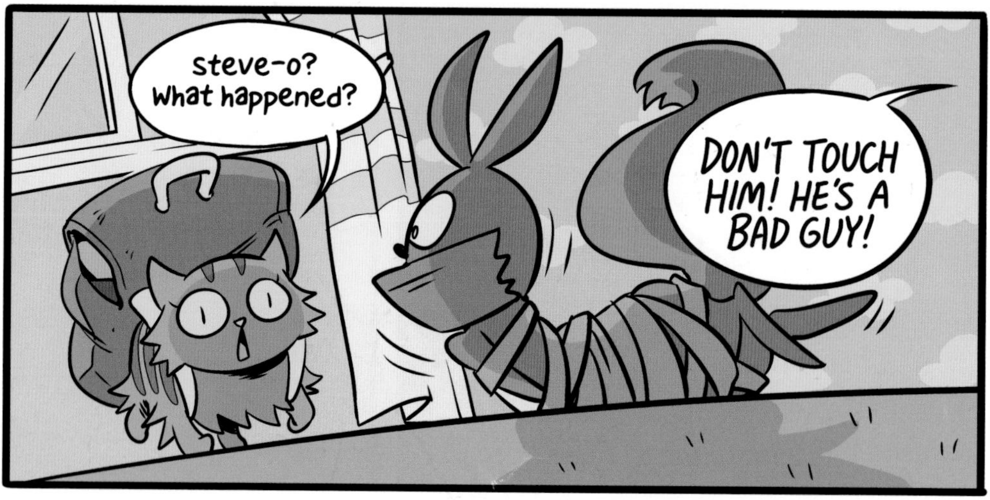
steve-o? What happened?
DON'T TOUCH HIM! HE'S A BAD GUY!

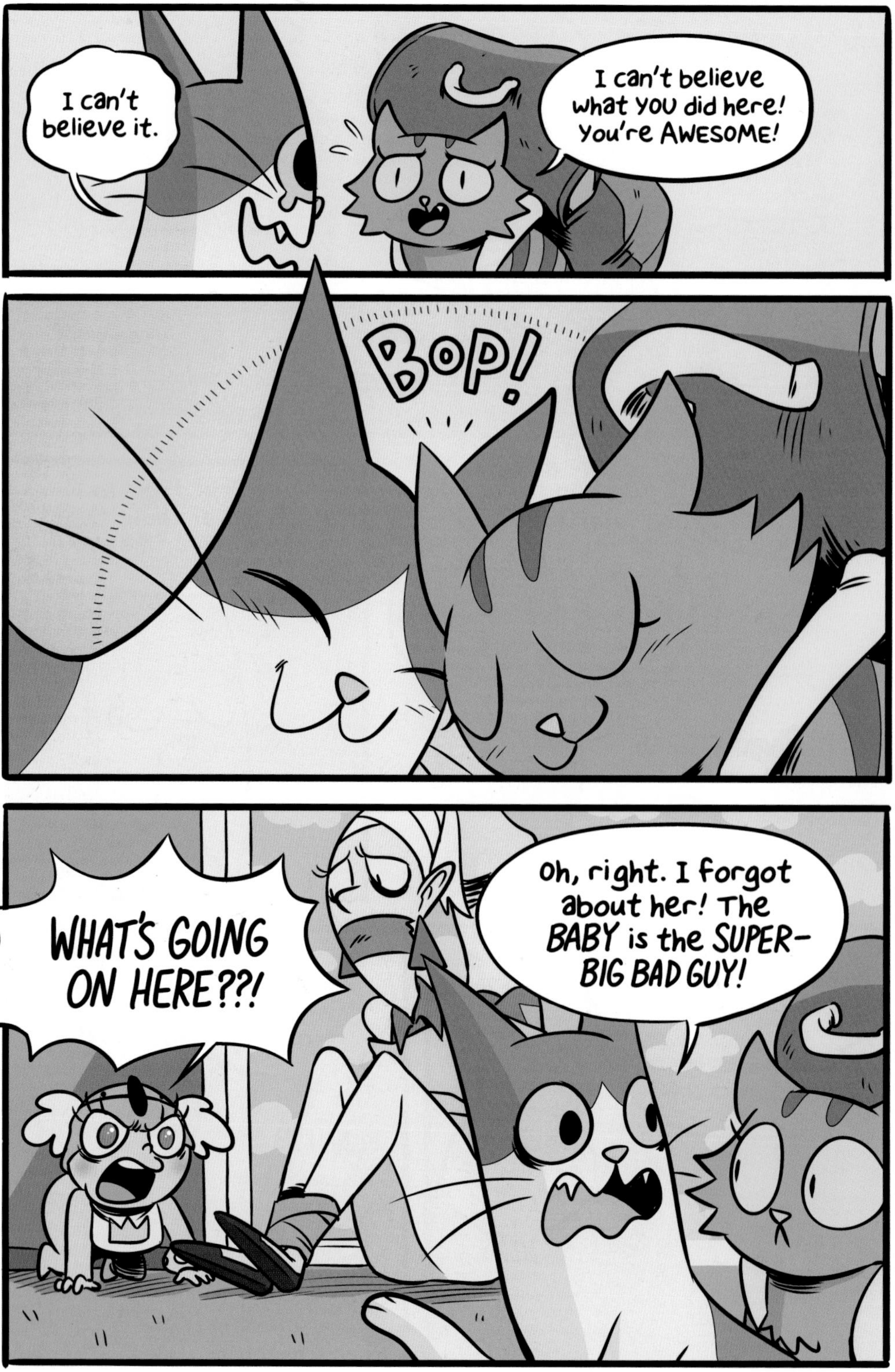
I can't believe it.
I can't believe what YOU did here! You're AWESOME!
BOP!
WHAT'S GOING ON HERE??!
Oh, right. I forgot about her! The BABY is the SUPER-BIG BAD GUY!

140

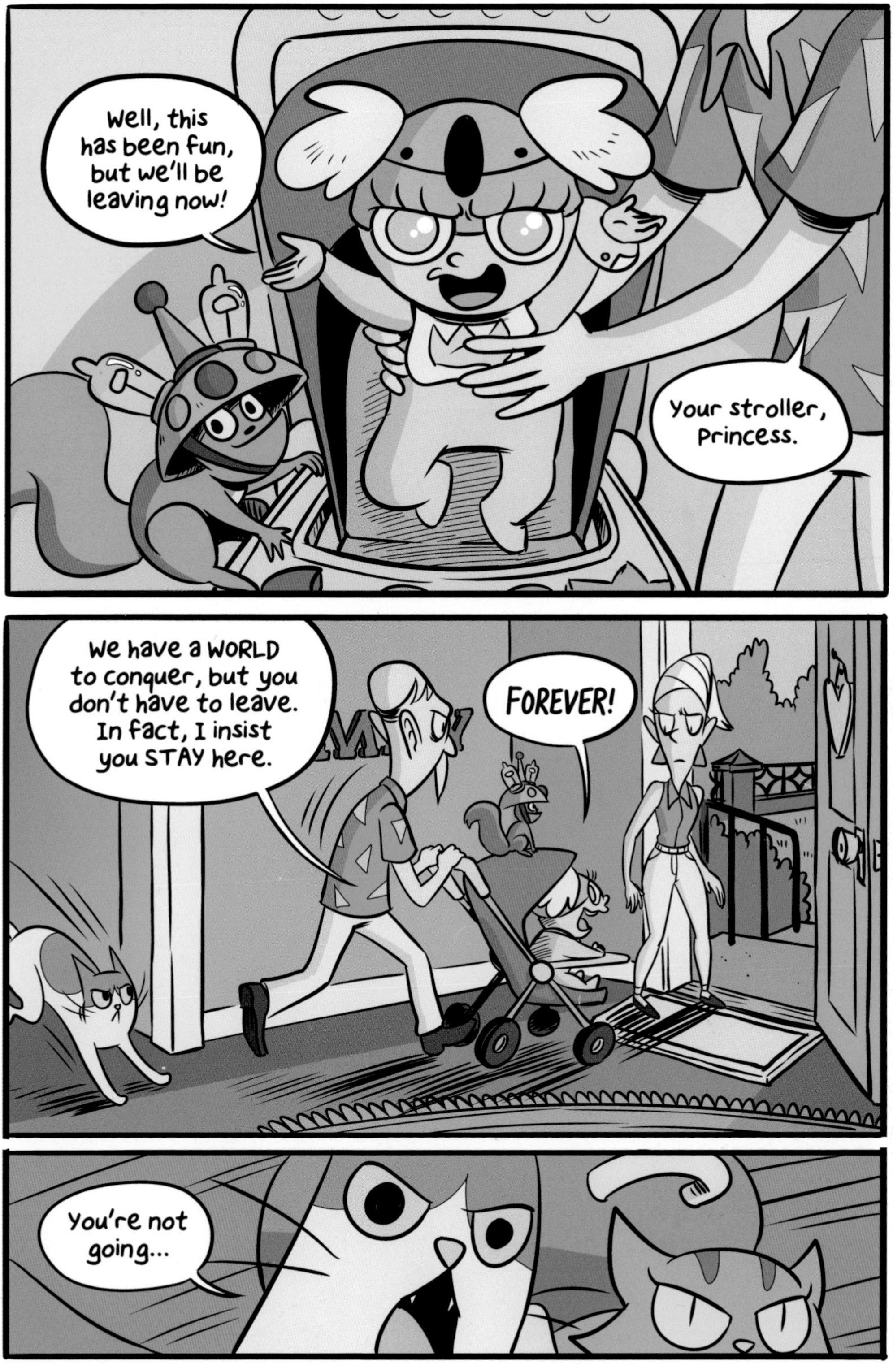
Well, this has been fun, but we'll be leaving now!
Your stroller, Princess.
We have a WORLD to conquer, but you don't have to leave. In fact, I insist you STAY here.
FOREVER!
You're not going...

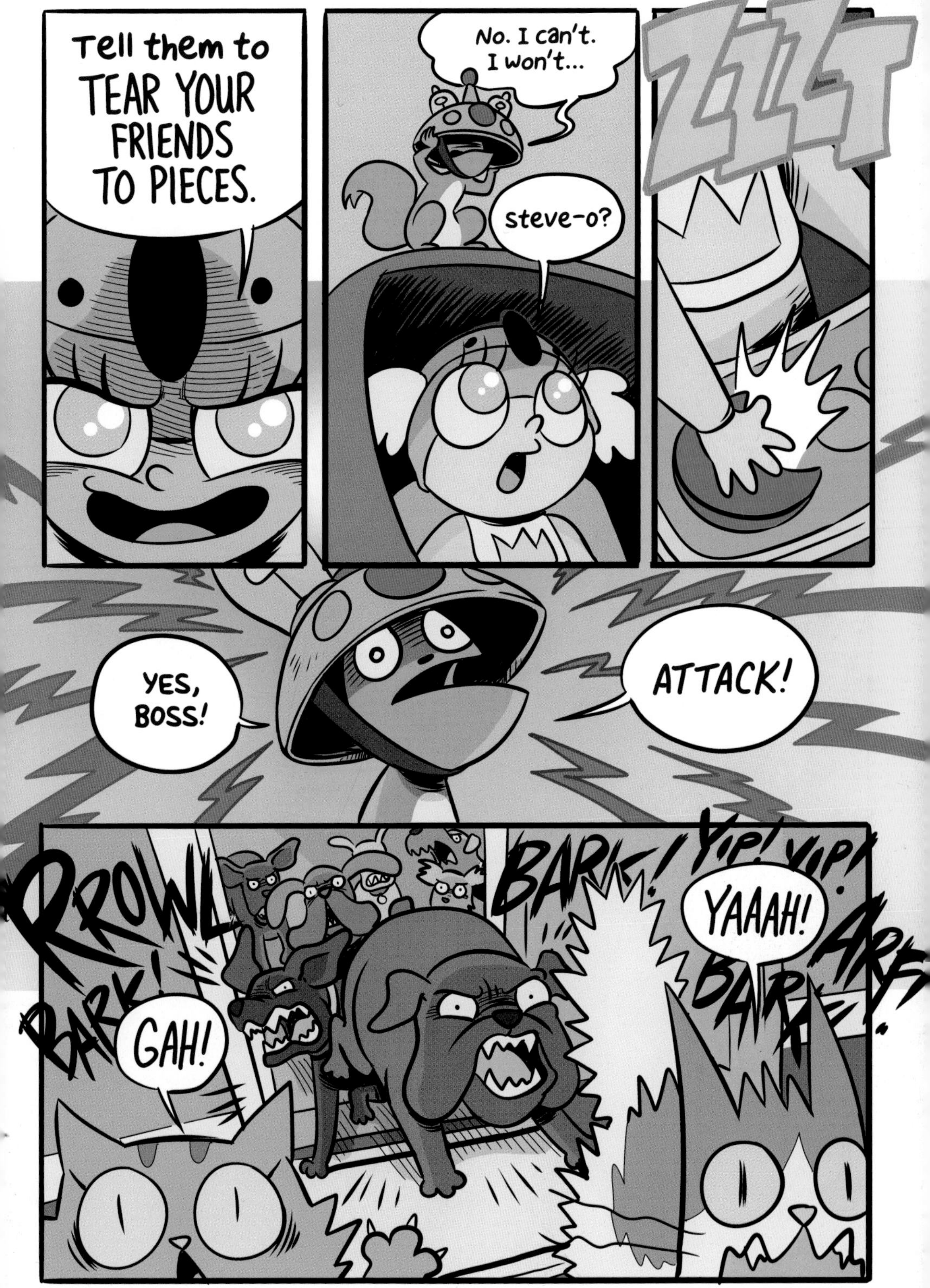
Tell them to TEAR YOUR FRIENDS TO PIECES.
No. I can't. I won't...
steve-o?
ZZZT
YES, BOSS!
ATTACK!
RROWL
BARK!
GAH!
BARK! YIP! YIP!
YAAAH!
BARK!

CHAPTER NINE

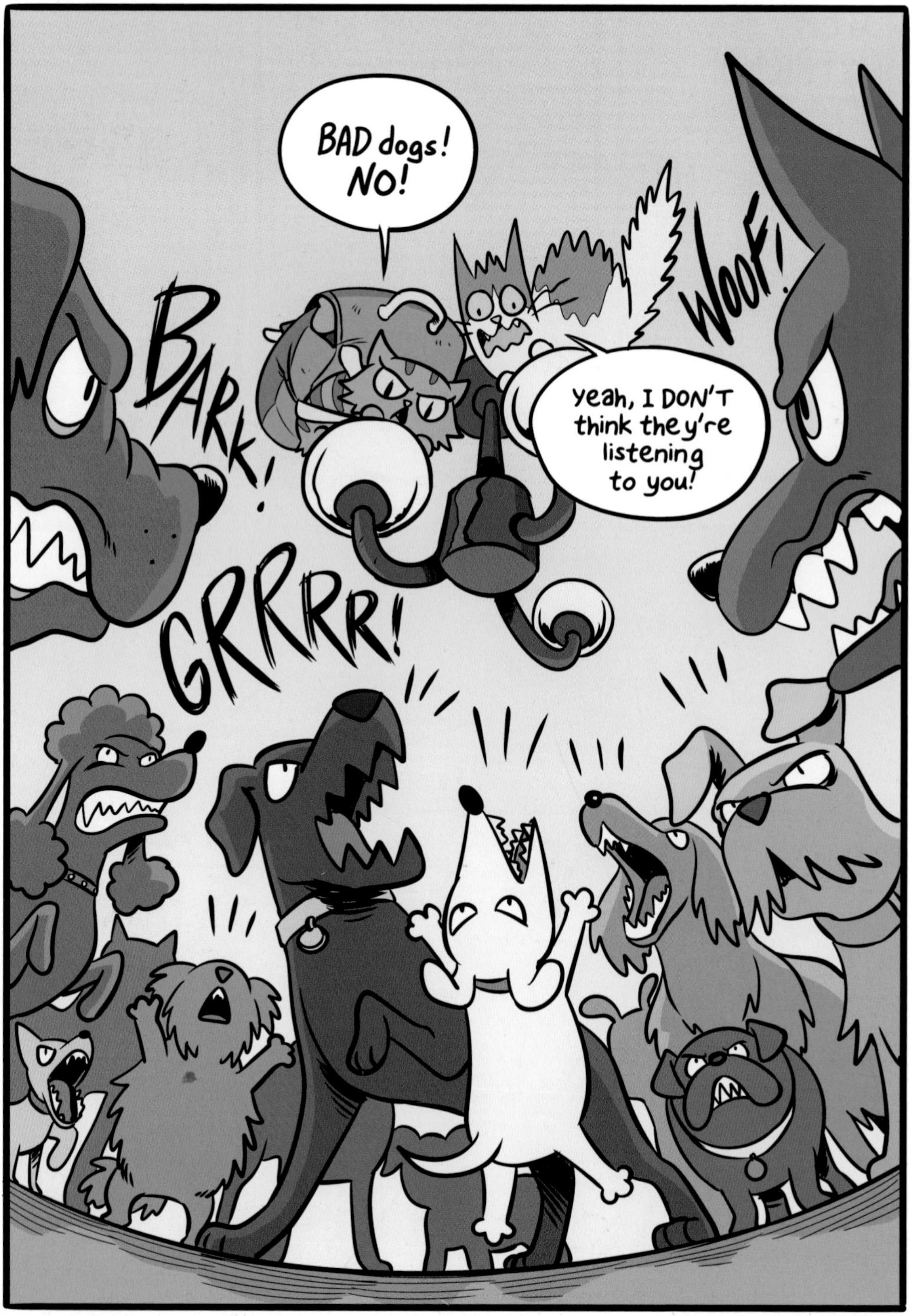

BAD dogs! NO!
BARK!
WOOF!
yeah, I DON'T think they're listening to you!
GRRRR!

145

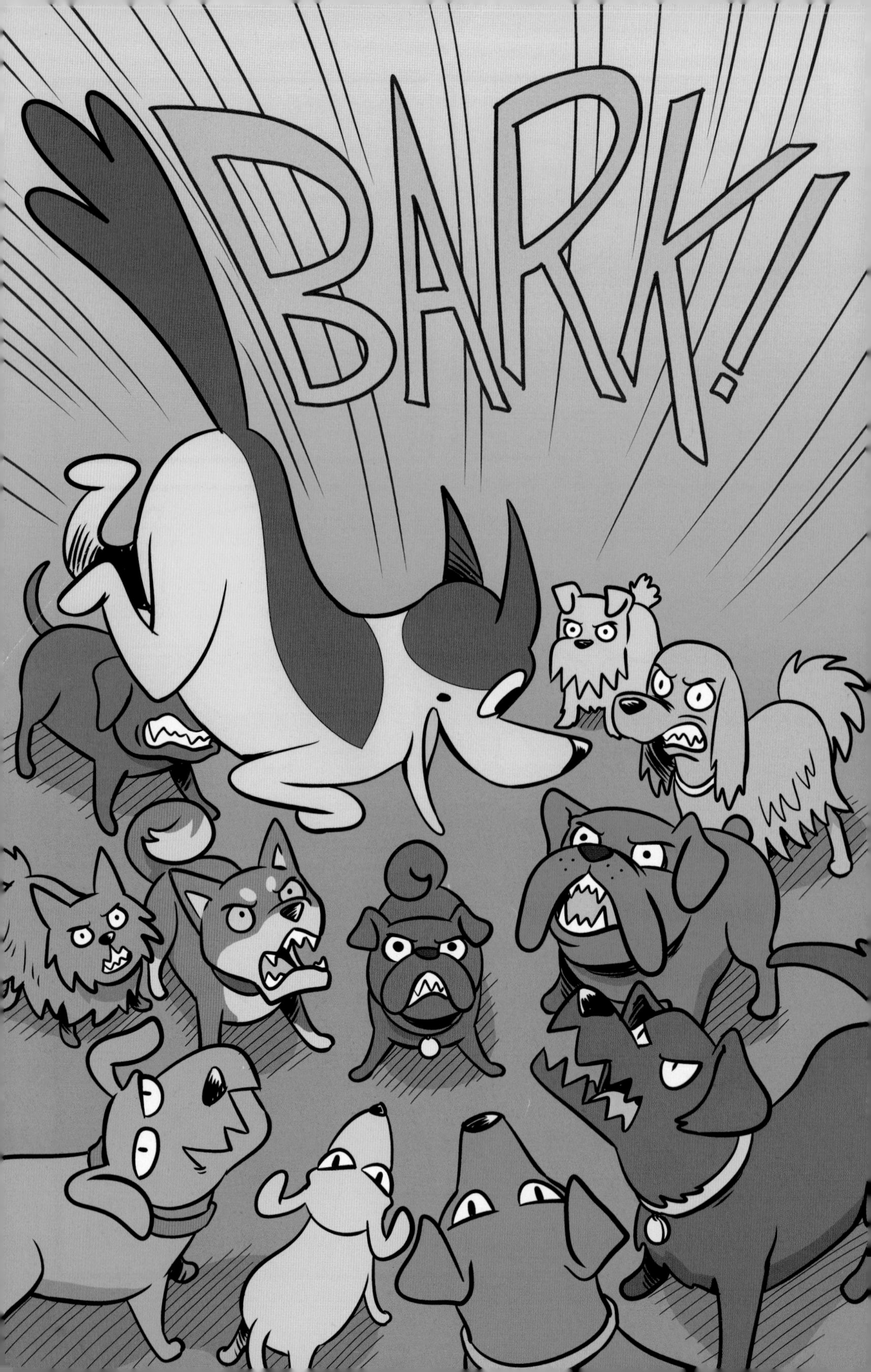
BARK!

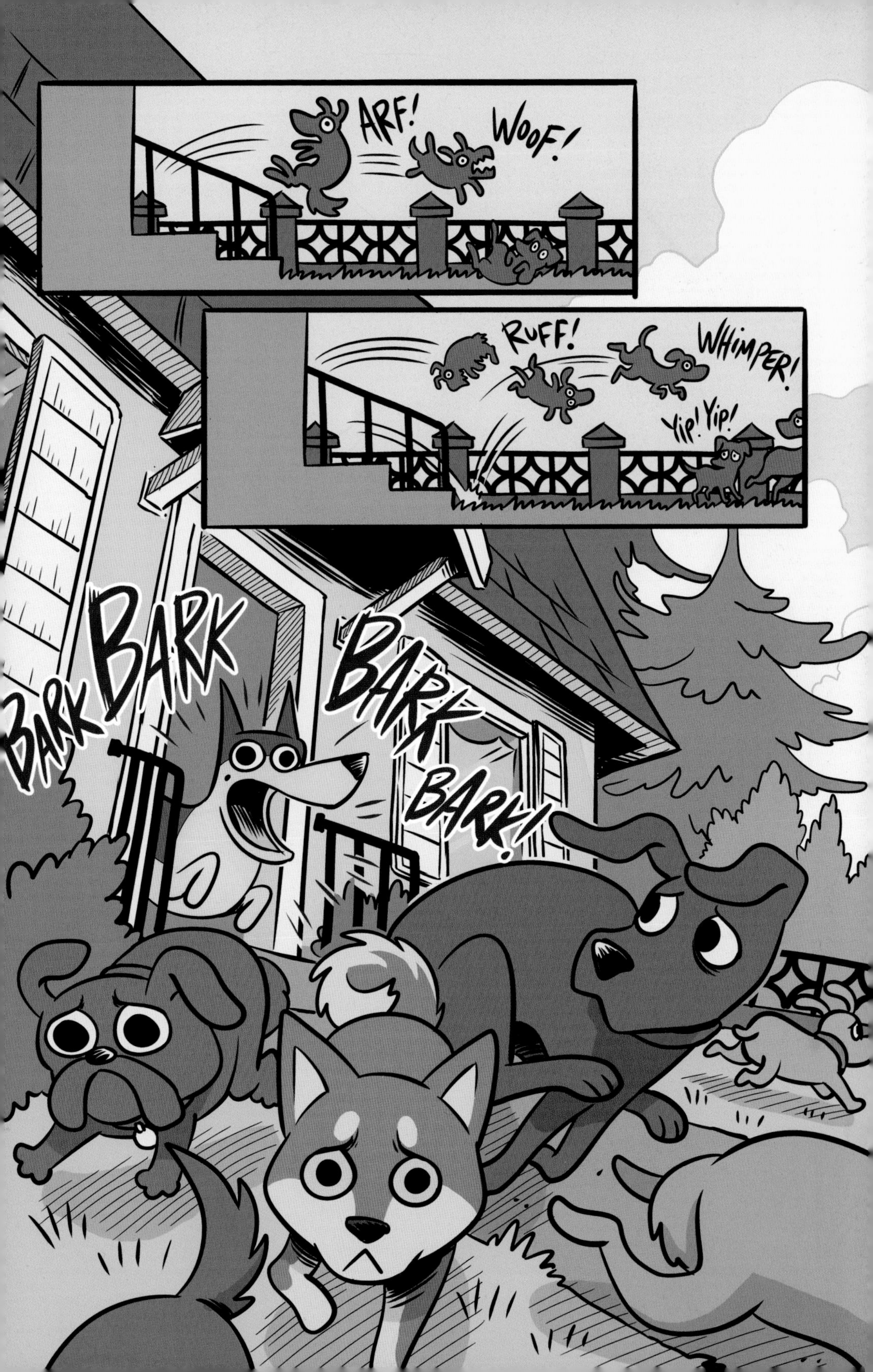
ARF!
WOOF!
RUFF!
WHIMPER!
Yip! Yip!
BARK BARK
BARK
BARK BARK!

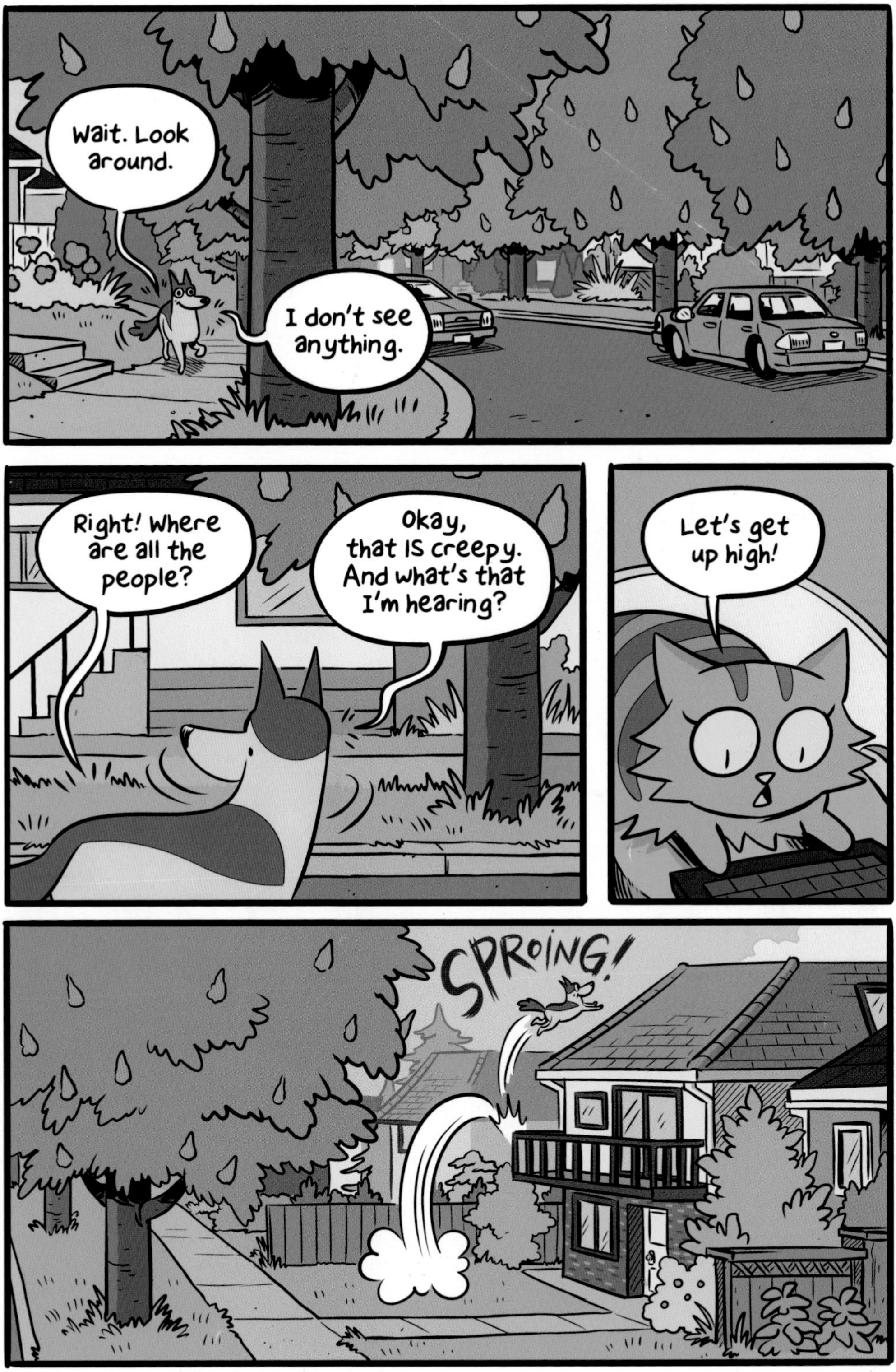
Wait. Look around.
I don't see anything.
Right! Where are all the people?
Okay, that IS creepy. And what's that I'm hearing?
Let's get up high!
SPROING!

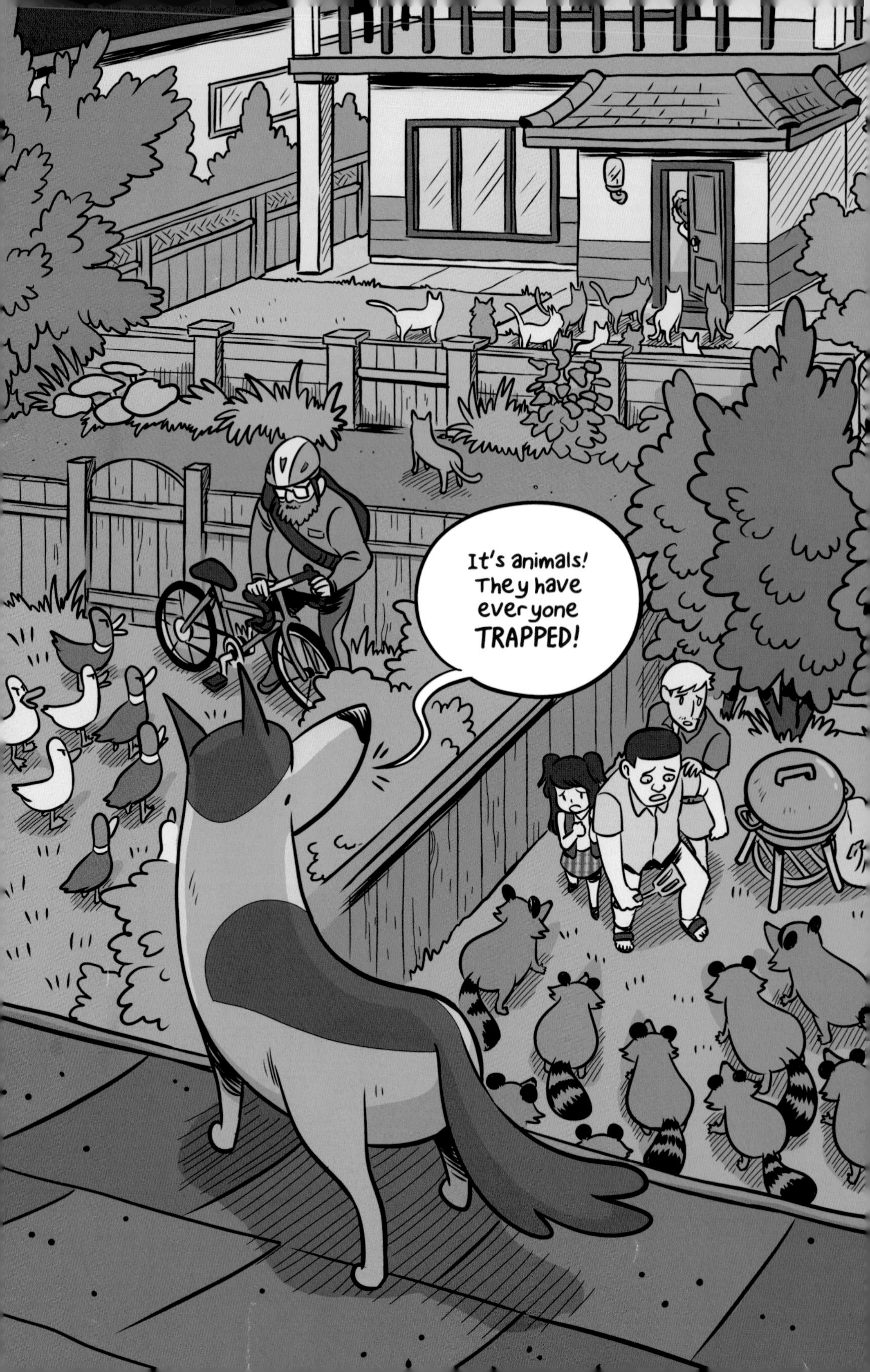
It's animals! They have everyone TRAPPED!

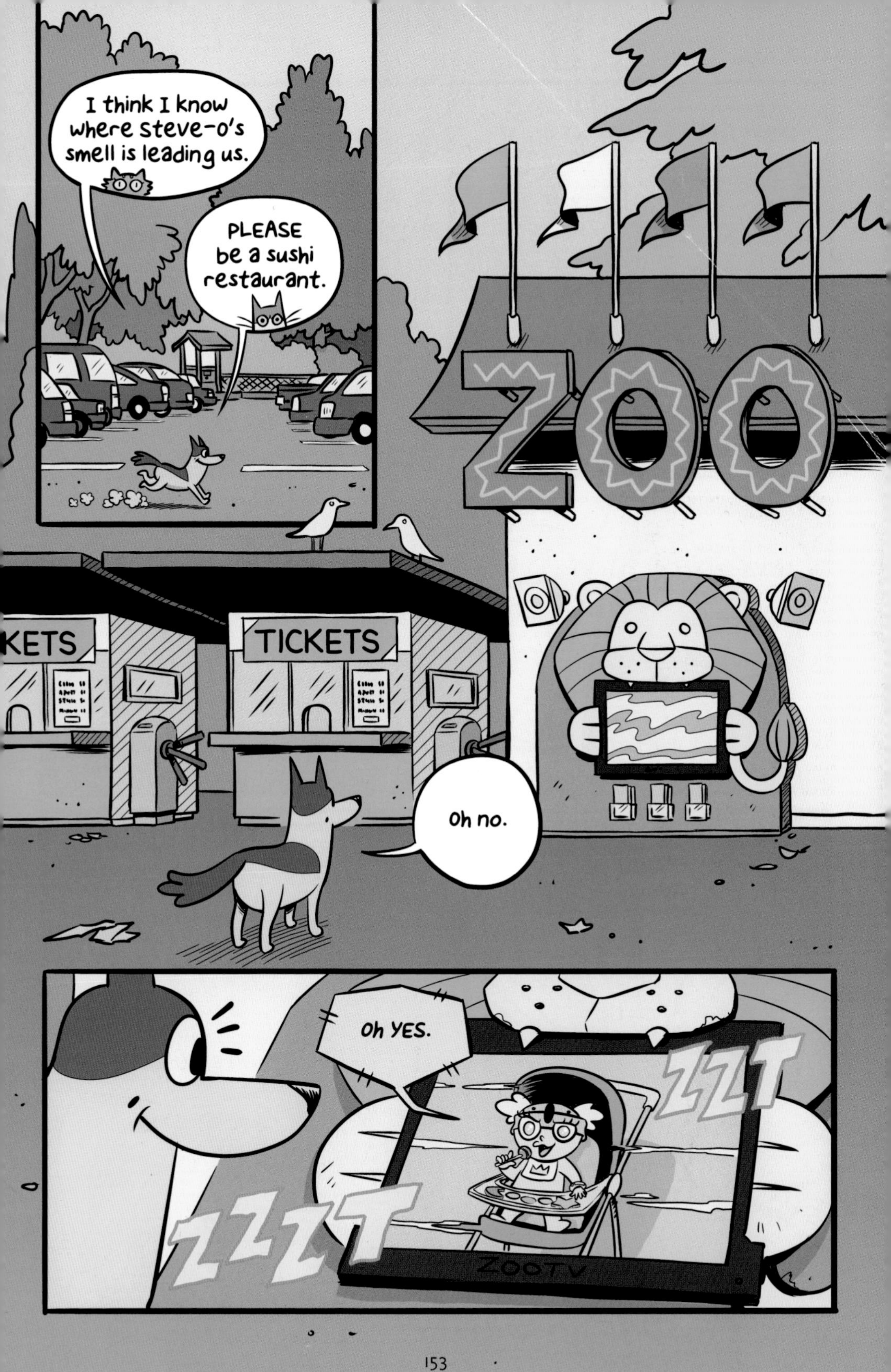
I think I know where steve-o's smell is leading us.
PLEASE be a sushi restaurant.
ZOO
TICKETS
KETS
Oh no.
Oh YES.
ZZZT
ZZZT
ZOOTV

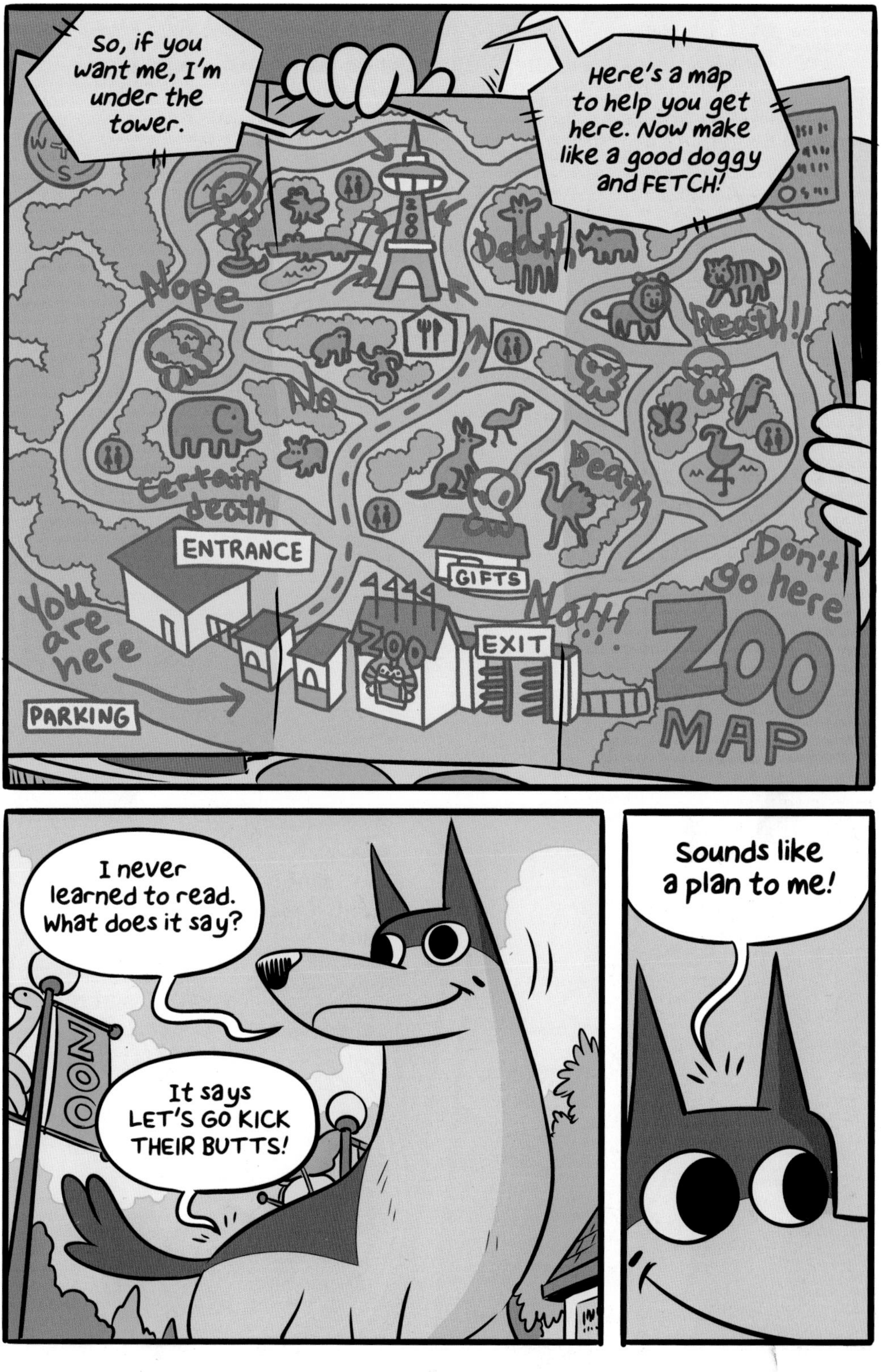
So, if you want me, I'm under the tower.
Here's a map to help you get here. Now make like a good doggy and FETCH!
Nope
Death!
Death!!
No
Certain death
ENTRANCE
GIFTS
Death
Don't go here
You are here
PARKING
ZOO
No!!!
EXIT
ZOO MAP
I never learned to read. What does it say?
It says LET'S GO KICK THEIR BUTTS!
ZOO
Sounds like a plan to me!

CHAPTER TEN

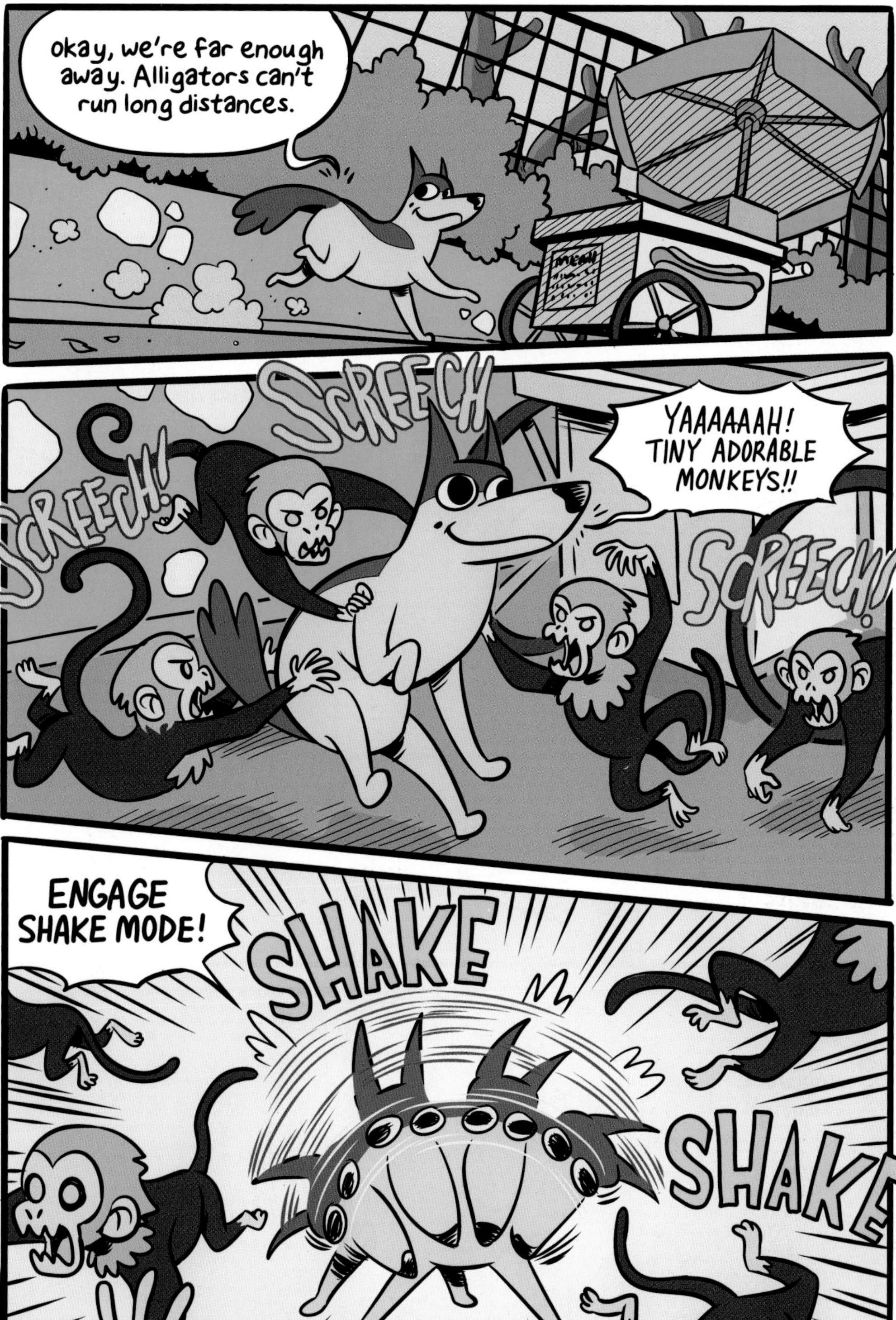
okay, we're far enough away. Alligators can't run long distances.
SCREECH
SCREECH!
YAAAAAAH! TINY ADORABLE MONKEYS!!
SCREECH!!
ENGAGE SHAKE MODE!
SHAKE
SHAKE

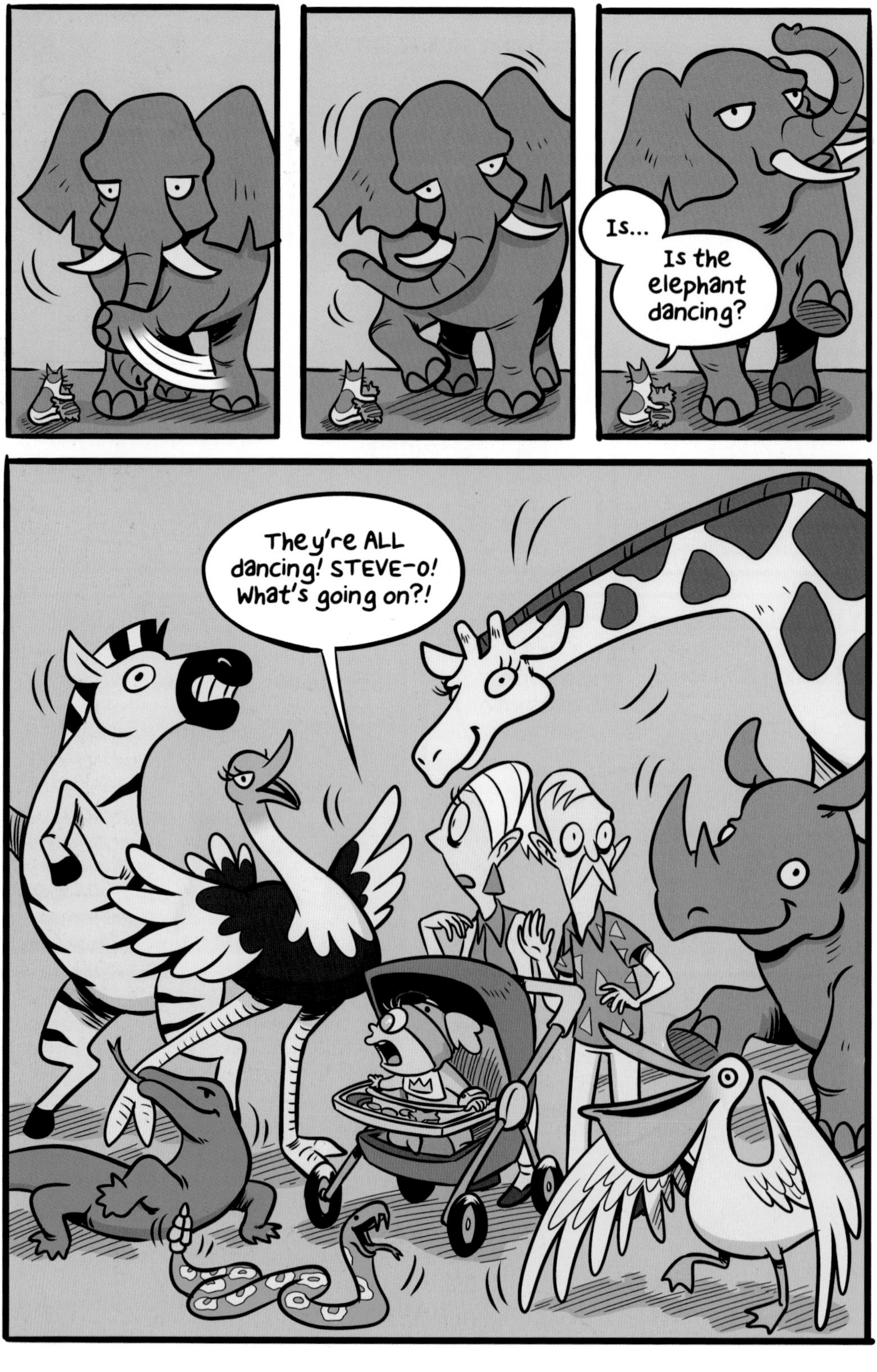
Is...
Is the elephant dancing?
They're ALL dancing! STEVE-O! What's going on?!

167

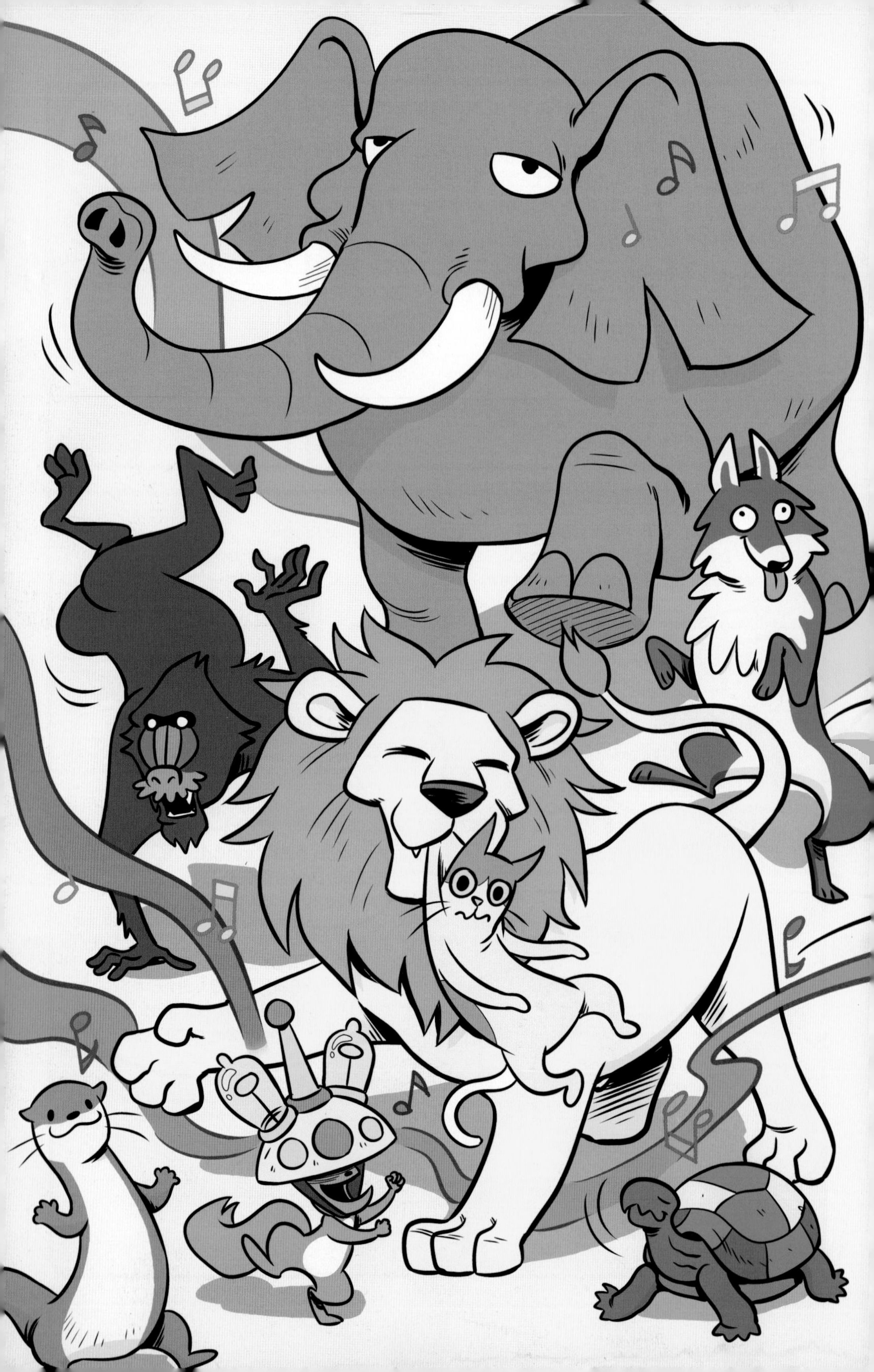

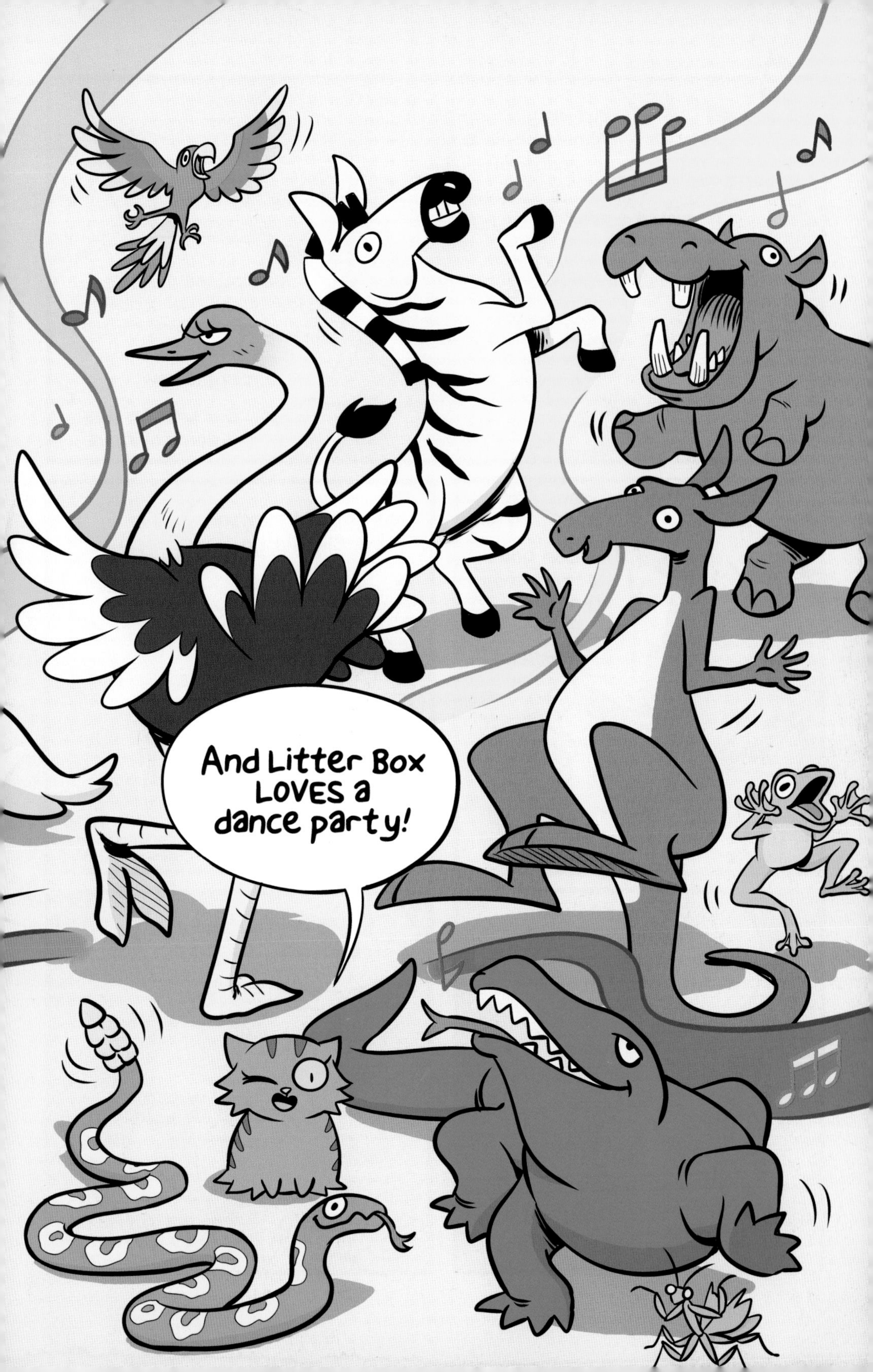
And Litter Box LOVES a dance party!

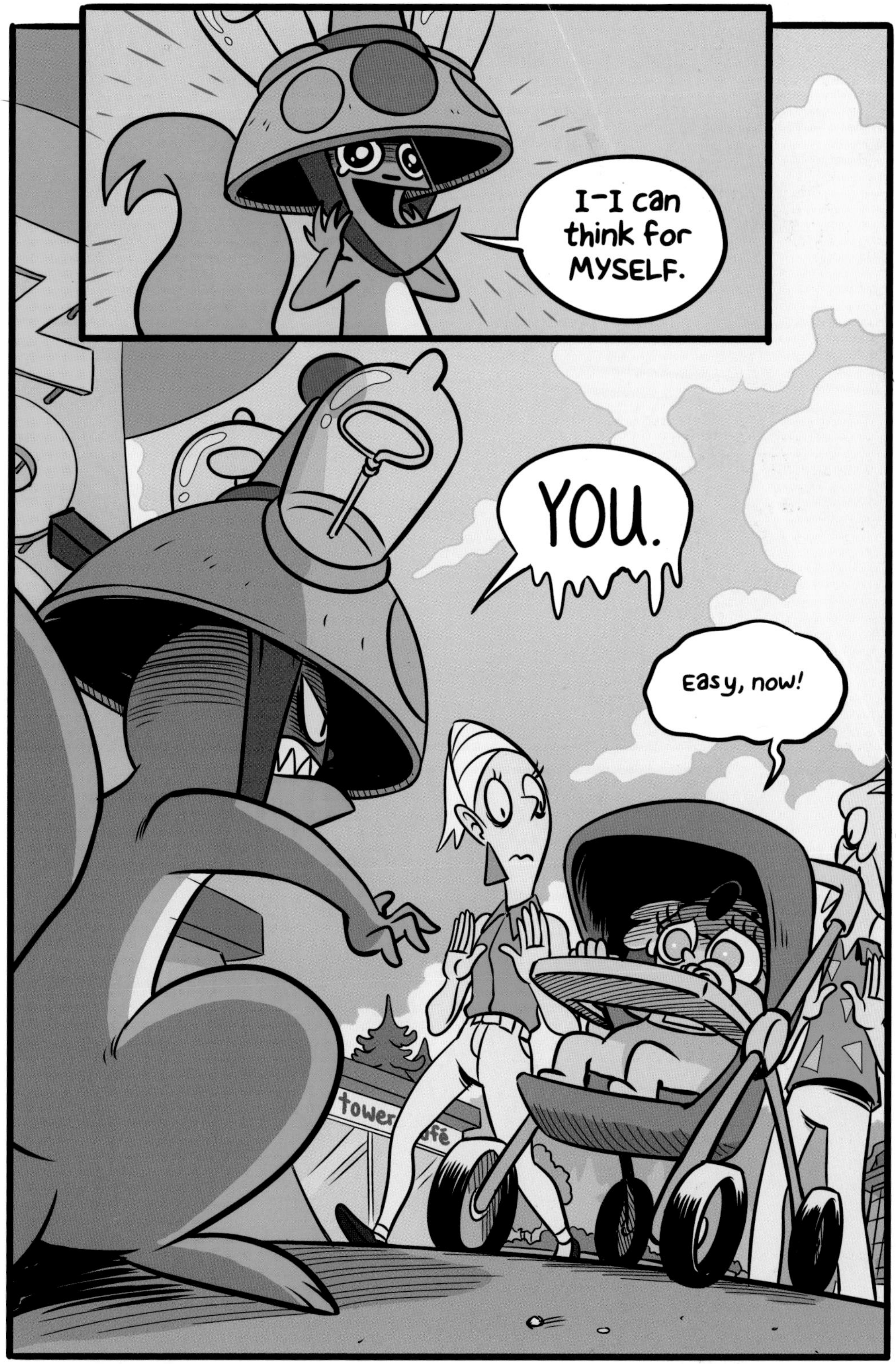
I-I can think for MYSELF.
YOU.
Easy, now!
tower

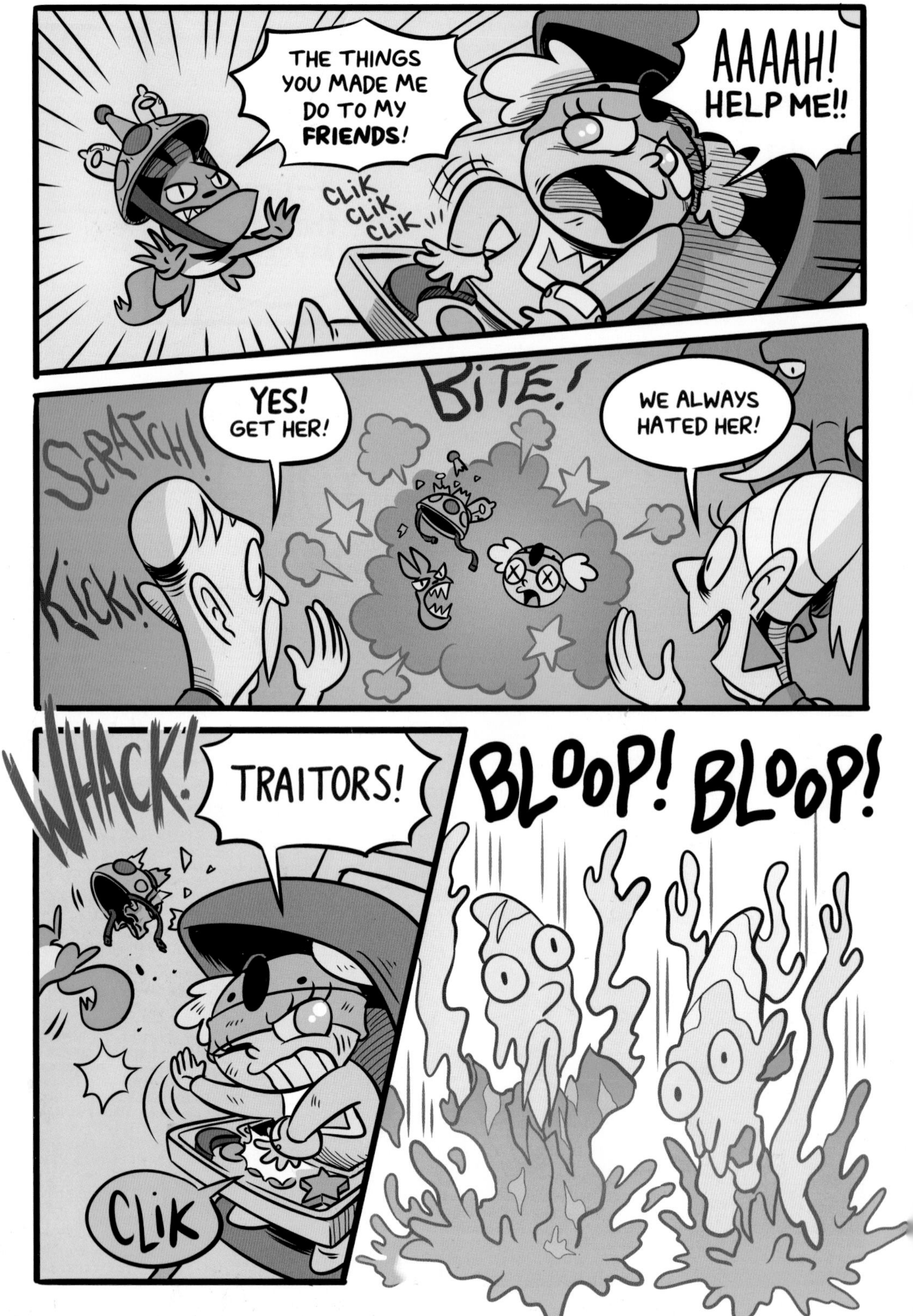
THE THINGS YOU MADE ME DO TO MY FRIENDS!
AAAAH! HELP ME!!
CLIK CLIK CLIK
YES! GET HER!
BITE!
WE ALWAYS HATED HER!
SCRATCH!
KICK!
WHACK!
TRAITORS!
CLIK
BLOOP! BLOOP!

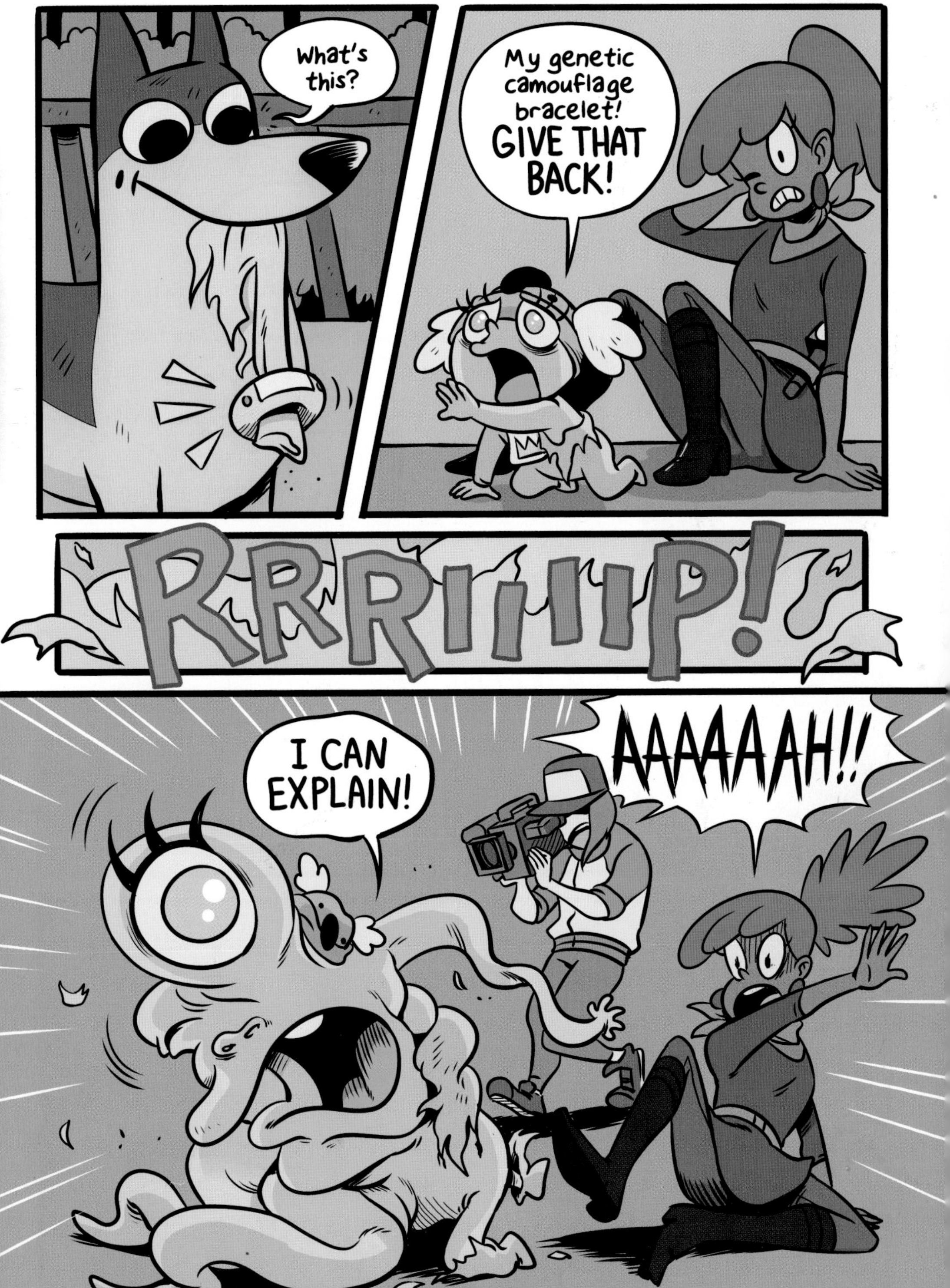
What's this?
My genetic camouflage bracelet! GIVE THAT BACK!
RRRIIIIP!
I CAN EXPLAIN!
AAAAAAH!!

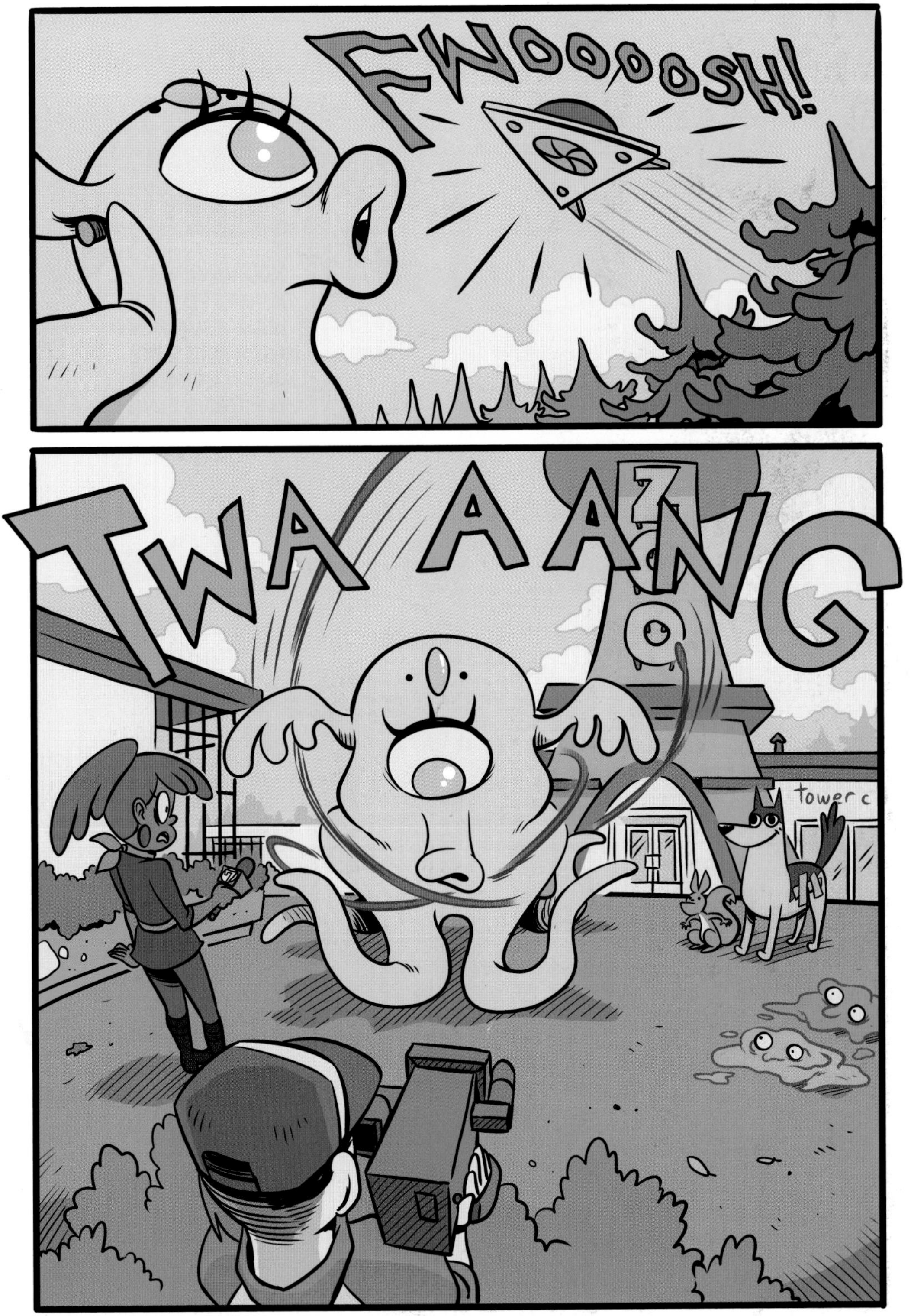
FWOOOOSH!
TWAAANG
tower c

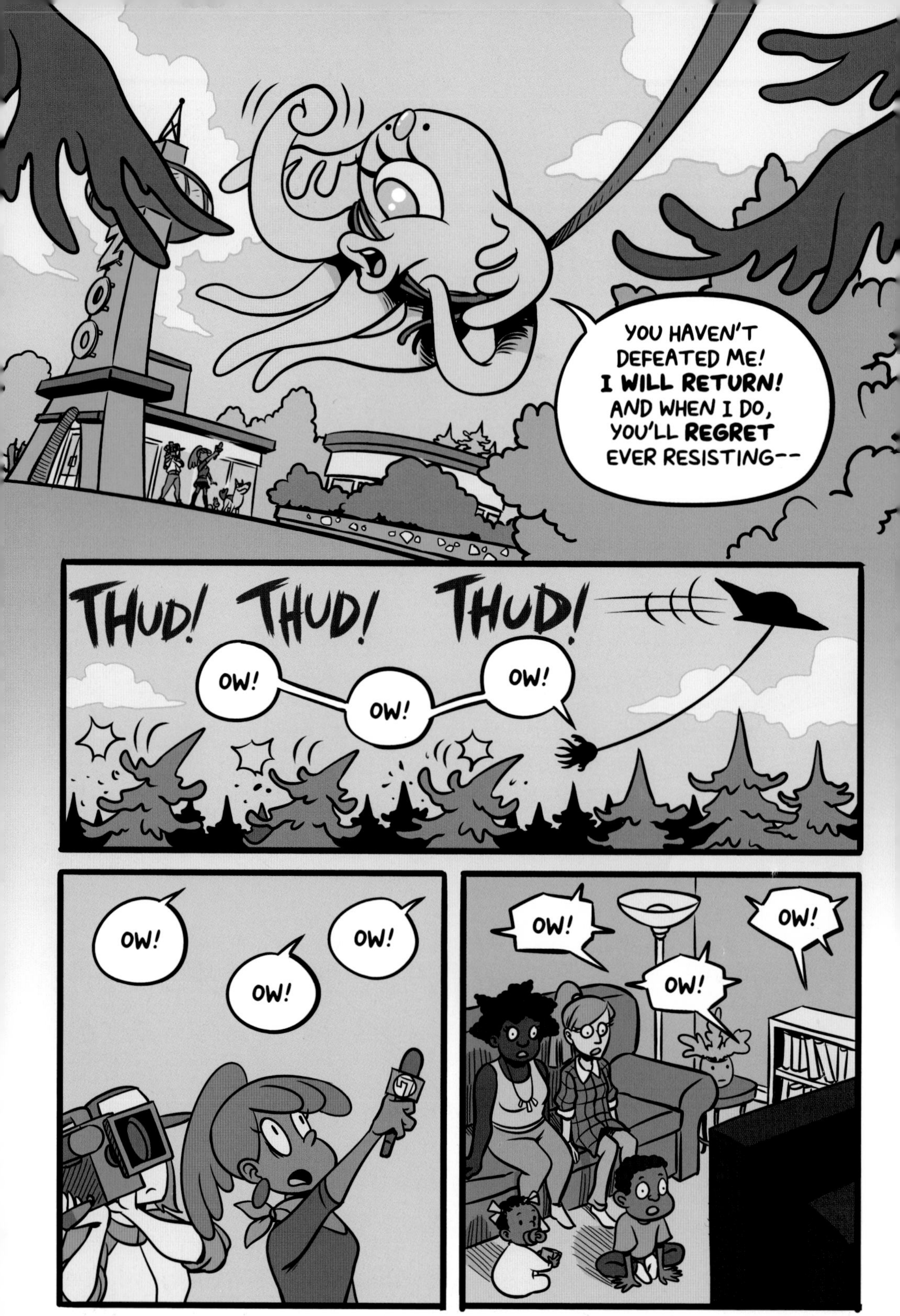
YOU HAVEN'T DEFEATED ME! I WILL RETURN! AND WHEN I DO, YOU'LL REGRET EVER RESISTING--
THUD! THUD! THUD!
OW!
OW!
OW!
OW!
OW!
OW!
OW!
OW!
OW!

180

CHAPTER ELEVEN

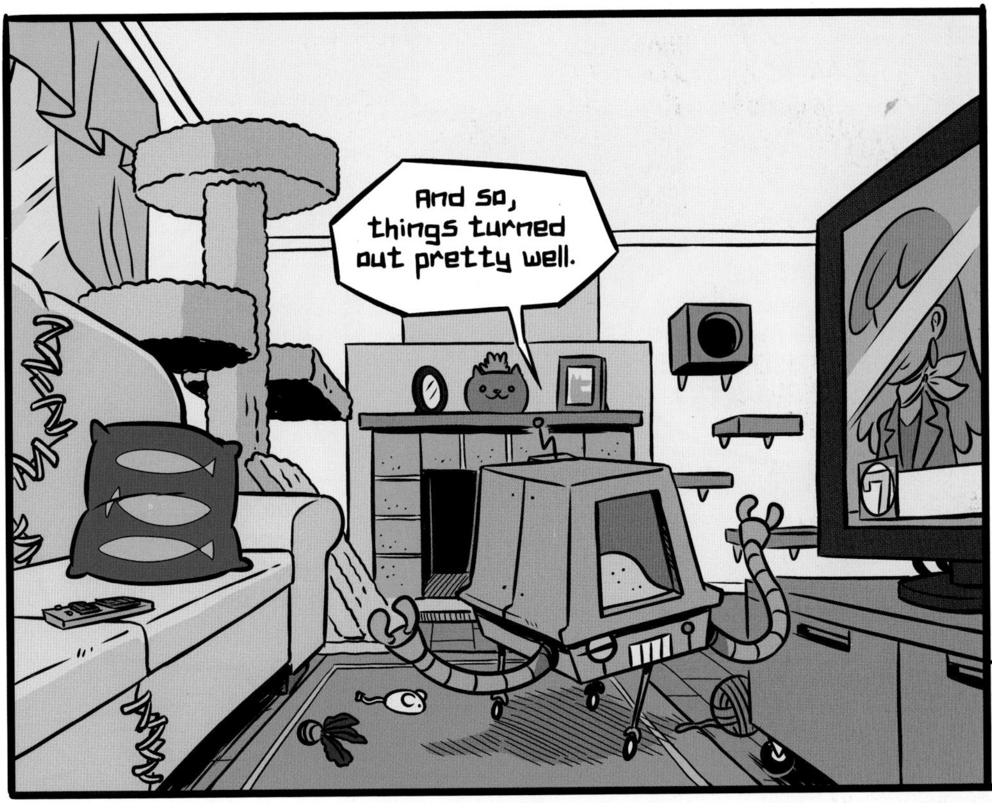
And so, things turned out pretty well.

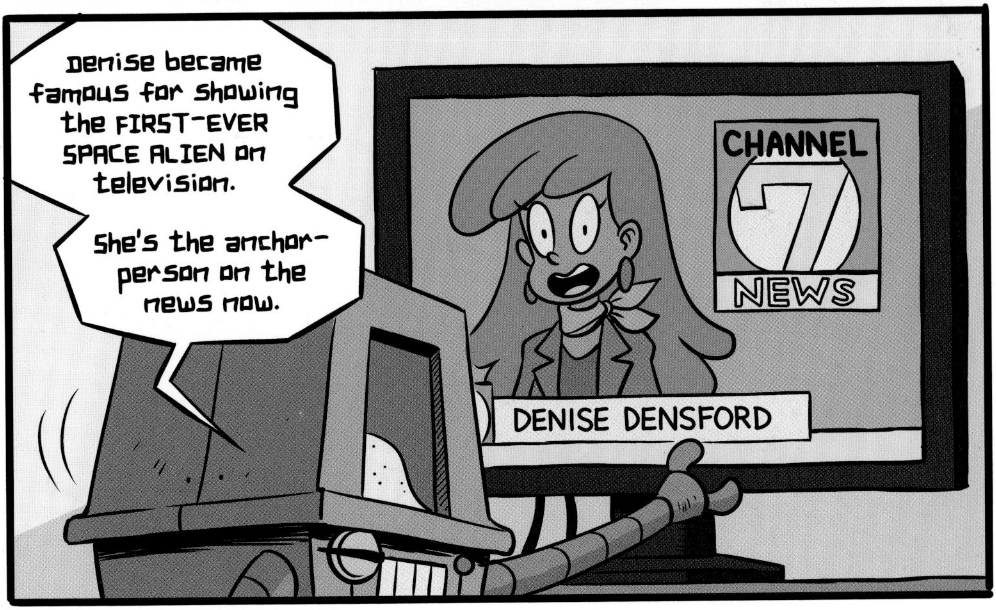
Denise became famous for showing the FIRST-EVER SPACE ALIEN on television.
She's the anchor-person on the news now.
CHANNEL 7 NEWS
DENISE DENSFORD

182

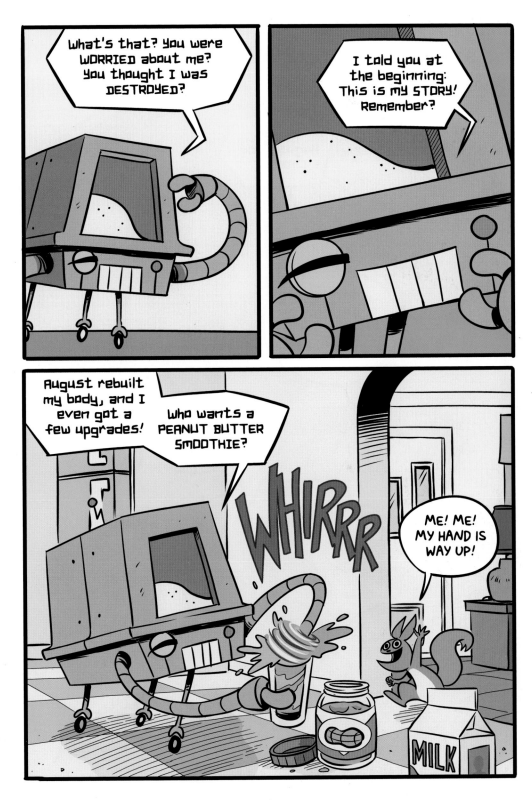

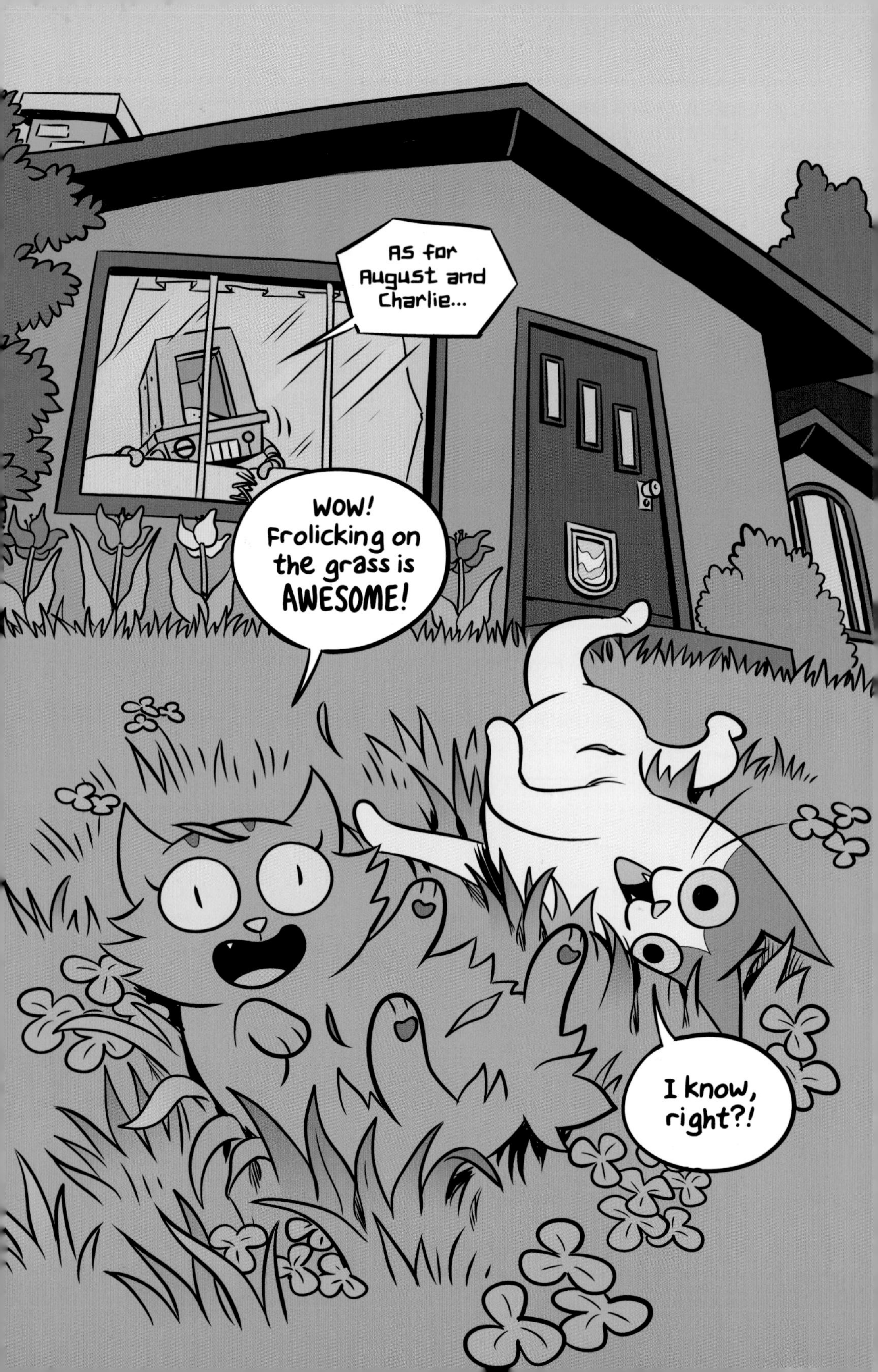
As for August and Charlie...
WOW! Frolicking on the grass is AWESOME!
I know, right?!

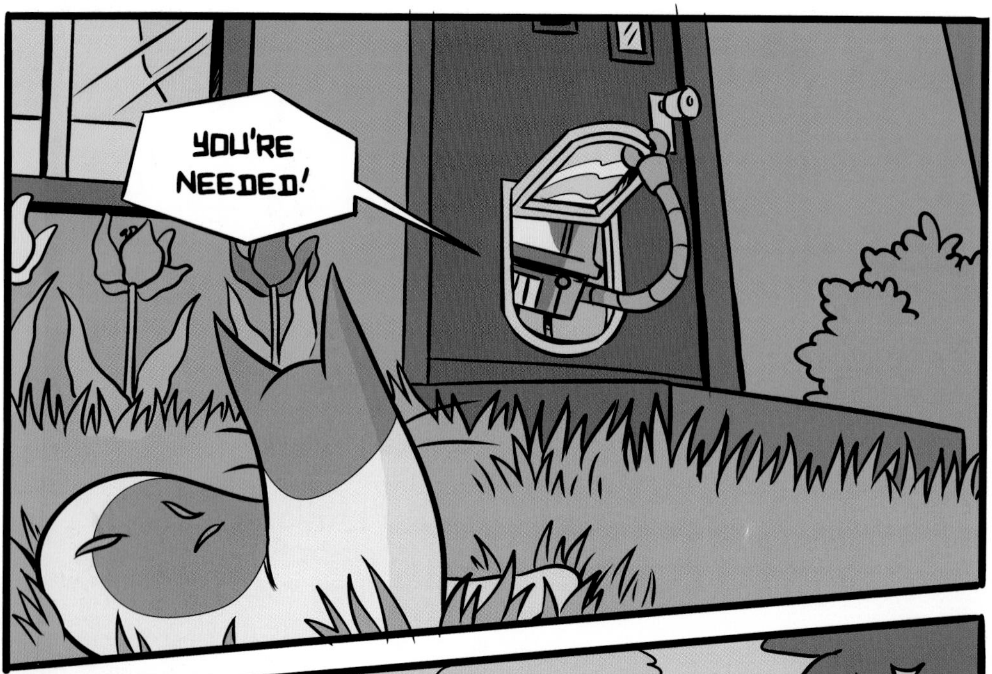
YOU'RE NEEDED!

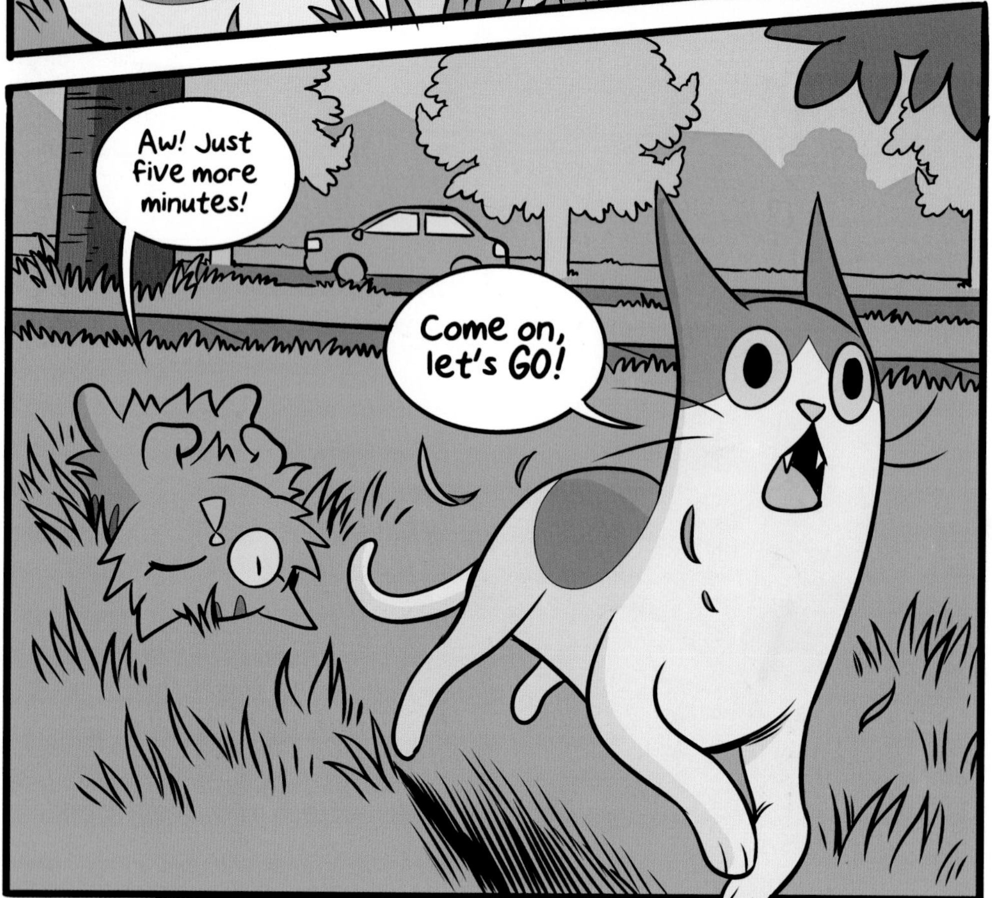
Aw! Just five more minutes!
Come on, let's GO!

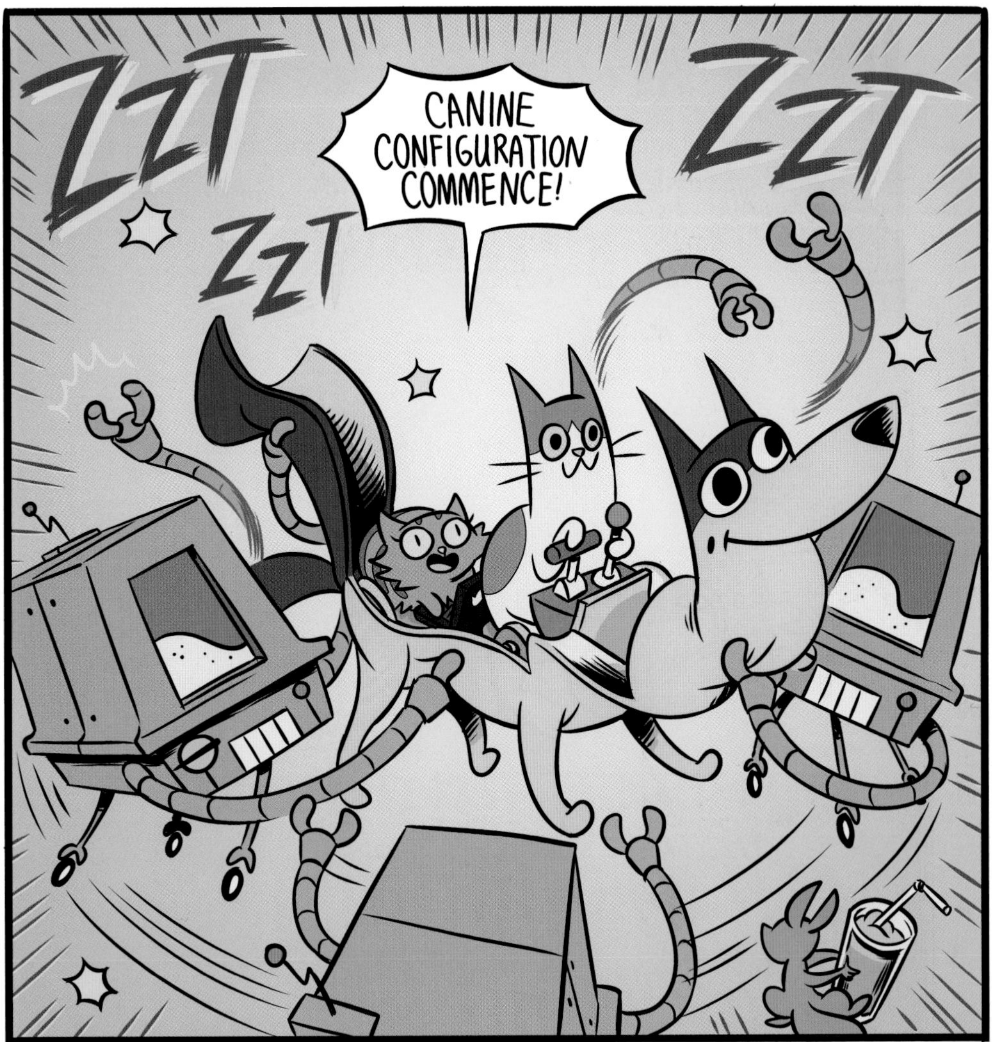
ZZT
ZZT
CANINE CONFIGURATION COMMENCE!
ZZT

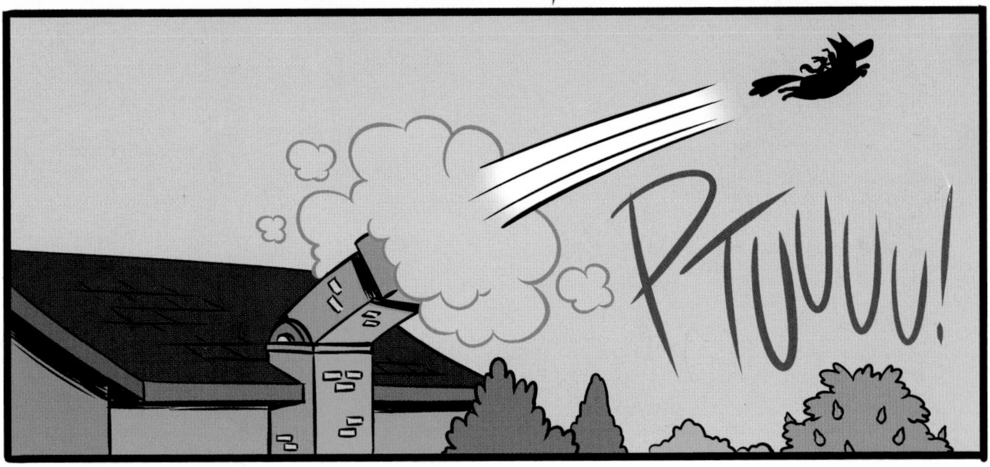
PTUUUU!

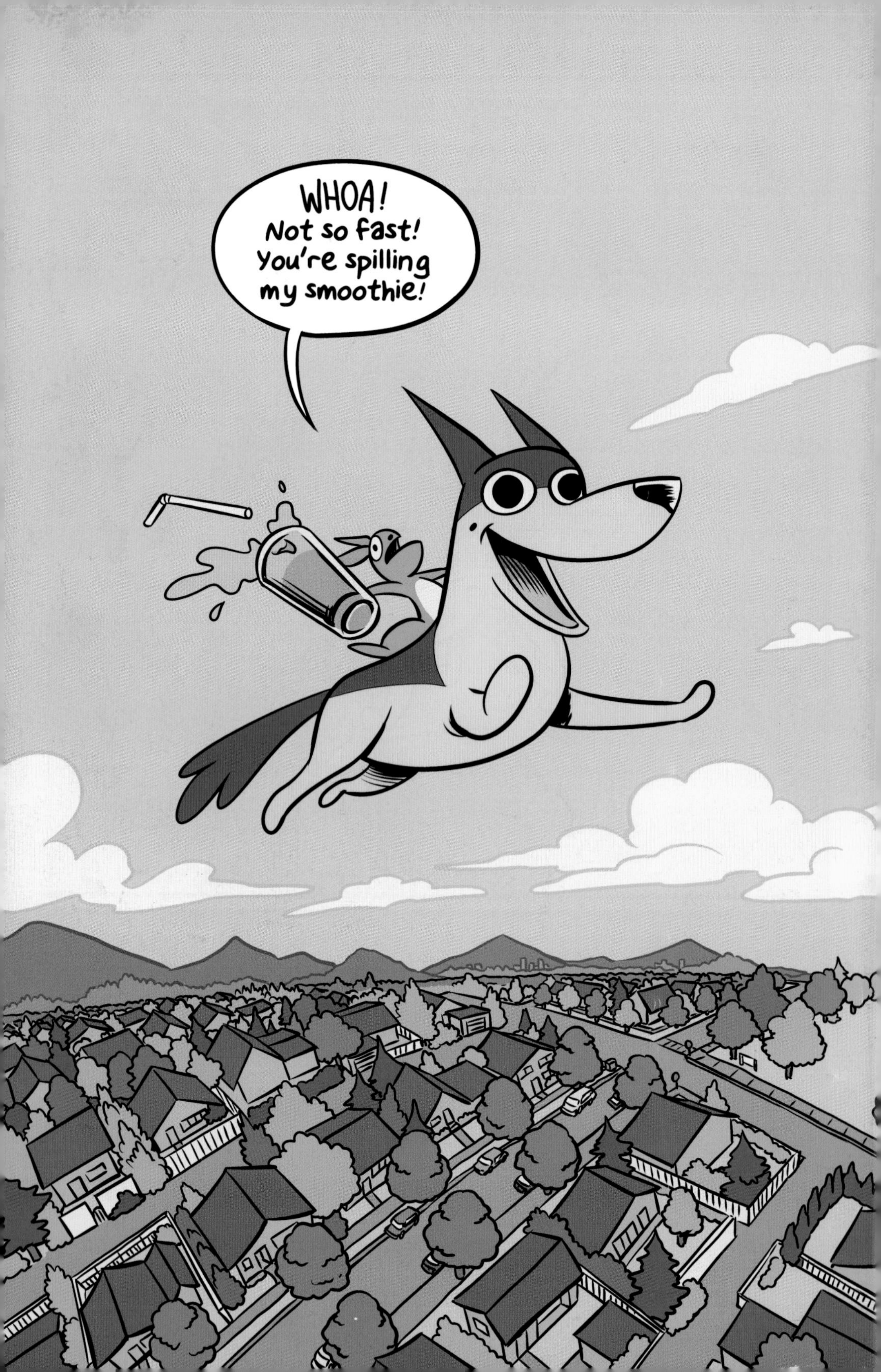
WHOA! Not so fast! You're spilling my smoothie!

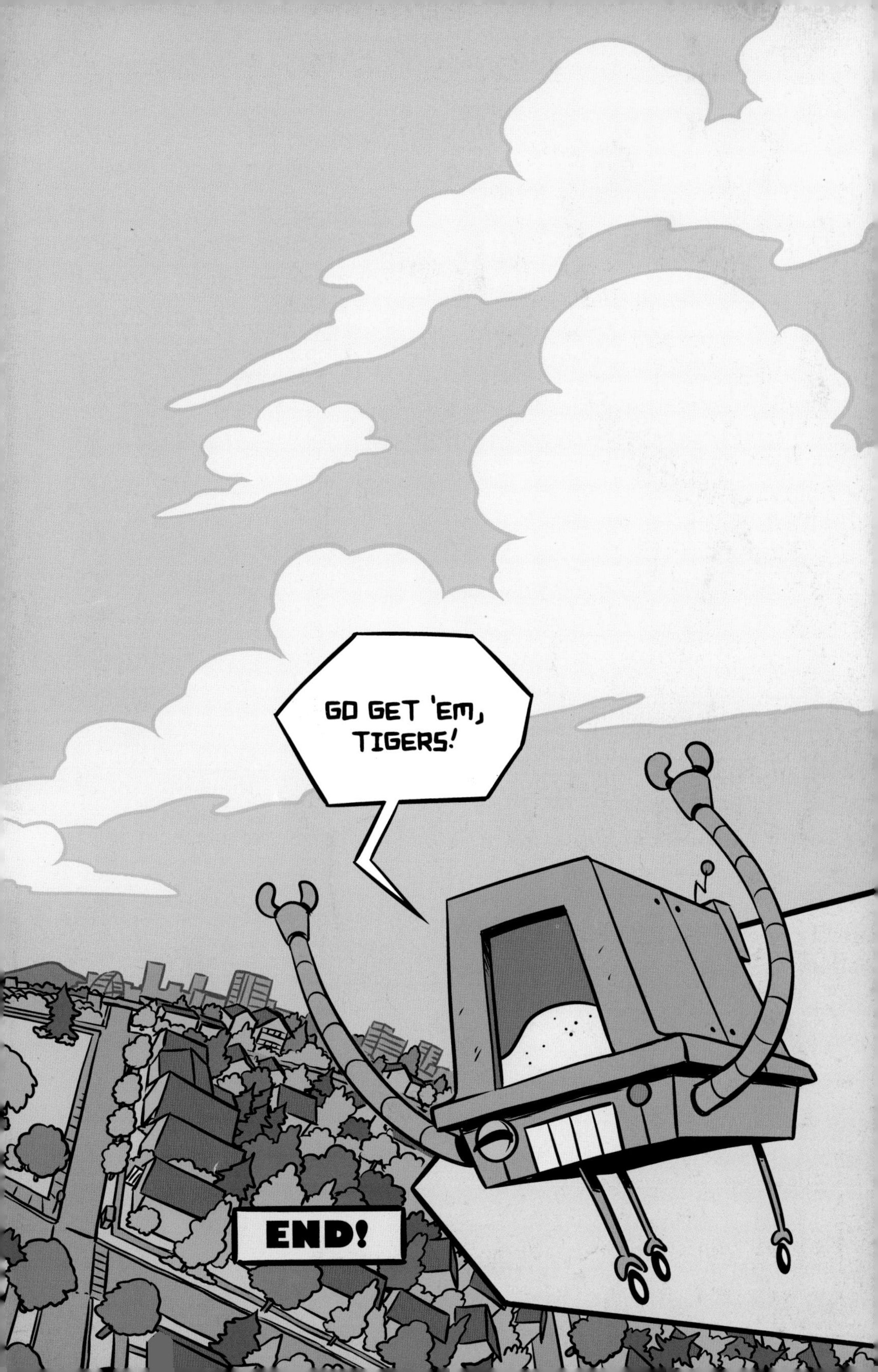
GO GET 'EM, TIGERS!
END!

IAN BOOTHBY has been writing comedy for TV and radio since he was thirteen and making his own comics since he was sixteen. Ian has written comic books for *The Simpsons*, *Futurama*, *Mars Attacks*, *Scooby-Doo*, *The Powerpuff Girls*, and *The Flash*. Ian has also won an Eisner Award for Best Short Story along with Nina Matsumoto, who you might know from being one of the other people with a bio on this page.

NINA MATSUMOTO is a Japanese Canadian who grew up drawing mostly animals, then mostly people, then back to animals again for this book. She pencils for Simpsons Comics and designs video game T-shirts for Fangamer. She created her own English manga series, Yokaiden, and drew *The Last Airbender Prequel: Zuko's Story*. In 2009, she won an Eisner Award with Ian Boothby, and they have been collaborating ever since. She lives with an aloof Shiba Inu that is most likely a cat in a dog suit.

DAVID DEDRICK has been writing and drawing funny pictures his whole life. He lives with his wife, two daughters, two dogs, one cat, and one pony. This is his first time coloring a book. Oh, and the pony doesn't live in the house.